GILEAD'S CURSE

The knight stepped in with the shorter blade, thrusting hard at Gilead's side, tearing his shirt, but missing his body by the smallest of margins. If Gilead had been built like a human, the knight would have connected with flesh, muscle, and perhaps even organs, but Gilead was half the width of a man, and had evaded another grave injury.

In response, Gilead thrust high and tight, making the knight duck to his left, as another slender beam of light cut its way into the clearing over the elf's left shoulder. The pike cut another narrow, shallow slice in the knight's arm, but it would take a great deal more than that to bring him down.

In the same series

GILEAD'S BLOOD
Dan Abnett & Nik Vincent

More elves from Black Library

ELVES
Graham McNeill
(Contains the novels *Defenders of Ulthuan*,
Sons of Ellyrion and *Guardians of the Forest*)

TIME OF LEGENDS: THE SUNDERING
Gav Thorpe
(Contains the novels *Malekith, Shadow King* and *Caledor*,
and the novella *The Bloody Handed*)

• TYRION AND TECLIS •
William King
Book 1: BLOOD OF AENARION
Book 2: SWORD OF CALEDOR
Book 3: BANE OF MALEKITH (December 2013)

• ORION •
Darius Hinks
Book 1: THE VAULTS OF WINTER
Book 2: TEARS OF ISHA (June 2013)
Book 3: COUNCIL OF BEASTS (2014)

• TIME OF LEGENDS: THE WAR OF VENGEANCE •
Book 1: THE GREAT BETRAYAL
Nick Kyme
Book 2: MASTER OF DRAGONS (October 2013)
Chris Wraight

A WARHAMMER NOVEL

GILEAD'S CURSE

Dan Abnett & Nik Vincent

BLACK LIBRARY

For Rebecca Alexander and Sarah Cawkwell, Nik's favourite beta-readers,
and for Andy Smillie, Gilead's greatest champion.

A BLACK LIBRARY PUBLICATION

First published in Great Britain in 2013 by
Black Library,
Games Workshop Ltd.,
Willow Road, Nottingham,
NG7 2WS, UK.

10 9 8 7 6 5 4 3 2 1

Cover illustration by Stefan Kopinski.

A CIP record for this book is available from the British Library.

UK ISBN: 978 1 84970 356 7
US ISBN: 978 1 84970 357 4

See Black Library on the internet at
www.blacklibrary.com

Find out more about Games Workshop
and the world of Warhammer at
www.games-workshop.com

Printed and bound by CPI Group (UK) Ltd, Croydon, CR0 4YY

This is a dark age, a bloody age, an age of daemons
and of sorcery. It is an age of battle and death, and of the
world's ending. Amidst all of the fire, flame and fury
it is a time, too, of mighty heroes, of bold deeds
and great courage.

At the heart of the Old World sprawls the Empire, the
largest and most powerful of the human realms. Known for
its engineers, sorcerers, traders and soldiers, it is
a land of great mountains, mighty rivers, dark forests
and vast cities. And from his throne in Altdorf reigns
the Emperor Karl Franz, sacred descendant of the
founder of these lands, Sigmar, and wielder
of his magical warhammer.

But these are far from civilised times. Across the length
and breadth of the Old World, from the knightly palaces
of Bretonnia to ice-bound Kislev in the far north, come
rumblings of war. In the towering Worlds Edge Mountains,
the orc tribes are gathering for another assault. Bandits and
renegades harry the wild southern lands of
the Border Princes. There are rumours of rat-things, the
skaven, emerging from the sewers and swamps across the
land. And from the northern wildernesses there is the
ever-present threat of Chaos, of daemons and beastmen
corrupted by the foul powers of the Dark Gods.
As the time of battle draws ever near,
the Empire needs heroes
like never before.

Chapter 1

I sat alone with the bard the night the cursed stories came. He was almost as ancient as I am now, and he had not the power to rein in his thoughts, nor to staunch the flow of words that tripped over his tongue into my innocent ears.

He had mentioned the cursed stories before, and the calamities that went with them. He was sorry not to tell tales of such daring and bravery that none could doubt the prowess of their elf hero: Gilead te tuin Tor Anrok, son, brother, companion, warrior. He was the fiercest and most loyal of his noble race, or so the bard would tell anyone who would listen.

I sat alone with the old storyteller. The delirium had taken him, and the women had worked their medicinal magic. I was to sop his brow with a poultice, rub his hands and arms with sappy oils, and sit awake for as long as I was able, while the women recovered their strength.

I was fearful, and his delirium was loud and fierce; there was no risk of my falling asleep that night. In the morning, he would be dead, and the cursed stories would be circling my brain, but not before the bard had rehearsed the curses over and over, between the more lucid moments when his eyes stared straight ahead and the stories came tumbling forth.

He had sworn he would not tell the cursed tales, but he was insensible and driven by unknowable forces. I had not sworn to block my ears against the telling, nor would I have known how to do so for I was no more than a slip of a girl.

I am ancient now and eager for the end to draw near. If I am as bewitched as the old man was, so be it. I would not pass his cursed tales to one unconscious of their significance or of the dangers inherent in hearing them.

I told the tales as a child. I talked of the curses until I was boxed about the ears, beaten black and blue and silenced by anyone scared enough to quiet a child with violence.

Leave now if you cannot stomach hearing these stories, recited not since I was an infant, told for the last time by me. Someone must keep them in his heart until it is time to pass the burden to a new generation, when, perhaps, a little of the curse will have withered away. When the curse is old and dissipated, man will hear the complete tales of Gilead, and in the meantime the great elf lord, the compassionate, stoic warrior, will add to this canon of adventures with feats so noble as to be almost beyond imagining.

Three generations of men have been born in my lifetime. I should have been a great-grand-dame, but it was not to be. The cursed bard himself lived a century through, and many of his stories came from generations of storytellers before him.

They say that elves live forever. I believe that Gilead lives yet, and I know that he has lived a dozen of our short, human generations, and more besides.

He would have been an old man when the cursed tales began, had he been a man. He was, instead, a tall, slender, fine-boned young elf of grand descent, fallen on the most desperate of circumstances. His home and his family were gone, his brother dead, his lessons in revenge learnt, and his honour restored.

His was never a tale of cruelty or neglect, except when it came to himself. He was the saddest of beings, the most bereft, the least heedful of his wellbeing. Some said his mind was so tortured that he looked long and hard for death, but that it eluded him, that cruel fate preferred to keep him in rude health while he fought against the fragile nature of his broken heart.

Be not a-feared. My first tale is not cursed. It is a preamble, a setting-up, a prologue. Hear it out, and then I will begin the cursed tales, for my time on the dirt of this realm is short, and I could not desire to live beyond the story's end.

Gilead fell into the practice of travelling for a little after the sun began to rise, or he began to journey before the sun had set. It was unpleasant always to sleep in the daylight and move through the darkness. It irked him to be always under a lightless sky. The shadows were long and lean, as he was, grey-on-grey in the twilight; that magic time when a thread each of black and white resonate with the same dull sheen when held against the sky. Any shadow was better than none at all, any light a blessing.

He travelled when the earliest risers were beginning their working day, and was aware of their heavy human scents and vulgar vocal tones. He had been alone so long that he was quite used to the meagre sounds of the natural world around him, the sighing creak of ancient trees, the tremulous whisper of fast-growing wild herbs, the fall of all kinds of rain, and the movement of the air. He heard the voices of the few remaining creatures, the hesitant mews of the deer of the forests, the swoops and caws of carrion birds, and even the rustle of insects foraging in the mulch that gathered in the undergrowth.

He did not need or particularly want human companionship, but his path inevitably skirted the more populous villages and towns. He knew better than to move openly among them, for their safety as much as for his own, and so that he could avoid distractions from his cause. Humans were creatures of urgent and consuming need, especially in these increasingly desperate times, and if they knew he was close by they would call upon him to make their pitiful lives more bearable. A thousand small acts of kindness might add weak smiles to some of the human faces that he so readily cringed from, but he had a mission that could change so much more, so much for the better.

'The shadow... It's too long. It's an omen... As bad an omen as you could wish for,' the woman whispered to her husband, clutching the child close to her skirts.

Her husband bent towards her.

'By Sigmar, you're a foolish woman, Brigida,' he said. 'The sun so low gives us all long shadows. Look at the bairn's, as tall as a willow-switch whip.'

The woman stopped in her tracks and picked up her only child, who was almost too big to be lifted, but who was glad to be carried, warmed by his mother's anxious body, and eager to return to a sleep so harshly cut short.

'Not our shadows, Ignaz,' she said. 'The other. Look to the edge of the ditch where the path loses its metal. Look to the shadow there.'

Gilead had not noticed his shadow and he cursed his carelessness, but he had already retreated from the road's edge, ducking between the trees that leaned out over it, windswept in the harsh, northern climate. He had crossed the Middle Mountains into Ostland weeks ago, and Wolfenburg was behind him to the west as he headed into the depths of Ostermark. He had travelled through the night, mounted on the fresh horse that he had procured in Altdorf the previous spring. He was fortunate indeed to get even this moderate palfrey, but the mare was young and even-tempered, and Gilead was spending whatever time he could on training the beast. She was a useful horse, clean and sound, not easily unnerved, and habitually quiet.

At sunrise, he had left her in a sheltered glade only a few dozen yards from the edge of the road, which was more or less straight and fairly recently metalled, with room for carts and carriages to pass easily, so there must have been regular traffic along it between villages and market towns. The air was cold and he could see his breath clouding slightly in front of him. All was quiet. He was tired, but content, and he had allowed himself to drift into memory, not of happier times, for there had been none these many decades, but of his people, at least.

He had been in a place very like this, at the edge of the Forest of Shadows, when the time had come for him to depart for the memorial. The similarity to those other circumstances so struck him that, in his imagination, he was back with his people, hearing the stories told by the women, examining the beautifully woven and embroidered shroud of the lost, casting his mourning cape around his shoulders and saying his farewells. Humans spoke so ignorantly of the elf, of his way of life and the manner of his death. The race was not immortal. An elf could and would die, perhaps not as readily as a human, who chased the narrow thread of his life away so quickly, but with his eyes so rarely facing forwards. A human life was so short that the future was as nothing. No man could rely entirely on being in the future of tomorrow, next week or next year, let alone the next decade or century.

Elves died too. Gilead had travelled a thousand miles, two, to return to the place of departing, to mourn his distant cousin. Death generally came only after a long life, and the fallen elf's noble deeds were celebrated in the times of departing, of the departed and of mourning. This death had come too soon.

The time of departing was for the closest family and friends. For anything between a decade and a score of years, depending on the elf's status and the size of his family or retinue, the fallen was considered to be in the departing stage of his life and death. He was still close enough to be spoken of in the present tense by those who had loved him the longest and most loyally. During the time of departing, the shroud was spun, woven and embellished with icons of the season and year of falling.

When this phase was complete, the wider elf community was brought in for the time of the departed, when the career of the fallen was celebrated, stories told, and the elf's embalmed, enshrined body finally dressed in his shroud. The second phase was shorter than the first, but equivalent in the hours spent. Ten brethren might spend ten years in the time of departing; one hundred cousins, six weeks in the time of the departed.

The elf population was small, in decline, and spread widely across the Empire and beyond. Intimate family groups were often made up of only two or three elves, and extended groups seldom had more than a dozen members.

The time of mourning was the last of the three phases, and would extend across centuries or even millennia. The time of mourning continued until the last of those present at the time of the departed entered their own time of departing. In the time of mourning, the fallen elf lived on in the hearts, minds and deeds of those who had known him, those fellow elves who had crossed his path.

Gilead had met his cousin, seventh generation removed, in that last time of departing. It had pleased him greatly for Fithvael's sake, for his old servant, friend and co-conspirator in the events that had followed his brother Galeth's death. That had been the beginning of it, when he had been the age of this young elf, this Laban te tuin Tor Mahone. The elf was young and eager, but respectful and gentle, and when the time of the departed was over, every old elf kissed him and smiled to know that, so long as this youth lived, their time would not be forgotten. Even Fithvael, among the oldest of them, could expect to live in this boy's memory for a thousand years.

Gilead's latest and most significant cause had been cemented in his will during the memorial to his old friend and cousin. It had been cemented with the knowledge that he must ensure Laban live a long life, that he might remember Fithvael for his allotted time of mourning. All hope would be lost if the elves began to fall to the evil that had cursed the weaker species of the world. Gilead would not allow it.

He knew not what was at the centre of all that was happening in the world, but he knew now that it was affecting every life force that inhabited every corner of every continent. How many decades ago had it started? Had it begun with the failing hedgerows and the meagre crops? Had it begun with the hunger that had caused so many fauna to perish? Once upon a time, the calls of the beasts and birds of the fens and woods, prairies and plains that he had traversed had been more than Gilead could stand. The abundance of layered voices, cries, caws, growls and howls had followed him everywhere he had travelled, and at night, a whole vast new array of beastly sounds filled the hours that should have been more restful. At the time, he had been able to find no peace; now he craved the sounds of a healthy and robust environment.

Livestock had been affected once there was no longer the excess of strong grass and grazing crops to feed them. They had grown tired and hungry, had withered to hide-covered skeletons and had died leaning against trees, walls and buildings, or had lost the ability to stand and had fallen dead to the bare earth.

The humans had struggled on. The very old and very young had died in greater numbers than they would have in times of plenty, but their lives had always been short and lived too quickly. Then the children stopped coming. Suddenly, even the youngest and most fertile of human women began to look drawn and wan and tired. Children came less often and families grew more slowly, and many of those that were born clung to the threads of their lives with quiet desperation.

Gilead's purpose was set in stone. It had led him across the Empire from the Loren Forest, north through Altdorf and on towards the Middle Mountains before his brethren began to suffer. Then his beloved cousin, Benath, had fallen. The time of the departed was spent speculating as to the cause of his death, and when no ready answer came, Gilead began to suspect that the plague that had befallen first flora and fauna, and then the fragile humans, might have taken his cousin and friend.

He had returned to the north with renewed vigour, determined to find the source of the evil that was permeating all strata of life. Nothing would sway him from his cause or from the course he must follow to track the evil force.

'It is gone,' said Ignaz, 'if it was ever there. Your imaginings will get the better of you, wife. You will scare the bairn to death.'

He stopped and gave his wife a rough hug. He had been too harsh with her, but he was fearful, too: fearful of losing his wife, and his child; fearful that his sparse and meagre beet crop might yet succumb to some blight or other; fearful that his one remaining milking goat had lost the will to bleat. More than anything, he was fearful that there would be no work for him or Brigida at the labour fair in Bortz, seven miles hence. A shadow, even a shadow so unusual that it had made his wife's face pale and turned her voice to a whisper, was the very least of his worries.

Brigida leaned her head into her husband's shoulder, and their child buried himself more deeply into the cocoon that their bodies made. Ignaz swallowed hard as he saw a long, grey shadow stop suddenly to the right of the road, and then ripple and wobble its way over the rutted ditch and disappear into the trees beyond. Apart from the effect of the terrain on the shadow, it seemed to glide as if by magic.

Ignaz held Brigida's head against his chest until the apparition had passed, and then disengaged, looking down at her, his pale face full of concern.

'I won't let any harm come to you,' he said. 'I promise you that on Sigmar's beard.'

'Don't promise,' said Brigida. 'Don't dare to invoke the great god's name. How could you stop it? The harm is already done.'

Gilead was roused from his reverie by Ignaz's reassuring words. He turned, unconsciously, towards the sounds the human couple were making, and caught sight of the low-slung sun, barely above his eye height, between the trees. He shielded his face for a moment and looked out across the road, a hundred yards or so behind where the couple stood, locked in their embrace. Their long shadows stretched away between their position and his.

Gilead waited for the little family to move away, aware of their heavy footfalls for several long minutes. The watery sun was rising slowly, and the shadows would be long for some time to come.

Tired, his mind dulled by the unravelling of recent memories and with a long night's journey, Gilead returned to the little glade where he had left his horse. He unburdened the palfrey of the few essentials he carried with him, rubbed her down with a handful of sickly, yellow strand grass, and threw a blanket over her. When his mount was comfortable, he swathed himself in the rough cloak, woven from contrasting threads, that he had bought when his beloved elf cape had become too fragile to wear for any but the most serious or sacred of occasions.

Gilead lay on the ground, sheltered beneath the greying canopy of a tree that was struggling to hang on to the last of its life. He could not sleep. He cast his mind back over the night's journey. It was a trick that Fithvael, his oldest, dearest, last companion had taught him, that his mind might not return to the darkest of places from which the old retainer had barely managed to rescue him. The night had been without event. He had travelled a long, narrow path through the woods, close to the edge of the road, staying in shadow, hidden from the twin moons that hung in the sky so high, for so much of the night.

Shadows. There had been talk of shadows. It was this morning. His mind was sticking on something that had happened this morning.

Gilead soon realised what it was, and knew that a sleepless day would follow, a day of information-gathering, of listening from the shadows, of moving among the humans, among their scents and sounds. He was loath to do it, but do it he must.

Gilead had not been slack or careless on the road that sunrise. He had not neglected to see his shadow running ahead of him, into the human woman's line of sight. He cast his mind back. It had been early, the sun low, so everything had been casting long shadows, but he had been moving to the west and south of the couple, and his shadow must have been cast into the woods, not onto the road.

Chapter 2

Gilead's tiredness ebbed away as this clue played on his mind. The palfrey needed to rest, if she was to be useful to him over the days to come, but she could sleep while he scoured the area for whatever had cast that shadow.

He hugged the edge of the ditch to the south and west of the road, keeping his shadow beyond the tree-line, while he reconnoitred the area. There was nothing in the road, no sounds of people or creatures anywhere nearby, and the only shadows were of the tree-line on the opposite side of the road. Gilead lifted his head to smell the lightly moving air, but there appeared to be nothing on the breeze. He could faintly sense the three humans that had walked the path before him, maybe an hour earlier, but he knew their scents and sounds, and was content to rule them out; he knew they had passed and moved on to their destination.

Several hundred yards further along, in the direction the

little family had taken, the road swerved gently to the left so that the tree-line's shade covered its entire width. Gilead crossed quickly, using the shadows to consume his own. His swift, silent feet barely seemed to connect with the hard, smooth surface of the road, and the air around him hardly moved at all. If he smelled of anything, it was of cool air and clean water, of the few foodstuffs that he had managed to forage and of the sweet hide of the beast that carried him.

No human would have detected his movement across the path, even if there'd been anyone watching. The few surviving local creatures, a scrawny rat picking at the dry remains of a bird carcass, while the bird's mate plucked sadly at its own battered feathers on the low branch of the nearest tree, didn't so much as blink at his passing.

Within the hour, Gilead knew that whatever had belonged to the shadow that Brigida had shied from was gone, or else had been a figment of her imagination. Everyone was jumpy. Everyone had been jumpy for a long time.

Gilead spent the next two hours foraging for what he would need to sustain him for the remainder of the day, since, once the mare was rested, he would continue his search for the elusive creature that had blighted the sunrise.

The soil was pale and poor, and would have been blown away on the breeze long ago if it weren't for the tenacious hold of the woodland trees' roots. They were stunted and twisted, wore greying or yellowing leaves, and their bark was pitted and sallow, but they clung on, the most ancient of life-forms, biding their time until the tide should turn and the world should be rid of the plague that spread insidiously across its lands.

The shoots and leaves that Gilead favoured to flavour his meals and provide aromatic salads had not been seen for a dozen seasons or more, and he had taken to foraging a little below the surface of the earth for the tubers, roots and corms that provided some meagre sustenance, though often their flesh was stringy and dry, and he had to pummel and mince them after long cooking to extract any nutrients buried within. He collected enough wood to make a small fire, the smoke from which would be dissipated among the lower branches of the trees, rendering his position undetectable from more than a dozen yards away. He drew water from an old, shallow culvert, the contents surprisingly fresh and sweet in the otherwise inhospitable surroundings; no doubt because there were neither humans nor animals in any numbers sufficient to deplete the stream.

Gilead bathed, ate, and refreshed himself, and, when the time came, he packed his belongings and led the palfrey out onto the road. He followed in Brigida and Ignaz's footsteps, keeping close to the ditch, crossing the road at its turns to ensure that his shadow was hidden, and keeping his mare relaxed and quiet.

He would be seen, and not seen. He would hide in plain sight, casting no scents nor sounds nor sudden movements into the air. The humans would hardly know he was there, yet, when they had need of him, he would respond.

His senses on full alert, Gilead tracked every sound, every movement, every scent on the air. As he came close to the subdued little town of Bortz, two hundred miles south-west of Bechafen, the natural smells and sounds of the open landscape drifted away, and the stink of fear and the sound of tremulous resentment tripping from the lips of the doleful humans filled his senses.

'They say Brigida saw a shadow on the road, this morning,' said one young woman as Gilead listened in.

'We're all seeing shadows,' said the old dame with her, 'and with good reason. Morr casts the longest shadow, and he's among us now. Sigmar help us all!'

'Don't say so,' said the younger woman, clutching the old dame by the crook of her arm.

'I do say so,' said the dame. 'I shall say so until I come to Sigmar's wondrous presence, and I shall be glad to go.'

Gilead moved on. This was only talk, an old woman frightening instead of reassuring the child. This was rumour, not fact.

'Not much of a labour fair,' said a young man, dragging a half-filled tarpaulin-covered cart in his wake.

'Nothing worth buying labour for,' said his companion, 'and the quality of the labour to be had, so weak and poor.'

'Shall it end, father?' asked the youth pulling the cart.

'Not in my lifetime,' said his father. 'Not while Sigmar gives me breath.'

As Gilead approached the main square of the market town that had clearly once been a busy, even thriving, centre of commerce, he heard the tentative dull clang of a handbell being lifted by someone inexpert at handling it.

The bell clanged again.

Gilead slid silently off the palfrey as the people around him stopped and turned to see where the noise was coming from.

Gilead watched as an old, bent man took the bell gently from the faltering hands of a tall, slender, tired-looking man, the man that the elf had seen on the road. Gilead watched as the old man lifted the bell to an inverted position in his hand and then relaxed his hand away, letting the bell drop onto its clapper, sending a clear, high note resonating across the square and out to the ears of the milling people.

More people stopped and turned, and, one by one, they began to move slowly back to gather in the square.

'Ignaz has something to say,' said the old man, inverting the bell and placing his hand over the clapper inside.

Ignaz coughed and wiped his mouth with the back of his hand, as if he didn't want to let the words out.

'I couldn't admit it before,' he said.

'Speak out, lad,' said a middle-aged woman from the rear of the crowd.

'I didn't like to admit it to Brigida, this morning. I didn't like to say it when there was no one to hear it, and us so vulnerable on the road alone.'

He coughed again.

'Only we weren't alone,' he said.

'Get to the nub of it, lad, the sun won't stay up forever, and you know it,' shouted the woman again, before one or two of the older men around her glared in her direction and shushed her.

'It's here,' he said. 'It's among us. Brigida saw it this morning, but I told her nay.' Ignaz gestured towards his wife, whose face turned an even paler shade of sallow, and the hollows beneath her eyes appeared to fill with greenish-black shadows. 'I saw it too, but I kept it from her.'

'Saw what?' someone called from the crowd in the shrill, tremulous voice of an eager boy or a terrified woman.

'Brigida saw a shadow. Then I saw it too.'

A murmur began to pass through the crowd. Some believed every word and were frightened of what might come out of the man's mouth next, while others were more sceptical, longer in the tooth or made of sterner stuff. Others still could feel their sap rising and their instincts to fight kick in. One or two shook their fists or howled improvised war cries.

'It doesn't sound like much... a shadow,' said Ignaz, 'but it was like nothing I've ever seen. It was too long and too lean, and too... too... It wasn't human.'

Someone shouted from the crowd: 'What time did you see your shadow?' Brave enough to heckle, if nothing else. 'Was it at dawn, perchance? "Oooh... Loook... Look how long the shadows are! Sigmar save me!" I'm sooo scared!' The voice broke into laughter, and Gilead watched unsurprised as a gathering of cocky boys started pummelling each other, playing at daemons because they knew not what else to do.

'It's here,' said Ignaz. 'The thing we've heard talk of. The rumours were true.'

The scents on the air grew stronger as the sky, filling steadily with clouds, darkened, and the lowering sun was swallowed into its grey depths. Gilead could smell their fear on the air.

He tugged ever so slightly on the mare's rein and turned into her body as she made a small circle to face the way they had come. The boy with the cart, and his father, were standing too close, and Gilead had to jink to avoid them. Their eyes were cast across the market square to watch as Ignaz tried to continue.

The palfrey was less lucky, and, as the tightening rein tugged at her head, she whinnied, her nostrils flaring slightly.

'Watch out,' said the boy, steadying his cart with the handrails he still gripped as the horse bumped against it. 'Look where you're going with that stupid beast.'

The boy was already unnerved by what was going on in the square. They were all in a state of tension from the rumours that were passing from one town to the next about the plague that was in their midst, and the daemon that rode in on its heels.

Once the cart was stable, the lad dropped his hold on the handrails, and it bumped onto its stop-feet, leaning slightly.

The boy slapped the palfrey hard on the flanks, and she skittered on her rear hoofs.

Gilead loosened his grip on the mare's reins, and turned to the boy, but the space around them was so limited, and the youth so agitated, there was nothing he could do to prevent what happened next.

The heckling boys were scuffling with each other, and Ignaz's voice was drowned out by the commotion that was gradually building. More of the locals were drawing close to see what the fuss was about, or to spread talk of what was happening. Gilead didn't like it. He was suddenly in the middle of a tight little group of stressed people; the situation was becoming less and less predictable, and he wanted to get him and his mount out of there.

The youth slapped the horse again, and she pulled her head up, extending Gilead's arm as he reached for a tighter hold, close on the horse's head. The boy was drawing attention to the mare, and the mare was drawing attention to him. He kept his head low and his grip on the reins steady, and worked his body away from the youth and his cart. There appeared to be no way out as the scuffling boys started to kick and punch at one of their number, falling against the cart, which inched across the paving stones with a squeak and a groan, blocking the mare's exit.

Gilead stood very close to the horse, his side against her foreleg, his shoulder against her neck. He leaned in gently and made soothing noises close to her ear. There was not room to mount her, and he didn't want more eyes on him.

Then he heard the odd clang, again, the sound of the bell being mishandled, and the market square was suddenly filled with the ringing of the bell, loud and shrill as someone swung it inexpertly and too fast.

The horse, already jittery and hemmed-in, tried to bolt, but got her legs caught in the hand cart. She panicked and struck out, kicking the boy who was being tortured by his friends, landing a heavy hoof on the victim's shoulder as he lay on his back on the cart. The boy yelped, and his friends stopped pummelling him, laughed, and tried to help him out of Gilead's way.

Gilead was impotent to do anything but try to keep his horse under control. He could not allow himself to be seen or recognised. He had to remain slumped under his cloak, his height disguised and his head covered. It was easier said than done.

Finally, the old man intervened. He grabbed the youth's hand as he pulled it back to slap the mare for a third time, and gave the cart a hard shove out of the way. The scuffling boys skipped off, dancing through the crowd, and Gilead breathed a sigh of relief.

The bell had quietened the crowd for the moment, and Gilead was sure that he could get away. He rubbed the mare's nose and patted her lightly on the shoulder. He turned the reins over in his hand, adjusting his grip, and clicked his tongue to encourage her to walk on.

Gilead did not see the child.

In the confusion of the busy market square, when things had begun to happen, a diligent father standing a few yards away had quietly picked up his child, lifted him over his head and sat him on his shoulders.

The child was suddenly the tallest person in the square, and watched, smiling, as the scene unfolded beneath him. He saw the boys arguing and the handcart getting bumped. He saw the skittish mare and the old man. He saw a hand reach up to the horse's head to hold the reins. He saw the long, tapering fingers, the narrow, elegant wrist. He saw the fine skin and the beautifully turned cuff of a type of garment that he didn't recognise.

All things are new and wondrous to a child. All creatures are fascinating.

Gilead did not notice the child, but, as he walked past, still soothing the mare, the child reached his hand out and gently tugged at the hood of the elf's cloak.

As the hood fell back to his shoulders, Gilead turned to see what had disturbed it. His eyes were more or less on a level with the child's, and his cold stare made the colour drain from the child's face, and his jaw quiver.

The child's face went from long and pale to red and round, and, before Gilead had time to lift his hood and drop into his knees to reduce his height, the child was screaming.

The child wailed hard, pointing all the time at where Gilead had been standing.

The crowd, hushed by the ringing of the bell, turned to look. The man with the child on his shoulders stared at Gilead for a moment before lifting the child from his shoulders to comfort him. He did not need to take action. He was not the only one who had seen what his child had seen.

One hand still tight on the mare's reins, Gilead turned his head in a slow circle, his body following. He came up to his full height, placed his feet shoulder-width apart and braced himself for what was to come.

Hours before, he had mistaken his shadow for that of whatever was terrorising these people. Now, they were mistaking him for their nemesis.

The first swing came, as it always did, from the youngest man, the cockiest, the keenest to prove something. Gilead dropped his shoulders back an inch or two, and the blow, which was never going to reach his face, was so poorly timed and imprecise that it failed even to connect with his chest. It did, however, turn the cocky kid and sent him staggering a step or two back into the tight circle that was forming around the elf.

Then a man stepped forwards, and the gap in the circle closed behind him. This must be their champion. He was a tall, wiry man, young, but by no means a boy. Gilead weighed him up in a moment or two, then lifted a hand in front of him, not so much a warning as a gesture of retreat. The elf would walk away if he were allowed to do so.

No one was going to allow him to walk.

The champion clasped one fist in the other, briefly, and danced a fast step towards the elf, swinging a left hook low into Gilead's body. Gilead moved deftly to the right, and the champion was surprised when his fist connected with fresh air. He swung twice more, and twice more Gilead ducked, while still managing to hold onto the mare's reins.

When the next blow came, it came from Gilead's left and a little behind him. It connected with his side, above his right hip. Gilead turned his head in time to see his assailant pulling a pained face and shaking out his punching hand.

It was two against one, if both the humans were prepared to continue.

Gilead handed his mare's reins to the old man with the kid and the cart. He took them without thinking, and then looked down at his hand, not a little surprised by the turn of events. He shrugged, shortened the rein and patted the mare on the shoulder to reassure her; after all, the horse wasn't his enemy.

Gilead wound his cloak into a long rope and secured it around his waist, lest he trip over it. Before he was finished, a third man had his fists up and a fourth was weighing a length of wood in his hand that looked like some sort of paddle.

The paddle came first, swung out low to take his legs from under him. Gilead stepped lightly over the paddle and waited for the next attack. The champion tried punching again, but there were five assailants now, surrounded by spectators, and the momentum was taken out of his swing when his fist, drawn back, landed in the armpit of the man next to him.

Gilead thought about turning and walking away from the farce, but that was impossible. The crowd was spoiling for a fight. The threat of the plague was bad enough, but to have the rumoured monster in their midst and do nothing was unthinkable. Any man would try to get his hands on the elf, and most of the women and children, too. Gilead must stand and fight.

When the next arm swung at him, Gilead caught it deftly by the wrist, turned it and its owner away, and shoved the man in the back, sending him sprawling into the arms of the crowd. Then he jinked to his left, and tripped the youngest and cockiest of his opponents. The boy landed on his face, bloodying his nose.

The man who had hurt his hand punching Gilead tried a double-handed swing at arm's length, but Gilead turned, and the fists landed in another man's exposed gut, doubling him over and making him retch.

Several men, watching the fiasco, began to separate from their wives and children, removed hats and jackets, and set pugnacious expressions on their faces.

Over the next few minutes, one or two blows found their targets, but none penetrated the elf's defences completely enough to cause him any damage, even fleeting. He caught swinging arms and legs, ducked imprecise blows from fists and feet, banged a couple of heads together, and sidestepped one woman who began angrily swinging a bundle that she'd been carrying.

More and more men joined the fight, but soon they were brawling with each other, fighting to get to their mutual enemy, sure that they might succeed where others had failed. Frustration and exasperation overcame them, rendering them useless in the face of the elf's vastly superior fighting skills.

Gilead had no intention of hurting any of them, and he'd rather not watch while they hurt each other.

The elf was ready when the old man dropped the mare's reins and jostled the man next to him, who had thumped his lad on his way into the fray. Gilead picked up the reins, ducked under the mare's neck, and led her quietly away.

His information-gathering exercise would have to be aborted, but it had borne some fruit. The locals were terrified. They were afraid of the plague visited on their land and livestock, but they were more afraid of the rumoured creature.

Death was not a ghost, a myth or an idea. Here, now, death came in corporeal form.

Chapter 3

Gilead retreated to the woods that bordered the town to the south. He lay low for days and then weeks, moving his small camp at regular intervals and leaving no signs of where he had passed or spent time. There were hundreds of acres of woodland to forage, and while food was not in plentiful supply, there was enough to sustain him for as long as he needed.

Gradually, he began to weave his way closer to Bortz. He needed more information if he were to change the fates of the people who lived there, but he dared not be spotted again.

He left the mare safely hidden in the woods and made several sojourns into the edges of the town where he would sit quietly in the corners of inns and drinking holes. On market days, he moved silently between barrows and stalls, listening to gossip, and, on the roads between the town and the local farms and villages, he tacked himself onto the ends of larger groups of traffic and listened to the stories that were spreading across the region.

Within a matter of weeks, as the days began to lengthen into a tired, pale form of spring, Gilead started to know who the enemy was and where he could be found. Whoever, whatever it was, clearly lacked Gilead's skills. It did not avoid detection by tracking. It appeared to return to the same haunts over and over again, approaching the town from the same direction, being spotted, or imagined, in a small area close to where Gilead had entered the town for the first time. The best, most reliable of the rumours all came from the same road into Bortz.

The spectre was humanoid, although its dimensions were exaggerated by the hysteria that had grown up around it. Had it been another elf, Gilead would have felt its presence. It had to be human, or some humanoid monster.

There were reports of it drifting away at twilight. It was said to be pale, deathly and ethereal, while being a strong fighter, and there were rumours of an impressive steed of the kind a warrior might ride.

Gilead spent two days in the woods tracking the creature. Its prints were clearly made by feet that were long and slender, large for a human man, but certainly not inhuman. Gilead tracked the horse, too, more often ridden than led, although, in the heaviest, most overgrown acres of the wood, two tracks wove side by side between the trees. The ground was otherwise undisturbed; there was no digging for roots to eat. Gilead found only the pale, scrawny carcasses of meatless rodents, bloodless and papery.

It was night when Gilead knew that he was close. It was the smell. It was like the smell of humans, but older and more decayed. There was a smell of dry graves, sepulchral almost. There was a mingled scent of horse sweat, warm leather and grease. The earth smelled of a fire that had been lit and extinguished more than once, but which had cooked nothing, and of blankets used too often between laundering. Gilead almost mistook the whole for the smell of death, but human death did not smell like this, nor animal death, either. This was the antithesis of the death-smell.

Gilead ducked between the lowest branches of the trees that surrounded the tight, narrow area from which the smell emanated. He saw the horse first, tethered to a tree, its head at full stretch trying to reach fresh sources of grass to chew on. The horse looked up for the briefest of moments, and then bowed again to its purpose.

Confident the horse would raise no alarm, Gilead looked through the darkness beyond it to the curl of grey smoke that rose a foot or two above the tiny fire pit that shed the only light for miles. A figure sat bent before the fire, its back to Gilead, its silhouetted elbow working small circles as its hands performed some monotonous task.

Gilead drew the shorter of his blades. There was little enough room to fight hand to hand, and none to wield a sword. He wondered for a moment whether a fight would be necessary. Could he not simply kill the man, quietly, while his back was turned? It was not the elf way. Gilead would stand face to face with any foe, believing that his greater skill and longer practice would lead to the defeat of any opponent he met in mortal combat.

He ducked under the last of the branches overhanging the space in the wood that hardly qualified as a glade, making no effort to quiet his footsteps. Gilead noticed the gleam of metal in the dim firelight. The creature was polishing a large

piece of armour, a cuisse or a pauldron. A helmet, adorned
with a battered plume, sat on one side of the figure, and he
appeared to be wearing a mail headpiece, although his chest
and back were covered in nothing more than a loose shirt.

As Gilead took another step, the war steed's head came up,
and its ears flicked forwards. The figure sitting at the fireside
turned towards Gilead, stepping swiftly to its feet. It dropped
the polishing cloth, and bent slightly at the knees to lower to
the ground the section of armour that it had been polishing,
keeping its gaze on Gilead.

Their eyes locked, and Gilead knew, at last, that this man
had transcended human mortality. It had been a man once,
but was no longer constrained by the passage of time, nor the
decaying of the mind or body. This sham of a man, this fac-
simile of a noble knight, had faced death and been reborn. It
was, perhaps, as long-lived as Gilead, and might live longer
than any elf, unless Gilead could put an end to it.

The first blow came fast and cruel as the knight turned,
swinging one foot high and wide to connect with Gilead's
shoulder. The knight had not removed his boots and a
gleaming spur left a tight row of pinprick holes in the flesh
of Gilead's arm. The elf had expected to land the first blow,
but he was quick to react, and blocked the knight's kick just
above the knee with his own foot, before too much damage
was inflicted.

The knight was caught off-balance when the side of Gilead's foot landed squarely against the inside of his thigh, and
he had to wheel sharply to bring himself squarely in front
of Gilead for another attack. Gilead brought his knife up,
and wove quick movements into his assailant's chest. The
knight ducked and backed away from two of the passes, but
a third made contact with the mail coif covering his head

and neck, but for which the blade would have sliced a convenient artery in the knight's neck.

The knight was strong and agile, and faster than any human, and it had been some time since Gilead had done serious battle. He had spent a considerable amount of time fighting humans, but always from a defensive stance, never intending to mark or maim, let alone kill.

Gilead caught the knight's wrist as it propelled a roundhouse punch in his direction, but the knight was too quick, and twisted his fist, loosening the elf's grip. Then the knight turned his back so that Gilead was behind him, at close quarters, and drove an elbow up hard under the elf's ribs.

If Gilead had been human, that blow would have winded him and probably left him badly bruised with a couple of cracked ribs, but Gilead was not human.

Reflexively, as Gilead bent to lessen the impact of the blow, he thrust his knife-hand out, hoping to make contact with the knight's hamstring. The knight had taken off most of his armour to clean it, so his legs were clad in nothing more protective than a leather-patched pair of breeches. He anticipated the elf's move, however, and sat into the knife, so that the flesh of his buttocks took the worst of the injury, leaving his muscle and connective tissues intact.

The wound should have bled, fiercely, but Gilead was not surprised when his knife-hand did not come away slick and hot with fresh blood.

As the knight turned to face Gilead, a weak stream of dark liquid trickling down the back of his leg, the elf flicked his knife deftly from his right hand to his left, and thrust hard into the knight's side before he had a chance to land another blow.

The knight barely faltered in his lunge towards Gilead,

wrapping his arms around the elf's waist and driving his protected head into his chest, bringing them both crashing hard to the forest floor. The mulch was not as rich and thick on the ground as it might have been ten or a dozen years ago, and the pair fell heavily. Gilead, with his wiry frame, the tensile strength of his narrow bones vastly superior to a human's, felt nothing very much, but the knight, landing hard, was winded. It gasped a stale breath of air up at Gilead, its eyes bulging slightly.

Only then did Gilead see the teeth. They were long and strong and as yellow as old ivory. In the split second the elf had to his advantage, he wondered whether this undead knight would bite him, whether one species could be sustained by the blood of another. Before the split second was over, Gilead rolled the body of the knight, until the elf was sitting on his chest, yanking the protective mail headpiece away to expose the knight's head and throat.

Rather than resisting the removal of the small amount of protective clothing that might save him from the elf, the knight brought his feet up and dug his heels hard into the elf's back, tearing Gilead's shirt and gouging long scratches to either side of his spine that would need good and careful cleaning if they were not to become infected.

The knight brought his hands up to grasp the elf around the neck. Gilead whipped his head around and brought it towards the knight's face in a swinging arc, hardly able to believe that he had been driven to head-butting the creature. This was not dignified. This was not how an elf warrior fought.

Gilead jumped to his feet, freeing himself from the knight's grasp. His shoulder smarted slightly, but adrenaline was kicking in, and he felt no pain.

The knight did not stay long on the ground, and the two warriors were soon circling each other, marking out an arena in the tiny clearing.

As he stood, the knight grabbed his discarded mail head-piece and wrapped it around his right fist. Gilead threw his knife from one hand to the other, preparing to strike. His first swing was met by the mail glove, which shrieked with the impact.

Gilead turned, kicked high and then thrust low with his knife, but the knight saw the kick, and countered it with a low, lunging punch. Both combatants were unbalanced, and whirled away from each other to regroup.

Keen to gain some small advantage, Gilead unsheathed his sword. He would have to keep its hilt close to his body, and limit his movement, but he could keep the knight at a greater reach, and perhaps control the outcome of the battle.

The knight's hand thrust down to the ground and scrubbed around for some kind of weapon. He was close to the fire, and a meagre pile of firewood. He picked a piece up, but discarded it immediately as useless.

As Gilead extended the tip of his sword towards the knight, ready to lunge, the knight's hand fell on the cuisse that he had been polishing, and he brought it up like a shield, deflecting the tip of the sword, sending it out wide, where it peeled a ribbon of diseased bark from a tree at the edge of the clearing. Gilead pulled the sword hilt back into his body and adjusted his grip, wrapping his fingers firmly around the guard, shortening the weapon's reach by several inches.

As Gilead worked his knife and his sword, flicking, extending, turning, jabbing and, from time to time, sending the short knife away in stunning arcs to give it the momentum to do real damage to flesh and bone, the knight lunged with his improvised shield, parried, stopped the blades with his mail-wrapped hand, and sustained no penetrating injuries.

Gilead brought the knife across the knight's cheek, taking off the tip of his nose, but he missed the eye entirely, and the wounds leaked only a little clear liquid. He brought the sword across the knight's body at an angle, and left a slice in his shirt and chest, but, again, no real damage was done. Gilead wanted to see pink flesh and white bone, and was a little perturbed when he saw only a greenish-grey flap of skin.

After twenty or thirty minutes of Gilead's fast-paced swordplay, and the knight's impressive defensive moves, after battling it out in the clearing for longer than any fight should last, someone had to break the deadlock.

Gilead willed himself to succeed, but the pace and rhythm of the fight had begun to stagnate and the adrenaline in his system was long gone. He found it almost impossible to increase his pace.

The knight wearied of playing the defensive game and finally stepped things up. He let go of the end of the coif, allowing it to drop in his hand so that he was holding one end of it. Without his head to shape it, the links of the mail fell into a rippling length of metal a yard long.

As Gilead thrust with his dagger, the knight swung the coif and brought it skittering against the length of the blade. The momentum of the swing wrapped the mail around the weapon and, to Gilead's surprise, dragged it out of his grasp.

The knight dropped the coif in favour of the dagger. Both combatants had a blade, and the knight still had the advantage of an improvised shield.

Gilead, in a desperate effort not to lose the advantage, tilted his sword up in front of him and drove at the knight with the full weight of his body. The knight was recovering his footing, having bent to pick up the blade, and was not ready for the onslaught. As he tried to remain standing, the knight dropped the heavy cuisse, and it crashed to the ground, tumbling over a pile of firewood.

At the edge of the clearing the war steed made itself as small as possible between the trees, and lifted its head in a sympathetic whinny.

The elf and the knight fought each other in the tiny clearing for another hour. Blows were traded, blades were thrust and parried, and, once or twice, the duellists were whisper-close to each other, the shorter knight's glowing eyes staring up into the elf's steely ones.

Gilead had flashes of his shadowfast capabilities, moments when he was everywhere at once, but still he could not best the fated creature that could not or would not die. They both bore wounds, some shallow and haphazard, others deeper and more threatening. The air was full of the grunts and cries of pain and triumph that punctuated their combat, and of a mixture of their scents: the sharp tang of adrenaline, the earthy blend of new sweat and old, and the sweet, clear-water smell that clung to the elf more strongly the harder he worked.

Then the dawn came.

Gilead did not see it, at first; he only heard it in the gentle early movements of the few creatures that still inhabited the woodland. Then he could smell the beginning of a new day, and feel it too. His senses better tuned to all things than a mortal man's would be, the elf knew that the day was breaking. He also knew that with the new day would come the end of one or other of them. He knew that if he did not kill the undead knight, he would perish at his hand.

For the first time in a hundred years, Gilead wondered

whether he could beat his opponent. If he did not, he would die on the blade of his own dagger, the weapon forged by his father's armourer and given to him in a ceremony by his faithful companion, Fithvael, on the completion of his combat training.

A shaft of light found a low angle between the trees at the edge of the woodland and speared across the narrow clearing. Morning had broken.

Chapter 4

Sleep comes at such awkward times when you're as old as I am. It matters little, now. I am refreshed and ready to begin again, just as soon as you fill my glass with a little tepid water, and perhaps bring me a morsel or two to eat.

It is a conceit, I suppose, to leave one's audience on a knife-edge, but it is not my way, I promise you. Now, where was I?

Gilead and the undead knight fought tooth and nail for long hours before dawn, and, as the sky was broken open by a new sun rising, the elf thought that he, too, would perish. He could not muster his strength. His elf abilities felt as if they were a million miles away. He sought to be shadowfast, but the skill came in such short bursts as to be irrelevant to the passage of the battle.

Gilead had not come across so practised a warrior in all his days. He had fought humans and daemons, monsters and beasts. He had fought creatures with brains and creatures with brawn, and once or twice he had done battle with beings of strength and sentience in equal measure. He had fought the spirited and the desperate, but he had never fought an equal.

With two blades, Gilead had not been able to bring down the knight. His undead foe had wielded no weapon in reply, but his skills in defence had proven his expertise in close-quarters warfare.

Gilead decided that whatever this being was, it was his equal in combat, and that was all that mattered on any field of battle.

A ray of clear, bright sunlight travelled between the branches of the trees, thrusting in at an angle to the ground, casting long shadows, and glinting dully off Gilead's blade.

Gilead and the knight circled each other, at too-close quarters in the confined space between the trees, looking into each other's eyes, searching for some weakness, some chink in the other's armour.

As the sun caught the blade of Gilead's sword, the glowing light in the knight's eyes dimmed and clouded.

Gilead thrust and swung, and thought, in the split second it took for the knight to parry, that his opponent might be slowing down.

Circling a little more, Gilead stepped between his opponent and the ray of sunshine, and the knight's eyes shone once more.

The knight stepped in with the shorter blade, thrusting hard at Gilead's side, tearing his shirt, but missing his body by the smallest of margins. If Gilead had been built like a human, the knight would have connected with flesh, muscle, and perhaps even organs, but Gilead was half the width of a man, and had evaded another grave injury.

In response, Gilead thrust high and tight, making the knight duck to his left, as another slender beam of light found its way into the clearing over the elf's left shoulder. The strike cut another narrow, shallow slice in the knight's neck, but it would take a great deal more than that to bring him down.

As Gilead drew his sword back to the centre, the new beam of light bounced off it slightly, and the elf noticed the clouds descend in the knight's eyes once more. He jinked to his right, so that the knight had no choice but to circle away from him, and Gilead made another strike. This time it was a feint, designed to make the knight move a little further around the circle and into the light.

The narrow sunbeam fell first on the knight's short dagger, and then danced from it to Gilead's blade. The elf went through an exercise series, one that he had practised a thousand times with his twin brother Galeth in the training yard at Tor Anrok. He sliced and jabbed, and made figures in the air, all designed to catch the light and throw it back into the knight's face.

The knight's eyes were dull and cloudy; nevertheless, he raised Gilead's dagger in a defensive posture and parried, while trying to find somewhere to hide from the light.

Gilead's next strike hit its target. The tip of his sword found the gap between the knight's ribs in the fourth intercostal space. It should have been enough to kill him.

The knight staggered back a pace or two, and fell against the sloping trunk of a tree in the grey shadow of its ragged canopy. His eyes glowed hot for a moment, and his fist clenched around his weapon with renewed vigour.

Gilead stepped back and took a long, deep breath, drawing the blade of his sword through a handful of cloth gathered up from his shirt to polish the elf-forged metal.

Gilead heard a distant whinny and then a weak bark. He swiped the blade through the cloth once more, and waited while the knight jerked his shoulder against the tree for leverage and took a step forwards.

The knight and the elf circled each other cautiously for a moment or two as they both heard movement in the woods around them. There was the sound of the dog barking, eagerly, but weakly, the sounds of boots stomping through dry leaves and mulch, and then came the calls, howls almost, as the local men urged each other on, building up their confidence to face their foe.

Gilead had not been the only one to track and find the knight. The locals, tired of living in fear under the threat of they knew not what, had banded together to attack their nemesis. They would kill him, or they would die trying.

The knight, clutching the weeping wound in his chest, looked from Gilead to his mount. A dancing beam of light caught the edge of his improvised shield, and, for a moment, he was blinded again.

The local men had mistaken Gilead for their foe once before, and the elf did not relish meeting this human force again, however much of a rabble it might be. He was exhausted from the battle, mentally and physically, and he had a number of wounds to clean and dress before he could leave these dark, cold barren woods of Ostermark for good.

As the elf made up his mind, the knight flung Gilead's dagger aside, and threw a bundle over his horse's back. Gilead swiftly and silently collected his weapon, and left the tiny clearing before the wounded knight could notice his departure. The knight struggled to mount his war steed, and the horse stomped the ground flat as it circled once and then twice as the undead warrior gathered his wits. Moments later, they too left the clearing.

Gilead knew that, wounded or not, the knight would best any human attack, that the local men were too weak and ill-equipped to defeat him, even in daylight. He trusted that the knight would lie low for long enough to avoid contact with the men, that he would do no more damage to the vulnerable humans than had already been done. The warrior must be as exhausted as Gilead was, and he would surely hide from the daylight and the human force, such as it was, in order to rest and recover his strength.

It would be up to Gilead to rid the countryside of the terrible scourge of the undead warrior knight. He would hunt him down wherever he fled or hid, and he would not fail a second time.

Gilead ducked and wove his way back to his waiting mare without disturbing a single twig or leaving so much as a footprint in the dry, grey mulch beneath his feet. It was as if he had never been there.

The humans passing nearby did not catch his scent on the breeze nor hear his footfalls, despite passing within yards of him. They were tracking their quarry deeper into the woodland, and it was not Gilead.

Chapter 5

Gilead washed rags in the shallow culvert with its sweet water, and used them to clean and wrap his wounds. His injuries were numerous, but none of them were deep; his concern was the malignant poison that must surround such an opponent, and the likelihood of succumbing to infection. Gilead sought out the cleansing herbs he would need to make a fresh and living salve for his injuries, but there were none to be found. He dug deep among the few remaining supplies in his pack and found dried versions of the leaves he needed. He knew that they would be less effective in this form, and spent some time rehydrating the herbs with clean water and drops of the more potent oils distilled centuries before by Fithvael at their home of Tor Anrok, the lost tower. He hoped the resulting unguents would be sufficient for his needs.

Gilead had never feared death; for many decades after his

twin Galeth's death, he had cynically toyed with it, dared it to take him from the cruel world and the fates it offered. After many adventures that had led him close to death, but closer still to madness, he had learned from his last and best companion, gone these many years, not to throw his life away. Fithvael had taught him to look after his health, both physical and mental, and to reward his body for its skills in combat by treating his wounds with the very best medicines that were available to him. Today, in this woodland, in these straitened times, the best medicines were those he had carried, ancient and dried to powder, from his homelands.

All that remained was for him to rest, and to hope that he would not fall prey to some alien fever.

Within days, Gilead was content to continue his quest. His wounds were healing slowly by his normal standards, but they were clean and free of infection. His horse, too, was rested and as well fed as anyone could hope in these times of virtual famine.

It was not difficult to pick up the knight's scent, literally and figuratively. He was not difficult to track, being less subtle than an elf, or even a well-trained human. The knight did not seek to hide his passage through the woodland, or the places where he had stopped to maim and bleed creatures to satisfy his appetites, and to allow his steed to rest or eat. Gilead was surprised that the knight had clearly covered a good deal of ground over the intervening time. The elf had wounded the knight seriously, if not fatally, and yet the creature seemed not to be slowed down by its injuries. It never stopped for more than an hour or two at a time, seemed not to need sleep, did not cook, and hardly rested. When it travelled by day, it did so more deeply in the forest, staying under the canopy where it was at its most dense, where shade from the sun was at its most complete.

Gilead tracked through areas of woodland that had been virtually decimated by the knight. He had taken almost a straight path during the daylight hours, hacking through branches and saplings rather than going around them. The ground was churned up in places, as if the knight had forced his steed to move faster than the terrain ought to have allowed. There were no signs of cooking, and none of the edible plants that still remained just under the earth's surface had been grubbed up or prepared. There were only the tattered, papery corpses of some of the more resilient local rodents, their flesh bled to a pale, stringy consistency. Gilead did not care to muse on the knight's tastes and urges. It was what it was, and Gilead would not stop until he had rid this northern winter land of its most feared predator.

Convinced that the knight was at the centre of all the horrors that had been visited on the Empire and beyond, determined that he must be caught and killed as soon as possible, Gilead rested little and rode his mare harder than he would have liked to make up ground.

In the northern lands, at the farthest north-east reaches of the Empire, in Ostermark, and farther north on the borders of Kislev, towns and villages huddled no more than a few miles apart. In such cold climes and rugged countryside, a man might walk half a day to cover six or seven miles. If he were to visit a town or market and return home the same night, his round-trip should not be more than ten or a dozen miles at most. Homesteads and farms also congregated in the countryside in this manner, so Gilead was never very far from some form of human habitation, and yet, he saw very few people. The further he travelled in the knight's wake, the fewer and further between were his human sightings.

On the third day of travelling, within a hundred miles of Bechafen, when Gilead felt that he was only a matter of hours away from finding his foe, he suddenly realised that he was totally alone. It was the elf's natural state to be a solitary individual, and he was used to going for weeks, sometimes months or even longer without seeing another sentient being. Wherever he had been in the Empire, at any time during the past several centuries, he had always been within the sight, sound or smell of some beast of the field, some bird, some creature, however small or humble. Now, there was nothing.

Gilead's path took him out of the edge of the forest at last, on to a stony pathway that bordered cultivated land. An hour later, he stopped the mare along the narrow track that he had been following across sloping farmland that was roughly divided into a series of strips. He was keeping close to the high, dusty hedgerows so as not to be easily detectable, but there was no one to see him. The fields were fairly recently tended. New crops, planted in the hope of a more abundant harvest next season, from diminishing stocks of precious seeds, were trying to force their way into the world. Gilead could not help but notice that their growth was patchy at best, that the soil was dry and had not been irrigated, and that the plants were fighting for the poor earth's nutrients with weeds that should not have been there. The small fields and narrow strips of land would each sustain only one family, and should be the lifeline to which the local community clung, but there was no one there. No one tilled the land or worked the tender young crops that were trying to grow there.

If there were no humans, why weren't the smaller beasts taking advantage of the young crops? Why were there not flocks of birds feeding on shoots and buds? Why were the shrews, voles and field mice not running amok? Why, if there were flora to feed the herbivorous creatures, were there no predators to feed on them? What had happened to the food chain?

Gilead wondered whether the humans had simply deserted the farms and homesteads that he saw scattered across the land, for they appeared to be intact. The humans, if they had left, must have done so recently for the crops were newly planted and not halfway to being harvested. But where would they go?

Something unthinkable had happened. Some terrible fate had befallen all living things.

Gilead left the path with its hedgerows for the nearest metalled road, which joined the larger villages and towns. He adjusted his grip on the mare's reins and brought her to a steady gallop in the centre of the empty road. The air was full of menace, not from a scent that he could identify, but from the lack of something. The air was too dry and stale, and Gilead felt death descending around him. The humans were dying. He was convinced of it. He was equally convinced that the undead knight had something... everything... to do with it.

Gilead rode into the outskirts of a market town called Omalk as the sun set, watery grey against a dull purple sky. He would normally have walked in, keeping to the meaner parts of town, to the alleyways and darker places. He did not hide now; there was no need for him to avoid detection for there was no one to see him. Many of the buildings, including the drinking holes and cook-shops where the poorer locals congregated to eat and drink, were locked up with their shutters pulled down, or were simply deserted.

Gilead dismounted and pushed open a door that had been left ajar some time before. The tables still bore the remnants of the last meals eaten there, although the food was cold and congealed on the assortment of mismatched, chipped plates. Ale had been drunk hurriedly, leaving splashes on the tables and one last swallow in the bottom of grubby glasses.

There was that smell again: the smell of old things, of death, and of human fear.

The men had left this drinking establishment, all at the same time, heedless of their meals and the few belongings that littered the room: a jacket slung over the back of a chair; a hessian bag, half-full of something-or-other, left under a table; a broken rake and a hoe with a split handle leaning side by side against the wide table that served as a bar.

Something had threatened these people. Something had threatened them with their very lives. Gilead could smell it, feel it on the air.

If he could smell it, he could track it.

Gilead could track as easily in the darkness as in the light, and much of the small town was in darkness. Chinks of light showed through in one or two places, from behind closed doors or around ill-fitting shutters. One or two windows had not been covered, nor the candles in the rooms inside extinguished, but they were few and far between. A trapdoor set in the pavement, close to a large building, showed light intermittently around its seal as someone moved around below. Then the light flickered and died.

Gilead did not need to disturb the inhabitants of the cellar to know that the place was full of women and children. He could hear the faint, shrill cries of small children and the murmurs of the women trying to soothe them. Once or twice he heard Sigmar's name invoked in desperate prayers.

He could almost taste the foetid smell of putrefaction on the air as he rode into the market square at the centre of the town. He expected to see death and devastation on a scale that few rarely witness, but the place was still and empty.

The smell came stronger than ever, and Gilead dismounted his mare to follow his nose.

He knew that the knight had been here. He could not see or hear him, but he found evidence of his mode of battle.

Gilead looked for and found a trail of destruction. He saw leaves on the ground from the surrounding trees that could only have been sliced off by a well-sharpened blade. He saw hoof-print patterns in the blue-green verges of tough nutsedge around the town square that bore witness to a well-disciplined war steed's wheeling and turning in response to his master's hand on his reins. He saw barrows and stalls haphazardly backed onto kerbs in avoidance of a raging battle, their meagre wares scattered across the paved streets.

Yet he saw no humans, and he saw no undead knight.

He could smell human blood, shed some hours before, and he found an abandoned shoe, and a button, sliced from a tunic. There was hair, too, a small clump of it with a scrap of skin attached, adhering to the bark of one of several trees that marked one end of the square. There were, however, no bodies, no wounded and no dead, despite the stench of mortality in the air.

The battle was over, or had moved on. This area had been cleared of dead and injured, and the women in hiding had taken their fallen men with them to tend their wounds or to prepare them for their graves.

The mare's ears pricked as a thin wail penetrated the still silence. Then came the faintest of sounds, as if a blade were striking off stone. Gilead could very nearly smell the sparks as they flew off honed steel.

He was close, but the battle didn't rage around him, it didn't rage in the town proper, nor had it left the area.

The battle raged beneath his feet, below Omalk's market square in whatever sewers, catacombs, cellars and underground sluices and passages occupied the spaces below the streets.

Gilead was struck by the thought that he should have known. He ought to have anticipated the knight's movements. Of course, he would seek out towns that had underground places. He would not fight above ground, unless he had to. He could not fight by full daylight, not as efficiently as he could by night, at least, and Gilead had known it all the time he had been looking for the knight.

Gilead did not know this particular town, but it did not necessarily follow that the knight had not sought it out because of the dark places beneath. Many towns and cities, especially those in the north of the Empire, had masses of underground byways, tunnels and even huge, open spaces beneath them, some caused naturally, others built, often by the skilled hands of dwarfs, who took great pride in hewing and dressing rock and stone of all kinds.

Gilead thought again of the basement on the outskirts of town where he had heard the women and children gathered. This place might have almost as much city below ground as above. There must be a hundred entrances and exits, and dozens of routes and chambers.

If the town below the town belonged to them all, and was in general and continuing use, then there would be plenty of access, and it would be close to the market square, close to where he was standing.

Chapter 6

Gilead tethered the mare and walked around the square, touching the door handles of buildings, looking through unlit windows into darkened rooms, and scanning the ground all the time with his eyes, looking for access to the buildings below street level.

He quickly found metal grilles set into the pavement right up against the buildings. They extended perhaps eighteen inches from the buildings they abutted, were a yard across, and they covered open cavities below so that no one could fall in accidentally. One or two of them looked like they covered chutes for goods to be delivered into waiting cellars, others looked like storm drains and overflows for collecting rainwater or to aid in cleaning and draining the market square. One was clearly a run-off from a slaughterhouse, with two well-worn, wide-brushed brooms leaning against the wall, and the faint smell of offal and old animal blood.

The smell of blood, fresh and human, was stronger on the west side of the square, and on close inspection, Gilead found that two of the grilles had removable bars. He only had to lift one of them out to be able to lower his body into the cavity. The narrow door that he found below street level showed no chink of light around it, and opened inwards.

Gilead carefully replaced the bar above his head to leave no trace of his entering the building, and then pushed gently against the door, turning the knob on the outside first one way and then the other.

The door opened an inch or two, but no further, and the strong, sweet, metallic smell of blood filled Gilead's nostrils. The elf listened for a moment, and smelt the air again, but there was no new sound or scent. He put his shoulder against the door and eased it open, pushing aside the body that barred his way.

Gilead rolled the corpse over. The kill was only a matter of a few hours old, and it was human. It had been cruelly and none-too-cleanly eviscerated, and the hard floor that it lay on was sticky with blood and gore.

A low, rumbling echo met Gilead's ears as he crossed the almost empty storage cellar, and he slowly, carefully, unsheathed his shorter blade, all the time edging towards the darkest corner of the room, eager to conceal his presence from anyone who might enter. He knew from experience that the knight was a fierce opponent, his equal in speed and grace with bladed weapons, and the elf wanted to meet him on his own terms, preferably by surprise attack.

Gilead backed into a dry, smooth stone wall, adjacent to an opening. He thought, at first, that it was an alcove, and glanced into it to see if it would offer him a temporary refuge, but as his eyes became accustomed to the gloom, he realised that this was the opening of a low, arched, brick tunnel. He also realised that this was where the sound was coming from.

He heard it again, but this time the low rumble was closer, and quite clearly a human moan, once the echoing nature of the subterranean corridor was factored in.

As Gilead stood, four-square, in the mouth of the tunnel, he glimpsed movement some thirty or forty feet away. A lurching figure staggered around a corner and fell against the right-hand wall of the corridor, clutching at its body with one hand. It groaned once more and slid to the hard, earth floor. Gilead almost felt the life force leave the bulky masculine body with that final groaning exhalation. He could do nothing for the human now.

Gilead ducked from his full height and moved stealthily, virtually silently, along the other side of the corridor, stopping for only the briefest moment to assure himself that the knight's latest victim was in fact dead. He looked down at the corpse still clutching at its gut even after death, trying to hold together a ragged tear that had allowed the contents of the man's abdomen to spill out over his thighs. The wound was not a clean slice or cut. It was not the product of fierce and lunging swordplay. Either the knight had lost his weapon of choice and had resorted to some other way to see off his human enemies, or he chose to kill this way, to hack and tear when he could have killed cleanly, both more elegantly and with greater respect for his opponents.

Gilead followed where the dead man had come from, turning left and right along corridors that smelt of recently spilled blood, stepping over more bodies with ragged mortal wounds ripped through torsos, necks, abdomens and faces. Some were cold, dead for several hours, others were warmer, and one or two still spilled blood, suggesting that they had not yet succumbed to their injuries, although they no doubt would.

The light in the tunnel was subdued and intermittent. At times, Gilead passed close to one of the pavement grilles, which would have allowed light to flood in during the day, but which afforded only the most meagre glow of luminescence borrowed from candlelit interiors, few and far between on such a desolate night, in a town whose population appeared to be anywhere but here.

There were torch sconces along many of the corridors he travelled, following his senses to where the knight must be doing battle. Some of them had lit torches in them, but they were clearly old and poorly made, using inferior waxes and oils, so that they smoked or burned with dull, green light, which cast gruesome shadows on all the surrounding surfaces.

The knight, with his glowing eyes, could clearly see more effectively in the dark, and, if Gilead's previous experience was to be borne out, was stronger and more able in every way when and where the sun didn't shine.

Gilead soon became accustomed to his surroundings. He adapted quickly and efficiently, using his heightened senses to compensate for any loss of visual clues.

Ahead of him, in the darkness, as Gilead approached a major hub where several tunnels of varying sizes and profiles and various degrees of importance met, he saw a figure scuttling from one opening to another, and back again. Three of the tunnels were lit, and glowed oddly, casting a collection of shadows around the figure that seemed not to resemble its form at all. The figure appeared not to know where it was or where it was going. It seemed confused and not a little afraid. It was literally jumping at its own shadows.

Gilead pressed his back lightly against the cool stone wall of the corridor from which he was approaching the hub, making sure not to cast a shadow of his own. He slowed his breathing and remained totally still, watching.

The figure was joined by a second, which hurtled out of the mouth of one of the darkened tunnels, almost knocking into the creature that was already trying to find its way. Gilead could only think of them as figures or creatures. They might have been men, but he couldn't be sure. They might have been boys, or even women. They were shorter than the average human male, and they were bent and ragged, the strange light conditions and multiple shadows hiding or distorting their forms.

As Gilead watched, the figure that had jumped at its own shadow suddenly lashed out at the other. It appeared to have a wide, short blade in its left hand, and moved quickly in frantic, staccato bursts.

It had clearly hit its target, because the other figure shrieked loudly, in obvious pain. It seemed to duck, and Gilead thought he saw it bare its teeth. Its head was entirely the wrong shape for a human, too flat on top and too narrow, and it appeared to end in an elongated jaw, too full of too-ragged teeth.

As the figures resolved, Gilead watched the creature under attack fill its maw with the other's arm, and thrash with extended claws, ripping at clothes and flesh, and tearing aside improvised armour.

Gilead allowed himself to breathe. The creatures, for it was clear that they were not human, were so caught up in their brutal skirmish that neither was likely to notice him.

The skaven beasts shrieked and clawed, turning and tumbling in a confusion of scrawny limbs, yellow teeth and claws, and mangy fur. Their blood, when it came, didn't smell like human blood; it reeked of disease and decay, of rot and putrefaction.

They were dwellers in the undercrofts, sewers and tunnels that lay beneath most human habitations, and where they could not adopt lost and forgotten underground byways, they dug their own foetid labyrinth of warrens. Gilead did not wonder what they were doing here, for they belonged here, this was their natural habitat, borrowed by the undead knight for his evil ends.

As the ratmen rolled into the entrance of one of the darker, dingier tunnels, Gilead stepped deftly past them, listening at the mouths of the various corridors for sounds of battle. The skaven looked and sounded as if they were well on the way to killing each other, and the elf wanted no part of it. He had more pressing business. He was obliged to help the humans if he could, but more than that, he felt confident that he was reaching the end of a search that had taken decades, scores of years of his life.

Gilead listened for sounds that he might associate with the undead knight, for the dancing footfalls of his fast feet, for the swish of a tempered steel blade cutting the air, for the *thunk* and *clang* of ill-aimed weapons falling against his shield. All he could hear were the shrill calls of ratmen and the anguished cries and grunts of human farmers and guildsmen turned hunters and soldiers.

Before Gilead could decide which tunnel to follow, the hub was suddenly full of bodies teeming out of two of the corridors to his right. Some staggered and lurched while the more able-bodied pushed and shoved their way out. Many of the humans had jagged flesh wounds and all had rents and tears in their clothes.

A skaven horde, dozens strong, followed its prey into the hub, and, as they rushed in, the two rats that had been fighting looked up in astonishment, one on top of the other. One of the larger rats kicked them, and they struggled to get up and join the fray, at least for as long as their tattered bodies would allow.

Gilead drew his dagger. He would have preferred to avoid this mayhem, but he could not exit the hub for the mass of bodies fighting there. Besides, the humans were being bested by the skaven, and the elf could not countenance the abject defeat of the local townsmen, knowing that their women and children were relying on them.

Gilead deftly cut the tendons in the back of one of the skaven's legs, bringing it down, and with it, two of its brethren, as it dropped its rusting blade to reach out for anything that might keep it upright. The human under attack turned in surprise, only to find himself at close quarters with another of the ratkind eager to finish what his comrade had begun rather than deal with a fresher opponent.

None of the filthy rodents wanted to face Gilead, and he found himself trying not to attack his foes from behind, blind-siding them. An elf warrior looked his opponent in the eye when he killed him.

A young man, slight of build, but quick and agile, a hoe held between his hands as if it were a staff, was thrusting his arms this way and that, whacking any rat that came within a couple of paces of him around the head, back and chest, or anywhere else that he might unbalance the foe. He soon realised that once any rat was on the floor it was unlikely to get up again. The skaven were weak creatures, feverish in their efforts, but shuffling and inelegant, and they were so short-lived by nature that they seldom had the chance to gain valuable experience in any sort of fight. They thrashed like fearful human infants, angry, petulant and entirely without discipline. It made them the perfect opponent in every regard, except one: they were unpredictable.

The young man swung his hoe, at waist height, once more. Gilead watched as the business end hurtled towards a rat. The creature was a particularly ugly specimen with tufts of patchy hair protruding at odd angles from its skull and bony shoulders. The thing did not duck, but neither did the hoe blade connect with the rat's torso, as Gilead had expected it would. The rat saw the swinging hoe, and thrust out its paws to catch hold of its shaft. The impact must have shaken the skaven's elbow joints horribly, but it hung on, nevertheless, as the boy wrestled with it for possession of the improvised weapon.

Neither the boy nor the rat was going to let go. Hanging on to his portion of the hoe meant that the boy lost all his agility and had to plant his feet firmly, shoulder-width apart, to stop himself tipping over. He stood his ground, determined not to be bested by the ugly rat. Gilead noticed other skaven creatures reacting to the situation. They redoubled their efforts to deal with the humans, scrapping harder and faster, and squealing more loudly as they exerted every ounce of strength they had to free themselves of their individual battles, either by besting their human opponents or by escaping from them.

One rat came up behind the young man and took hold of the hoe's handle, making it even more awkward for the boy to wield. Then two more came in low and began to bite and scratch at the boy's ankles and legs. Seconds later, another rat hurled himself at the boy's back, landing there, wrapping its ersatz arms around the boy's neck in a chokehold.

Gilead switched his dagger to his left hand and drew his sword. He began to attack the rats closest to him, cutting them down with one swing of his sword or one deft thrust of his dagger, regardless of whether they were facing him or not; most of them were not. He made his way towards the boy, whose face was turning pale, but who stood his ground. The boy had two choices; he could keep a firm hold on his weapon and suffer the wounds that the other rats were inflicting on him with their snapping jaws and greasy claws, while the two on either end of the hoe disabled him, but he would surely die. Alternatively, he could let go of the weapon and have nothing left with which to defend himself against the massed skaven attack.

Gilead separated another rat from its life force, thrusting his dagger into the main artery in its groin and leaving it to bleed out, and he was right in front of the boy. The boy went from looking washed out to looking preternaturally pale. He had been heroic in his battle with the rats until they had found a way to get the better of him, and he still showed more courage than most, despite the colour draining from his face. The elf was another matter entirely. Every sensible human was in awe of the elves, in awe of their stature, their prowess, and their long, long lives; in awe of their legendary standing.

Gilead saw mingled fear, respect and even hero-worship in the boy's eyes. Then the elf swung his sword at an angle and connected with soft tissue. The rat holding the bladed end of the hoe suddenly let go. As Gilead withdrew his sword for a second swing, the skaven clutched its paws to its belly and looked down at the blood and viscera leaking out of its abdomen.

The boy blinked, and a little of the colour flushed back

into his cheeks. His eyes glistened and he nodded slightly at the elf, relieved to find an ally.

Without turning, the young man shoved the shaft of the hoe back into the rat behind him, winding it and snapping its fragile ribs, causing it to fall over the pair of skaven that were shredding his trousers and boots. He kicked them off, and then turned and backed hard into an adjacent wall to dislodge the creature from his back.

Encouraged by the boy, some of the men rallied and redoubled their efforts against the skaven, but the ratmen, if not stronger, were, at the very least, wilder, more ruthless and more accustomed to fighting. There were also a very great number of them.

Gilead continued to kill and maim the creatures in short order, but his real mission was to find the undead knight and prevent him causing any more damage. The skaven were opportunists, surely? Gilead thought it unlikely that they were in some way allied to the knight; he was a beast of an altogether different breed. He was as immortal as they were short-lived, as skilful in combat as they were clumsy, and as intelligent as they were brutish. The knight was more akin to the elf than to these sorry creatures.

The boy stayed close to Gilead, his new hero, wielding his hoe with innate finesse, felling a number of skaven while not actually managing to kill them.

'Flee!' Gilead said, the word alien in his mouth. He seldom spoke to humans, although he was able, preferring simply to listen to their conversations than join in with them and endure speaking in their ugly guttural language.

The boy looked at him, unsure what to think as the elf's dulcet tones struggled with the human word.

'Flee?' he asked.

'Flee,' said Gilead, again, severing a rat's sword-arm from its body, as it swung its spiked mace in a haphazard arc, trying to get under the elf's guard.

Gilead and the boy were subduing the skaven horde more successfully as the elf fell into an easy rhythm and the boy's confidence grew. Some of the men, on hearing Gilead speak, took the opportunity to follow his instruction and leave the skirmish, while some simply stared at the elf in awe and wonder.

Gilead pointed at a fallen weapon, a long, wooden handle with a blade strapped to one end with greasy twine and rags. It had belonged to a skaven rat, but Gilead indicated the boy might find it useful. The kid shook his head and rotated his hoe over his hands, showing how well balanced the tool was.

'No,' said the boy.

Gilead was left in no doubt what he was being told 'No' to. The boy had no intention of fleeing and none of giving up the hoe he was using as a weapon.

A high-pitched war cry emanated from one of the tunnels, echoing around the hub, causing the skaven to stop fighting, and giving the few remaining live humans another opportunity to leave the scene.

The cry sounded again, closer and more urgent, the shriek a mixture of fear and loathing, distress and zeal.

Gilead cocked his head for a moment, assessing where the noise was coming from and at what distance. Then he nodded his head very slightly towards two of the tunnels to his left and one opposite. When they came, and they would come very soon, they would emerge from those three tunnels, and they would attack in their dozens or scores.

'Flee!' Gilead said again, but he knew that he was giving the order too late. He also knew that the brave boy would choose to stand his ground.

Gilead shrugged. He wanted to confront the knight, but he had no choice but to deal with the ratmen.

Then, at the edges of his hearing, Gilead detected the ping of tempered steel sparking off stone, and the swish of a deftly controlled blade cutting air. Perhaps the skaven were fighting alongside the undead knight after all, for Gilead knew in his heart that his enemy was bringing up the rear of the rat horde, careering down the dank tunnel towards him.

The first of the skaven emerged from the tunnel opposite Gilead's position. They were smaller but firmer than many of the others, younger perhaps, less diseased, faster and more eager to defile the humans. They carried bladed weapons with long handles, and wore improvised armour, spiked headpieces and cuffs. Several of them also carried more of the torches, which glowed green and gave off a sickly sweet smell. The waxes and oils they used were neither fresh nor free from impurities.

As the skaven surged into the hub, they looked this way and that, and acted hastily rather than in concert. They touched their torches to anything that would burn. Soon, many of the corpses on the earthen floor, both human and skaven, were burning slowly, flames licking lethargically through fur and cloth. One of the rats even managed to set fire to itself as it lowered its torch too close to the filthy rags that wrapped its backwards-jointed legs. Gilead last saw it hopping and skipping about as if trying to escape the flames, but, instead, setting its twitching, frantic tail on fire.

Gilead watched for what felt like long moments as he counted the skaven pouring out of the tunnels, and assessed what damage they could do and what danger they were to him and to the humans still caught in the hub. He counted the torches, too, and worked out how long they might burn for and at what temperatures. He assessed how many of the humans would die or suffer lasting injuries, and decided that the figures were too high to be borne.

Gilead had not been shadowfast for many years, and had almost forgotten what it felt like. By turns it was liberating and tedious, exhausting and exhilarating. The elf had all the time he needed to prepare to fight the skaven, and all the time he needed to achieve the desired outcome of the battle. His sword and dagger moved faster than the eye could detect, even the flitting, nervous eye of a skaven. He cut them down as if they were nothing. He thrust and swung, lunged and flicked both weapons, never needing to parry, since none of the skaven were able to detect the movement of the blades in time to see them, let alone with time to mount a defence.

As Gilead worked his magic, and the few remaining humans did their best to keep out of his way, the skaven began to turn, feebly looking for an escape route back the way they had come. Ratmen began to push and shove their brethren into Gilead's path in order to avoid the elf and his scything, invisible weapons.

Then he saw it.

High over the heads of the skaven, standing tall and lean and menacing, his eyes glowing in the low, green-tinged light shed by the skaven torches, stood the undead knight, fully armed and armoured.

Gilead spun out of the path of a pair of skaven, turning and barrelling into a mass of clawing limbs and piercing squeals, and cut down two more of the ratmen who were try-ing to flee. His head came up for a moment, and he breathed deeply, steadying his senses as he harnessed his shadowfast capabilities to home in on the knight and his actions.

Gilead watched as the knight brought his sword around

past his shoulder, giving his swing enough momentum for the blade to cut down two skaven at once, slicing across one belly and one back, severing a spine and gouging a gut, disabling both of the ratmen.

The knight fixed Gilead's eyes with his own, and, shadow-fast, the elf looked deeply into the warrior's glowing orbs for what felt like several minutes. He saw there fierce determination and the will to kill, but he also saw a kind of nobility, compassion even. Despite everything, despite the nature of the creature and his legacy, somehow, the undead knight felt like nothing so much as his ally.

The skaven were caught between two deadly foes, falling to the knight and the elf in roughly equal numbers, both warriors showing unheard-of prowess in the field of combat.

The young man stood by and watched in awe, raising his fist once or twice in celebration at some particularly powerful or subtle strike or blow, and filling the echoing chamber with prayers to Sigmar.

Short minutes later, large numbers of skaven littered the hub and the entrances to all of the tunnels and corridors that led away from it. Some had managed to stagger away injured and dying, and one or two even showed some bravery, or perhaps foolishness, as they fought to the death, regardless of being seriously outclassed by their opponents.

The last of the skaven dealt with, Gilead turned his back on the small group of humans that remained underground, guarding them, his dagger and sword raised and ready before the knight.

The elf and the knight locked eyes once more as Gilead eased out of his shadowfast state. He did not need the skill; the very thing that would have surely overcome the knight in the glade those many days ago, and which he was now able to harness with ease, was no longer necessary. It was for the best.

The knight raised his sword vertically in front of him, the hilt at his abdomen, the tip reaching beyond the top of his helm, in salute to Gilead. The elf sheathed his dagger and raised his own sword in a mirror image of his opponent. The knight closed his eyes and then opened them again slowly, and the elf nodded slightly, keeping his eyes on the warrior. The salute complete, Gilead sheathed his sword and turned to the boy.

'You should have fled,' he said.

'Thank you,' said the boy.

'Go now,' said Gilead, and turned down the tunnel up which he had come.

'It was the ratmen,' the boy called after him. 'By Sigmar's beard, it was always the ratmen.'

Chapter 7

'He will come, so he will. He will come. When he comes, for come he will, I'll live forever. I won't live for now, not just for now. I'll live forever,' the words tripped out over a narrow, dry pink tongue, through V-shaped rows of bright, sharp dentition.

His gleaming black eyes, like onyx marbles lapped to a mirror finish, shone back at him from the many reflective surfaces of the object he held between blackened claws as he gabbled. His words came in a torrent, spoken almost without punctuation, without pausing for breath, fast and uncontrolled.

'He will come, so he will. He will come,' he said, but there was no one close enough to hear his speech, only the artefact in his hands and the air moving in response to his words.

The scratch of claws and the groan of leather armour creaking around bobbing heads as his attendants sniffed at the foetid air and rotated their ears, listening for the things they must listen for, drew his attention. He ran one soft, pink palm over the vibrating earth wall of his antechamber, and then dropped the artefact on its plaited hair-ribbon back under his coat. It hit the soft, short fur of his belly, where it had grown anew over the last few days, and began to heat and then wither the fur until the smell of slowly burning hair drifted up to his nostrils, making him turn his head this way and that, eyes wide.

The undercrofts throbbed with the movement of hundreds... thousands of his minions, their whispered exchanges creating a susurrus that filled the air and the mind. He could sense it all as they gathered in the vaulted chamber of an ancient crypt, built by man-things a millennium ago, inhabited by his own kind for almost half that time. He would go to them in a few minutes more, go to them, show himself and speak the words that would galvanise them. He did not need to hear the words they spoke to one another in fast, clipped tones; he needed only to feel the air move around him, vibrating the coarse whiskers that sprouted from his brow and maw.

One conversation came to him, and then another and another.

'The gold is there, the gems, the wealth. Gold and more gold, and gems and gold. Piled, piled high and wide, piled everywhere, the gold and the gems and more gold.'

This was his power. These were his lands, these walls, these tunnels, caves and warrens, these fissures through the earth. All that was sky-less belonged to him, and all those who thrived sunless and moonless in his nether-lands bowed down before him.

They were ratkin in their dirt-lined warrens, tunnels and

burrows, living in the warm embrace of the earth, lean and sleek, fast as fast, eager to serve, eager to get closer to their lord, to the centre of things. They were the whisperers, the collectors of information on the movements of men, of beasts, of higher beings. They were the stalkers, the followers, the gatherers of intelligence. Every time man or beast undertook a journey, the whisperers knew about it. They could read the vibrations in the ground. They knew whether a warrior travelled alone by the weight of his warhorse's hoof-falls, knew how far and how long he had travelled, and how burdened he was. They knew when carts rolled to markets, laden with the new fruits of the surface fields, fruits too young, not ripened to the putrefaction of the flesh they thrived on, not brown and grey and fizzing with fermentation, but bright and clean and anathema. They knew when the dirt was tilled and when it was dug, and they knew the purpose of the tilling or the digging. They knew the difference between deep holes dug for bodies and those excavated for hiding treasures, wealth, things, objects, artefacts, the wonders the air-walkers worshipped them with.

They were ratfolk in their brick-lined burrows, with their dripping moss-covered walls, and low-vaulted ceilings, nothing but brick below, around and above them. Their warrens rich in midden-pickings from above, they were closest to the top-worlders, the surface-dwellers, the crust-livers, the air-walkers. They lived so close to the streets, houses, workshops and hostelries inhabited by species that had solid ground only beneath their feet and never above their heads; the rest was air. By contrast to the ratfolk, the air-walkers were robust of constitution, slow of wits, hairless and sluggish, and abominable.

They were squatters and vagrants in their rock-hewn

fastnesses, stolen away from the ancient race of dwarf masons who had quarried the stone, and built the halls and corridors and vaulted spaces. They were skirmishers and assassins. They had outnumbered the dwarf-men, out-manoeuvred them, bested them and stolen from them. They were thieves and liars, wielders of knives and blades, and they were ruthless.

He had learned about the air-walkers. He had learned so much about so many. He had learned that they were not all alike. The dwarfs were few; an old enemy, irrelevant. The humans were the worst, the ugliest, the most stupid. The humans were to be despised and to be pitied. They would fall as the dwarfs had. They were as nothing compared to the Fell people. The Fell people were fast like he was, but long-lived, longer-lived than the humans... much longer...

He placed his hand over the smouldering flesh of his belly, filthy black claws extending almost the full width of the spongy swelling below his narrow ribcage. He felt the incessant bump of his blood organ, ticking his existence away.

The vibrations were growing, the waves pervading his senses, intersecting to create patterns in the micro-movements of the air in his waiting room, the antechamber that led directly out onto the mound of earth raised at the near end of the crypt, the mound from which he would speak to his followers.

He smoothed his coat over his chest, pressing the amulet a little deeper into his fur and skin. He clenched his teeth together and rotated his jaw several times as if chewing, and he lifted and bobbed his snout and whiskers.

Timing was everything.

He took the staff in his left hand, and wrapped the tattered ribbons of cloth that clung to it around the flesh of his paw, protecting the soft parts while exposing the black claws. He cast his eyes over the runes that ran the length of the staff, and concentrated for the briefest of moments, almost as if in silent prayer.

He left the antechamber by its only exit, and climbed the short spiral of stone steps that would lead him onto the mound. He tapped his staff down hard on each step, quieting the crowds that could hear his approach and feel the vibrations he was summoning from the staff and the old worn steps. There was menace in every footfall, and more in the deliberateness with which he placed his staff, not to aid his climb, but to instil fear and wonder in the waiting audience, his congregation.

He stood on the dais in the pale ethereal light cast by a hundred lanterns, fed with low-grade vermin-fat, which had been hung not for their light, for the congregants did not need it to see by, but for their effect. The chattering that had ebbed away as he climbed the steps came to a dead stop as he planted his feet firmly at the centre of the mound. He was surrounded by his bodyguard, the strongest, bravest and most ruthless of his followers, who stood lower on the sides of the mound, their backs turned towards him.

A head, below and to his left, situated almost directly under a lantern that swung lazily back and forth casting its low, tremulous light, twitched, as if its owner might dare to look over his shoulder, might presume to defy an order.

He took one step off the apex of the mound, one step down and to his left.

The attack was swift and deadly, the blades of his staff whirring through the air, cutting the vibrations into bright new patterns. He destroyed the guard who had dared to twitch, his right-hand rat, his captain, his champion, with a series of slices from the long stiletto bound to the end of his staff. Then he sawed into his remains with the broad, serrated blade that protruded from the haft of his weapon at a twisted but pleasing angle.

No human would have detected a sound as the congregation held its collective breath, but to these creatures the air was filled with waves of tension and noise, and movement crashing through their numbers, driving them to respond with fear and wonder. Their leader returned to his position at the apex of the dais mound, blood gleaming on the blades of his weapon in the narrow beams of faint lantern-light.

He watched the throng.

Beyond his ring fence of bodyguards closest to the mound stood his most trusted lieutenants, warriors and fang-leaders; beyond them gathered their loyal followers, and beyond those great swathes of young clanrats, eager for blood, swarmed in loose groups. It was there, at the edges of the congregation, that the violence began.

The blood thirst was upon them as their whiskers, snouts and ears responded to the waves that their leader had sent through them. The stench of blood, the movement in the air as thousands of them exhaled almost in unison, the vibration under their feet as their leader pounded the end of his staff into the earth of the mound, conspired to generate a wave of fear and loathing that roused them to acts of unfathomable violence. When their leader cut down the lieutenant who had been plotting against his reign, reasserting his strength and wisdom, and rightness, the youngest of the congregants, the most eager, neurotic and most easily influenced, turned one upon another, needing no further excuse to wreak a debt of violence on their weaker companions.

The bodies would not lie in their stinking filth and blood

for long. The wounded and dead would be consumed with gusto as soon as the niceties had played out.

In the minute or two that their leader allowed to elapse, dozens, perhaps hundreds of the most pathetic, had been hacked to pieces or maimed; ears, eyes and limbs torn to shreds, guts and skulls opened.

In the last moments before their ruler brought the meeting to order, two clan leaders did bloody battle, surrounded by a heaving crowd of baying followers. They thrust and scythed their weapons at each other, blades clashing and arcing, leaving shadows in the air as they sped to their targets. The smaller but bulkier of the two, hunched at the shoulders and wide of stance, took the bloodiest wound low in his gut or perhaps high up in his thigh. The resulting spurt of blood probably emanated from the femoral or iliac artery. His opponent stepped to one side and raised his arms in triumph, only to be cut brutally across his narrow belly with the serrated blade wielded by one of his henchmen. The victor took two steps up the side of the mound, and the last place in the circle of bodyguards was won and filled, the ring of warriors completed. Their leader had asserted his strength and power, a scheming underling had been dealt with and replaced, and all had been accomplished in an appropriate bloodthirsty frenzy on the grandest of stages.

His position thoroughly reasserted, the leader threw back his head and squealed with laughter. The sound was high and shrill and filled with breath, like a shriek or a screech. The cacophony erupted in the space and fractured the atmosphere, which was still filled with the sounds of clamouring, skirmishing young ones. The air splintered and trembled as it was cleansed of the sounds of close and brutal combat.

The congregants loosened their grips on their weapons,

shrugged back into postures and stances that roughly signified attention to the dais, and, most of all, they fell silent.

He told them. He told them all, his warriors and his workers, his spies and his whisperers. He told them this, as he had told them before, long and often.

'They love us and loathe us; love and loathe.' He snickered, and his whiskers wove intricate patterns in the air as he proclaimed this lesson to his gathered masses.

'They worship and defile us. Worship us. Worship me. They give into the earth all the things they despise on the earth, and all the things they treasure beyond everything. Their treasures are our treasures. They dig our dirt and deposit their treasures in the earth to worship us. My treasures. The gold is mine, and the gems; the gold is mine and ours, and all to my good. The gold and the gems. And the secrets. The dirt holds their secrets.'

The skaven masses hissed their approval as the Rat King laid claim to all that was below the surface in every crevice, nook, hole and grave dug by man or beast.

'It is the Fell One,' he said. 'The Fell One must be mine. The Fell One must be my newest treasure. Behold his powers. Behold how fleet he is, how fleet. The Fell One must be mine. Seek him. Seek him out, and I shall lead him here. The Fell One shall fall at my feet and call me master. The Fell One shall fall, and I shall be his merciless captor. Behold how fleet he is, how fleet. The long-lived one, the Fell One, shall fall. When he falls, for fall he will, I'll live forever. I won't live for now, not just for now. I'll live forever.'

There was movement among the skaven crowds gathered in the crypt before their Rat King. They shuffled and elbowed one another at this strange turn of events. They bared their teeth, and hissed, and kicked. One went down at the edges of the gathering, and then another. They were restless, and their ruler seemed not to know what he was saying. The atmosphere filled first with motes of dust, disturbed into flight by the action of rat-feet on dry, subterranean dirt. Then the air began to move with the breath of the ratkin and the palpable tension among them; their snouts could not help but shrug and twitch, their whiskers tremble and their ears rotate. Their blood organs could not help but flutter and fibrillate. Their energy made the motes dance and weave in intricate, delicate patterns, writing the courses of their fates in the air around them. No mortal man could read the prophecies written there, but the dancing collections of motes began to mesmerise the weakest of the skaven. Only the initiated, the ancient, the leaders and kings of other worlds and other times could truly read the hieroglyphs created in the air, the omens and oracles that spoke of the true and honest states and fates of their kind.

The Rat King looked out over the heads of his followers, out into the depths of the crowd, as whispers approached him. He heard disappointment, disenchantment, impatience and dread. He heard the disaffected whisperings of the very young and the moans of fear from the old.

'Gold and gems,' he heard. 'Gold and gems.'

'Gold and gems,' he said, lifting his weapon in his left hand, allowing the runes carved into the surface of its haft to glint in the low, yellow light of the smoking lanterns.

The skaven hordes quietened a little, and he felt rather than heard the whisper come again. He seemed not to be able to speak his own mind.

'Gold and gems,' he said again.

And then again, 'Gold and gems.'

He felt the ache in his belly, and smelt the musky, acrid scent of his body hair singeing and his skin scorching beneath the amulet.

'Gold and gems,' he said once more as he thrust his hand under his coat to extract the amulet.

As he lifted the hair-ribbon over his head, the amulet felt dull and cold in his paw, no more interesting than a lump of coal or chalk. He could not feel its facets, nor imagine the reflective qualities that it had possessed only minutes before. It felt dull and soft and crumbly. Fear struck deep in his blood organ as he clenched his clawed paw around the amulet. He felt the power drain out of his hands, and thought he might stagger or fall. His left hand gripped the staff of his weapon more firmly, and he allowed it to take his weight as his right hand rose before him, without him exerting any of his will upon it.

His head was suddenly full of words that he did not understand and could never have enunciated. He wanted to copy the words, say them aloud from his twisted maw, but none would come.

He heard a hum, a tune, almost a melody. It was a lullaby, and then it was gone, transformed into a frantic crashing wave of discord that emptied his head of all right-thinking.

Then the motes in the air began to dance to a different tune, to no tune at all, only to the noises in his head.

The Rat King wanted to hold his paws over his ears and over his eyes. He wanted to still the insistent twitch of his whiskers and the rotating of his ears, and yet he had no power over his movements.

Finally, he felt the amulet grow so cold in his paw, so insubstantial, that he thought it would fall to dust. He wanted to clench it more tightly, to hold onto it, never to let it go.

It sustained him. He knew not how, but it was because of this object that he had grown and thrived and lived so long among his brethren.

He clutched the staff in his left hand, driving its end so firmly into the compacted earth floor of the mound that it made a small, perfectly hemispherical crater that began to radiate odd cracks in the surface of the dais. His weapon took his entire weight, for he felt as slow and heavy as death. His blood organ boomed, low, within his body, ponderous as a human's.

His head turned to watch the movement of his right arm as it stretched out to his side, parallel to the floor. He looked at his paw, glowing and translucent, the veins showing like threads of pink light through the padding of his paw palms. The veins pulsed, long and slow. The involuntary twitching in his snout and whiskers slowed so dramatically that he thought he had been stilled, that this was all some terrible dream-state, or some unasked-for condition that afflicted any hapless being who came into ownership of his amulet: the magical talisman that had shown him his path to great age and even greater power among his kind.

He could do nothing but watch and trust.

At the furthest reaches of the congregation, skaven began to keel over where they stood, falling to their deaths as their blood organs slowed to nothing, or trilled to a frequency beyond the capacities of their bodies to tolerate. There were no signs. There was no way to know which of them would succumb or why they were dying, but die they must, in their dozens and hundreds. They expired staring into space, without a mark or a spot of blood appearing on their bodies.

Then, the air sucked away the swirling motes from around the corpses. The particles grouped and banded together and moved around the crypt in waves until all eyes were fixed on the dancing display of light and dust above the skavens' heads. The spectacle drifted up towards the vaulted masonry high above them, casting shadows and spots of light onto the surfaces of the stones, making them glisten and glitter.

A galaxy of motes and particles, forming an array of symbols in three dimensions, settled in a broad halo around the mound with the Rat King at its centre. Then he was bathed in light as the specks reflected and refracted all the illumination they could summon from the lanterns that flickered their smoky flames into the cavernous ceiling space.

The throng was agog, the skaven staring at their leader and at the story that was playing out over his head.

The Rat King watched as his right paw throbbed with the pink light that seemed to be coursing through his veins, and he sucked in a shocked breath as he watched his claws spread and his palm open.

He waited, his blood organ stopping entirely, true silence falling all around him as the motes stopped their merry dance, each coming to a dead halt in the air, all shining their reflected light down on him.

If there had been any capacity for rational thought in the Rat King's mind, in that moment, he might have believed that he would never take another life-sustaining breath. Indeed, many of his kind would be dead by the time the drama had played out, and he did not doubt, in that moment, that he would be one of them. If he survived, he knew that he would live a longer, more satisfying life than all of his predecessors, perhaps than all of his predecessors combined.

He dreaded dropping the amulet to the earth floor at his feet. He dreaded that it would wither to dust, that it would cease to protect him, cease to strengthen his reign.

He wanted to close his eyes against the sight. He wanted his blood organ to begin pumping again. He wanted to be one of them, one of the horde, a simple skaven without the wit for ambition, without the secret of longevity.

He could neither blink nor twitch a whisker, nor clear his parched throat. Terror and anticipation filled him with wonder and horror and glee. The amulet had woven its magic before in ways that he had never understood, but he had kept it, cherished it, allowed it to burn his hair and brand his flesh, tolerated it filling his mind with unfathomable sounds and words and songs. He had fallen under its spell, and he had benefited and suffered for it in almost equal measures.

The Rat King's claws peeled away from the charm, and his pink palm throbbed.

He was no longer holding the amulet in his paw, and yet, it did not fall.

The charm hung for a moment in the air, and then brilliant light exploded from it in a million prismatic sparkles, brighter and more ethereal than the dust motes held magically still in the air above his head. He thought that the charm had splintered and broken, its otherworldly elements rending it asunder in a miasma of blinding shards of luminescence.

When all the light had dispersed into the vaulted ceiling of the crypt, and his hand closed again, involuntarily, around the air, he felt something cool and solid and slick where he had expected to feel nothing at all. The amulet felt hard like stone, but greasy like the pelt of a well-fed and well-serviced brood-mother. He could not determine whether it was the faceted mineral that it had appeared to be in its most recent incarnation, and he could not open his paw again to look upon it.

He stared out over the congregation of rats, at their faces

upturned to look at the light display whirling above their heads. Then, deep in the gloom at the furthest reaches of the crypt, he saw a pair of pink eyes shining out at him. Their gaze held as the Rat King called upon this, his minion, to do his bidding, to find the Fell One.

Suddenly, there was a picture in his head, a glowing image of the tallest, most slender and upright being that the Rat King had ever seen. The biped stood as high as two, if not three, skaven, and it was straight, without the angles for shoulders and elbows and knees and heels that typified the ratman's physique. It was more like the hairless, human air-walkers, while being taller than the tallest man-thing, longer of neck, more elegant, half the width and so uncannily upright. The Rat King knew that this was his target, this was the Fell One, this was the creature that would help him to live forever. He knew not why, nor how this could be achieved; he only knew that it was his destiny. He only knew that he had clutched the amulet, and that he had sensed and seen his very being projected into a wondrous future, to a time when he would be worshipped by everything below ground in the Under-empire, by everything above it and by all that lay between.

At the very moment when he wondered whether he was dead or in some mortal trance-state, the glitter dust that the charm had produced whirled and cycled in the air before him, between his position and that of the skaven who had locked eyes with him. He could no longer see the young pup, for he was blinded by the perfectly realised hologram that the brilliant sparks had generated, the perfect vision of the Fell One.

'He will come, so he will. He will come. When he comes, for come he will, I'll live forever. I won't live for now, not just for now. I'll live forever.'

He heard the words, both in his head and in the air around him. The voice sounded like his, but he could not remember forming the words, either in his mind or in his maw.

'He will come, so he will. He will come. When he comes, for come he will, you'll live forever. You won't live for now, not just for now. You'll live forever.'

The words were real, the whisper coalescing around the astounding form of the Fell One that began to change colour and slowly revolve in the air before him.

It was the pup, speaking.

The Rat King's eyes, open wide in a blinkless stare, could see the suggestion of movement in the pup's jaw, and sense the tremor in the air caused by his whiskers as he shaped his maw to produce the words.

Then another voice spoke up, and another.

Eyes began to turn towards the figure of the Fell One with its white head-fur cascading from its high crown, with its intricately woven cloak of the strangest iridescent cloth, with its weapon so fine, so light, burnished so bright as to defy usefulness. Unblinking eyes shone pink, whiskers twitched and maws chewed and flexed and whispered.

The susurrus of the thousands of voices moved the air such that the detail in which the Fell One was wrought became increasingly profound. It was possible to divine individual hairs on his head and stitches in his garb, to see flecks of a million colours in the bright irises of his almond-shaped eyes and to stare into the eternity reflected back from their fathomless pupils.

Chapter 8

The news radiated outwards from the crypt.

The skaven followed their burrows and tunnels back through the nether-lands to where they had come from, all the while monitoring the movements in the earth above them, searching for the sounds of the Fell One, reaching out to feel his alien vibrations in the micro-movements of the dirt around them.

Competition was fierce, and the eager skaven fought one another tooth and claw for the best avenues, the shallowest fissures, the places under the earth that resonated most profoundly with the waves of movement on the surface. They defended the spaces where earth tremors intersected to pinpoint exact locations where the Fell One might pass. Some chose their positions and stayed there, fighting off all-comers, and touching, testing and sniffing the dirt endlessly, confusing their senses and rendering themselves helplessly insane, often in a matter of hours.

They would begin by trying not to affect the area where they stood sentry, fighting the urge to twitch or move or even breathe. They could not risk hunting, did not dare to leave their posts in search of food or drink, so that when the supplies that they carried ran out, they didn't think to replace them. Many died of starvation without eating the rations they carried lest they miss some tremor in the air because they disturbed it with chewing.

Others of the skaven scurried back and forth, hither and yon in the dirt tunnels and warrens of the nether-lands, searching for the Fell One by covering too much ground too quickly. They collapsed, exhausted and confused, or fought for access to the narrowest and least-used of the tunnels below ground. Their accelerated metabolisms meant they could cover a great deal of ground quickly, but also meant they needed to eat and drink often. Many were so intent on finding the Fell One, so driven by their Rat King's mission, so eager to please their lord and to benefit from the capture of so rare and wondrous a creature that they too forgot to feed their bodies.

Violence had been the most common form of death among the skaven for centuries, violence from outside forces as much as violence from within their ranks. There was no understanding of familial relationships, no sense that they were brothers-in-arms, no loyalties, no ties, and no love lost between them. They fought each other, and killed and died, for any reason and for no reason at all. Now, they died from starvation and insanity, or they were ground down and eaten up by the amulet; that magical device that gathered up souls, devoured them, and distributed their life and longevity back to the wearer.

The Rat King felt it all. Every road, every path, every warren, every space led back to his crypt, back to his anteroom, back to him.

Any skaven that learnt anything, either by good luck or hard work, or by means of stealing from others of its kind, came scurrying back to its master, and the whispers began finding their way back up the chain of command to the Rat King.

He felt their conversations in the air, knew when they were close and when they were on wild-goose chases. He could tell by their manner, their bearing, the way they whispered, as much as by what they whispered, whether they were onto something or not.

Then he heard about the human. He knew from the side-by-side rhythms of the human boy and his master the Fell One, that he had found his quarry. The contrast between the vibrations they caused and the echoes these sent down through the fissures and burrows, down through the dirt and the earth back to the Rat King, was the most telling clue of all. Each vibration was identified by a comparison to its companion.

The boy defined the Fell One.

There was blood on his hands. There was skaven blood on his hands. The boy had killed a ratman. He had killed rat-men. He would kill them again.

The Rat King did not care. The loss of one of his kind was as nothing. He could devour a thousand of them, a thousand thousand, and still not consume a life force to equal that of the Fell One. Let the boy kill, let him kill them if it brought the Fell One closer.

Closer he would come, closer and closer.

'He will come, so he will. He will come. When he comes, for come he will, the Fell One will come too.'

In the dark little antechamber of the crypt, the Rat King sat on a throne cobbled together from the broken staves, hafts and blades of a dozen weapons or more, the rusted, useless, broken blades jutting out at angles in all directions. The joints were made with greasy twists of cloth, ribbons torn from rent and bloodied garments, wound tight, lacing back and forth around the sticks of wood. The hafts and staves were worn smooth, black and shiny by the filthy grasps of their many former owners, the runes crudely carved into them many years before honed by time and silky to the touch.

The Rat King's refuge was at the centre of his world. It was, so far as he knew, the only space for hundreds of underground miles, the only place in the Under-empire that had only one entrance and one exit, and those two the same opening. He was the only skaven that lived in private, that could not be taken by surprise, whose space was sacrosanct and could not be penetrated by new digs or the reopening of old tunnels. He lived at the end of the maze, at the vanishing point, and all roads led to his door. He lived at the epicentre of all vibrations, of all movement, and all sounds travelled to him.

The stories of the boy came thick and fast, that he was with the Fell One and then at a distance, then close again. Every time the boy was mentioned the Fell One was felt, his rhythm denser and slower and more mediated, harder to detect, more economical. He was beyond the boy, and then ahead, and then behind him, to his left or right. They wove, together, a beautiful, intricate, crossing pattern with loops and whorls like the subtly winding paths of the pad prints from a skaven's paw, and their vibrations made intersecting wave patterns of delightful complexity.

Hundreds of sightings over days and weeks came together in the Rat King's mind. His leaders, his champions, his warriors and his minions each had small pieces of the puzzle, and the further up the food chain the skaven were, the more pieces of the puzzle they had, but none could put together a complete picture. None had all the information.

No individual would share information with another of the same standing in skaven society. Lower-ranking ratmen would share only with those of higher status. The minions fed the warriors information, the warriors fed the champions, and the champions fed information to the leaders. Each of the dozen or so of the Rat King's closest aides collected his own cache of information of sightings, of vibration paths, but none trusted his equals enough to share that information.

Once the Rat King had got what he wanted, he pitted his underlings against each other, filling their heads with stories of treachery, backstabbing, spying and stealing. No one survived for very long with any amount of information.

The strongest of the leaders, those who survived the deaths of their colleagues, came under special scrutiny from the Rat King. He promised them much.

The first of his lieutenants entered his antechamber as he sat on his throne, facing the single portal that kept him the safest and best-protected of them all in his uterine cul-de-sac.

He motioned for the large, red-eyed skaven with the thick covering of coarse, dirty black hair to kneel before him.

The skaven did not argue with him, despite being beyond grovelling to anyone, including the Rat King that he would happily conspire to dethrone. Something compelled him to take orders from the wizened old Rat King, whose wrist was adorned with the hard, dull amulet, which seemed to throb, lighting the kinks and curves of hair in the ribbon that held it in place.

The Rat King held his hand in front of his kneeling lieutenant's face, the charm suspended from it.

The lieutenant remained still, but the air around him began to bend and throb, vibrating the Rat King's whiskers and filling his mind's eye with a hundred images. The lieutenant began to speak, although all of the information was already suspended in the air between them, making his speech redundant. His eyes glazed over and he recounted, in automatic tones, all of the information that had been fed to him through the channels of his command. He had thought to keep something back, not to tell the whole story but to leave gaps in the tale that might confound the Rat King's intention to track the Fell One for his own ends. However, as he knelt in the small antechamber, the lieutenant had no choice but to tell it all, and to share the conclusions that he had drawn from the wealth of information that had come his way. With a broad overview, he had seen connections that others with less knowledge had missed, and he added these to his recitation of events.

The Rat King absorbed the account of the Fell One's movements, along with the lieutenant's thoughts on their significance, and all of the information that floated around in the air between them, with the amulet as his guide.

When it was done, the lieutenant continued to kneel before the Rat King, unable to move unless instructed to, his gaze caught in the impenetrable depths of the charm stone.

The amulet twisted and rotated on its hair-ribbon, as the Rat King brought his hands down onto his lieutenant's face, one paw on each of the skaven cheeks.

The Rat King began slowly to apply pressure with his

opposable claws, above the ridges of his lieutenant's cheek-bones. Seconds later, with a pair of quick explosions, there and gone in no time, he caught two pink, wet flesh marbles in his palms. The Rat King tossed his lieutenant's eyeballs casually to the earth floor and muttered for him to leave the antechamber.

The lieutenant stood and turned, crushing one of his eyes under a paw as he did so, and stepping on the other as he moved tentatively across the room.

The second of the Rat King's lieutenants lost his hearing when his master punctuated his eardrums with the same claws that had blinded the first.

The third lieutenant was relieved of his tongue, sliced deeply and cleanly away.

The fourth lieutenant lost his most precious sense when the king excised his whiskers, plucking them one at a time from his maw and brow, and then had his paws burned to thickly scarred stumps incapable of feeling the subtlety of a vibration through any wall made of earth, brick or stone.

The lieutenants relayed their information and, maimed and helpless, were returned to their men. None would last out the day, and, with their deaths, all the information they had gathered was lost back to its sources, sources who could not be induced to share anew.

The Rat King was all-knowing. He was the repository of all information pertaining to the Fell One and his unlikely companion.

Chapter 9

The watched ones, the Fell One and the boy, had nothing in common. They did not sleep or eat at the same time, or with the same frequency; they moved at different paces, often in different directions; their bodies had no rhythms alike, nor had they similar needs.

And yet.

'He will come, so he will. He will come. When he comes, for come he will, the Fell One will come too.'

The words echoed around his antechamber as he awaited more news, more sightings, more information to add to the labyrinthine light map that he cast his black eyes over.

He did not read it consciously. The skaven were a simple, brutal race. They kept smells and vibrations in their heads, they recognised things intuitively. They knew fear when they saw it and the blood thirst. They registered anger and resentment, hunger and mirth. They instinctively knew where they were, underground, at any time, however far they had travelled through the tunnels, however injured or frightened they were; a skaven could never be lost in his natural habitat. Maps of the Under-empire were redundant, and it was a simple fact that no one had ever seen fit to draw one. Maps of the top-world were known to exist, but the skaven turned their noses up at the thought of them, preferring to rely on the solid evidence of ancient and immovable landmarks.

A three-dimensional map made of dust and specks of light would be as alien to the skaven as flying. And yet, there it was, suspended in the foetid air of the Rat King's underground lair, a living, breathing, cycling representation of all the routes and paths the Fell One and the boy had taken in their travels.

The Rat King disturbed the air gently with the claw of his left hand, amending the details on the map with hieroglyphic notations, while his right hand swung the amulet from its hair-ribbon in a fast, short, pendulum motion that seemed to rearrange the dust in subtle, but important ways. He did not fully understand what he was doing, only that he was responding to the whispers in his head, the urgings and admonitions that he must listen to through all his waking hours, and all of his hours were wakeful.

All the time that the Fell One had been in his sights, all the time that he had been accompanied by the human boy, was time that appeared to have been spent in some kind of search, some quest that led the old being in a tacking course from one point on the surface to another. He was an air-walker, a crust-liver and yet he wove a path from one point of egress to the next across the skaven nether-lands.

Every point of egress from above ground to below, every portal, every burrow entrance from which a skaven might exit onto the dirt or enter under it, was marked by a sighting of the Fell One and the boy.

Other sightings put the boy at the site of an ancient tree or a known well, and still more put the Fell One at the entrance to a basement or the site of an ancient burial; places known to the skaven, landmarks for them in the confusing light and air of the top-world. Whenever the Fell One's path entwined with the boy's, wherever they joined forces, they did so where the skaven world met the surface.

The Rat King saw it all. Suddenly, all he could ever want was right there in front of him.

Everything fell neatly into place, and the Rat King clapped his paws together in glee, the claws clacking against each other in a staccato sound that tore tiny holes in the fabric of the air, disturbing the map that shone and glittered before him.

They were hunting. They were searching for skaven to kill. The tiny, dull lights, flitting aimlessly in angry little batches, congregating in the dark places on the Rat King's map, were their prey. The skaven were dying, their blood was on the Fell One's hands, and on the boy's.

The dull lights began to wink out one at a time, and then by twos and threes. Some continued to throb faintly for several seconds before blinking out, and some hurried away, returning to the nether-lands and to safety.

They were not safe, however. The skaven were not safe. They were not safe from their Rat King, and they were not safe from the Fell One; they were not even safe from the boy.

The boy was the key, the boy and his companions.

He could have him. He could have the Fell One.

'He will come, so he will. He will come. When he comes, for come he will, the Fell One will come too.'

He spoke without realising that he was doing so, and as he spoke, his black eyes clouded a little and his gaze seemed to fall short of the map that was slowly disintegrating back into its component parts.

The amulet, twisting and pulsing on its hair-ribbon, seemed to slow down, no longer rocking back and forth like a relentless pendulum marking time, but coming to a gentle rest.

'I will bring him, so I will. I will bring him. When he comes, for come he will, I'll live forever. I won't live for now, not just for now. I'll live forever.'

The Rat King unwrapped the hair-ribbon from around his wrist, hung it around his neck and dropped the amulet down under his coat. He could feel the flesh of his belly warm with the contact of the charm, and could smell the searing of his hair. His snout twitched slightly, and if his long maw with its rows of sharp teeth could smile, a smile was what appeared on his face.

He placed his fleshy palms flat on the walls of his ante-chamber and felt the vibrations building. They built so fast and with such intensity that his palms curled involuntarily, and his claws dug deep gouges in the mossy stone walls.

He shrugged his coat more comfortably around his shoulders, and took the haft of his weapon in his left paw, using his right to wrap the strips of ragged cloth around the soft parts of his palm while exposing the blackened claws, sharpened by their recent contact with the stone.

The ground beneath his feet throbbed, and he could hear the treads of thousands of pairs of feet as his minions drew closer.

The message had been subliminal. He had not even been aware that he was summoning them, and yet summon them he had, in their hordes. Every tribal leader, every champion, every lieutenant had taken up his clarion cry, and soon they would fill the crypt and stand in awe as they listened to his orders.

He had sacrificed so many of them to his cause, and each of their lives had lengthened his by a breath or two, by half a dozen beats of his blood organ. Their lives were cheap.

It did not matter how many of them he sacrificed to ensure his immortality, there would always be more of them. Every time he killed a champion, every time he slaughtered a leader who knew too much, every time he tore into a warrior who coughed at the wrong moment, or turned his back, or showed the slightest disrespect to the Rat King, another happily took his place. They lived fast and they died young. The brood-mothers, serviced by all and any who could fight their way through the throngs to get at them, simply produced more. The nurseries were full of them, teeming with the little bastards who would fight and die, even as pups, for the sake of violence.

There would only ever be one Fell One, and he had a plan to take him captive. He had a plan that would decimate his hordes of ratmen, but it would never exhaust their numbers entirely.

He did not know how long he stood in the antechamber, mesmerised by the voices in his head, and by the plot that was forming from the strange words. When his senses returned, the Rat King could hear the sounds of skaven jostling for positions in the crypt. They had answered his call. They had come. He could sense that the lanterns had been lit, and that his bodyguard, none of whom had served him for more than a few days, and none of whom would serve him for many more hours, were in position.

He left the antechamber and climbed the short spiral of stone steps that led to the mound.

He needed no words to silence them. They stood in rough ranks, facing him. They stopped jostling and pushing. They did not elbow, or shove or trip one another.

The Rat King's snout twitched slightly in air that felt thick with fear and awe, fear and awe for him, and for the power he was about to wield.

The Rat King spread his arms to his sides, his left clutching the haft of his weapon. He looked down on the backs of the heads of his bodyguard; none twitched. They were still and they were silent.

He looked out over their heads, watching pairs of red and black eyes glinting and throwing light in the great space. The air above their heads was dense and dark, and full of presentiments.

The Rat King took hold of the amulet and lifted it out of his coat. He didn't wind the hair-ribbon from around his neck, but simply tugged on it, and it came away in a small cascade of drifting hairs. He held the amulet high above his head, and opened his hand.

The charm spun slowly in the air, and then faster and faster, casting brilliant light into the darkest of corners. Then the voices began, chanting a strange incantation that made some of the minions furthest from the dais sweat and gag, and fall dead to the earth floor beneath their feet. Finally, the chanting stopped and a single voice echoed around the great hall.

'I will bring him, so I will. I will bring him. When he comes, for come he will, I'll live forever. I won't live for now, not just for now. I'll live forever.'

The skaven joined in, first singly and in small numbers,

and then in groups and tribes, and soon they were all reciting the words.

'We shall bring him so we shall. We shall bring him. When he comes, for come he will, you'll live forever. You won't live for now, not just for now. You'll live forever.'

As they spoke, the miasma of their breath, finding its way into the vaulted space above their heads, augmented by the ethereal, brilliant light from the amulet, formed shapes and patterns in the air until the entire plot was drawn in stark detail before them. The boy was there: the bait. The Fell One with his sword stood out in stark detail, defending the human boy. Some of the skaven tittered and gurgled odd laughing noises as they witnessed the Fell One's unfounded loyalty to the ugly, slow, smooth-skinned human boy. They laughed less when they witnessed the speed and savagery of his weapon as it cut down their shadows right above their heads.

The plan was laid out before them. Their mission was etched indelibly on their collective mind. They would obey their Rat King and master, even knowing that they would die doing his will.

A young skaven, maddened by the sights before him, clutched his bladed weapon in both of his hands, like a scythe, and swept through the legs of a dozen of his nearest compatriots before he could be stopped. Another ratman, a frenzied tribal leader with a deep battle scar cleaving his brow that should have left him dead, drew a thick-edged serrated blade across his own throat until bright pink blood gouted from his carotid, signalling his death.

Many succumbed, but those that remained were galvanised by the experience. It was all before them. They had a mission and they would give their lives in the quest for its completion.

They began to turn from the Rat King as he held his arms aloft and stared deeply into the light show high above him in the vaulted ceiling of the crypt.

Gradually, the amulet slowed in its spinning motion, and the light began to disperse from it.

The hordes banded together and chose their routes out of the crypt, their feet pounding on the earth floor, and their voices echoing down the tunnels as they departed.

As the last of the skaven made ready to leave, and the Rat King's bodyguard turned to him for permission to fight for his greater glory, the amulet stopped dead in the air. The Rat King did not reach out to take it.

There were no more than a dozen of them in the crypt, standing around and on the dais mound, when the amulet began to revolve in the opposite direction; it began sucking light back into its core, began to regenerate, just as the Rat King was revitalised by the losses of the lives around him.

All of the energy in the room was gone, and the darkness turned to something beyond dark, beyond the densest black darkness that the skaven were so familiar with in the depths of the dirt.

The amulet began to suck the light out of their eyes, catching the gleams that bounced off their claws and teeth, and sucking the refracted pinpoint luminescences from the drops of saliva that coated their tongues.

It began to suck the light from the air among the hair on their bodies, and from the pores in their skin.

Then it began to draw light from the dressed stone of the crypt, from the vaults and buttresses, from every mason's cut and mark.

* * *

When it was done, the amulet was dull and cloudy, and looked utterly unremarkable, aside from the fact that it sat in the air where there was nothing but necromancy to keep it aloft.

When it was done, the Rat King closed his hand around the amulet and stepped from the top of the mound towards his antechamber. As he left the crypt, he turned to look at the desiccated corpses of his bodyguard. Then he turned to look back into the crypt, to take in all that had occurred.

The light was low, but that did not affect his sight, or what he saw.

The crypt was wrought anew in obsidian, blacker than any stone hewn with a mason's chisel had any right to be. It was dull and black in an infinite, endless way that would endure beyond anything that the skaven had ever known.

Whatever happened in the nether-lands, whatever became of the Rat King, of his minions and of his kingdom, the crypt would remain forever.

Chapter 10

I dreamt, I think, a strange and brutal dream. I sleep so little now that I am ancient, and when I do, I find myself riding the night horse with a vigour that belies my age and sex. The boy was right, it is always the skaven.

The stories I have heard and told of the skaven cause me to wonder yet if they are not the most damned of beasts, the most cruel and vicious of races; certainly, they haunt me still.

'Go home,' said Gilead, mildly revolted by the feel of the human words on his lips. 'Return to your family.'

'I have none,' said the boy. 'I was the last of them. My brothers, older and younger, and my baby sister... All are dead,' he said, with a catch in his throat, making the words sound even more guttural and ugly to Gilead's ears than they might otherwise.

'You have a homestead, somewhere,' said Gilead. 'A village... a town.'

They were more words than he had spoken to another living soul since he had left his brethren at the funeral, more words than he cared to speak in the ugly human tongue.

'All gone,' said the boy. The catch in his throat had cleared. He spoke in a matter-of-fact tone without any discernible effect. Gilead turned to the boy, surprised by such composure in one so young and so unutterably related to the coarser species.

Gilead had been sitting before a small fire at the edge of one of the roads that radiated out from the dreadful, defiled town. He had not gone back into the woods; there was no need. The remaining humans were resting and regrouping and mourning their dead. They would not miss the elf, and neither would they travel at night.

Perhaps he had come there on purpose. Perhaps he had made it easy for the human boy to follow him and come upon him so easily and so quickly after the battle. He looked at the boy who stood a little way behind him and to his right, at the edge of the road. He said nothing, and then turned back to the simple meal that he was cooking at his fire. He pushed the point of his knife into the glowing orange-grey embers under the fire, spearing something that nestled there. With a flick of his wrist, the elf sent the object arcing through the air. It landed in the boy's outstretched hands, but he had to toss it from one hand to the other to prevent it burning his palms. Ash dropped away from the small tuber, and the boy popped it into his mouth, biting hungrily into it. It was too hot, and he spat it out, the two pieces landing unceremoniously in his hands, the bright pink insides fluffy and steaming.

When the first tuber was eaten, Gilead tossed the boy a second. It was sweeter than the first and dark purplish-red in hue. After biting into it, the boy looked from its exposed flesh to Gilead, a question in his eyes.

'It's good,' said Gilead. 'Almost anything can be made to be edible.'

The boy smiled and took another healthy bite from the tuber.

The tea that Gilead handed to the boy in a horn beaker that looked more like a thimble, even in his small, feminine hands, tasted slightly bitter, but wonderfully aromatic. He did not know what it was made of, only that it was intense and warming, and unlike anything he had ever tasted. Somehow, it quenched his thirst too, despite being so meagre in quantity.

'It is cleansing,' said Gilead. 'A little is enough.'

When he had finished drinking, the boy ran his little finger around the inside of the beaker and sucked on it, eager not to miss a drop of the delicious liquid.

Gilead did not smile; at least, if there was a smile somewhere within him, it did not find its way to his lips.

'Sleep,' he said. 'Tomorrow, we shall talk.'

'Then I can stay with you?' asked the boy.

'Tomorrow, we shall talk,' said Gilead again.

The boy looked at the elf's face and saw that it was useless to ask his question again. He looked into a face that frightened him a little, but which was also reassuring. He knew what an elf was; everyone knew what one was, but no one that he knew had ever met a member of the ancient race, and he doubted that anyone he would ever know would find himself in the position of being the guest of one.

The countryside was full of them, and yet they went undetected by the human boy, until they were pointed out by

Gilead; but the child was clever and eager, and he soon learned the signs that would lead him underground, into the realms of the skaven.

The ground was often built up around the entrances, which appeared on the shaded sides of mounds constructed by the ratkind, or in convenient natural slopes. They were generally not to be found in dense or difficult ground, so rarely very deeply into woodland where tree roots would make it difficult to penetrate easily underground.

In open country, it was easy enough to locate entrances to the burrows and warrens that the skaven excavated and then made their homes in, nor was it difficult to work out whether the entrances were currently in use or had been abandoned some time previously.

Gilead was a skilled tracker and was endlessly patient. He would watch and he would wait for clear evidence of skaven movement. He was capable of sitting in hiding, lying in wait, for hours or even days at a time, despite cramped or difficult conditions.

The boy, once shown how to identify possible entrances to skaven lairs was sent out into the surrounding countryside to locate new positions. He travelled on foot over several miles each day, taking arcing paths in previously determined sectors. Gilead told him where to go, pointing out landmarks, and the boy covered the ground.

He had told the elf warrior his name once, but had never heard it spoken back to him. They did not talk. Gilead tolerated his presence because he was useful.

'Aargh!' he cried.

It was dusk and he had quartered a large area of pasture on the north slope of a wide shallow valley. The tree-line had been cut back decades or even centuries ago and the land had clearly been used for common grazing. The animals were gone, the livestock long dead, either slaughtered to feed the famished locals or starved to death for the want of enough healthy grass. The boy had been up to his waist in weeds that were clumping in odd formations and showing small flowers that were almost grey. Hungry, the boy had pulled a handful of the tall, slender stalks, but when he put the plant up to his nose it stank of putrefaction, and he tossed it aside in disgust.

It was late and he had not found any evidence of excavation, so the boy was hurrying back to the elf, through the last section he was supposed to be examining, convinced that to stop and study the land properly would be a waste of his time. Besides, the elf was bound to have something for him to eat, and it had been several hours since he had almost eaten the weeds that grew in this area.

He was embarrassed by the scream. He had placed a foot without looking, and it had dropped away beneath him, startling him into crying out. He had landed hard on his backside, but his foot had not touched the bottom of the hole, so there was no damage to his leg or ankle. He withdrew the leg and, still seated, began to part the weeds to expose a ragged, almost elliptical hole in the gently sloping ground.

The boy dropped his head closer as he saw the faint twinkle of a light somewhere below the opening, and then he cried out again.

Claws reached up to clutch the boy's head, dragging him by the neck into the darkness. Then he heard a shriek close to his ear and another fleshy paw, complete with needle-sharp black claws, began to swipe and tear in the general direction of his face.

The boy grabbed the haft of his hoe close to the head, and drove it hard into the hole. He couldn't see to aim the blow as his face was half-covered in grappling paws, but he could feel the end of his hoe meet the resistance of flesh-covered bones. Something squealed and bucked in a frenzy of movement. The boy could feel the ground beneath him vibrating with the violence of the skaven's fit. He could not believe that the frenetic shrieking, bucking and clawing were deliberate.

The boy shook his head and neck clear of the flailing claws, but not before he had taken several deep scratches to his face and neck; one, connecting with his mouth, had left a flap of skin hanging from his lower lip, exposing the pink of his gums. He backed away from the hole, watching intently for evidence of another attack from the rat.

He saw not one pair of shining eyes, but three. Or, at least, he counted five sparks of light glinting off five eyeballs, suggesting the presence of three of the skaven in the hole. Then he saw the flash of small, bright white claws, when previously he had seen only black talons. The squeals were pitched higher than he thought possible, even for the ratmen, and he could discern very little fur. He reached out to take a tuft of fine hair that had been torn out on the ragged lip of the hole, and rubbed it between his fingers; it was as fine as a baby's breath, and, when he lifted it closer to his face to get a better look at it in the failing light, the hair was pale and silky, and it smelt sweet, like overripe fruit.

There was another shriek, and the boy thrust his hoe into the hole once more. He was less afraid for his own life, and more concerned about what was happening in the dark shadows of the burrow.

A claw reached up, took hold of the haft of the boy's weapon and started yanking at it. The boy pulled back hard on his end of the staff, leaning his back against the slope and bracing his feet. After four or five seconds of stalemate, he suddenly let go his grip on the weapon, making his opponent fall abruptly backwards deeper into the hole. Then he renewed his grasp, burning his hands slightly as the wooden haft slipped through his grip. Finally, he held it firmly again, close to the end of the long handle, but determined to make ground. The skaven who had fallen back into the hole must be hurt, surely? The boy pulled and thrust on the haft by turns, knowing that he couldn't risk letting go of his only weapon and losing it forever.

There was more scuffling and squealing in the hole, and more evidence of flashing eyes and claws as the light began to ebb out of the air. Then something was bundled out of the hole onto the slope close to the boy's feet. He peered at the bloody mess, not sure what to make of it at first. It might just have been an old fur made into a bundle for storage, but it had new pink blood on it. Then he saw a black claw at the end of a deep gash, ripped out, no doubt, by the force of the blow that its owner had struck, and he knew that he was looking at the victim of vicious skaven infighting.

He kicked gently at the bundle of fur, and it rolled clumsily over. The boy wanted to gag.

This was not a skaven soldier, an adult that could fight for itself in the scuffles for supremacy that occupied much of their time and thinking space. This was not a warrior being punished for some scheming insubordination. The skaven rat lying in a bloody heap at the boy's feet was an infant. The skin on its belly had not yet grown hair and was still pink; where its hair had grown, it was soft and downy and a delicate colour. Its new claws, not yet the killing weapons that they might have become, were clean and white and almost transparent.

The boy sat dumbfounded for a moment. He knew that they were vicious and evil, but, until that moment, he had not realised just how ruthless the skaven were.

The first skaven to emerge, alive, from the hole in the ground was large and grey, and had only one eye in its misshapen head. The eye glinted blackly at the boy, caught off-guard by the horror of his realisation.

Before he knew what was happening, the boy was pinned to the cold earth beneath him by the handle of his own weapon. He looked into the one good eye that the ratman still owned, and braced himself for the onslaught to his olfactory senses that was bound to occur if he followed through with the thought that was forming in his mind.

He held his breath and kicked out in the direction of the ratman leaning on the handle of his hoe. It was his intention to dislodge the hoe and bring the ratman down on top of him so that he could fight it on his own terms. He had not factored in the possibility of the haft flexing and snapping off a couple of feet from his shoulder.

When the rat landed on him, it did so by impaling itself on the jagged end of the broken hoe handle. Its body thudded down on top of him, expelling in a foetid gust the last of the stale air in the skaven's lungs.

Pinned to the slope, the boy thought once again that he would gag, or even faint at the stink that assailed his senses. Beyond that, he knew that he'd have to dislodge the surprising dead weight of the ratman in order to crawl out from under the corpse. He tried to bring a hand up to cover his face, pinch his nose, and cut off the stench, but both of his arms were pinned down. The corpse was leaching blood from the site of its fatal wound, and the putrid, diseased smell of its insides added to the malodorous fog that was threatening to make the boy puke; a most unpleasant prospect when he had no way to turn his head.

Suddenly, the smell had abated, and the cold air hit the boy hard in the chest, leaving the creeping sensation of someone else's blood cooling and congealing on his shirt.

He heard a yelp as he rose on his elbows to see who had rescued him. The last of the skaven, jaws wide in the midst of a death-scream, was run through on the point of Gilead's sword, as the elf lunged effortlessly towards the ratman emerging from the hole in the ground. A deft shove, and the newly dead skaven fell back through the hole, folded almost in half, its clawed, hoof-like back feet the last of it to disappear below ground.

The one-eyed skaven was not nearly as dead as the boy had imagined. It yelped as it rolled over, the haft of the hoe clearly visible protruding through its back. It crawled away, grabbing the dead infant under one arm and trying to scurry off down the hole. It was a pitiful sight. Its life force was all but spent and its blood organ was pumping wildly, desperately trying to enable the skaven's escape.

Gilead only wiped the blood from his sword. The rat-thing was dead already; he wasn't going to waste his efforts killing it again.

The elf sheathed his sword and looked at the boy. He did not speak, but it was enough that he had heard the commotion and come to investigate. The boy scrambled to his feet, wiped the worst of the blood off his face with his sleeve and pulled the blood-sodden shirt away from the sucking contact it was making with his skin. It disgusted him for a moment. Then he saw the remaining broken piece of his hoe, and the skaven's putrid blood was all but forgotten. The hoe wasn't a weapon, not really, and yet it's balanced haft and sharpened blade had stood him in very good stead over the days and weeks that he had used it to combat the cursed skaven. Now it was broken and useless. He had not the tools to mend it, and even if he could, the balance would be lost in the repair. Besides, he didn't relish going after the one-eyed skaven to retrieve the missing section of handle from its corpse.

Gilead picked up the end of the broken hoe with the head attached and weighed it in his hand. Then he signalled for the boy to follow him, and they walked towards the small camp they had made where the slope of the land met the tree-line. The boy thought they must be returning for their supper, and could see the welcoming drifting smoke of the small fire that Gilead had lit some time before. He had become used to the tubers and corms that the elf cooked for them both, looked forward to them, even.

As they reached the tree-line, Gilead wove a path among the saplings that grew close to the edge of the wooded area. The woods had clearly been cultivated and used, but coppicing appeared to have stopped two or three years earlier. In these times of famine and plague, the boy was surprised to realise that Gilead had a wealth of young trees to choose from. The elf selected one that was growing straight and true at the centre of a clump that needed to be thinned out if any of the healthier saplings were to grow on unchecked. There were no woodsmen left to thin and coppice and manage the woodland, but there was at least hope that the woodland would survive and even thrive, eventually.

Gilead cut the sapling low to the ground, and examined the wood where it had been sliced into. He discarded the sapling briskly, and the boy noticed that there was rot at its base. Perhaps it was an illusion; perhaps the woodland was not as healthy as it appeared to be. Gilead cut two more saplings from the central growth, but both were equally rotten. Then he selected a sapling from the outer circle of growth. He cut the young tree away above where it curved at the base to accommodate the growth of other branches. He weighed the length of raw wood in his hands and nicked off the one or two side shoots that were developing close to its tapering end. The cut end was clean and white, and the grain tightly packed.

They walked the hundred yards or so back to the camp, and Gilead sat down by the fire. He retrieved what looked like a paring knife from his pack. When he began to strip the bark from the sapling, the boy wondered whether the tool he was using was appropriate to the work, but he had already seen the wonders that could be wrought with an elf-made blade and thought better of questioning Gilead. The boy coughed. Gilead looked up from his handiwork and nodded at the embers of the small fire, encouraging the boy to finish preparing their meal while he worked on.

Chapter 11

When the boy woke the next morning, Gilead handed him his hoe. The haft was smooth as silk, glossy almost, and had been finished with some sort of wax that smelled fresh and sweet. The hoe gleamed with a high shine and was almost too sharp to the touch; it had been fixed to the handle with perfect dome-headed pins of a type that the boy had never seen on a farm tool, although he had once seen something similar in the pommel of a greatsword.

The boy didn't know what to say. He simply looked at Gilead, who stood more than two heads taller than he was, and smiled up at the elf. He didn't know whether Gilead had slept that night. He didn't know how long it must have taken to produce something so perfect. To whittle and carve the haft should have taken a mere mortal a day or two, and to clean, straighten and hone a blade on the hoe at least another day. Gilead could not possibly have completed the work and slept, and yet the elf looked rested and alert.

'We begin today,' said the elf.

The boy looked at him, an eyebrow raised, questioning.

'They know we are here,' said Gilead. 'We have sabotaged as many of their entrances underground as we are able, and now we attack.'

'We're going underground?' asked the boy, his mouth wide with fear and wonder.

'If the skaven are to cease their persecution of the humans, we must penetrate to the source of their evil and destroy their leader.'

'We're going underground,' said the boy.

Gilead and the boy had sabotaged dozens of openings in the ground over the past weeks, cutting the skaven off from their prey above ground, and leaving them without escape routes. Gilead knew the lie of the land, knew every inch of hundreds of acres of pasture, scrub and woodland. He knew which entrances underground the skaven used most often and which had been abandoned or were used only in the direst of emergencies. Gilead and the boy had collapsed several of the portals, digging away at the earth around them. They had filled others with vegetation and rocks, and even rotten trees and branches torn from the woodland. Some they had turned into traps, using tripwires and hidden obstacles that would bring the skaven crashing to the ground and cause lethal injuries.

Gilead and the boy had skirmished at the edges of some of the burrow holes. They had injured some of the skaven, and killed several, but they had never before sent their victims back down their holes, and, last night, the one-eyed ratman had crawled back into his warren with a hoe handle through his torso.

When they climbed down into the hole in the slope where the boy had seen his first infant skaven, where the one-eyed ratman had retreated to die, they found nothing but a clump or two of grey fur and a broken, rotting leather thong that might have been part of some padded armour. They could smell death, putrescence and corruption, but the scent was hours old and mostly distant.

The boy didn't care to think what had happened to the corpse of the infant skaven, and there was no time for misplaced sentiment.

It quickly became clear that there was no space underground with a ceiling high enough to accommodate the attenuated height of the elf, but Gilead seemed to lose none of his stealth or speed simply because he could not stand upright. The boy felt clumsy by comparison, even though he barely needed to drop his shoulders, let alone stoop, to walk unobstructed along the skaven-built tunnels and burrows.

It also became only too obvious that the boy could not function in the pitch-darkness that soon engulfed them below ground. The skaven were adapted to the lack of light, and Gilead seemed to manage well enough, but the boy soon found himself tripping over his feet. Gilead handed him what looked like a rush lantern, but on a much smaller scale. It had a brass reservoir in the lower half, shaped like a bowl so that it wouldn't stand on a flat surface, with a small crystal cover above and a wick between the two that was barely thicker than a strand of strong hair. The boy wondered whether it would show any light at all, and if it did, for how long. Nonetheless, he held the cover open while Gilead lit the wick, and was soon surrounded by enough soft light to show the earth beneath his feet for a pace or two, the walls at his sides and the ceiling pressing down on his head. The light seemed not to bleed at its furthest reaches, but to stop abruptly at a radius of about a yard and a half.

Gilead was the first to sniff out skaven scum, and he killed the ratmen they came across with consummate ease. The boy raised his hoe only once in the first few hours of their exploration. They had come to a junction, a place where one path forked into two, one tunnel rising steeply away, back to the surface, to an exit that Gilead knew he had booby-trapped with stakes thrust into the soft earth at dangerous angles, should the skaven happen to trip or fall into them. Gilead dealt swiftly with the two ratmen that emerged from the right-hand fork in the tunnel, which led deeper into the earth. He did not see the small, hunched figure of a third skaven as it peered around the edge of the tunnel that led back to the surface. The boy turned in that direction, something catching his eye in the darkness, and he was upon the skaven, thrusting the newly-sharpened blade of his hoe at an angle deep into the creature's side. It did not cry out, but simply folded in half with the exhalation of a shallow, forced breath, and collapsed at the boy's feet. The sound that followed could not possibly have been caused by its demise, could it? Was it a sound?

The boy looked to Gilead for guidance, and the elf raised a hand to indicate the boy remain still and silent.

The elf felt it through his feet, like a roll played on an impossibly deeply tuned drum. He felt the faint throb of dozens of scurrying feet thundering along pathways, tunnels and corridors, without knowing what it must mean.

The boy's eyes grew large.

'They're coming,' he said.

The noise did not grow louder, however, and the vibrations did not increase. The skaven were not running towards the elf and the boy, but away from them.

The elf and the boy continued deeper into the labyrinth of warrens and burrows, always taking the path downwards when given a choice.

Once or twice, the tunnels opened out into excavated caverns and caves, which might have been rooms if the skaven lived like any other civilised race. They found crude seats made from mounds of earth with planks placed on top, or from short planks simply wedged into the hard walls of the burrows at sitting height. They saw bundles and piles of leather scraps and cloth, and shallow bowls full of foul liquid grease used to oil leather armour or as fuel for the clay lamps that sat in niches higher in the walls. In the darkest and dampest corners, they found foodstuffs stored and piled, fermenting into heaps of unidentifiable vegetation. Once or twice they saw young skaven foraging at the edges of the mounds for the liquescent treats they clearly craved. Gilead ignored them.

Sentries were posted only intermittently, mostly where the tunnels met or branched out. They seemed to have been chosen from the oldest and youngest of the active rat-warriors, from the sickest and least able. Gilead wasted little effort, simply running them through or cutting their arteries and letting them bleed out where they fell. They were no competition for him.

'Why are they so few?' asked the boy. 'Where are the rest of them?'

Gilead looked at the boy and tipped his head slightly on one side as if in thought. Some of the burrows and tunnels had clearly been deserted for some time, but many of them still held the appalling scents of the skaven, and some even harboured the warmth of their recently retreating bodies.

The ratmen were short-lived and unsubtle, and could not possibly have any sort of plan. They had simply moved on, or were retreating for fear of their adversaries. Their kind had seen what Gilead and even the boy could do with a little brute force and effort and a decent weapon, so perhaps they preferred not to meet them in hand-to-hand combat. Perhaps they were cowards, after all.

They were not cowards. They were brutal, ruthless killers, and, for the only time in any of their short lives, they had a leader who could formulate a plan and, having done so, a leader who could compel the skaven horde to carry out that plan.

There were ratmen who could not, would not, concentrate for long enough to hear the plan. There were those who wanted nothing so much as to follow their senses, track the intruders into their tunnels and bring them crashing down at the mercy of their blades and claws and teeth, however unlikely that outcome might be. There were those who could not sit still, but broke away from their tribes and scoured the tunnels for prey. There were those too long in the tooth to leave the posts they had defended all of their meagre lives. There were those too stupid to live. There were those whose thoughtless acts would lead the Fell One and the human boy ever closer to the heart of the underground compound that they called home. Dozens would die bringing the Fell One to the skaven Rat King, but their deaths would not be in vain, for they were, unwittingly perhaps, doing the better part of his bidding. There were any number that could be sacrificed, any number that would sacrifice themselves.

The remainder of the skaven, the vast majority, had congregated once more in the great crypt. They had fought their way there, jostling one another, beating a path when the call had come. The traffic through the burrows, tunnels and warrens had been fast and dense and had left bodies in its wake.

Gilead had still been on the surface, mapping the entrances to the burrows, sabotaging them and planning his assault on the heart of the warren. Only the weak, the sick, the young and the disabled skaven remained close to the surface. He had killed the one-eyed, old ratman with ease, had run through his companion, and the infant had died only moments after the boy had extricated his foot from the hole in the ground. The skaven Rat King had left traps like this one, close to the surface, all over the plot of land that Gilead and the boy had quartered and examined. It mattered not which bait the Fell One took, it only mattered that his boy was a clumsy air-walker of the human kind, and would lead the elf into the snare that awaited him. Every hole in the ground, every entrance to a burrow was rigged to bring down the clumsy boy; every hole had a small skirmish party ready to respond when the entrance was breached. Wherever the boy came down, the Fell One would follow, and he would attack.

Gilead and the boy worked their way deeper and further into the network of tunnels and spaces below the ground. Gilead felt his way through the soles of his boots and the palms of his hands, mapping in his mind all the tunnels he had passed through, which directions they had run in, where they had intersected and what they were made of. The boy kept pace only because of the lantern in his hand, by its faint pool of concentrated light. He remained behind the elf, where he had been told to stay, in touch, but out of danger.

Gilead turned abruptly when the light behind him suddenly went out. He did not need it to see by, and he cast a hand along the passage behind him, marking out the yard, less than his arm's length, between his position and where the boy should be. He was gone.

The elf heard a gasp, but it sounded as if it were several yards to the left of his position, eight to be precise, and, in his situation, it paid to be precise.

For a split second, Gilead was torn between continuing on his quest to find the leader of the skaven, and any loyalty he might have to the boy. He had not asked the human to follow him, and yet he had been content to use the boy when it suited him. Was the life of one mortal human more important than the lives of thousands, perhaps millions of his species? The Empire was at risk, had been for decades, and in the past few years had been plunged into a combination of plague and famine that seemed impossible to escape. Gilead's loyalty was to his quest; his obligation was to save the race, not the individual.

Almost unaware of what he was doing, Gilead strode the eight yards to his left where he had heard the boy inhale a frightened breath, drawing his sword and assessing the width of the tunnel from the curvature of the earth floor beneath his feet and the echo of his own light breathing, undetectable to whoever else might be in the tunnel.

The sound of leather kicking at earth, behind and to the right of Gilead's position, told him that the boy was being dragged away against his will, but that he was conscious and fighting.

Gilead did not think to question why the boy was not dead. He knew why.

The elf wondered where he had gone wrong, how he could have misjudged the skaven so badly, how he could have underestimated any creature that could successfully lead such a massive horde of unpredictable, infantile, erratic followers.

Gilead had used the boy to halve his workload, and his enemy had used the same boy as bait.

All the elf could do was walk into the storm that was to come, alert and prepared to fight off a thousand ratmen with their glass-marble eyes and their foetid breath, with their squeals and claws and tearing blades.

He was not afraid for himself, and he cared little enough for the boy.

Gilead followed the sounds of scuffling as they echoed through the tunnels, leading yet further down into the depths of the earth. There was nothing to see, but the elf could smell the anticipation of a gathered army. There was nothing as profound as the aroma of eager expectation in the minutes before adrenaline began to pump and blood began to flow, and a hundred new scents pervaded the battleground.

Suddenly able to stand fully upright, Gilead broke into a measured run, the sword held firmly in the on-guard position in his right hand, his left hand dragging lightly against the tunnel wall, balancing his footfalls and honing his sense of direction. This was no time to trip or fall.

Then there was light, and there was sound.

The sound was the rapid breathing of several thousand skaven bodies made restless by the passage of time that had brought their foe to them. Their patience, always limited, was being controlled by their sovereign, standing proud at the centre of his mound, a dishevelled mess of a boy prostrate before him.

The light was the greenish glow of a few dozen lanterns strung around and above the mound, lighting the Rat King of the skaven, not in a spot of light, but in a sickly haze.

As Gilead stepped into the vaulted crypt, the crowds parted. One or two of the skaven were driven mad by the sight of a foe they were not allowed to touch, and they twitched and danced in front of him, frothing at the mouth, chittering and clutching at themselves. Some could do nothing more effective than rend their clothes and pull out clumps of their hair as their eyes spun in their heads and their blood organs burst within their chests.

As they died, the elf stepped over them, walking deliberately towards the mound.

As they died, the boy lifted first his scratched, torn and bloody head, then his shoulders and torso from the ground at the Rat King's feet. He had no hope of living. He did not delude himself; the elf was a wondrous being, but there was little enough chance of him escaping death, let alone of him saving the boy, too.

Finding his way onto one knee, and then hoisting himself painfully upright, the boy did himself proud, looking across the gap that divided them, out over a sea of mangy grey heads. He nodded to Gilead.

'Quirin,' said Gilead, fervently, but almost under his breath. The boy heard the elf speak his name, and his eyes were suddenly full of life, even though the skin on his face, where it was visible between tears and scratches, was so pale in the greenish light as to be almost grey. Gilead saw that the boy was sweating, too, and knew that he could not live for long.

A score more of the skaven died of shock on hearing the elf uttering a word in his elegant, resonating tones, and hundreds ducked and shoved their way further back into the crowd.

Every single skaven, including the Rat King, would have stood in abject fear before the Fell One in any other arena, but in this place, at this time, the group mind had taken over. They were not singular, they were not fighting for their own sakes; the horde was greater than any individual, and no one would die in vain. They knew not what they died for, but they were accustomed to the brevity of their lives, and killed and died by instinct, because that is what they'd done for thousands of years: killed and died and made more ratmen, and that was all.

Somehow, against the odds, the boy had held onto his hoe during his abduction. It lay on the mound before him, light playing off the blade-edge that Gilead had honed during the previous night.

The boy stooped to pick up the hoe, but was slow and unsteady, and was quickly surrounded by several of the Rat King's bodyguard.

The Rat King laughed, and waved a hand over the boy as if to suggest that his guard should not defend him against the human.

Gilead's pace towards the mound increased, and with the movement of his body through the air, the skaven stepped yet further back, forming a wide aisle for him to jog down. The air was overflowing with the stench of the liquefaction of stomach contents as skaven lost control of their bowels and gag reflexes. Several reached filthy claws up to ears and nostrils that had begun to trickle with dirty black blood. Still, they did not seek to attack the elf.

The boy lurched towards the Rat King with his hoe held out in front of him. The king ducked and wove and danced a jig around the boy, laughing and squealing in delight as his guard looked on. The boy staggered, one eye glazing over with the fever in his brow, the other filling with the blood that was oozing from several wounds in his face and head.

As the Rat King ducked and danced, he turned his weapon over in his hands, slicing lightly, rapidly through the air, impossibly close to the boy's staggering body.

The boy tripped a little over his feet, and took the haft of his hoe in both hands, holding it vertically so that he could lean his weight down on it without falling to the floor.

As the blood began to seep from dozens of shallow slices in the boy's skin, as the cloth of his shirt began to fall away in long ribbons, exposing the grey skin of his torso and the hundreds of wounds inflicted there, Gilead made a last effort to reach the mound, the boy he could not save and the Rat King he intended to kill.

The elf feinted towards the skaven lining his route, watching for an opportunity. Before they had a chance to retreat, Gilead found a skaven leg joint to step on to elevate himself, a stooped shoulder for his next step and a head for his last, and he was up and over the bodyguard surrounding the Rat King. His eyes blazed as he confronted the ancient creature, but he held his sword away from his body to the right.

The Rat King did not dance or weave or squeal. He stood before the elf as still and silent as any skaven might be, yet Gilead could feel the creature tremble, despite the bright flashes of light that reflected off the marble surfaces of his eyes.

The Rat King dropped his weapon and fussed with something hanging around his neck, a length of ribbon or leather, perhaps. The Rat King pulled on the length of braided hair and the amulet tied to it. He clutched it in both paws and raised it above his head.

The skaven were fast because they were short-lived creatures. They had no capacity for reasoning, so every action was a staccato reaction, a primal response.

Gilead was fast too.

The attack came from behind Gilead to his left. It was a brutal, badly timed lunge, and Gilead deftly tripped the bodyguard and pierced his chest before he could rise from where he had fallen on the earth mound at the elf's feet.

A second guard attacked with the length of his staff weapon, a cross between a scythe and a halberd, an ugly hybrid clearly concocted from the blades of two older weapons and the handle of a third. Gilead disarmed him with a flick of his wrist, and the weapon spiralled away into the crowd that was gathering around the focus of the fight. It took out three more ratmen, two of them at the knees, and a third because he was pushed into the fray by the skaven behind him. The last tripped over his feet, falling onto the curved scythe blade that jutted from the weapon's handle.

Each skaven bodyguard that fell was replaced by another of his tribe, warriors all. Gilead found time to unsheathe his short blade, and a weapon in each hand, cut and sliced his way through skin, bone, flaking leather armour and the putrid strips of rotten, greasy cloth that the skaven wound their hands and feet in.

Gilead blinked and could see it all. He could see the faces of hundreds of skaven on the slopes of the mound below him and out on the floor of the crypt. He could see nothing in their eyes but a lust to destroy. They were jostling and breaking into skirmishes among themselves, since they could neither reach their enemy, nor, if they could have come face to face with the Fell One, would they have been allowed to kill him. He saw a kind of uncontrolled primal frenzy that he had not known existed, despite the stories he had heard about the rat-creatures.

He also saw the boy. He saw him look at the elf, his hero, and then he saw him close his eyes, involuntarily. The blood-shot orbs rolled back into the boy's head. Somehow, the boy held onto the handle of his hoe, and it kept him upright for what seemed like minutes. It was almost comical, the way the boy's... Quirin's... corpse was suspended, half standing, half kneeling, propped up by the weapon that Gilead had remade for him. Finally, the moment was over, and the boy was slumped on his face on the dirt mound.

Gilead wanted revenge, not only because the skaven had killed the boy, but because he had allowed it to happen, and his guilt and anger could result in nothing short of devastation for the skaven.

Gilead was shadowfast.

While he ducked and dived and sliced and lunged, and thrust his blade into squealing ratmen one after another, he looked around for the leader of this debauched race. He saw that the sea of rat-faces looking up at the mound had become much denser, those twitching maws and marble eyes closer together. The crowd was surging towards the dais mound, dragging its dead and wounded with it, crushing the weakest among its mass. As it moved in an unstoppable wave towards Gilead, the Rat King rode on an impossible wave of rat-arms away from him, shaking the double-paw in which it clutched its magical amulet.

Gilead thrust with his short blade into the side of a rat that had changed its mind about doing battle with the elf, and was turning tail, attempting to run away. The blade ground on something as it punched through the leather armour, skin and bone of the creature's torso, and, as the skaven turned, Gilead lost his grip on the weapon, his hands slick with the gore of dozens of the dead.

Without a thought, he scooped up the boy's hoe and began to turn it over in his hand, weighing its usefulness. Gilead's second weapon was gone, rendering his primary blade much less useful against so many attackers.

The elf sheathed his sword, grasped the hoe haft with both hands and began to wield it expertly. The handle end broke sternums and winded rats to death, or tripped them off their hind feet, tumbling them to the ground where they met their deaths by being trampled. The sharpened head of the hoe cut through limbs and arteries, and even sliced a scraggy grey neck clean through, the rat's head falling in one direction and its body in another.

They came at him over and over again, barely lifting their weapons to the elf before dying at his hand. Gilead looked around again at the circle of assailants pushing and shoving each other, either to take their turn at fighting him or to get away from his thrusting attacks. They were poorly armed. Many appeared to have broken their weapons deliberately. There were stringy ribbons of greasy cloth where once a blade had been wrapped to a staff, many of the blades looked old and dull and well beyond use, and those skaven with decent weapons turned their blades away and attacked with hafts and handles.

Gilead looked at the mass of bodies around him, which was vast, despite the fact that the ratmen were clearing bodies away from the focus of the battle as fast they could manage. Then he looked out again at the Rat King riding above his followers, relying on their loyalty to keep him aloft.

They did not see him move, they did not feel his footfalls
pass over their heads and shoulders as the Fell One found a
path out over the crowd towards the skaven sovereign. He
could not lose the battle by killing all day and all night, and
for as long as it took to decimate the skaven horde. He could
not lose the battle when none of the creatures were able or
willing to even attempt to kill him. Despite it all, he knew
that this was a battle he could not win.

In the blink of an eye, the Rat King, with the experience
gleaned through years of life that he should never have lived,
homed in on the Fell One, and knew what he was doing. He
cried out at his followers below him, and, letting the amulet
fall to the length of the plaited hair-string that it hung from,
he began to spin the charm around his head.

The mesmerised ratmen watched as the great vaulted ceiling of the crypt, black and sparkling, filled with thousands
of pinpricks of bright light. Some died on the spot; many
opened their own veins, driven by wonder and awe to end
their lives at this zenith of their sovereign's power. The Rat
King was returned safely to the dais on a wave of rat-paws,
where he stood at the centre of the bloody mound. All of his
bodyguards were gone, not even their bodies remaining on
the mound, although much of their blood had been spilt
there. Every tribal leader, every champion, every lieutenant
had been killed by the Fell One. Every one of them would
add to the Rat King's longevity, but they were as nothing
compared with this great catch. The Fell One was in their
midst, and the Rat King had the ultimate power over him.

The Rat King cried out high and loud and long. The rats
responded vigorously, sloughing off their mesmeric states to
do their leader's bidding.

Shadowfast as he was, Gilead did not expect the ratmen

to know that he was using their heads and shoulders as stepping-stones, but the Rat King was preternaturally fast, too, and he could feel and read every vibration and every movement in the air. He had monitored the Fell One's every move, and it was time to best him, to capture him and to harness his life force.

Without warning, the sea of bodies under Gilead's feet disappeared, the rats answering the clarion call to disperse with all haste.

Gilead fell, suddenly, but not far. His drop was almost vertical, and, under other circumstances, he would simply have risen on his knees, his weapon in his hand, and fought on.

As Gilead hit the ground, the ratmen piled on top of him in a mass of sheer numbers that weighed him down, crushing him to the earth floor of the crypt, disabling him. His ability to be shadowfast was knocked out of him as his concentration broke in the fall, and it was as much as he could do to fill his lungs so that he would not be killed by the black mass of stinking bodies that lay on top of him.

Gilead could not move, and the mass of bodies above him did not move.

Dozens of rats died in the scrum that brought the Fell One down to earth and kept him there, hundreds had died in combat with him, and thousands had died in setting the trap and luring Gilead into their midst.

The Rat King looked down on the Fell One as he lay on the floor of his antechamber, tied every which way with leather thongs from old armour, with the greasy rags that the skaven used in the construction of their weapons and in their sovereign's throne, and with lengths of strong sinew cut from skaven corpses.

The Rat King did not count his dead. He could not count, but he knew in his thrumming blood organ that if he could, he would take great pleasure in counting the scores, perhaps hundreds of years of life that this great bounty, this Fell One, would secure for him long into the future.

Chapter 12

By all that's good and holy, by Sigmar's beard and Ulric's teeth, and by blessed Aenarion, it pains me to repeat the events and traumas that Gilead suffered at any hand, but these cursed tales are the most hellish of all to tell. Were I not on my deathbed, facing the end of my time in these environs, I would not choose to recount such stories, but I am honour-bound by the tenets and laws of the bardic guilds to impart all that I have learned and all that has been entrusted to me by those that came before, however addled their minds in the telling and however young I might have been in the hearing.

Listen if you dare, but be aware of what you will hear and how it will affect your lives. Pass this dread mantle I must, but with a weary heart made heavy by promises pledged too easily, many years ago.

* * *

Gilead lay too long in that place. He was bound so tight that it was impossible for him to move. He was barely able to breathe, and if he had not had his wits about him, and inhaled deeply as soon as he was aware that the skaven hordes sought to bury him beneath their combined weight, he would surely have died of asphyxiation, either at the time of his capture or shortly after his bindings were secured. There was barely an eighth of an inch movement in the bindings of his chest, so his breaths must be shallow and controlled, and no unnecessary energy must be expended before he was able to escape his captivity.

The first time he gained consciousness, Gilead kept his eyes closed while he carried out a detailed inventory of his ailments, wounds and vulnerabilities. They were many and took some time to enumerate and assess, but the worst of them was the tight, restricting bandage of greasy cloth, sodden rope, and leather straps and thongs that held him in the tightest of grips. He could neither straighten his knees nor flex his ankles. He could not rotate his wrists, tied tightly behind him, nor push his elbows away from where they were strapped to his sides. He could not turn his head nor flex it back or forth on his neck. He could not take a deep breath to settle his mind or relax his body. He could barely breathe deeply enough to lift smells out of the air around him. He could see, if he chose to open his eyes, but, most importantly of all, he could hear. He could hear, but he could not respond.

'He has come, so he has. He has come. Now he has come, for come he has, I'll live forever. I won't live for now, not just for now. I'll live forever,' said the skaven Rat King.

Gilead did not need to open his eyes to know who was speaking. The rat's voice had become impossibly high-pitched with excitement, and the words kept tripping out of his mouth, over and over, the speaker apparently caught in some spell that made him repeat the little speech, ad infinitum, as if it were some kind of unholy mantra.

Gilead did not open his eyes. He did not respond. He continued to take shallow breaths. His mouth was dry and somewhat tacky from the noxious smells that he had inhaled underground and could not rid himself of, but he did not swallow, nor did he lick his parched lips. His mouth remained firmly, but casually, closed, as if he continued in his unconscious state in some still and dreamless existence. The skaven had not killed him. Their king had been stronger and more powerful than Gilead could ever have expected, more in control of his horde than any Rat King had a right to be, and far more cunning than the average enemy creature, and yet the elf had not died at their hands. Since he was not dead yet, the skaven clearly had other plans for the elf. He knew not what they were, but he did know that there was time enough to find out, and, in the meantime, his best course of action was to rest as much as he could, regain some strength, and formulate a plan of escape.

Gilead rolled his closed eyes back into his head, and adjusted a twinge or two with some small exertions and a little fine muscle control. The Rat King could, no doubt, detect his movements, but dormant creatures stirred too, and the skaven would surely think nothing of the elf moving a little in his sleep.

The elf fell, voluntarily, into a restful and invigorating sleep-state, one from which he could wake at will, should the need present itself.

* * *

Gilead woke again when the chanting stopped. He lay still for an hour or two, listening, and opened his eyes only when he knew that he was likely to remain alone for some time to come.

Aware that the skaven could detect the smallest of movements through the vibrations carried by earth, brick and rock in their underground fastnesses, Gilead made no attempts to free himself from the confines of the ties that bound him. He did not thrash or squirm. He lay as still as he could and felt the earth floor beneath his body. He had to concentrate long and hard to feel any vibrations at all, and when he did feel something, he was able to deduce that the crowds in the great hall had dispersed and there were few or no skaven close by.

Gilead had been lying on his side, curled slightly, as his bindings pulled his knees towards his chest. He opened his eyes into the faint green light that hung in the air of the antechamber. He could see very little apart from the legs of an oddly formed piece of furniture close to his face. The Rat King had clearly taken pleasure in looking down on the elf's face, for Gilead cast his eyes upwards to see that the tangle of wood and blades and handles, and parts of tools and weapons strapped together, formed an impressively grotesque throne, of sorts.

The faint smell that drifted around Gilead as he flexed the muscles down the left side of his body in an attempt to roll onto his back, told him that the Rat King had left the room four or five hours previously and had not returned. There was only one scent signature in the room, so the king was clearly a lone creature, keen to maintain a private space. There could be only one reason for that.

Gilead flexed again, breathing out as hard as his bounds

would allow, and slowly rolled off his side and onto his back, trapping his hands beneath him. His feet were raised slightly off the ground and his knees tucked up. It was not the most elegant of postures, but it was a possible position of strength against the bindings when the time came.

For the moment, Gilead allowed the back of his head to rest on the cold dank earth and began to cast his eyes around the room, since there was very little movement in his head and neck.

The room was spartan. It had only one door to serve as both entrance and exit, so must be an antechamber to a larger space, possibly the great hall, since the few sounds that came to Gilead appeared to do so from an echoing distance.

The room held only the chair for furniture, but was too small to be used as a throne room for the skaven to kneel and bow before their leader; besides, Gilead had already determined that the room had only one inhabitant. As his eyes grew accustomed to the lack of light in the room, Gilead began to cast his gaze into the deeper recesses. He could not see into the corners beyond his head, at floor level, but he could look up into the low ceiling of dark, crusting earth above him. He followed the line of the ceiling until he was able to peer into the corners, albeit there were only three of them and they curved away rather than met the walls at regular angles. Then a dark spot caught his eye, just below the rim where the ceiling met the curving, irregular wall to his left. He cast his eye further along the wall and spotted another dark spot, and then a lighter one. He counted six anomalies along the top of the wall.

Concentrating first on the lightest of the patches high on the wall, Gilead quickly realised that he was looking at an opening or a niche from which a small amount of light was emanating. He took two or three shallow breaths and blinked twice, taking his time to examine the area of the wall, thoroughly.

He saw a faint spark, and thought he heard a low hum. He stopped breathing and closed his eyes for a moment so that he could concentrate on fully hearing the sound. It was a click, so slow and pitched so low as to be almost inaudible and easily mistaken for a low buzz or hum. Gilead took a breath, drawing in as much of the stale air around him as he could, and listened again while he exhaled impossibly slowly.

There was a pattern to the clicks, a rhythm, a pace, not like a heartbeat, but more like music, like a skilled percussionist picking out a complex tune with intricate phrasing. It was beautiful, and Gilead found his mind following the pattern, trying to decipher its meaning. It must mean something.

His eyes firmly closed, his breathing abated and only his hearing informing his consciousness, Gilead was mesmerised by the sound until he stopped counting the clicks, stopped trying to work out the pattern, and simply became absorbed by it. It filled his mind's eye with a swarming carpet of gleaming, glossy carapaces, an oil-slick of rainbow colours refracting impossibly from the backs and wing-cases of a tidal wave of chittering insects. Suddenly, the low click separated into thousands, millions of squeaks and squeals as armoured limbs rubbed against one another and proboscises and antennae twitched and flexed.

Then, at the apex of the crescendo, a thousand million wing-cases unfolded, releasing gossamer wings in thousands of shades of blue, yellow and green. The sound changed again as millions of pairs of wings extended into the air, moving great swathes of it and causing a deafening susurrus as if an exodus were under way.

Gilead wondered in the moment, afraid of nothing, steeped in the pleasure of so magical an event.

Eventually, the elf had to breathe again, and his mind returned to him, only the low hum and the greenish light a reminder of what he had witnessed. He blinked and an image flashed against his retina. He could not see it, not from this angle low to the floor, and yet he knew that the niche from which the faint greenish light emanated held a bell jar in which was imprisoned a single, mature, winged beetle of a type that he had never seen before, and which he believed he would never see again. It was magical, talismanic and beautiful, and it was as far from home as he was, and almost as ancient.

Gilead cast his eyes along the wall to the left of the lit niche, and concentrated hard on the first of the dark patches; if the lit patch was a niche and in that niche was the captive insect, what else might the Rat King have collected? What else could Gilead learn about his captor?

Gilead concentrated for what, to skaven scum, would have seemed like a very long time, but Gilead was a mature example of one of the longest-living of species, and minutes, hours, days, even, were as nothing to him. Time was always on his side. He dilated his pupils as far as he could, until his vision became slightly blurry at the very edges, casting an aura around the niche he was focusing on, making it appear even more magical, more dreamlike. His flexed pupils grabbed all the light that they could out of the air, deep in the shadows of the niche in the wall, and he began to discern a shape there. He saw a 'V' of some lightweight chain or other, from which hung something so fragile it seemed to shift in some invisible, imperceptible breeze in the room, although it was only the smallest movement in the air caused by Gilead's measured, shallow breathing. It looked like a feather... No, a lock of hair. It was a lock of the finest, brightest, lightest of hair, like the down that grew on the most precious of elf-infants' heads.

Gilead's blink captured everything the elf could wish to know about the pale lock of hair, the single sweeping curl that hung by the side of a glorious face... glorious even for a human, for the curl did not belong to an infant elf, but to a beautiful human girl. An abundance of soft curls crowned a delicate, porcelain-perfect head. Suddenly, the face broke into a stunning smile of perfect pink lips and tiny teeth, plumping and rouging apple-cheeks and reaching into the palest of pale blue eyes, with devastating effect. The girl tossed her head, and the cascading curls bounced around her face. Gilead noticed a discreet circlet of fine gold wirework with pink sweet-water pearls and an abundance of pave-set diamonds. The hair did not belong to any beautiful girl, it belonged to a special girl, a girl of fine breeding and finer habits, a girl of great expectations and exemplary deportment; it belonged to a singular girl, a girl who could change the Empire forever.

Gilead's eyes opened at the end of the blink, and he sighed slightly. The girl, so clear in his mind, so complete, so real, was gone, and he was back in the dark, underground bolt-hole of the skaven scum.

Gilead wondered whether he wanted to look into any of the other niches in the wall. He had seen such wonders in the first two, and did not want to break the spell, and yet, he needed to know, felt compelled to scrutinise the niches, not only for the sake of the Rat King, not only because he thought he'd gain a greater insight into the machinations of the creature, but for the sake of the objects themselves, so that he might experience their wonders.

An hour passed in the moments that Gilead took to prepare himself for another bout of concentration, and for the possibility of losing himself in his mind once more.

As Gilead looked up at the third niche, a warm, orange-red glow began to emanate from it. The glow trickled and then poured out of the wall. It appeared to turn into a stream of clear orange liquid, and then began to steam and coalesce, and before he knew what was happening, Gilead was being drowned in a confetti of cascading leaves. They were red and yellow and a bright, sappy green. The light seemed to come from within them, flickering brightly, making the leaves seem transparent, showing the skeletons of their perfectly symmetrical veins. The leaves continued to fall, pouring from the niche as if blown through it in great gusts.

Gilead was soon covered in the leaves, too light for him to feel them falling, but warming him in a blanket of feathery silk. When they fell close to his eyes, Gilead barely needed to breathe out to shift the trajectory of the leaves, keeping his face clear of them, although a little part of him longed to be buried forever in the subtle, comforting embrace of whatever natural force had created such a wonder.

He continued to watch, unblinking, as more leaves were ejected from the niche, but, as they met the foetid air of the antechamber, they began to spark and dance. One by one, the leaves began to ignite in bright, smokeless flames. They changed colour to subtle ashy greys and blues, and then floated up into the curved ceiling before their lights were extinguished and they vanished into the air, leaving behind only the faintest whiff of warm clouds and clean ozone.

As the air cleared, more and more of the leaves began to ignite. They jumped and skittered over Gilead's form like benign fleas before combusting and floating away in brilliant, waving, dancing patterns before his eyes.

As the last of the sparks and flames and the last wisps of light disappeared, Gilead saw the outline of a climbing plant imprinted on the wall. It was like a sky clematis, espaliered against the wall in an endless ladder formation, branches twisting, and tendrils sending out enough shoots to accommodate the abundance of leaves that had been shed into the room. The illusion was there in the last flames of light, and gone just as quickly. The niche held... what? A single leaf? No, Gilead saw that the niche contained a tall glass vial sealed at both ends, suspended in a soupy shaft of light that almost obscured the contents: a single tendril with a lone bud-node and a barely formed leaf.

The fourth niche, the highest and largest of them, was more than simply a cavity, with its cleanly defined arched shape and its protruding shelf. Initially, Gilead could detect nothing there, except the shadow of something ancient, cold, long dead. The shadow began to dissipate and the air to flex and, suddenly, Gilead was looking at a reflection of himself in a dense, smoky pane. The reflection stood to the foreground, and beyond it, the elf could see the antechamber with him lying on the floor looking up at the niches, each glowing brightly, displaying its wares. The arched niche through the glass was reflecting light and the faint image of another supine Gilead.

Gilead did not dwell upon the images, but something primal made his mind stir, and, for an instant, he felt the urge to shiver. There was not room to accomplish the feat in the confines of the ties that bound him, so he contented himself with the sensation of someone walking stolidly over his grave.

The fifth niche was a ragged black hole in the wall. Gilead stretched his mind into it, dilating his pupils and concentrating for several minutes in an unblinking state. He was shadowfast in his will, lying perfectly still, but performing a great many checks and manoeuvres in his mind to eliminate the possibility of anything at all emerging from the fifth anomaly in the wall, barely a niche, just a roughly scooped-out hollow. In those several minutes, the niche disclosed nothing of its contents, past, present or future. It was as if it had never held anything, including the hands and tools that had dug it out of the wall, and that it never would house anything. Gilead had never witnessed anything so empty; it was as if the very air refused to fill the aperture.

With some unease, Gilead relaxed his mind away from the niche, pushing his head gently into the earth beneath it in order to relax the muscles in his neck. They had become firm with his extended bout of concentration, not that he had been able to move his head more than a fraction of an inch, but the fine muscle control was part of an elf warrior's training and it stood him in good stead. When the shackles came off, when the bindings were cut or unravelled, he would not rub at sore joints and creak at the knees and elbows, his head would not ache from the pressures on his neck and shoulders, and he would be able to stand both feet firmly on the ground without tendons and ligaments crying out for mercy.

The rest he had taken had worn away to nothing as Gilead dissected the contents of the various cavities in the antechamber's wall. He cast his ears out of the space once more, listening for echoing sounds of life in the great hall and the warrens, corridors and burrows beyond. Hearing nothing, he rested again, turning his eyes back into his head and succumbing to the self-induced sleep-state that would refresh his mind and body.

Chapter 13

Gilead woke. For several seconds, he thought about nothing except what might have disturbed his sleep. When he did think, it was to assess his position again. He was well rested, and, from his condition, he deduced that several more hours had passed. A quick check of his physical state confirmed that he had sustained no lasting injuries, but that some of the many minor wounds inflicted on him by the skaven were beginning to fester with the inevitable infections that their filth bred.

He could only guess to the nearest hour or two what time it was. He did not know for sure whether it was daylight outside or for how long he had been tied up and left on the cold earth floor, but it must have been some time, as the ground beneath his body had taken some of his heat and he no longer felt the dankness there. Sleep and hyper-consciousness, and the shifts in time they caused, elongating or diminishing it, like a

149

concertina being played by some over-zealous drinking-hole musician, made time almost infinitely flexible.

Gilead waited for whatever had woken him to stir again, but nothing happened. He felt none but the faintest of vibrations through his back and his hands trapped beneath him, between his spine and the floor of the antechamber.

He looked up at the last of the niches, but could barely discern its outline against the dark, uneven wall. With half of his faculties directed at the possible return of the Rat King, looking into the niche was proving impossible.

Gilead rocked slightly, releasing the increasing pressure on his hands, lifting his head off the floor in a series of complex callisthenic micro-movements. Despite being locked in bindings so tight as to make almost all movement impossible, the elf had rested his body well, and was not suffering stiffness, muscle cramp, loss of blood flow or any other minor ailments that might afflict humans, or even other, older, less fit elves.

Satisfied that his body was sound, and that there was no immediate threat from the other side of the antechamber door, Gilead allowed his mind to concentrate entirely on the final niche. The others told only parts of stories, and not the whole, and the elf believed that the artefacts collected by the Rat King would afford him a greater insight into the ratfolk leader's intentions, and a better opportunity to defeat him and quash his obvious ambitions.

Gilead breathed rhythmically, closed his eyes to focus on listening, and then opened them wide, concentrating on his sight at the expense of his other senses. His eyes penetrated the darkness and within moments it was as if he were standing with his chin at the lip of the niche, peering in, with an unhindered view of what was inside.

Two small objects lay in the aperture, side by side. To begin with, Gilead could not see a connection between them. The first object was a small, perfect sphere hewn from some kind of stone. It was unexceptional, save that it was lapped to a mirror finish so bright as to surpass understanding of the craftsmanship that must have gone into making it. The second object looked like an entire eggshell with the egg removed. It was white and matt, and so transparent that Gilead could barely follow the curve of its form. There was a tiny pinprick hole in one end that allowed a fine shaft of light to penetrate it, and it sat on a larger hole in its flat end.

Gilead breathed in and concentrated harder. In the next instant, he was trying to pick up the tiny sphere. Its surface was so smooth as to make it impossible to get a grip on the little object, but it was cold and preternaturally hard. At once, Gilead knew that the little ball was made of the rarest of all rocks, carved by a dwarf craftsman of the very first and finest order. Instinctively, he knew what the other object was. It was not an eggshell at all. The other object was the antithesis of the first. The little rock ball was the most perfect sphere with the most perfect surface made of the densest, hardest and heaviest of all organic rocks. The egg, though also made of stone, was hewn from the lightest, softest and most friable of the organic rocks, also carved by a fine craftsman, probably the same man who had carved the sphere. These two objects represented the alpha and omega of the stonecutter's craft. Gilead knew without further investigation that he could never lift or hold the sphere; that its smooth surface would roll it out of his hands, even if he could hold its weight. Nor could he touch the egg without it crumbling to dust before it fell into his open palm.

Gilead was reminded of the great hall where he had been captured by the skaven rat hordes. The high, vaulted ceiling was beautifully, perfectly carved whole out of the rock. The walls were as smooth as silk and the floor was flat and level. The great expanses of the room were almost impossibly large between the pillars that held the ceiling aloft, and this, too, reflected the dwarf stonecutters' arts.

As his mind moved around the great room, Gilead's ears pricked. He could hear an odd rhythmic chant, a strange ululating call, and the echo of it across the space. Then he heard footfalls, clicking with claws in a scurry that could only be made by skaven feet, punctuated by the rhythmic tap of the Rat King's staff, like a third foot beating syncopated time.

'He has come,' he heard.

'He has come, so he has. He has come. Now he has come, for come he has, I'll live forever. I won't live for now, not just for now. I'll live forever.'

Gilead opened his eyes and ears, and found himself back in the antechamber. The Rat King was returning, and the elf planned to be ready for the hunched, hairy, grotesque figure to walk through the door.

Gilead expected the chant to end. Surely the Rat King couldn't keep up his singsong prognostications indefinitely?

Then he realised that the chant was in the air, embedded somehow, in the room around him. It was as if there were a zone around the skaven leader that followed wherever he went. The surest evidence of it was the chant, the mantra that alluded to Gilead. He wondered if there had been other chants for other missions, for it was clearly the Rat King's fervent wish to trap the elf in some demeaning form of servitude or, perhaps, as some captive specimen.

Gilead breathed in as long and deeply as he was able, and

then breathed out again. He emptied his body of every last atom of air, and relaxed his muscles until they were almost unbearably slack. Then he repeated the exercise. He did this three, four, five times more, and then listened again.

It was taking some time for the Rat King to cross the great hall, but Gilead was in no doubt that he was heading for his antechamber, and for the elf.

One by one, Gilead tensed all of his muscles individually, beginning with his hands and feet, and working his way towards his body mass and his centre of gravity. When he had tensed all the muscles individually, he tensed them all in unison, breathing in as deeply as he could while doing so.

The bindings around the elf's body felt extraordinarily tight, and, where they were of the narrowest gauge, they began to cut into his skin and the almost imperceptible layer of subcutaneous fat that covered his muscles.

The elf was not concerned that the Rat King could hear him, only with what he could hear of the Rat King. He was still minutes away, and the chant continued unabated.

Then Gilead felt a breeze on his face, and looked up at the door to see if he could locate the source of it. The door was firmly shut, but Gilead could see the shadows of leaves, falling on a breeze. They were the same leaves that had cascaded down on him from one of the wall-niches. The same, but different. The leaves were not red and yellow and sappy green, they were brown and black, like gossamer lace, ragged and punctured with ugly holes.

The leaves fell around him, disappearing in the air, leaving a putrid smell behind of rotting vegetation, and, oddly, of stale urine. He looked around, trying to work out what was going on, and saw a massive root system growing down through the ceiling from the earth above, into the room. The roots appeared to be growing strong and true in the same ladder-like formation as the plant above ground, except that dozens of rats were playing around the roots. They were pulling on the finer filaments, as if they were playing some strange game of tug-of-war; they were scratching away at them, trying to gnaw through them, and pissing on them. Several young skaven were laughing and playing, and seeing who could piss the highest up the root system. Where their urine fell, it burned like acid, making the roots shrink and fume with the reek of ammonia and sulphur. Where there were tooth marks in the roots, and chunks bitten away, the white fleshy part of the plant was turning brown and shrivelling before Gilead's eyes. The magical tree did not stand a chance under the skaven onslaught, and they seemed to be treating the destruction of the beautiful, rare and ancient organism as a game.

The odours in the room thickened as the tree, first the leaves, and then the branches, and, in what seemed like no time at all, the entire plant, roots and all, turned to dust and ashes.

Gilead turned his attention back to his predicament. He was bound with ropes made of hemp, leather and rags. The rags were heavily greased, and much of the leather had mouldered in the dank conditions underground. Some of the hemp ropes were little more than oakum ready for the picking. The rot and filth of the skaven existence below ground, and never far from the water table, meant that conditions were forever dank and moist, and that all organic materials rotted easily and quickly.

The ropes that were whole, complete, were new to a life below ground, unwilling to fall apart and shred; nevertheless they had a deep and penetrating dampness about them that made them soft and pliable. As Gilead breathed in and flexed his muscles over and over again, he began to hear the creak of the ropes as they flexed and stretched.

The whisper of dying leaves and crumbling roots subsided, and beyond the sounds, Gilead heard a faint, pitiful cry. He smelt a salt-sweet tear cutting across the malodorous plant smells of organic death and ammonia, and he saw a tendril of silvery hair bobbing. The cry gave way to wracking, wretched sobs, and Gilead saw a bubble of saliva finding its way between lips that should have been pink and pert, but were, instead, pale and pursed in a grey, frightened face. Only the eyes, the huge, pale blue eyes of the child princess, were as he had seen them before.

Then he saw a pink, fleshy, padded paw with black claws and scrappy grey-brown fur, and he felt wet onyx eyes staring malevolently into the porcelain-blue ones. One claw traced a trail down the girl's cheek. The girl closed her eyes, squeezing her nose up so high that it looked for all the world as if she were baring her small, pretty teeth in a state of panic. The claw that had grazed the flesh of her cheek, however shallowly, now went to work on her hair and on the pale, silky sheen of the fabric of her simple dress, trimmed with lace too old and too perfectly and intricately made to be of recent manufacture, and the colour of good paper to prove its age. More padded paws with more filthy claws began to grab at her hair and clothes. She screamed, shrill and sudden, and a gold wire circlet of pink pearls and glittering diamonds dropped to the floor with a sound like tiny bells, scattering gems everywhere.

As the Rat King wove his path across the great hall, the images in Gilead's visions became bigger and more garishly coloured, and the sounds resonated less hollowly, seeming more real. Gilead could almost see the waves of scents on the air, the sweet, honeyed aroma of the girl's peachy skin and recently laundered garments, the clean salt of her tears, and the smell of her horror. If the skaven hadn't chosen to kill her, the experience very well might have. Gilead confronted the events, knowing that they had happened deep in the past, and that there was no way to change what had gone before.

The Rat King's past actions, the means by which he had retrieved the various strange, magical objects that occupied the niches in the wall above Gilead, hung heavily in the air.

Gilead breathed again, deeply and quickly, swelling his torso and making hard bunches of the muscles in his arms and legs, putting pressure on the bindings until wrinkles and then cracks began to appear across the leather thongs that bound his legs. As much as it was possible to be still and yet shadowfast, the elf had achieved that state. He used his speed to flex and relax his muscles, spasming them at an alarming rate in order to manipulate the ties and thongs that bound his arms to his torso. Finally, one by one, the leather straps began to twist, and stress fractures began to appear in several places in the ties around his wrists and elbows.

Then the knocking began, the sound of axes against rock, of wedges and pegs being driven into fissures with hardwood mallets, and of water dripping from rotary drills driven into rock by short, heavyset creatures with stone in their hearts. Gilead saw the sheen of sweat on low brows topped with abundant hair, and droplets forming on full beards and moustaches. Then he looked down at his hands, and they were the hands of a dwarf, holding a diamond file in his right, and his left stained with the lapping powder that had been scattered onto whatever he was holding in it. Gilead blinked hard, and looked around. The faces of a dozen dwarfs around him, each mason wielding a tool of his trade, began to fade and flicker out, until Gilead was alone. He looked down and saw that he was sitting at a bench on which sat the eggshell that he had seen in the niche. The elf was disconcerted for a moment to see through the eyes of a foreigner, but he persisted in opening his left hand and looking down at what was held there.

He caught the merest glimpse of a small, hard spherical object, and then became aware of its extraordinary weight. Gilead loitered for a moment in the nameless dwarf's mind, and there he saw the great sadness of a man who had lost his companions. This dwarf was the last of them, the others all lost in battle to the hugely abundant ratkin. It was a war of convenience; the skaven were multiplying beyond all that was reasonable, and sought to annex whatever underground spaces they could colonise. The dwarfs had been the greatest architects of the Empire for millennia, but they were a dying breed, and the skaven were willing and eager to capitalise on that.

With no one to defend him from the hordes, the dwarf fought bravely and well. He would not have had the opportunity to fight at all if Gilead had not been in his head when the skaven ambushed him, but the elf could not fight for him. Gilead blinked hard and stepped out of the dwarf's mind.

The skaven quickly disarmed the dwarf of his file, but not before he had brained several of the marauding ratmen.

When all that remained to him was the little ball of heavy stone in his left hand, the dwarf closed his fist around it and punched his way through the heads of a dozen more of the rat-scum before he was overwhelmed and taken down. After the dwarf had fallen, the Rat King pried his fingers aside to expose the magical sphere of rock. It took several of his coterie to roll the little ball onto an improvised litter so that it could be transported back to the Rat King's lair. Gilead could not bear to watch what became of the dwarf's body, but when next he opened his eyes, there was no dwarf corpse to be seen among the dozens of dead ratmen.

Gilead returned, resolutely, to the antechamber and to his corporeal form, bracing himself for what he must do to escape his bindings once and for all. The elf concentrated on his breathing again, and every new breath that he took came longer and deeper into his chest until he no longer needed to rely on filling his lungs to expand his chest, but only had to flex his muscles. In a matter of a few minutes all of the leather ropes and thongs had torn through under the pressure of his muscles under tension, and he was moving freely. Only the oiled rags resisted stretching and breaking, but once the leather and hemp ropes had been desiccated and destroyed, it was only a matter of a few minutes and a little extra exertion before the elf was able to shrug off the stinking rags.

Gilead got to his feet and kicked the ropes, thongs and cloth bindings that had held him so rigidly into a corner out of the way. There was no getting away from the filth and stink of the ties that had bound him from his neck down, but he took a moment to straighten his clothes and to run his fingers through his hair, which appeared to be yellowing from the miasma of greasy smoke in the atmosphere.

Gilead's weapons had been wrested from his hands as he'd fought to breathe beneath the dozens of writhing bodies that had pinned him to the floor of the great hall. He did not know or care how many of the ratmen had died, suffocated or crushed to death in their efforts to subdue him. He did care that they had managed to take his weapons from him, but the Rat King was clearly a scavenger, a collector of objects, and elf-made blades must surely be as prized as any other artefact. It took Gilead a matter of moments to find his sword and dagger slotted into gaps in the throne chair. He was surprised that he had not seen them there sooner among the poorly made, rusting and broken pieces of weaponry from which the chair was constructed.

As he passed the flat of the blade against his thumb, reassured by the cool, smooth steel, he heard the whisper of gusting breath between the words that the Rat King was still mouthing.

'He has come, so he has. He has come. Now he has come, for come he has, I'll live forever. I won't live for now, not just for now. I'll live forever.'

The Rat King held his amulet in his left paw, and sniffed and twitched at the smell of burning flesh that emanated from it. He could not stop grinning, nor could he stop repeating, over and over again, the words that meant so much to him.

He clipped down the short spiral staircase to his little chamber, and pushed at the door with the end of the staff that he held in his right hand. He could not wait to cast his eyes down on the elf once more. He had almost been too excited to leave him, but he had had no choice but to appoint new men at every level of his horde. So very many had died for him in capturing the Fell One, so many little sparks of life force had been gathered and added to his immortality. They had died for him, but he had to be certain that others would do so, and that required a hierarchy. If his captains, lieutenants and leaders were not in place then the skaven would turn on each other in a free-for-all of devastating proportions. The Rat King's power base, painstakingly built up over years, decades, would be lost forever if he had no one to keep the troops in line.

He had spent most of the previous day watching fierce young skaven clawing and hacking each other to death in a series of gladiatorial bouts that ended with the last ratmen standing being awarded the highest military honours and the best positions in the Rat King's bodyguard.

He was going to live forever, and the Fell One would keep.

Gilead did not wait for the door to open to take up a belligerent stance with a weapon in each hand. He only wondered that the Rat King did not feel the need to bring a phalanx of fighting men with him.

The door swung open, and the hunched figure of the Rat King appeared in front of Gilead. He was not armed, except for the long staff that he used as a walking aid, and for ceremonial appearances. It was a badge of office as much as it was a useful weapon, and he was certainly not wielding it in anger, or using it as a defence as he walked into the antechamber.

Gilead could not see what was in the Rat King's other hand; nevertheless, he knew that it was the reason he was in the skaven stronghold. He also knew that the Rat King believed the object could control the elf, and hold him in its thrall. Gilead knew no such thing. After all, had not the amulet

given him visions of the Rat King's little collection of artefacts? Had it not opened his eyes and ears, and warned him
of the Rat King's return?

Gilead looked hard into the Rat King's eyes, but heard only
the words tripping inexorably from the foul creature's maw.

'You have come, so you have. You have come. Now you
have come, for come you have, I'll live forever. I won't live for
now, not just for now. I'll live forever,' it said.

Gilead saw the little skip in the Rat King's step as if it
were attempting to dance a jig, and detected a greedy glint
in its eyes as it looked down at its paw, where it held the
single perfect curl from the girl's innocent head. The lock
of hair bounced and jiggled as the ratman's body jostled
up and down to some rhythm all its own. He saw the battered corpse of the girl-child at the Rat King's feet, and he
saw the group of skaven fighting to be the first to taste her
sweet flesh.

His sword still drawn, Gilead held his stance, but could not
move to attack the wretched creature that stood before him.
The curl was gone from the Rat King's paw, and in its place
was a great handful of brilliant red and orange leaves, spilling
over and falling to the ground. As they fell, they blackened
and smoked with a noxious, greasy gas. The Rat King rubbed
the leaves in his paw, and a rope of drool dripped from his
canines and landed in the vegetation, the acidic spittle ignit-
ing the foliage in a flaring blue flame that made the leaves
fizz and wither.

Gilead wanted to save the leaves, rescue the magical plant,
but he knew that it was long gone. He wanted to kill the Rat
King, too, the monster who had wrought such evil madness
upon the noble, the innocent and the magical. His vision
shifted and rippled in front of him, and he stared deep into

the Rat King's eyes once more. The beast appeared to be laughing at him, its eyes wide and glistening, its teeth bared and its tongue dancing around in its maw.

The Rat King let something drop from his paw. The object was suspended from a length of ribbon, apparently made from intricately plaited hair, and it swung and twisted slightly.

Gilead could not tear his gaze from the Rat King's eyes, but in those eyes he began to see flashes of bright light, sparks bobbing and dancing in the onyx orbs. The sparks coalesced into soft, white lights that seemed to fall on a complex tableau, a fully formed picture of some moment far in the future, appearing simultaneously in the Rat King's marble-like eyeballs, in stereo.

Gilead wanted nothing more than to kill the Rat King and to destroy the sparkling amulet that was sending shafts of light into the creature's eyes. The elf did not know whether the amulet was in thrall to the rat or the rat was in thrall to the amulet; it mattered not, for both must perish.

He thought to raise his sword, to lunge, to attack the Rat King, to best him before his loyal horde stormed the ante-chamber, for he knew now that the ratmen had gathered in vast numbers, beyond, in the great hall. He did not know how the knowledge of their gathering had eluded him, only that it had.

The warrior elf knew that if he killed the Rat King and destroyed the amulet, the spell would be broken and the rat hordes would fall into desperate disarray. He would not have to fight his way out of the warrens and burrows below ground, for the ratmen would not choose to fight him and die if they could fight one another and live.

Gilead had to kill but one creature. He looked deeper into

the Rat King's eyes, searching for the motivation to seize the moment and end whatever new tragedy was to come, before it had begun.

Gilead beheld the image of a vast, ancient ratman with sleek white fur, glistening teeth and gleaming eyes. The ratman was standing on a mountain of corpses of mesmerising proportions. This was the future if Gilead did not act to end the Rat King here and now.

'You have come, so you have. You have come. Now you have come, for come you have, I'll live forever. I won't live for now, not just for now. I'll live forever,' said the Rat King.

Chapter 14

Mastering the bardic arts requires such discipline, such breadth and depth of understanding that it falls to the very few, to the most learned, and to those truly in their unfettered prime to invoke a character that is *other*.

I fell upon my profession as a child at the bedside of a teller of the most magical of elf tales, and I have tried my humble best to invoke the ancient race honestly and honourably.

I weary now, and know that it will take all the energy I have to do justice to this portion of the tale, this most pained and painful of subjects, this creature of the endless night, of enduring darkness, of pity and of pathos.

Forgive me if I falter, for so desolate a character never walked the Empire but he filled these bardic veins with bloodless ice. I feel a glacial blast at only anticipating unfurling this tale. Stir the fire, for my chilled hands will not hold

the poker steady, and swathe my shoulders in another of
your fine blankets, and I will do my very best.

> *Hail mine liege lord the night,*
> *Hail mine liege lady the moon.*
> *Hail mine steed of might,*
> *Hail mine blades of doom.*
> *Hail mine eternity of life,*
> *Hail mine eternity of death.*
> *Hail mine duty of strife,*
> *Hail mine sacrifice of faith.*

He spoke the words over and over, first aloud, and then
silently. For the first half-hour of silent repetitions his lips
moved, but, gradually, the words became a mantra, a medi-
tation in his exhausted mind. Then, his lips were all but
stilled, the top, so pale that its edge was invisible, the lip
and the surrounding skin the same bloodless, grey hue. His
bottom lip swelled slightly at the centre, dark and moist, as
if a great black ball of blood were trying to leak out from
between his teeth. It quivered from time to time. He longed
to feel the words as he had felt them a thousand years ago,
but he felt nothing now, nothing but the futility of an existence devoid of all meaning.

He sat in a small clearing with his back exposed. He had
long since given up the practice of sitting with his back
against a tree or wall, or into the corner of a room. He had
long since abandoned any desire to defend himself. He relished his vulnerability, however artificial it was. He knew
that if he were attacked from behind, he would surely hear
his adversary, be on his feet before the attack had happened,
and would probably have run his assailant through on his

sword before the poor deluded fool had had a chance to parry or counter-attack.

He was the consummate fighting machine. He had no heart, no fear, no weaknesses, and above all no worthy opponent.

Everyone was his enemy. Every mortal creature despised him, as he despised himself. Every sentient race cursed him, cowered before him and condemned him, as his own kind had condemned him to this endless round, this interminable existence.

He was nothing. He had nothing. Time had taught him that as it had taught him little else of any value.

He was merely a construct, only the sum of the parts, parts that had been so key to his life once, long ago when they had meant something. He had been battle. He had been armour and blade. He had been nobility. He had been service. He had been honour, loyalty and faith. He clung to the tenets of his long-dead existence, not lest he should cease to exist, for he knew that he could never cease to be, but lest his existence become not only futile, but also structureless. The routine was all that remained. The observances were all that reminded him of what he had once been. He knew not how to pray like a Bretonnian knight, but he knew that a Bretonnian knight must pray, and so he prayed the only prayer that he knew. He knew that a Bretonnian knight must be noble, strong, faithful and brave. He knew that he had once been all of those things. What he was now, what he had been this past millennium, was none of those things. That he could act as if he were what he had once been must be enough.

He had not died an honourable death. He would not die in honour now, and so he must make his observances, follow his routines, and preserve a receding corner of sanity in his hindbrain.

He settled a camp, not because he needed to rest, but because he had been taught how to settle and strike a camp in preparation for his first crusade. He lit a fire, not because he needed the heat or the light, or to cook food, but because fire was the essence of life. He mended his clothes, cleaned his armour and oiled his blade, not because those things made a difference to his capacity for combat, but because the routines made him feel alive, human, humble again for a moment, as if his continued existence mattered, as if he had a cause, a reason for being.

He sat before the fire he had built, a neat, perfectly symmetrical cone of twigs giving off a warmth that he could not truly feel, and worked lapping powder into the smooth, curving steel of his cuisse. He wove small, regular circles across the metal to the rhythm of the words in his head, trying to think of nothing else.

It was impossible.

He had been sitting like this when the elf had come upon him. He had used this same cuisse as a shield when he was forced to improvise to save himself from the great warrior's onslaught.

To save himself.

How had he come to save himself?

Why had he fought to save himself?

The Vampire Count sat still, silent, without even the words in his head for company, without the mantra, the improvised prayer that kept all other thoughts from his fragile mind. He polished the armour only because that was what he did, and now the very act that helped to keep him sane brought with it the madness of the question, 'Why had he fought to save himself?'

The humans were as nothing. He had never been a man in

the prosaic sense. A knight is not a man, for he is so much more, and so much less than other men. He had not sought to defile humans in the way that had been so popular among his kind for so long. He had taken the solitary path. He must battle when the battle came to him, but he would not raise the dead nor bring with him the destroyed. For those who were less than nothing, the hordes that were destroyed only to be brought back to destroy anew, were less than pitiful, less than pathetic.

He had fought to save himself because he could not fail to do what he had been schooled to do. He could not fail to be that knight, that paragon, that exemplar. Decades as that living, breathing knight could not be wiped away, not even by a thousand years of undeath.

The elf, whose name he knew not, was the closest he had come in a thousand years to real, final, ultimate death.

His face showed no expression. His lip did not quiver, nor did his pupils dilate. His nostrils did not flare, nor did his brow rise. The thought in his head was not visible on his face.

The Vampire Count began his mantra again, his lips working the sounds of the words that he spoke fervently, aloud, filling the clearing with increasingly stentorian tones. With every repetition his voice grew stronger and firmer.

> *Hail mine liege lord the night,*
> *Hail mine liege lady the moon.*
> *Hail mine steed of might,*
> *Hail mine blades of doom.*
> *Hail mine eternity of life,*
> *Hail mine eternity of death.*
> *Hail mine duty of strife,*
> *Hail mine sacrifice of faith.*

He knew what he must do. He must fight to the death for the right, the privilege, of being expunged, of being removed wholly and completely from existence. He could not sacrifice himself, so he must find a worthy opponent and die at his hand. He must find the elf. He must challenge him, and he must trust that the magical being would finally best him in combat.

The knowledge freed the Vampire Count from the pall of ages, liberated him from the threat of eternal life, and lifted him. He did not know what it was to feel happiness or even contentment, and he did not feel them now. He did feel a little less dread, a little less resignation. He wondered if what he felt was hope, but he dismissed the thought almost before it had a chance to come to life in his mind. The rhythm of his mantra was broken for a moment, and his voice faltered. The feeling did not last, and the undead creature began his prayer again, from the beginning, as he kicked over the remains of his fire, folded away his tin of lapping powder and his polishing cloth, and took up the first piece of armour to strap to his body.

The elf had sought to destroy the skaven. The Vampire Count resolved to descend below ground, and, perhaps, the skaven would find they had an ally, after all.

Despite there being little to party with, there was great reason to celebrate, and so they must.

Dozens of their men had been returned to the community, both to the town and to the surrounding tracts of farmland. The men had returned and borne with them tales of the rout of the skaven.

They did not know who had slaughtered the ratmen in such numbers, or how he had done it. Only one or two of them had seen the warrior, so tall and lean, so ethereally handsome. A very few had seen him wield his weapons, killing and maiming with every thrust and strike. Those few told their stories long and loud to whoever would listen. Their audiences of women and children were large and growing, and within a day or two all the men were claiming to have seen the wondrous creature. Some even dared to call him an elf, although so rare and extraordinary a creature had never been seen by any of them before.

Most claimed to have seen him, some claimed to have been standing within feet of him when the tide of skaven was broken on his blade, and a few even claimed to have fought alongside him. One told of how he had been back to back with the elf, of how he had been urged on by the creature and then praised in dulcet tones for his bravery.

'"No man ever fought so bravely", that's what he said,' said Varn Holst, a short, portly man, who had come away from the undercrofts with a long tear in the skin of his shin, which was red and raw and infected. He'd taken the injury falling over a skaven blade abandoned in one of the underground tunnels before he'd even joined the fray. He'd lain low after taking the injury, and had only begun to run for his life when he heard the cries of his fellow humans behind him. Just a few days later his mother-in-law removed the leg below the knee, and only a week after the battle with the skaven, Varn Holst died of a fever. He'd had his moment of glory, had told a good yarn, and there was no shame in that, but everyone knew that if he'd ever actually seen an elf, at best he would have soiled himself or fainted clean away and at worst he would have died of fear where he stood.

The merrymaking continued for days, half-festival,

half-wake. There was little enough to eat at the best of times, but someone somewhere was always willing to brew beer, and even harder stuff, from whatever rotten peelings, unripe fruit, or flaking tree-bark might be available, so there was a surfeit of alcohol. Several of the younger men and one or two women were made sick by ale that was too young to drink, after all the properly brewed stuff was gone. For the rest, there was more than enough alcohol of the kind that burnt all the way down and then all the way up again, and might cause temporary blindness in anyone who had the constitution to drink more than a pint of it. Indeed, it had been a huge help to poor old Varn when his leg had to be amputated.

They did not know what the rout of the skaven meant for the land, for their families or for their futures, but for now, for these few days, the townspeople and folk from the surrounding countryside were content to make merry and celebrate the victory bestowed on them by the mysterious warrior.

They did not notice the strangers in their midst. They did not see the tall, elderly man or his taller, younger companion. They did not lower their voices when the slumped, hooded interlopers sat quietly in the corners of their drinking holes.

The strangers watched and listened and registered everything. They heard the humans' drunken stories, as incoherent and elaborated as they often were, and they pieced together some semblance of the truth.

The creature the humans had mistaken for the villain plaguing them, the mysterious figure they had shrunk from and feared, the ethereal being that they had credited with the decimation of the land and all the other hardships they had suffered these many years, had become their hero, his praises sung in every word that passed their lips.

The unlikely pair of strangers watched and listened. They entered and left the cookshops and drinking holes without being confronted, or even noticed, and they moved from street corner to street corner, from farmstead to lowly hovel, to garner as much information as they could. They were not disappointed.

Some of the stories were contradictory, for what elf could be hunted and tracked by the coarse humans? Some tales were embellished to the point of being almost comedy, for what elf had ever worn full plate armour of the type described by one over-zealous storyteller? And still there were mysteries left unanswered.

There were dozens of stories of bravery and derring-do, all involving the mysterious, fearless warrior, often with a phalanx of eager humans in support. There were dozens of descriptions of blades flashing faster than the eye could follow, and of ratmen being killed and maimed in the onslaught, or running screaming from the valiant swords-man. One human, surrounded by an eager audience, even blew out every lamp in the windowless hovel that was his theatre, putting the very last and smallest, with its meagre glow, between his feet under the table so that everyone could experience the miserable dark below ground in the tunnels that made up the labyrinthine warren the skaven inhabited.

The strangers left under the cover of darkness, after the story-teller began to weave tales so absurd and unbelievable that the older of the two could hardly contain his mirth, while the younger was filled with scorn and indignation.

'They talk of him as if he had wrought some great magic,' said the youth.

'They should,' said his older companion. 'He does that.'

'They do not talk of where he is,' said the youth, 'nor of what happened after his great victory.'

'No,' said the other.

'It is him, though?' asked the youth.

'You've heard the stories. He is the subject of tales that will be told and retold for a thousand years by the humans. If we cared to tell his tales, we would tell them for millennia.'

'But the discrepancies? There are so many, and they are of the strangest kinds,' said the youth.

'The humans tell stories in a particular fashion; the truth is less important to them than the romance of the tale. They know not what an elf truly is, and so they embellish, ornamenting a character in their own terms, in ways that define the sense of a being rather than the reality of it.'

'So, it is him.'

'It is him,' said the older man as they walked into the darkness away from the edges of the town.

'Do you know where to find him?' asked the youth.

'He said that he would find me,' said the other, 'but since there is no sign of him, and no word of him leaving the skaven warrens, I fear we shall have to follow him underground.'

The old man stopped suddenly, and watched for a moment or two as the youth, failing to notice that his companion was not at his side, strode purposefully onwards.

'So like him,' the old man said to himself. 'So young and tall and headstrong, and so very, very like him.'

The youthful figure stopped and turned to face his old companion.

The old man lifted a hand in acknowledgement, and began to walk towards him. He dropped his head, so that no part of his face was visible beneath his hood, and he muttered under his breath, 'Where are you, Gilead te tuin? Where are you, my old friend?'

Chapter 15

The Vampire Count had very little in the way of tracking skills. He was drawn by blood, and could smell it on everything; creature, monster, human. He could smell the difference between the carrion-eating, lower mammal life-forms that he had been forced to feed on in the past few years, and the sweeter, subtler aroma of the grass-eating mammals whose blood he preferred. The skaven smelled like the lower orders, like the rodents they took their common name from, but even more vile. Nothing would induce him to sate his appetite on those loathsome creatures. Humans, while they had their uses for many of his brethren, did not represent the richest of pickings for him, their omnivorous appetites and their indiscretions with alcohol, tobacco and other drugs making their blood tannic and greasy. A young, female human who did not sully her blood with drugs and drank only water was the highest prize of all, and virtually impossible to resist, but there were so few of those around that he had not partaken of one in more than a decade.

The elf had not smelled of blood at all, and was so skilled at leaving no evidence of his existence that the only trail he had left was one of bodies, of skaven dead.

The Vampire Count stopped for a moment while he allowed this thought to ferment. If he could not track the elf by his blood scent, nor recognise the clear, spring-water smell of his adversary, he would simply follow the trail of rat bodies, for the elf would surely be found at the site of the biggest pile of slaughtered skaven.

Fully armed and armoured, the Vampire Count stowed his belongings and stood beside his war steed, waiting for the sun to set. His best chance to track down an entrance to the skaven labyrinth below the earth was on open ground, since the ratmen were too lazy to dig through the roots of trees. He would have to wait for several hours in the woods before emerging at twilight, but he was used to the passage of great tracts of time and could wait out these hours without recourse to thought or movement, food or rest. As he waited he would recite his mantra over and over again, and try to remember the true meaning of honour.

> *Hail mine liege lord the night,*
> *Hail mine liege lady the moon.*
> *Hail mine steed of might,*
> *Hail mine blades of doom.*
> *Hail mine eternity of life,*
> *Hail mine eternity of death.*
> *Hail mine duty of strife,*
> *Hail mine sacrifice of faith.*

* * *

'Tell me of the skaven,' said the youth, as the companions sat together over a small fire, eating the roasted flesh of the tubers and corms that grew in the mulchy layers of earth close to the surface.

'The ratmen?' asked the older man. 'They live no life at all, but fill what little time they have with wretched thrashing and mewling and scavenging for carrion. Their weapons are primitive and their usage crude, yet predictable. But talk is meaningless. You are well trained and will confront the ska-ven soon enough.'

The stench in the air was of putrefaction, animal and veg-etable, but there was no smell of fresh blood or of living beings, not even of the skaven.

The Vampire Count stood soft in the knees and low at the shoulders in a dark, earthy tunnel, his eyes glowing, shed-ding enough light for him to see a yard or two of the path ahead. He could hear nothing, and his touch was impeded by the ancient plate that encased his body. He must rely on being able to smell and taste the air to find his quarry.

The Vampire Count did not draw his weapon in the con-fined space, since there was nothing nearby to attack nor to defend himself against, but he was eager for the fight. He could move more easily in open spaces, and in tunnels built of brick or hewn from rock rather than dug out of the earth with claws. At every junction, the fallen knight took the wider tunnel with the higher ceiling, while still working his way down into the earth.

The scents changed little, but the confined spaces seemed to concentrate them. Many of the smells were as old as time, unable to escape and dissipate into the air above ground. None of the smells were dry, none clean, none fresh or enticing. The tunnels stank not of sweet earth or baked brick, or hewn stone, but of rot and decay, of damp and infection and death and putrefaction. It did not dawn on the Vampire Count to wonder what he smelled of. It did not occur to him that his body reeked of age and death, of disease and fear.

None stopped his passage through the tunnels and burrows that drew him deeper underground, for there were none to stop him.

The first skaven that the Vampire Count encountered were a clutch of mewling infants, pink and mottled of skin, crusted of eye, transparent of claw. He ran his sword through their pitiful bodies not in self-defence but in revulsion. They made no sound as they died. The only sound the Count made was to exhale with the stroke, as he had been taught hundreds of years before, despite the fact that breathing was redundant and his lungs were petrified, rendered useless at the time of his undeath. He had maintained his habits forcibly at first, afraid that he would forget his old self as his undead state took precedence over everything that had gone before. Now he wished that he had forgotten, that he could forget. Nothing in his undead life gave him pain so much as the loss of the old way of living.

The Vampire Count took hold of the neck of his scabbard in his left hand, preparing to replace his sword, when he heard a faint, distant scratching noise that brought his nose up to meet the movement in the air to detect any fresh odour.

The smell was of carrion flesh and infection, but newer, more immediate, and more likely to be alive than dead.

The Count adjusted his grip on his sword and surged into the darkness, down a sloping corridor that gave way to another and then another. Two minutes later, he found himself at a junction of four corridors, one sloping upwards, two low and dark, but the fourth... the fourth was wide of mouth and sweeping of curve.

The Count heard a crash and a tumble, and the shriek and screech of narrow jaws and unsheathed claws. He was almost bowled over by a scratching, screaming bundle of skaven bodies, hurtling from the tunnel like cats in the middle of a fight.

A pair of bloody, shiny eyes looked up at him, and the head they belonged to was suddenly still at the centre of the mayhem. As the ratman opened his mouth to shriek a warning to the other members of the ragged ball of fur that constituted their several bodies, the Count brought his blade across its jaw and out through the back of its head. In one sweeping motion, he separated the ratman from its life by dividing the crown of its head from its mandible. A second skaven lost an eye, and while it was lamenting its fortune, was lanced through the belly on the end of the Count's rapidly swinging sword.

The Count misjudged his third stroke when one of the ratmen moved faster than he had anticipated, and he took two limbs from the skaven, a lower and an upper on its left side. The ratman tried for a moment to run away from its attacker, but became confused, and could only perform a ragged circle before it bled out. The Count thought he had seen off the last of the clutch of skaven when the fourth clamped one paw to its face and another to its chest and literally keeled over in front of him before he had even swung at it. Then there was a fifth, who had separated itself from the melee at the first opportunity and was fleeing back down the tunnel, squeaking as it went.

The Count followed it, not so quickly, but with steely determination. Any survivors would surely lead him, eventually, to the great skaven killer that was the ethereal elf.

The pair of figures, tall and slender silhouettes in the fading light, struck camp as soon as they had finished their meal and cleaned their utensils. The elegant dishes went back into their packs, and they left the site of their meal as it had been when they had arrived. The last of the fire was brushed back into the earth and carefully kicked over, and the companions left no trace of themselves as they went in search of an opening in the ground.

Their eyes adjusted quickly from the twilight to the underground gloom, and they soon found themselves navigating a series of earth tunnels, moist to the touch, but eerily quiet.

The older, shorter of the two figures led the way when the tunnels and corridors were too narrow for them to walk side by side, and their exceptional height meant that few of the burrows were tall enough for them to stand upright in. The older man kept his entire torso low, so that his head remained upright and level, and the youth behind him followed his lead, soon matching his stride, and growing increasingly confident.

'How do we track him?' asked the youth.

'We don't. We track death.'

'Because of the humans?'

'Because of the humans' stories,' said the older man. 'If he defended them, if he slew even half as many as they say, if he is still beneath the ground, then we will find him where we find death.'

'Deeper then?' asked the youth, as they came to a fork in the tunnel. He hesitated for a moment, resting the palm of his hand against the dark, packed-earth wall, and looked hard at his companion, as if concentrating. 'There's movement.'

'Deeper,' said his companion, already leading the way.

At the next turn in the tunnel, in a shallow alcove to the left of them, they saw their first dead.

'What is it?' asked the youth, steadying his breathing, lest the stench of putrid flesh overwhelm his senses.

'These,' said his companion. 'They're the young. That's what their offspring look like, such as they are. Not very different from the adults, smaller of course, but equally pestilential.'

'He did this?' asked the youth.

His elder dropped to his knees to look a little more closely at the bundle of blood and downy fur.

'The kill is clean, efficient, executed with a honed blade. He could have done this. No... he must have done this, for who else in these parts would wield a blade so elegantly? Certainly not the skaven, and the humans carried more tools than weapons below ground when they went into battle.'

'It isn't the work of a human hand,' the youth agreed.

'The rest might be due to fatigue or the confines of the space. The strokes do not quite conform to his usual pattern of attack, but in the absence of an alternative, we must believe that it is him.'

The pair continued for another quarter of a mile of tunnels, turning this way and that, following the vibrations in the walls. Then the older companion stopped suddenly as he felt a series of thuds through the earth floor.

'Bodies?' asked the youth.

'Falling. Creatures are dying.'

The youth made to hurry forwards, but the old man

extended an arm to prevent him. There was a strange, animal cry, and then nothing.

'He doesn't need our help,' said the old man. 'The battle is over, until the next time.'

'Should we let him know we're behind him?' asked the youth. 'Should we call out?'

'Subtle as ever,' said his companion. 'He'll know we're here. We're not hiding our footfalls, and we're speaking together freely. Even an idiot human would have no trouble tracking us down.'

Minutes later, they came upon four skaven corpses, variously annihilated with some bladed weapon.

'Look here,' said the youth, pointing to a corpse that had died of its injuries, the limbs on its left side cut cleanly from its body. 'This is not the work of a consummate warrior.'

His companion looked down at the corpse.

'No,' he said, 'but the skaven are surprisingly fleet, and singular of purpose. If this rat creature darted swiftly and suddenly enough, especially with a kick of adrenaline behind it, there is just a chance that even an experienced swordsman might miss his target once in a while.'

'It seems so unlikely,' said the youth.

'Perhaps,' said the old man, 'but he has been below ground, fighting a massed horde of skaven, for several days, and none of us is perfect... Not even–'

The skaven was almost past them before they had seen it, crossing the junction where they had found the corpses. The youth drew the shorter of his blades, but his companion had drawn a weapon and driven it through the creature, high against its collarbone, before he had the chance to wield it.

The skaven remained standing, clutching at its shoulder as the older man twisted his blade and opened the wound, making the ratman shriek and fall.

'You're right,' said the youth, 'they're fast.'

'Still not fast enough, though, lad.'

Chapter 16

The Count turned as he heard the sudden shriek of a skaven, a ratman under attack. Moments later there was a thud, and the faint sound of words, or perhaps humming. He bent his ear and concentrated on the sounds, but they were not words in any language that he recognised, and nor were they the sudden squeaks and squawks of the skaven. He wondered for a moment if the words might have come from the elf, but dismissed the thought. The sounds came from behind and above him, and the great warrior was surely deep among the ratmen, killing and maiming, and, besides, the elf had been alone, with no one to talk to.

The next junction was a dog-legged right turn down another slope, a marriage of stone and earth that included several ragged steps. The Count cloaked himself in the shadows at the bottom of the steps and waited.

He heard steps, not the scamper of claws, but the definite

strides of upright bipeds. The strides seemed long for any but the tallest human, yet light and confident, more like a dance with a regular beat than simple walking. There were, however, two distinct walkers, the rhythms slightly different.

The strides sounded at first close by, but then deviated before coming back at a right angle to their original positions. The corridors were irregular, labyrinthine, and sounds echoed and bounced around in the spaces in a manner that the Count found confusing. He did not trust them.

He moved away down the sloping tunnel that had begun with the stone steps, and could hear nothing.

He stopped again, and the footfalls were audible once more.

He walked back to the steps, and the footfalls stopped.

The Count was sure that he was being followed, his pursuers stopping to listen for his footsteps, and walking towards him when he moved on.

He knew that he could not mask the sound of his steps, or the vibrations he made in the tunnels. He was not built for subtlety, and his armour would not allow for it, but he was built to fight, and he would be ready and waiting for the battle when it came to him.

'Do you hear that?' asked the youth. 'That is not the sound of his stride.'

'Nor that of a skaven,' said his companion.

'A human, then?'

'More than human if he was responsible for the killing we've seen,' said the old man. 'A true warrior. I doubt such a man would exist in the towns and villages, among the people we have seen here.'

'A traveller, then, a mercenary?' asked the youth. 'But why

did the locals tell tales of an elf and not of this mortal?'

'An exceptional man might seem like an elf to some of them, and might easily become an elf in the telling of their tales. The humans call it "hyperbole", and they're wondrous accomplished in the use of it.'

'We should leave then?' asked the youth. 'We should search for him elsewhere?'

'Why "elsewhere",' asked the old man, 'when there is no word of him anywhere but here? Besides, even the most resourceful human might benefit from our assistance against the skaven.'

'Have we not a purpose of our own?' asked the youth.

'Our purpose has ever been to serve,' said the old man, 'and serve is what we shall ever endeavour to do.'

A sheen of red light penetrated the air as the Vampire Count blinked. He knew that they were close, and he knew that he had no choice but to confront them. He expanded the muscles in his chest as if breathing deeply into stone-hard lungs, and he felt a calm descend around him. He would fight. He knew that he would fight, but for the first time since he had been immortal he also knew that he could fight and lose.

The youth looked at his companion, his mouth open slightly as if to say something, but his feet stilled against crumbling earth. The passage was to his right, stone steps leading down into it at an angle. He had seen something.

His old companion looked steadily into the youth's eyes, forbidding him to move or speak.

The reddish light shone faintly but steadily to their right, a little below their head height, but the steps surely allowed for that. The old man moved silently against the wall opposite the tunnel mouth and waved a hand for the youth to stand beside, but behind, him.

They both concentrated hard on the dull light that went out and then returned as if in a blink.

The two men unsheathed their short blades, swords being too long and unwieldy in the confined space.

The youth gestured with his head tilted in the direction of the light, as if asking a question.

His companion shook his head, keeping his eyes on the opening to the tunnel.

Whatever was waiting in the entrance to the tunnel was not human, nor was it the elf they sought. Whatever was waiting in the entrance was not skaven. It was assuredly not a friend, and so it was almost certainly a foe.

The old man adjusted his grip on his weapon and, as swift and silent as he could be, he flew down the steps, straight at the red light, ready to defend his life and that of his companion.

A blade came to meet his, mere inches from their faces, as the elder got his first look at his opponent. The youth followed his companion with all haste, but stopped dead in his tracks on the bottom step, stunned by what stood before him.

The youth thrust haphazardly with his blade, but not before his adversary had unsheathed a second weapon, parrying both blades, and turning both of his opponents' weapons away.

The youth looked from his friend to his foe and back again, unsure of his standing. Should he fight alongside his companion, or should he wait to see what transpired between the two combatants? Honour required that only one of them should do battle with their adversary, that he stand down in favour of the older, and the first to attack, but their assailant looked like a fierce creature, the stuff of legend.

The old man tossed his short blade to his left hand and drew a second with his right. He did not draw a sword, knowing that it would become an encumbrance in the limited space, and he was not eager to blunt it on steel and stone. The knife he drew from his boot was an all-purpose tool more than it was a weapon, but its long, grooved stiletto blade was honed to an edge for skinning beasts and stripping the bark from saplings, and wielding it would double his chances of striking the Vampire Count a fatal blow.

The Vampire Count came on fast and sure, and the old man had to duck and parry fast and aggressively to prevent the first three strikes of the Vampire Count's blade from finding the flaws in his defence. Then he was on the attack, looking always for chinks in the warrior's armour as his blades flashed left and right, aiming at joints and the soft places under the arms and thighs and in the groin. He did not expect to land blows against a swordsman who was clearly more than capable, fast, strong and determined, but he might put the beast on the defensive and slow down the chances that a counter-attack might prove fatal.

The youth had never seen his companion sweat before, and was surprised to see it now. He was even more surprised by the Vampire Count's prowess with a blade, and his confidence, especially when face to face with so masterly an opponent.

The Vampire Count grunted and feinted, and then came in at an angle across his foe's body, and the youth finally realised that his companion might be in real trouble. The blade in his hand was ready, and he was as capable as one so young and untried could be. He had certainly proved himself in training, and had taken more instruction on their arduous journey to this place. He cut in, instinctively forcing the Vampire Count's blade wide of his target, slewing the steel across the undead's body at a clumsy angle, unbalancing him.

The old man got a blade in low, and felt sure that he had torn into the Vampire Count's calf, despite there being no blood to show for his effort.

The Vampire Count didn't falter, but stepped into the youth's next lunge, bringing them virtually nose to nose with each other.

The youth breathed in as he prepared to break and thrust, and almost gagged on the rich dry smell of death mixed with the sweet aroma of lapping powders and the musky scent of the fine chamois that the Vampire Count had used to polish his armour.

His old companion came to his rescue, blindsiding the Vampire Count with a sweep and a lurch, bringing the blade in his left hand up clumsily, but effectively, into range of those fierce red eyes.

The Vampire Count ducked the older warrior's strike, and the youth rallied.

The youth's next thrust was fierce, but ill-considered. He wanted nothing more than to maim and kill the vile creature, but his disgust had got the better of his fighting prowess, and his desperation to succeed led to a clumsy attack that was easily parried away. The youth found himself without his blade, and had to step back to regroup while his companion held back the Vampire Count as effectively as he could.

The fight slowed.

The old warrior brought both blades to the battle, lunging and crossing, the first blade skidding off the curving steel of a cuisse, the second barely making contact with the inside of the Vampire Count's left forearm. The undead warrior parried lightly, making no attempt to separate the old fighter from his weapons, and failing to take advantage and counter-attack.

The fight slowed further, the warrior testing the Vampire Count's resolve to do him real damage, leaving an opening here, an undefended flank there. He took a tear in his cloak and a nick to an earlobe for his trouble, but no final swing, no fatal blow was struck.

The youth stood and watched, aghast, before coming back into the fray, at which point the Vampire Count doubled his efforts.

'Fight, fiend!' declared the youth, appalled that such a creature should dare to patronise not only himself, but his revered companion. 'Attack!'

The eldar simply stepped back, leaving the youth to do his best. His best was fine, good even, but it was not the stuff of great legends.

'Desist,' said the old warrior.

The youth fumbled his parry and was rewarded with a long scratch down the length of his right arm, as he reacted in disbelief to his old friend's command.

The red-eyed creature desisted at once, sheathing his weapon and taking a short step backwards.

The youth attacked once more, a combination of frustration and desperation getting the better of him. He sliced a neat gouge in the Vampire Count's cheek, and watched, horrified, as it failed to fill with blood. A thin trickle of yellowish liquid eventually drizzled out of the curving gash, and the folds of skin separated slightly, but, by that time, the Vampire Count had taken hold of the youth by his shoulders and was holding him at arm's length. The Vampire Count's eyes, still red, did not shine as brightly as they had before, and the youth thought he saw melancholy in them.

Then the moment had passed. He shrugged the Vampire Count's hands off his shoulders and took a step back to stand next to his companion.

The Vampire Count began to turn slowly, confident in the knowledge that he would not come under attack a second time. He felt as weary as he had ever felt, his existence perhaps more futile than it had been only an hour or two ago. He had thought to meet his nemesis, and he had found only another enemy, a worthy enemy, who had given him a fair fight, but these two would have to work longer and harder if they were ever to find a way to best him. The old one, perhaps, for he had clearly been a great warrior in his time, but the youth had a very great deal to learn, and the Vampire Count would rather be a part of that education than end the youth's life before it had begun. Mortality seemed even more precious to him now, when he viewed it in the eager eyes and strong young limbs of the youth.

If he had been capable of shedding a tear, the Vampire Count might have done so then, but only for himself, and only because he was thwarted in what might prove his last chance to meet a worthy adversary. Perhaps in another hundred years the youth would be up to the challenge. He did not want to wait another hundred years.

The Vampire Count had taken two or three steps forwards before the old man called out to him.

'Wait,' he said.

The Vampire Count half turned, but made no move to walk towards his adversary.

'You are not he,' he said over his shoulder, his voice deep

and hollow and his tones heavily accented with a guttural intonation that the youth had not heard before.

The old warrior thought for a moment, and the Vampire Count waited for him to formulate his thought, standing in impressive profile before them.

'I am not he,' he said.

'Nor neither of you be,' said the Count.

The youth tried to untangle the oddness of the phrase, which even by the standards of human language felt like a form of torture to his ears. Then he looked from the Vampire Count to his companion.

'He has seen him,' he said.

The Vampire Count, failing to understand the youth's alien language, made to turn from them again.

'You have seen him, then?' asked the old man, using the only language the two had in common.

'Him?' asked the Vampire Count. 'I sought out the ancient one, sought out his valour and his wondrous swordplay. I sought to expire at his hand. I sought to count him mine liege lord of death.'

'You have fought him, then?' asked the youth.

The Vampire Count turned to face them both, intrigued.

'Thou art brethren to the ancient one?' he asked. 'Brethren, and yet lesser warriors than thou shouldst be.'

'Older,' said the warrior, 'or younger.' He gestured to the youth.

'Cousins,' said the youth. 'I believe we call each other cousin. I am his cousin, and my revered companion is his teacher... and mine too, should I impress him.'

'Thou, teacher, hast been bested,' said the Vampire Count, without irony.

'I was bested a great many years ago,' said the elder,

sheathing his blade and then sitting on the step behind him, stretching his left leg in front of him and pushing his second weapon back into the inside edge of his boot.

'You are alive,' said the youth. 'How come you to be alive? Why would he not kill a monster such as you?'

The elder looked up at the youth.

'A little respect for the warrior,' he said in their own language. 'Talk of being bested might give him cause to best you yet, and me too, should it fall to his will.'

The Vampire Count turned and took a step away from the pair as the youth also made to sheathe his blade. Death would not release him from a thousand years of unlife today, and he was tired of talk made so difficult by the version of his language that they spoke, but which he hardly recognised.

Then came the sound.

It filled the corridors with a booming rush that resonated at a frequency lower than anyone would expect from a skaven horde. It was, nonetheless, a cacophony of voices baying and calling as one mind with one intention.

The Vampire Count stood still amid the wave of sound as it rolled over him, and then turned to the others. The older warrior was standing with one hand against the stone wall beside him, and the youth had armed himself and was trying not to cower against the onslaught that was the ferocious cacophony, while clearly intent on getting away from it as fast as he could manage.

The elder stayed the youth with one hand on his arm, a touch both reassuring and commanding. Then he looked hard into the Vampire Count's eyes for a moment before asking his question.

'Do they call for him?' he asked. 'Is the ancient one still below ground?'

The Vampire Count had an image in his head of Gilead standing in a broad, dark, stinking space, surrounded by tunnels, cutting down ratmen two, three, even four at a time. He remembered the baleful cries as the ancient one wrought his destruction on the petty vermin. He remembered, for a moment, the duel in the forest, and he knew not how the elf had been taken, but every ounce of magic left in his veins told him that he had, that the ancient one would be found below ground, deep in the heart of the Rat King's empire.

The Vampire Count said nothing; he simply turned on his heel and lumbered off down the tunnel towards the deafening roar that once more assailed their senses, beckoning as he went.

'No!' shouted the elder, behind him. His hand was still against the earth wall, and he let go of the youth's arm in order to point in a direction at a steep angle to the tunnel they were standing in.

The Vampire Count knew that the warrior was better equipped than he was to judge the distance and direction of the sound, for he knew something of the constitution and skills of the elf-kind.

The three unlikely companions turned as one, climbed the steps out of the tunnel, and turned into a narrow earthwork, one at a time, descending steeply into they knew not what.

The old elf, Fithvael, thought of Gilead, his companion and friend.

The youth, Laban te tuin Tor Mahone, who had attended Benath's funeral and had been given into Fithvael's care, thought of the legend that was his great cousin, Gilead, and hoped that he could somehow prove worthy of the trust that had been placed in him by his community, and of the family connection to his hero, however tenuous it might be.

The Vampire Count thought only of an all-embracing nothingness that would end his misery forever.

Chapter 17

Don't clamour so. I promised to finish my story and finish it I shall. Then I can end this sorry existence and join that great brigade of storytellers that shines so brightly in my memory. I am rested and eager to continue, if you could just remind me where I left the story off. It seems like years since Gilead's name passed my withered lips, and yet I know it was mere hours ago.

The skaven had congregated beneath the ground in the great hall with its crystallised vaults and buttresses and its great, arching black ceiling above. None remained but the youthful and exuberant. All the chaff had been separated; all the old and infirm, and the cowardly, were dead and gone, mostly into the stomachs of the survivors.

All that a skaven had to do to survive was to kill and maim and incapacitate his brothers and cousins, his father and uncles and grandfathers, if he knew who they were. The rat-men were all of one cruel and vicious kind, and gave no thought to the complex biological relationships that might otherwise have tied them to allegiances they hadn't the capacity to understand.

The only skaven of any age among them was their king. He had been their master for as long as any of them had lived, and for longer than any of them could remember. There were no legends extant of any other ruler. He was all and everything to them. Their stories were short and brutal, their myths bloody, and all contained but one name, and his name was 'King'.

Gilead stood and flexed as the Rat King entered the room. He had sloughed off the ties that bound him, body and mind, and was refreshed and whole again. His senses were alert, and he was ready to do battle.

The Rat King raised one whiskered brow; his jaw moved quickly back and forth, and around and around, but without making any words.

'I have come,' said Gilead.

'So you have,' said the Rat King.

Gilead expected more. He expected the ratman to twitch and fidget, and to trip over its words, but it did not. Even its jaw had settled and was still, its whiskers unmoving.

The Rat King took a long, deep breath, and then looked from side to side, as if suspicious of what was happening to him. His eyes swung from left to right, rather than darted, and then they fixed, unblinking, on the Fell One.

'You are not what you expected to be,' said Gilead.

The Rat King felt his mind homing in on Gilead in a way that it had never managed before. He found that he was concentrating, taking in the tall, lean figure of the elf, scrutinising his prisoner's features and stance, and trying to work out what thoughts were in his head.

The Rat King shook his head slowly and blinked hard.

'I have come,' said Gilead again.

'So you have,' said the Rat King, looking startled at the sound of his own lowering voice, his words enunciated more roundly and not repeated.

'And?' asked Gilead.

The Rat King sat in the strange throne of weapon blades and handles, staring at Gilead.

'And I shall live forever,' said the Rat King.

He had stopped chewing out the words between jaws that twitched and gnawed at an alarming rate. He had stopped blinking so much and so often. Images came to him whole, not broken and strobed by the constant flickering of his eyelids.

The Rat King grasped the arms of his throne with his clawed paws and breathed deeply once more, unused to the flow of air through his lungs and the rush of oxygen into his bloodstream.

The Rat King swallowed. The pink rims of his eyes, the red of his gums and the puce flesh of his tail paled visibly before Gilead's eyes.

One side of the elf's mouth curled in a wry smile.

'Are you quite well?' Gilead asked the Rat King. 'You look rather pale.'

'I shall live forever,' said the Rat King. His voice was deeper even than it had been moments before, and he spoke more slowly, with greater purpose, as if, for the first time, he was formulating words and listening to what he was saying. He had stopped repeating himself over and over, ad infinitum.

'Is this what it feels like?' asked the Rat King, turning his paws over in front of his face, examining them as if he had never seen them before. 'Is this what being immortal feels like?'

'I am not immortal,' said Gilead. 'I will live only as long as any of my kind, if I am allowed to expire of old age. You plan to kill me, and, if you succeed, I shall prove very mortal, very quickly.'

'You have come,' said the Rat King, looking hard at Gilead, who stood over him.

'Yes,' said Gilead, 'I have come.'

Fithvael and Laban dropped to their knees and followed corridors, tunnels and burrows, following the rumble of thousands of bickering jaws and the vibrations of as many twitching, fidgeting bodies. The Vampire Count was slower and clumsier, his armour making his body bulky and awkward. Fithvael was cautious of their new ally, happy that the Count struggled to keep pace.

'How could we have mistaken such a beast for our fine cousin?' Laban asked Fithvael as the two forged ahead.

'Do not underestimate the Count,' said Fithvael. 'He is our ally for now, but soon he will be our enemy once more. He is a fine exponent of the blade arts, and it is incumbent upon you not to forget it, lad.'

'I meant no disrespect,' said Laban, colouring slightly as he turned to his teacher, and promptly tripped over an exposed root under his left foot.

'We are all capable of being clumsy,' said Fithvael, stifling his mirth.

Fithvael and Laban stopped in their tracks, and the Count blundered towards the elves as a great wall of sound came up around them. They had never heard the like of it before, as it boomed and echoed down the tunnels of the underground warren, coming at them from any number of impossible angles. It was rhythmic and shrill with a bass note of thousands of stamping paws as they pounded into the hard, earth floor of the great chamber.

'Come we close?' asked the Vampire Count, breathing hard onto the back of Fithvael's neck in the darkness of the tunnel.

Fithvael placed a hand on the wall beside him, although he could feel the vibrations so strongly through his booted feet that there was no doubt in his mind what awaited them if they continued into the great vaulted space at the centre of the warren.

They had passed no live skaven on their journey into the depths of the earth. The weak and dying had been taken or devoured, and every last remaining ratman had gathered in one place: the one place to which the three unlikely companions were heading.

'What do we do when we get there?' asked Laban. 'We should have a plan.'

'We have come to attempt to rescue our friend,' said Fithvael. 'I have no sense of him in the turmoil that the ratmen are creating.'

'The ancient one resides in these stricken realms,' said the Vampire Count. 'He resides at their centre. I know not how I know it, but know it I do.'

'That still isn't a plan,' said Laban, who appeared to have shrunk as the noise around them grew louder. 'We cannot simply walk into the gathered hosts of skaven. We will surely die.'

'There is much cunning in their characters,' said the Vampire Count, 'and guile aplenty, yet they greatly lack real intelligence, and are frantic and graceless in battle.'

Fithvael turned to the Count.

'We can kill them?' he asked.

'We three can kill and maim their host in great numbers,' said the Count, drawing his blades.

'Great numbers, perhaps,' said Laban, 'but hordes?'

The Rat King sank back into his throne and did not move for some time. Then, he pushed one paw down inside his clothes and pulled out a long ribbon of plaited hair with a jewel hanging from it. He held it up before his face and watched it, unblinking, for several seconds.

'Nothing,' said the Rat King.

'What did you expect?' asked Gilead.

'Something,' said the king, looking up at the elf. 'I expected to know something. Now that I stop to think about it... There is nothing to think about.'

'What did you expect?' asked Gilead again.

'Something,' said the Rat King again.

'You were going to live forever,' said Gilead.

'Not just for now,' said the Rat King, looking from Gilead's face to the gem as it turned slowly on its hair-ribbon.

'You are not what you expected to be,' said Gilead.

'It's made of hair,' said the Rat King, peering at the curving locks of the ribbon. He looked sharply up at Gilead again. 'Whose hair?'

'I know not,' said Gilead. 'Does it matter?'

'Whose hair was woven into this ribbon?' asked the Rat King. 'Why? Is it just any hair? Or is it the hair of someone who matters... or who mattered once?'

'I know not,' said Gilead, watching the Rat King carefully.

The Rat King brought the ribbon up to his nose and sniffed at it.

'It is the hair of my brethren,' said the Rat King. 'Of my kind... But whose? Who gave this hair to make this ribbon? Is he dead? Did I belong to him? Was the hair given freely, or taken? Does it matter?'

Gilead did not mean to answer the questions, thinking them rhetorical, but the Rat King looked up at him, sad longing in his eyes, and asked again, 'Does it matter?'

'Does it matter to you?' asked Gilead.

Gilead had never feared for his life, and he did not fear for it now. He took his mortality entirely for granted. He knew that he would die one day, soon perhaps, and it couldn't matter less. That he was mortal was a blessing to Gilead, for only in death could he overcome the enduring sadness of too much life lived and too much loss lived through. He thought of Tor Anrok, of his family, and of his twin, Galeth, dead these many years. He thought of Fithvael and the agonies they had endured in each other's company. He remembered Benath and the funeral rites of his dear cousin and honoured friend. He thought of the oldest of his kind and of the youngest of his kin, and he remembered. He knew that with remembrance came knowledge and with knowledge remembrance.

Gilead understood what had befallen the great Rat King, the beast who had dared to live forever, at any cost to himself, at any cost to his kind. He knew that the changes creeping into the Rat King's consciousness were irreversible, that his skaven adversary would never be the same again. He could not know what effect that would have on the Rat King or on his own mortality.

Gilead looked down into the Rat King's unblinking eyes as great pools of water gathered in their lower lids. The water brimmed, and yet the Rat King still did not blink. When the tears fell, they fell fat and heavy, and ran off the greasy hair that clung to his thin cheeks, or caught in the great whiskers, riding their lengths and falling, pregnant, from their tapering ends.

The Rat King was crying.

Gilead had not known that was even possible.

The Rat King unwound the hair-ribbon from around his neck, and patiently unwove the strands of hair so that the loop became one long plait from which the Rat King removed the gem at its centre. Then he dropped the gem to the floor and began to wrap the plait carefully around his wrist, as if it were the most precious thing in all the world.

'They are dead,' said the Rat King. 'The skaven that gave their hair for this ribbon are dead and gone, long gone, or not so long, they live such short and hectic lives.'

The words seemed incongruous in the skaven's maw, misplaced and formal, and his tone seemed alien, as if some human was hiding behind the Rat King's throne, speaking for him in some grotesque joke.

'You must help me,' said the skaven, standing suddenly from the throne. He grabbed Gilead by the front of his shirt, looked up into the elf's eyes, and shook him. 'You must help me to help them.'

Gilead covered the Rat King's hands with his own and pried them away from their hold on his clothing. Then he placed the paws together in front of the ratman and let them go. The Rat King held his hands before him, where Gilead had left them, and did not move.

'Help you?' asked Gilead, his words dripping scorn upon the Rat King. 'Nothing and no one can help you now.'

'We must know one another, of course,' said the Rat King, looking beseechingly up at Gilead. 'We must know ourselves and our brothers and cousins. We must know one another.'

Then the ratman sat down suddenly on his throne. He would have fallen had not the throne been directly behind him. It was as if he'd had a sudden shock and needed a moment to recover.

The moment came and went as Gilead looked from the Rat King to the gem that lay between his hind paws. The Rat King looked at his wrist and then covered the plaited ribbon tied there with his other paw, and groaned. The rims of his eyes and the pads of his paws grew whiter than ever, and then he closed his eyes and sat very still.

Gilead watched as the hairs on the Rat King, every last one of them, stood on end. His whiskers did not arch from his snout, but stood straight out like needles. He bristled all over as if gooseflesh were keeping the follicles taut, causing the hairs to stand proud, making the ratman an inch bigger in every direction. The effect was freakish, and Gilead wanted to look away, but found that he could not. Then, every single hair on the Rat King's body blanched white from the root to the tip, before Gilead's very eyes.

The elf could not tell what had caused the change, whether it was just another side effect of the amulet that seemed to be ruling the Rat King's thinking, or whether this was happening as a direct result of the ratman's constitution.

The Rat King opened his eyes and looked once more at Gilead, with wonder and longing rather than with the empty expressionless eyes that the elf had become used to. This new animation was disconcerting.

'Are you quite well?' asked Gilead, the smile returning to his lips; the irony of the situation wasn't lost on the elf.

He bent at the waist, ostensibly to be on a level with the seated Rat King, but also so that he could retrieve the gem from the floor at his feet.

'I must know,' said the Rat King, a vision of pure, ethereal white. 'I must know it all. I must know who I am and whence I came. I must know all that has gone before me, and all that I can expect from the future.'

'I have come,' said Gilead.

'But can you tell me everything?' asked the Rat King.

'There is nothing to tell,' said Gilead.

Chapter 18

'If we can hear nothing but their shouting and stamping, they can't hear us at all,' said Fithvael, striding down the corridor that gleamed with a faint, greenish light from the far end.

'But how will we defend ourselves against so many?' asked Laban.

'We won't need to,' said Fithvael. 'You'll see, lad.'

'If we are to find my cousin, Gilead, what makes you think he's down among them?' asked Laban.

'I don't think it,' said Fithvael, turning and staring hard at the youth. 'I know it, and so does he.' Fithvael gestured beyond Laban to the Vampire Count, who stood several yards distant.

'Your cousin is among them,' said the Count. 'Had he died at their hands, there would be a riot of celebration.'

Fithvael gestured, waving his hand before them.

'That is not celebration,' he said. 'That is blood lust.'

'And yet you urge me to walk into it,' said Laban, standing his ground.

'It's not your blood they're baying for,' said Fithvael.

'You're not nearly as important as your fine cousin,' said the Count, coming up behind Laban, and patting him heavily on the shoulder.

Laban turned to look at where the gauntleted hand had touched him, and tried to hide the shudder of revulsion that passed through him. By the time he turned back, Fithvael was a dozen yards farther down the corridor, his back resolutely turned on his companions.

Laban felt something trickle down the back of his shirt, and raised his hand above his head. At first he thought that water, or condensation, had gathered and was falling on him. Many of the underground tunnels were wet and muddy, and once or twice he'd heard a drop of water fall into a puddle below, the sound echoing through the tunnels. Even standing directly below the drip, Laban could hear nothing but the roar and shriek of the skaven horde.

There was no drip. Laban pushed his fingers below his collar at the nape of his neck and felt slightly moist grains of sandy earth. Then, before him, against the greenish gleam at the end of the tunnel, he saw a fall of gritty particles. The young elf touched the arching ceiling of the tunnel and felt a fissure opening in it as the whole structure vibrated with the pulsing throb of the restless crowd.

There was no point calling out, for Fithvael would not hear him, so Laban te tuin darted the length of the corridor and touched his teacher's arm. By the time Fithvael had turned, there was no need for Laban to point; they could both see the Vampire Count stepping through a moving curtain of dust and grit.

There was a booming thud, and the Count was enveloped in a great sooty cataract of dark, moist dust and particulates as the tunnel directly behind him collapsed under the pressure of the skaven vibrations. The Count stepped through the cloud, his armour dulled and marred by the shower, looking more sinister than ever.

'Well, there's no turning back now,' said Fithvael, drawing the shorter of his blades.

'Onwards!' exclaimed the Vampire Count, raising his sword in salute to his companions.

'What is our aim?' asked Laban.

'The same as it ever was,' said Fithvael, 'to find Gilead and to ensure his safety.'

'How do we do that?' asked Laban.

He need not have asked. The Vampire Count had skirted the two elves, standing side by side in the broad entrance to the great chamber, and had begun cutting down the ratmen that stood in his path. They fell one after another, one on top of another, as the Count carved a path through the throng.

Many of the skaven were not aware of the Count cutting through them until it was too late. They were facing the mound where they expected their great King to emerge, to lead them on to greater battles against wondrous foes. They expected to attack, not to be attacked.

Fithvael and Laban had no choice but to follow in the Count's footsteps, bringing up his rear, and defending it so that he could not be attacked from behind and have his efforts wasted.

The ratmen were almost too easy to kill. Their attacks, though frantic and unpredictable, were generally poorly aimed and haphazard; as many strikes missed as hit, and when they did strike they tended to be wide of the desired mark, so that Fithvael and Laban defended more attacks to their limbs than to their torsos or heads. The ratmen were also just as likely to attack each other as the elves, either by accident or by design, and fights soon broke out among the skaven closest to the Vampire Count. A wide 'V' of bodies was scattered on the floor behind him, like the wake of some great sea-going vessel.

Of the skaven who saw their attacker, many fell dead before they were touched, their blood organs giving out under the pressure of fear and panic. An increasing number of the beasts rendered insane by the power of the rhythm stamped out by their kin, and by the ululating and shrieking of voices, sat among the corpses gorging themselves. The sight sickened Laban, who took considerable pleasure in smiting the cannibals, adding more carrion to the feast.

Several long minutes passed as the Count made progress towards the great mound where the Rat King would appear to address his host. He cut and thrust, and swept through dozens of ratmen; blood ran from his sword and sprays of it clung to the filth on his sullied armour, yet he made little impact on the horde as a whole. The damage he could do, even with Fithvael and Laban at his back, was limited to an insignificant area, to one small section of the crowd.

It would take one Vampire Count and two elves days or weeks to plough through the entire skaven horde. The task was impossible, but there was no sign that the Vampire Count would stop fighting until all of the ratmen were destroyed. There was no subtlety to his craft; he was a killing machine, an automaton, merciless and unmoved by the destruction that surrounded him. He had nothing but contempt for these pitiful creatures, and would gladly kill a thousand of them, or more, for the opportunity to stand opposite the great elf in combat.

'Your people await,' said Gilead.

'Me?' asked the Rat King, turning the plaited hair-ribbon slowly around his narrow wrist. 'Perhaps they can tell me.'

Gilead handed the Rat King his staff, which had been propped up, forgotten, against the back of the throne. The King grasped it firmly in his hand, and hoisted himself up. His old body was not suited to the slow, ponderous movements of a beast deep in thought, and he seemed not to be aware of the patterns of vibration in the antechamber, which Gilead feared might crumble to dust under the waves of pressure that were bombarding it.

The elf withdrew his sword from its place in the tangle of broken and discarded tools and weapons that comprised the skaven throne, and sheathed it. The Rat King arranged his robes around his body and slowly gathered his newfound wits. He did not see that Gilead was newly armed.

Gilead watched a drizzle of grit fall from somewhere in the ceiling and land on the Rat King's shoulders. Then he heard the *whump* of collapsing earth, and a light in the antechamber was extinguished as the first of the niches, high in the chamber wall, collapsed under the weight of vibrations that were thrumming through the underground structures.

The Rat King left the chamber ahead of the elf, climbing the steps and walking out onto the mound. As the skaven host saw their king emerge, the ratmen nearest the mound redoubled their efforts to stamp and wail. The wave of sound rippled through the host, and soon the noise was beyond anything that Gilead had ever encountered. He looked out over the Rat King's head, across the tightly packed crowd, and watched as gaps began to appear between the ratmen's heads. Hundreds of the skaven died on their feet, crumpling to the ground to be trampled underfoot. The noise and wonder, the heat of so many bodies, and fear of anything and everything, killed them by the score.

Gilead's eye was drawn further and further into the crowd as the wave of death spread outwards from the epicentre that was the mound and the royal rat that stood on top of it.

Then, slowly, a kind of hush began to fall.

The Rat King did nothing. He did not twitch or sniff; he did not fidget or shuffle. He did not blink, and he did not speak. The blood organ in his chest was beating remarkably slowly, and he wondered that everyone around him could not hear it thump incessantly, instead of flickering like the buzzing wings of some carrion-eating insect. He did not know if he could stand the beat of his own heart. The quantity of blood reaching his brain was too much. He had too many thoughts, too many questions, and there was no one to answer them. He looked out at the snouts raised before him, but could not find a single pair of eyes that would stay open for long enough for him to focus on a single face, and talk to a single one of his followers.

The skaven were filled with such unfocused expectation that they were lost in a miasma of frenzy. They were born for destruction, and without a leader, any leader, they would destroy indiscriminately.

They did not recognise their Rat King as he stood before him. He did not look like one of them at all. He should have been a blur of bristling fur and blinking eyes, of gyrating maw and hopping hind paws. He should have been spilling words out at them, over and over, feeding their bloodlust, rallying them to vicious acts of wanton death and destruction, even if it were only their own.

The Rat King turned to look at Gilead, who slowly dropped his head in a deliberate nod, keeping his eyes fixed on the ratman. This seemed to fill the Rat King with more confusion and fear, and he tore his eyes away from the elf's lean, perfect face and cast them up into the vaulted ceiling. The glossy crystalline surface far above their heads sparkled and scintillated, reflecting every speck of light back into the chamber. The Rat King lost himself in those sparkles for several long moments, composing himself. He wished for the hundredth time that his temples would stop throbbing and his heart would stop beating so heavily.

When he dropped his eyes back to the crowd, the Rat King finally found something that he could focus on. At the distant reaches of the great space, he saw a pair of glowing, red lights at the head of a deep 'V' of fallen bodies, bathed in a bloody sheen.

The phalanx of bodyguards standing in a broad circle on the slopes of the mound was facing outwards, into the crowd. They remained tense and fidgeting, their whiskers and tails twitching, their paws jerking and flexing the weapons that they carried, ready to attack. They hissed and snickered, and blinked hard and often, as the skaven before them stopped stamping and wailing, and shuffled and sniffed and became agitated instead. Scores of the ratmen in the first dozen tightly packed rows began to point and chatter, and elbow one another. Several tried to scale the mound, but were cut down by the strongest and meanest of the bodyguards.

Gilead unsheathed his weapons. He knew what was to come, and he knew his part in it.

The Rat King stood rigid in front of the elf, his snout point-ing a little to the left in the direction of his fixed gaze. Gilead followed the Rat King's line of sight, and then wondered why he had not seen it before. Someone was carving a path to the mound, someone was decimating the skaven horde, killing and maiming his way to… to whom? To the Rat King, in order to destroy him? Or to the elf?

Then Gilead saw the edge of a long, narrow blade as the green lantern-light slid off its surface. He knew the blade, and he knew to whom it belonged. He watched for another moment, tracing the arc of the weapon, knowing that his old friend yet wielded it. Fithvael was in the great chamber, fight-ing his way towards Gilead.

The moment was lost as Gilead lunged to his left, driv-ing his sword through the torso of the skaven bodyguard pounding towards him. The ratman had turned to see what the hordes were fussing about, and he'd seen what they had seen. Gilead got between the Rat King and his bodyguard-turned enemy.

The Rat King would have to suffer a little more, a little lon-ger, before he was put out of his misery. In the meantime, there was a battle to be joined.

There was much confusion on the mound, but at its epi-centre the Rat King stood absolutely still, his eyes fixed on the Vampire Count. The only being in the room who didn't need to blink.

The skaven host had been of one mind. Their leader had made them strong, and they were granted their powers by him. As individuals, the ratmen had no minds of their own, but were drawn to their king, eager for a taste of his power, instinctively knowing that there was no other course for them. They lived only to do his bidding. All the time that the Rat King rallied his host, whipping it into a frenzy with one mind and one body, nothing could defeat his cause.

As the skaven looked up at their king, covered in the white fur of the weak and old and infirm, as they took in his immobility and his silence, some knew that his time was at an end. For every ratmen with the instinct to attack the old and weak and feeble, their king became just another target.

At the foot of the mound, jostling and bustling turned to nipping and clawing, and then to savage fighting, resulting in mass skirmishes between the ratmen. The pounding and stamping and wailing continued throughout a large portion of the great chamber further from the mound, and the whole room shook with the impact of thousands of paws and the waves of sound that battered every surface.

Gilead looked up to see that the lanterns lighting the space were swaying as if even the great, dwarf-hewn ceiling above was heaving and flexing to the beat of the skaven paws.

Then, in the far right-hand corner of the chamber, ratmen began to surge into the backs of their kin, and a wave of bodies tightened its formation, heaving a more solid mass of ratmen towards the mound.

Between cutting and thrusting his blades through the bodies of all and any who would stand against him, Gilead glanced across the chamber as the air in the room flexed with a great *whump*. Dust and debris were thrust into the chamber from the pressure of another tunnel collapsing. There were many entrances into and exits from the great chamber, but one by one they were collapsing. One by one, the underground corridors, the burrows and warrens, the labyrinth of connected passageways, all were succumbing to the vibrations caused by the massed skaven. The pounding and stamping, and the shrieking and screeching, had hit the perfect frequency to resonate through the earth, shifting and vibrating stone and bricks and soil, moving the dirt and rocks that supported the tunnels, rendering them weak and feeble, and drilling away at their capacity to keep the rooms and chambers and the corridors and passageways open.

The great, vaulted chamber was a remarkable feat of engineering, dwarf-built, hewn from rock to withstand the massive tonnage of earth and stone above. Yet the crystals in the ceiling shifted and sparkled, scintillating with the micro-movements that were being felt even in this underground fortress.

Through dint of greater fighting prowess, luck and lunacy, any one of the ratmen might come to lead the skaven; instinctively, many of them knew it.

There was more than one battle to be fought. Any being who was not a skaven must be a foe, so Gilead, Fithvael, Laban and the Vampire Count were all under attack as chaos spread throughout the chamber. The skaven no longer had one single purpose, to follow their king, but each had his own purpose, to survive against all-comers. Any ratman with the instinct for ambition or the lust for power must find a foe in every other ratman. Then there was the Rat King. The horde was divided. Many knew only one king and did not question his supremacy; they would fight and die for their leader. The rest thought nothing of renouncing their king for being old and still and alien to them. Skaven was set against skaven.

Chapter 19

The mood changed in the chamber.

Gilead fought on the mound, taking on any and all. He sliced through arteries in necks and groins, cut weapon-wielding paws from limbs, plunged his blades into torsos, and cut down the bodyguard one at a time, one after another, and then the swarming masses that began to rush the mound in twos and threes. Every stroke met its target and no energy was wasted in dispatching the skaven beasts. As the bodies piled up, the elf wove a path across the mound, keeping the Rat King in the corner of his vision, conscious, even in the heaving throng of bodies, that one body was singularly still.

Gilead knew not why he was keeping the skaven leader alive, other than to have the pleasure of dispatching the evil creature when the time came. In the meantime, every ratman that tried to get close to his king, to assassinate his erstwhile leader, was met with the controlled fury of Gilead's intent.

Halfway across the chamber, and making faster progress as the skaven turned on each other, the Vampire Count continued to plunge onwards. He was no longer simply cutting down bodies, for some of the ratmen, no longer in thrall to their king, were turning to fight back; yet the Count was in no danger.

He stood tall and proud in his filthy armour. The damp earth and grit that had fallen on it, covering it in a layer of dust, were caught in every joint and seam of the burnished metal, grinding and marking the armour with a myriad of tiny scratches that would take a week of careful rubbing, and a tub of good lapping powder, to polish out.

Every time the Vampire Count raised his blade to the foe, it came back bloodied. Every time skaven blood gouted from the hundreds of wounds he inflicted, it arced through the air, coming to rest in splashes and droplets all over the armour, smearing the dirt that was already there. He was a gruesome sight to behold. He strode on, hacking and driving through the crowd, one after another of the skaven horde falling to his sword, many before they had a chance to defend themselves.

One at a time, or even in skirmishing groups, there was no hope of the skaven doing the Vampire Count any lasting damage. He took a jolt to a greave from the studded end of a spear haft, and a dink to a rerebrace from a poorly judged swing of a mace, but none of the ratmen came close enough to do any real or lasting damage. If he'd had living flesh beneath the armour, he would have hardly suffered a bruise, and certainly no broken bones.

Other hearts beat at their own rates: for the skaven, fast enough to kill the creatures that owned them, for the elves, in the calm, measured manner that allowed them to fight on through the long minutes, balancing the rhythms of their bodies with the swing, thrust and slice of their bladed weapons. The Vampire Count had no heart to rely on, and yet he, too, fought to some internal beat, some rhythm of his own.

'How long must we do battle?' asked Laban, swinging wildly, and taking down two more skaven.

'For as long as it takes,' said Fithvael, inhaling as he withdrew his sword from the side of the skaven that was convulsing on its short fall to the floor of the chamber.

'There are so many of them,' said Laban, 'and they are so easy to kill.'

'Pathos,' said Fithvael, 'can occur on a battlefield. Feel it when we are done with this. Do not succumb to it here, or now.'

'They are so wretched,' said Laban as the figure he was lunging at fell hard on its back, clutching its chest; it avoided being skewered, but only in the act of dying. Dying on the edge of an elf blade would have been an honourable end, if the skaven had cared anything for honour.

'And *he* frightens me,' said the young elf, breathing as he spoke, not entirely effortlessly, for he had a blade in each hand, and, though his lower body was moving only a small pace at a time towards the mound, his shoulders, back and arms had built up a fast-paced rhythm. The skaven were coming to him, but their attacks were so ineffectual that they might as well have been throwing themselves on the elf's blades.

'Gilead?' asked Fithvael, driving his short blade into the skaven scrabbling at his boots, trying to pull itself upright without thought to how it would survive standing before a well-armed elf without a weapon in its paw.

'The Count,' said Laban, thrusting his sword across the old elf, and turning his wrist, disarming the skaven on Fithvael's blind side.

'You should be afraid of him,' said Fithvael, stepping back to give the young elf room to complete his manoeuvre.

'What will happen?' asked Laban, sidestepping away from Fithvael and making a quarter-turn to stop three more skaven in their attack, disabling the first before killing the second with a slash to the jugular and the third by disembowelling, the blade flashing across the rounded, grey-furred belly of the old ratman.

'We finish this, and then we'll see,' said Fithvael, quickly taking two steps backwards as the space between him and the Count opened up. 'The Count is cutting a swathe; keep up, lad.'

Laban noted the glimmer of a mocking smile cross Fithvael's lips, and realised that the old man was enjoying himself.

The Count glanced unblinking up at the mound, and locked eyes for a moment with the Rat King. He knew instinctively what the creature was, but felt nothing more than idle loathing for it. The skaven could not, did not, defend themselves against his sword and blade, and he did not need a shield at all. They fell away to left and right, yet more climbing over their kin to fall at the Count's hand. There was an array of dozens, scores, hundreds of dead behind him in a great wake, but bodies were falling harder and faster, so that they were beginning to fall one on top of another until they were two, three or four deep in places. The Vampire Count was literally up to his waist in bloody bodies.

The Vampire Count did not relish the exercise of slaughter, nor did he care who he killed, or how, or how many. He had but one objective; to face the warrior elf, to kill him or die at his hand. There was almost nothing left of the great knight that he had once been, but there was just enough to drive him onwards. His one ambition to die, his one hope to meet his match, to meet Gilead and battle to the death.

The mound was being assaulted from all sides, but the ground was shifting, and part of the dais fell away, taking a score of skaven with it. A fissure opened in the ground, wide enough for clumsy, skittering ratmen to fall foul of its edge and find themselves swallowed into the earth beneath.

Gilead felt the movement in the earth and took his fight to the slope furthest from the Rat King's antechamber. He remembered the silty earth trickling from the ceiling and saw in his mind's eye the niche in the wall collapsing under the pressure of the vibrations. There was no stamping now, no wall of sound, but the worst of the damage was already done, and Gilead knew how fragile the underground structures had become.

As he dropped his shoulder and brought his sword-hand up from his knee, through flesh and air, and out above his head, raking through a skaven diagonally from hip to shoulder, Gilead caught the flash of light bouncing off his blade and up into the vaulted ceiling above. The crystal forms scintillated back at him, and the elf was reminded of the gem that the Rat King had worn as an amulet, from which he had cast the magic that had altered the structure of the underground chamber. He remembered the niches and the things they contained, and he knew all and everything that the Rat King had done to preserve his life force indefinitely.

Gilead planted his feet squarely as he turned his body, swinging his sword at waist height, carving the blade through the spines of two more ratmen. So much had been lost to the Rat King's ambition, ambition that Gilead knew could never be realised. The Rat King was not capable of sustaining a long life with all that entailed. It was not a matter of a body outliving its usefulness, it was a matter of the mind. The Rat King had not the mental capacity to learn or to understand. The creature could not stand the beat of its own heart, or the blood-flow to its brain, an organ it had never used for anything more complex than a reaction, an instinct.

Gilead could never forgive such a monster. He could not forgive him for ravaging human history, for unravelling magical nature, for sullying ancient races and their achievements, but most of all he could not forgive him for crumbling under the weight of his stolen longevity. Time had been a curse to Gilead for much of his long life, but whether it felt like a curse or not, it was always a responsibility, a responsibility that those who understood it took seriously.

Gilead turned and wove a dance around the Rat King, making smaller and smaller circles around the great bulk of the stationary figure clad in its coat of white hair, staring, catatonic, into the crowd.

At every completion of the circle, Gilead cast his gaze once more out over the heads of the remaining skaven, looking for Fithvael, looking for the Count. With every turn of the circle the elf locked eyes with the Vampire Count, for the merest moment. Gilead knew that the Count understood. He understood a term of years, the sentence of a long life spent alone with thoughts raked up and processed over a millennium or even longer. There was sorrow in his heart for the undead monster, sorrow and sympathy.

As Gilead let his eyes return to the battle, to the next skaven sacrifice and the next, and the one after that, the mound shook once more and the earth began to slip from its sides, reducing its height dramatically. Then came another great crash, not the sound of falling earth, but the rumble of masonry dislodged, an avalanche of dressed stone and old brick that burst into the chamber from Gilead's right, cutting off another exit, filling the chamber with more of everything, more dust, more sound, more debris, and more dead bodies.

Fewer than one in three of the skaven still lived. They were the weakest and the most cowardly. They had kept to the edges of the crowd, their eyes and ears closed as much as possible. They had moved when the crowds moved them, but ducked under arms and crawled between legs so as not to come face to face with any adversary, even their own kind.

They were running, searching out the few remaining exits, trying not to encounter each other at close quarters, running and squealing. They emerged from under bodies where they had twitched and sniffled, hoping beyond hope not to be noticed. They were desperate, and climbed on each other's backs to find routes out of the chamber. Another tunnel collapsed, and another; the vaulted ceiling seemed to shimmy and then spread, lowering the surface. Fault lines began to appear in the sparkling black surface. The air shifted in the chamber once more as the steps to the antechamber collapsed, sucking air and dirt and bodies into a hole in the ground that was several yards across. The turbulence made the lanterns swing, and then blew them out in a stinking miasma of some combination of gases that was barely breathable.

Gilead tore a rag from his sleeve and wrapped it around the lower part of his face.

Somehow, the elf knew not how, the Rat King was still standing. His kin had given up attacking him. There was nothing left to fight for if they were going to have to dig themselves out, one at a time, over hours or days, simply to survive.

Fithvael and Laban ran through the last of the skaven, the few remaining who, finally understanding their plight, turned to the Fell Ones for their salvation. Fithvael tried not to pity them as he ran them through, but Laban could not countenance killing the ragged, sorry creatures at all, and it was Fithvael and the Vampire Count who finished the last of them, humanely, with single killing strokes.

The Vampire Count shifted slightly in his armour and began to stride the last few yards to where the mound had once stood, with Gilead upon it.

'What's he doing?' asked Laban.

'He plans to challenge Gilead, of course,' said Fithvael, matter-of-fact.

Laban shrugged, speechless.

'After all we have been through?' he asked. 'After all the killing?'

'The death of the many means nothing to a warrior such as our beleaguered knight,' said Fithvael. 'The death of the one is all that will satisfy him.'

'He must die,' said Laban, slowly. 'He must die, and Gilead must kill him.'

Fithvael looked up, as if at the heavens, but the black firmament with almost no light in it felt oppressively close to their heads, despite what little light there was still sparking off the diamond crystals.

'We shall all die,' he said, 'if we don't get out of here.'

Gilead stepped between the Rat King and the Vampire

Count. He stepped close to the ratman, so close that the skaven could do nothing but blink long and hard, and then look into the elf's eyes.

'You have come,' said the skaven.

'I have come,' said Gilead.

'I cannot live forever,' said the skaven.

'No,' said Gilead.

Gilead drew his sword and looked hard along the length of the blade. It was in imperfect condition, having been well used over the last few hours, and for the many hours before that it had been left to rot, thrust into the haphazard web of weapons that made up the skaven throne. This king would not sit on that throne again.

The Rat King watched as Gilead pulled his blade through a strip of cloth and looked at it once more. It looked clean to the Rat King; he wondered at its cleanliness. He wondered how anything might be kept clean. He wondered how he might keep himself clean. Then he saw the blade coming towards him. He had nothing but time. He had the time to step away from the blade as it sliced through the air towards him, but he did not use the time to take a step. He used the time to wonder why he had wanted to live forever. He used the time that Gilead took to arc his blade through the air, horizontally, on its path towards the Rat King's throat... towards his own, white-furred throat... He used the time to wonder that he knew nothing, and that it was right that he should never know anything.

The blade of Gilead's sword connected with the fur of the Rat King's neck a mere inch or two below his snout, for he had no chin to speak of. The blade cut through the fur, and clumps of the stuff, less than half an inch long, fell to the floor, drifting through the air, heavier than feathers, but not so heavy as to fall quite vertically. Then the blade touched flesh and cleaved a path through skin, parting the layers of the dermis, almost bloodlessly. Still the Rat King did not flinch. He knew that the skin of his neck was being parted by the blade, not because he felt it, for he felt nothing, but only because he knew it must be so.

The first and last thing that the Rat King felt was the blade cutting the artery in his neck. He felt the cold of the elf-folded steel, and the heat of his skaven blood. He thought that his blood smelled somehow unclean, but he did not know why.

The Vampire Count stopped two or three yards from Gilead, who had his back turned to him. The Count could see the Rat King's eyes, but they were no longer staring at him. He had never been the Rat King's foe, not as the Fell One had been. He would not interfere. He knew the outcome of this encounter. He knew that this was an execution and, as much as he could relish anything, the Vampire Count relished the thought that the elf was capable of executing the rat-monster; for if he could execute one beast, he could surely execute another.

The Vampire Count waited for the Rat King's head and body to fall. They fell separately, the head to his left, bouncing and rolling several yards from his foot. The body fell hard and suddenly to the right. It did not bounce or roll, but landed with a thud, throwing up a low cloud of dust.

Gilead nodded to Fithvael and cocked a questioning head at Laban. Then he looked directly at the Vampire Count, and sheathed his sword.

'Not here,' he said. 'Not now.'

Fithvael and Laban looked at each other and then back at Gilead, who had crouched and placed his hand flat on the floor. He stayed there for a moment or two and then darted a look towards the collapsed antechamber. He stood and pointed.

'We must leave,' he said. 'This way.'

Chapter 20

You couldn't think that was the end of the tale. There's always more to come, and Gilead te tuin Tor Anrok will be making new legends for new storytellers long after I am no longer of this world. Leave now, and you will miss the best of it… or the worst. It is true, I must rest often, but an hour's sleep here or there is nothing more than anyone of my great age might expect to be allowed.

Draw closer, for if you give me leave to rest easy in my chair, and speak softly, I will preserve my strength and get to the end of the cursed tales before your patience runs out. There is nothing left to me but the tale, and the telling of it at the proper pace. Heed or heed not, I can do no better.

Laban did not want to sheathe his blades while the Vampire Count was their companion, but he soon discovered that he would need hands, feet, knees, elbows, and in some places his fingertips to follow Gilead back above ground.

Gilead led the way, followed by the Vampire Count, with Fithvael and Laban behind. They had fought the skaven long and hard, without sustaining a single meaningful injury between them. They were, nonetheless, weary, and as thousands of corpses were buried beneath as many tons of earth, rock, brick and dust, they faced the arduous task of finding a way back to the surface. The skaven were dead, or buried alive. They had lived below ground and had died below ground. There was nothing to be said about it, and no one to mourn them.

Gilead found portions of tunnels and corridors that had not entirely collapsed, joined by voids and cavities that remained because of the integrity of the great dwarf structure, hewn from the earth and turned to obsidian crystal by the Rat King's amulet. Gilead wove his way along tunnels, slid between fallen rocks and found cavities behind decaying walls that he dismantled one crumbling brick at a time.

He was conscious, all the time, of the Vampire Count, of his gleaming red eyes on his back, but he felt no threat. The creature would not blindside him; it would not be in its best interests. He was more concerned about his young cousin, Laban, who might seize an opportunity to be a hero. Gilead owed the Vampire Count, not much, but, at the very least, a little respect for his dignity.

At a particularly narrow fissure between the remains of a stone wall and a rock fall, the Vampire Count halted. Gilead had stepped easily through the gap, but even sideways the Count was wedged solid before a third of his body had passed to the far side. He turned to Fithvael, behind him, who shrugged.

When the Count continued to look at Fithvael, the elf

moved closer and began to examine his armour. It was old, but well cared-for, and of a standard human type with fastenings at the sides of the body and the insides of the limbs that had not changed much over the centuries. The armour had been well looked-after, by the knight's squire a millennium ago, and by the Count for many scores of years. The ancient leather straps were supple, as tough as steel, but shaped by the hands that had fastened them over decades. They must have been replaced many times, but the buckles and fastenings had been removed from the old straps and reused on their replacements. The patina of a thousand years made the metalwork smooth and soft, and an impossibly deep colour. As Fithvael's nimble fingers worked the buckles and straps, he realised that they didn't feel clumsy and bulky in his hands as most products of human manufacture did. He wondered, for a moment, where they had originated, but it did not matter.

Fithvael eased the straps on the body armour down the Count's sides, allowing him to become an inch narrower; it was enough to free him from the clutches of the walls to his chest and back, but did not allow the two parts of the cuirass to collapse far enough for him to pass through the gap.

'You must remove your armour,' said Gilead, 'and quickly.' Then he placed the palm of his hand on the low roof of the cavity he had climbed into and felt the pulse of the earth around them moving. 'Help him,' the elf urged his companions.

The Vampire Count stood with his feet apart and his arms raised, and Laban and Fithvael worked one on each side of him to remove the metal pieces, after first disarming him of a small arsenal of weapons. Laban was surprised at how warm and smooth and ancient the elegantly curved and worked sheets of metal felt; nevertheless, he didn't care to hold them for any length of time. He was also careful not to touch the flesh of the Count or the clothes he wore beneath the metal. He could feel no life, no warmth, no pulse. The armour was radiating more heat than the body inside it.

Fithvael began the work of strapping the separate pieces of armour together to make a series of bundles that could be carried. For several seconds, the four of them could hear nothing but the sound of metal on metal, and of old leather being threaded through buckles. Then there was a low rumble, and a series of distant *whumps.*

'Fear not,' said the Count, looking at Fithvael. 'I will have no further need of my armour. There is but one fate remaining to me to be fulfilled, and my nemesis will join me in battle equally ill-equipped.'

'Your trust in me does me much honour,' said Gilead, looking directly at the Vampire Count. He looked smaller without his armour, but equally stoic and serious. Somehow, the leather and linen garments that he wore beneath his armour showed only the marks and wear of polished metal. There were no rings of grime at collars or cuffs, no yellow sweat stains beneath the arms or low in the back. There were no oily finger marks, nor blood, saliva, nor any marks made by any bodily fluids.

This was a knight who did not sweat, whose heart did not pound, nor bowels nor bladder open to humiliate him. This was a knight who had been taught how not to shed a tear as a child, and who could not shed one now, even should he desire to do so.

'You should pass, now,' said Fithvael, standing the Vampire Count's breastplate upright against the nearest wall, as if it were some kind of memorial to the creature who had cheated death. There would be no other.

The Vampire Count held out his hand to Laban, who was holding his weapons. The elf looked warily at the Count, and then to Fithvael, who shrugged, and finally to Gilead. There was another rumble, and silty dust began to fall onto the Count's shoulders, marring his shirt.

'Quickly, cousin,' said Gilead. 'Restore his weapons.'

'But,' said Laban, twisted the sheath of the sword in his hand, as if trying to wring something from it.

'But me no buts,' said Gilead. 'Sir Knight will have need of his weapons before another dawn. We can do without our armour, but surely not our swords.'

The Vampire Count bowed his head, and then looked into Gilead's eyes as he took his weapons from the young elf.

Without the armour, the Vampire Count was firm and sinewy, longer and leaner of frame than he had first appeared. He did not pass as easily through the gaps and fissures as the elves did, but a little manoeuvring, stretching a limb here, folding at the waist there, and he managed to keep pace with Gilead as they clambered up through ruined passages to reach the surface.

When he saw light for the first time, Gilead blinked and smiled. He was on his hands and knees in a sharply sloping space, the brick floor kicked up, broken and uneven, buckled and shifted by the movement of earth all around. The shaft of light came between two rocks above. It was little more than a pinprick that cast a pool of light on the floor below, no more than the size of a small coin, but slightly elliptical.

'It is full sun,' said Gilead, 'the noon of the day.'

The Vampire Count looked at Gilead and nodded.

'There will be time enough,' he said. 'I shall remain below ground until the dusk.'

'Indeed,' said Gilead.

'You'll have to get out, now,' said Fithvael. 'There is no path to bypass you, sir, and the lad is weary of the confines below ground.'

Gilead crawled under the light, so that it shone an oval on his shoulder. Then he reached up and carefully began to remove bricks and rocks from close to his head, until his entire head and back was bathed in the hard northern sunlight. When the hole was wide enough to allow his shoulders egress, Gilead lifted his hands above his head and stood to his full height, so that half of his body was above ground. The space occupied by the Vampire Count, Fithvael and Laban below was thrust back into darkness as Gilead's body shut out the light. The Vampire Count's eyes gleamed and glistened in the darkness, apparently full of life after the draining effect the sunlight had produced in him.

Gilead lifted himself out through the hole, and quickly unwrapped his cloak from around his body. He covered the opening with it, so that no more sunlight could penetrate.

He had emerged in a shallow, waterless ditch that ran along the edge of a dry, dead field. No crops had grown there for years and the ditch, which had once been for irrigation, was sandy and smelled of dust. There was no cover, apart from the depth of the ditch and the hedgerow running alongside it. Standing, Gilead could see and hear for miles, and he did not fear being seen. All was still and silent.

A few moments passed, and then Gilead's cloak lying in the bottom of the ditch began to bulge and move, as if it had a life of its own.

Below ground, Laban had insisted that the Vampire Count hand his weapons back to him. It did not matter that the Count would be weak in the sunlight and quite ineffective in a fight with Gilead. It only mattered that Laban keep his cousin safe and protected, and, to that end, if the Vampire Count were the next to pass out into the world above, as he must be, the young elf was not prepared to take any risks. He and Fithvael would not be able to climb out of the hole in time to fight off the Count if he chose to attack Gilead.

The Vampire Count, stripped of his armour and his weapons, lifted his hands above his head, as if in surrender, and pushed up through Gilead's cloak. He preferred not to be exposed to the sun if it wasn't absolutely necessary, as it made him feel weak and ill, sending chills through his body and slowing down his responses.

Gilead watched as his cloak began to take on the shape of the man beneath it: first the hands and then the head and shoulders. Finally, the Vampire Count pulled the rest of his body up into the ditch and sat against the side of it, several feet from Gilead, never shifting or removing the cloak from around his head and torso.

Then Fithvael and Laban emerged into the sunlight. Laban blinked and smiled. The sky was clear and grey and as bright as a northern sky could be with the sun directly overhead.

When they were all in the ditch, Gilead touched the Vampire Count's shoulder through the cloth of his cloak. The Count moved back over the hole, lowering his body into it, and disappearing, leaving the cloak covering the aperture.

Laban reached out a hand to draw the cloak towards him, thinking that he would fold it and return it to his cousin.

'Leave it,' said Gilead. 'Let him rest peacefully until dusk. I owe him that. We all owe him that.'

The three elves climbed easily out of the ditch and set up a small camp close by, shielded from the worst of the cold wind in the lee of the tall, sparse hedgerow. The straggling, thorny shrubs were pale and almost barren, but in one or two places Gilead was able to scratch the surface of the twigs and branches and find patches of green flesh beneath. The hedgerow was alive, if barely, so there must be enough plant material in the area to sustain them for a day or two, if the need arose. For now, they were content to rest and recuperate, and to prepare for what was to come.

'My cousin,' began Laban.

'Cousin, indeed,' said Gilead, smiling slightly and reaching his arms out to embrace the youth. Laban looked startled for a moment and then walked shyly into the embrace.

'You honour me, my lord,' he said, bowing his head.

'You brought the boy, old man,' said Gilead, embracing his mentor, servant and faithful friend for the first time in a great many years, for only the third time in their lives.

'You are much changed, Gilead,' said Fithvael, surprised by the unexpected warmth of their reception.

'Not so very much,' said Gilead. 'Enough, I hope. Now, explain yourself, old man; why have you brought the boy?'

Gilead, Fithvael and Laban talked, rested, ate and prepared.

As Fithvael honed the blade of Gilead's second weapon and Laban adjusted the cuffs of Gilead's shirt so that they would fall away from his wrists if he were wielding his blades, Gilead spoke to them of the amulet.

'The boy,' said Gilead. 'I shall never forget that boy. "By Sigmar's beard, it was always the skaven." That's what he said. It was always the skaven. He was wrong.'

'The plague?' asked Laban. 'He thought the skaven had caused the plague? How could that be?'

'It was not so,' said Fithvael. 'Gilead has told us that the boy was wrong. What he has not told us is why he was wrong, or why the boy believed that the skaven were responsible.'

Gilead reached two slender fingers into the top of his boot and, a moment later, pulled out the amulet that had hung around the Rat King's neck on the ribbon of plaited hair. He turned it over and over in his fingers, examining it. It seemed inert; it did not sparkle or glisten, nor did it seem to absorb and deaden the light that hit it. It was matt and darkly colourless. It looked like a rock, a pebble, perfectly elliptical, but unassuming.

After looking at it for several moments, Gilead flicked it at Fithvael, who caught it deftly in his left hand, his right still holding the whetstone with which he was restoring Gilead's blade in preparation for what was surely to come.

'What is it?' asked Gilead. 'Why would it change the skaven king?'

'Change him?' asked Fithvael. 'How did it change him?'

'He was old and slow, and confused.'

Fithvael held the amulet up to the light between his thumb and forefinger. It did nothing. He tossed it back to Gilead.

'He might be able to shed some light on this,' said Fithvael, gesturing towards the cloak that still covered the hole in the ground.

'You would rely on a Vampire Count for information?' asked Laban. 'That way foolishness lies, surely, cousin?'

'I have followed a path through the plagued lands for more than a decade,' said Gilead. 'They brought me to the creature. I thought he must be an instrument of misery in the lives of the humans. I thought he must be a catalyst for all that has befallen the lands and the crops and creatures. And yet, he fought at my side against the skaven and now he seeks me out to do battle to the death.'

'What of the stone?' asked Fithvael.

Gilead held it to the light as Fithvael had done and then dropped it back into a pouch.

'There is power in it… The power to show me great arte-facts, fine wonders of the world, wondrous objects of great significance. It showed me how they had been collected. It showed me that it was the greatest of them,' said Gilead. 'If you had only seen what I have seen.'

'Yet I have not,' said Fithvael.

'Nor I,' said Laban.

The older elves looked at the younger, and he returned to his chore.

'By Sigmar's beard, it was always the skaven,' said Gilead. 'They stole the amulet. The Rat King stole the power of eternal life.'

'If you deduce correctly,' said Fithvael. 'We know the "what" and the "why", but not the "from whom". Where did the amulet originate? What is its purpose? Are there others?'

'Its purpose is evil,' said Gilead. 'I have followed the plague, and the amulet is all I found.'

'The amulet and the Vampire Count,' said Fithvael.

'He found me,' said Gilead.

'Did he?' asked Fithvael. 'Are you sure of that? Was he looking for the same thing you were looking for, or was he hunting the skaven for some other end.'

'He is already immortal,' said Gilead. 'He sought me out, that he might meet his nemesis, and finally rest.'

'That's what he found,' said Fithvael. 'But are you sure that's what he was looking for? Are you sure he followed you until he found you, or did he find you while pursuing some other end?'

'I know not, old friend,' said Gilead.

'Then, may I suggest,' said Fithvael, 'that you find out?'

The conversation ended, and the elves returned to their tasks.

'How will you kill him?' asked Laban, finally.

'You assume that I will kill him, and not be killed by him,' said Gilead. 'Your confidence is misplaced.'

'You have fought a thousand enemies before,' said Laban. 'You fought a thousand in one day, killing the skaven. How would you doubt your combat skills?'

'I have fought the knight before, and could not get the better of him.'

'You walked away from that battle,' said Laban.

'And so did he,' said Gilead. 'The way to win in combat is to respect your opponent... every opponent. Treat every battle as if it is your last. Fight every inch in every arena. Tire not. Surrender no quarter. Expect neither defeat nor victory.'

'Show neither fear nor contempt,' said Fithvael.

The two men were reciting a form of mantra, a prayer.

'As my master taught me,' said Gilead.

'Who was your master?' asked Laban.

'You are looking at him,' said Gilead, and he turned his head to look at his teacher, and in so doing, directed the young elf's eyes to his mentor.

'The old servant?' asked Laban.

Gilead glared at the youth, who blushed.

'Begging your forgiveness, sir,' said Laban.

'You'll do more than that,' said Gilead, tossing Laban his shorter blade.

Laban caught it from the air and looked at Gilead, puzzled.

Gilead smiled at Fithvael.

'Show the boy,' he said.

'It's neither the time nor the place,' said Fithvael, chuckling.

'But I need to rest,' said Gilead, 'and what is more relaxing than watching a great show of combat skills? Indulge me.'

'Hand me the knife, lad,' said Fithvael.

Laban stood and offered Fithvael the blade, hilt first.

'You'll need this, later,' said Fithvael, sheathing the blade and handing it to Gilead. 'We will work unarmed.'

Fithvael was on his feet, facing Laban, his stance broad, his shoulders square, his hands hanging loosely by his sides.

'Need you prepare?' he asked the youth.

'For what?' asked Laban.

'You heard our master,' said Fithvael. 'Let us indulge him with a little play. I ask again. Is there any preparation you would like to do before we commence?'

Laban looked from Gilead to Fithvael. They were both smiling, and the old elf seemed relaxed and unthreatening.

Laban looked down at his body, and at his empty hands. He was unencumbered by a cloak, and his well-fitting travelling clothes did not impede his movements.

'What are you waiting for, boy?' asked Gilead.

Laban looked from Gilead to Fithvael again, and Fithvael made a slight gesture with both hands, beckoning.

'I don't...' began Laban.

'Ah,' said Gilead, 'but you must.' He smiled again. 'Don't hurt him, old man,' he said.

'Not for anything,' said Fithvael.

Laban te tuin Tor Mahone took a step towards Fithvael, keeping his knees soft, and then threw a punch in a long arc into Fithvael's chest. Fithvael dipped his chest away, bending backwards from the waist. Laban's fist did not connect. He had not thrown the punch hard for fear of hurting the old elf, but he was humiliated and his face flushed slightly as he cupped his fist in his hand. Next he threw a tight jab to Fithvael's gut, but with one step the old man turned his body sideways and grabbed the jab before it landed against his hip. He threw the fist back at the young elf.

Fithvael stepped into the next punch, stopping Laban's forearm against his upper arm, and planting a sharp slap on his opponent's cheek, as if teasing him. Laban countered with a jab and a hook. Fithvael ducked so that the jab cleared his shoulder, throwing Laban against his chest, so that the hook sailed around the old man's body, and they ended up in a clinch. Fithvael lifted Laban slightly and planted him back on his feet.

He slapped the boy again, once on each cheek, before Laban was ready to be joined once more in combat.

'You'll have to do better than that,' said Gilead. 'Use your speed. He is old and past his prime.'

Laban looked at Gilead, encouraged, and changed his tactics. He flew at Fithvael, turning in the air with a high kick. Again, there was no impact as Fithvael danced away from the blow, but, having turned, the mentor caught the youth's foot out of the air and twisted it. He brought Laban down to earth, so he landed heavily on his chest, his foot still in Fithvael's hand. The mentor turned the foot, obliging Laban to turn over so that he was lying on his back with Fithvael standing over him.

'You're dead,' said Gilead.

'I didn't want to hurt him,' said Laban.

Fithvael let go of the youth's foot, and gestured again for Laban to rise and attack.

'Catch your breath, and try again,' said Fithvael, standing before the youth, feet shoulder-width apart, arms crossed over his chest.

Laban stood, wary. Then he lunged at Fithvael, head down, as if to throw his shoulder into the old elf's gut, in a wrestling hold. In one elegant movement, Fithvael ducked low and under Laban, and lifted him off his feet and over his back.

Fithvael came up into the standing position, his arms still crossed while Laban sprawled on the ground behind him.

Gilead laughed a low chuckle, which made Fithvael turn for a second in wonder. Laban saw the old elf turn, and chose his moment, hoping to catch the old elf at the apex of his turn, off-balance and off-guard. Fithvael was old, but he was long practised in the arts of combat, and what he lacked in strength or speed he made up for in cunning and an economy of movement. He was neither as off-balance nor as off-guard as Laban had believed him to be, and he snapped back to his stationary position, using the youth's momentum against him, causing Laban to stagger out under the old elf's arm to sprawl on his belly at Gilead's feet.

'The boy has much to learn,' said Gilead. 'When do you begin?'

'I believe I just began,' said Fithvael crouching at the fire they had built, digging in its embers for the tubers roasting there. He flicked one out with his knife, in Laban's direction. The youth was sitting on the ground close by, and caught it in his hands.

'Lesson number two,' said Gilead as Laban dropped the tuber and began to blow on his scorched fingers. 'Think twice before you ever catch a hot potato.'

Chapter 21

Dusk came early in the north, and when it was impossible to distinguish between threads of black and white in the waning sunlight, Fithvael looked to Gilead for permission to lift the cloak from the hole in the ground.

Fithvael and Laban had taken an hour to clear a flat area of ground for the combat to take place in. They had grubbed up the last of the pale weeds, removed the few rocks and stones that had found their way onto the fallow land, and raked through the dusty earth with bunches of hedgerow twigs to level it. There were no makeshift weapons hidden in the ground, no rocks that could be used to add weight to a fist, no lost blades, no detritus of former skirmishes. There were no roots to fall over, and no shade advantage, since the sun was all but set; the moons were high in the sky. The space was even marked out at a distance from the ditch so that no accidental fall could put one or other opponent at an advantage.

Gilead had eaten a light meal and was well rested and in good spirits. He did not, however, take advantage of Fithvael's presence and run drills or sparring practice. He would take no advantage that he could not offer to his adversary.

'Will you talk about the amulet?' asked Fithvael. 'Will you ask the knight's knowledge of it?'

'If it will further our ends,' said Gilead. 'If it will help to banish the plague from these lands... from all land, I will ask. I will not beg.'

'You won't have to,' said Fithvael, straightening the back of the elf's shirt. Gilead examined the cuffs that Laban had adjusted and nodded his thanks to the youth.

'You make a fine seamstress,' he said. 'Your wife need waste no time in sewing for you.'

Laban dared not scowl.

'I've rarely known you in such high spirits,' Fithvael said to Gilead. 'Should I be concerned?'

'Only for my life,' said Gilead. 'I do not relish the thought of my own demise as once I might have, but it holds no fear for me, and still offers some blessed relief. I'm sure you'd rather have me smile in the face of death, than sigh, or cry out.'

'Is he truly so able?' asked Fithvael.

'You saw him,' said Gilead.

'I saw him plough through young, stupid creatures, without an ounce of finer feeling,' said Fithvael.

'I am sure,' said Gilead, 'if he has any feeling at all, it is of the very finest sort.'

They turned to watch as the Vampire Count's hands emerged from the hole in the ground, holding a sword and a shorter secondary blade. The hands were white, and the fine-boned digits ended in thick, cruel talons, shaped like teardrops, as if filed to points. The weapons were those of an ancient Bretonnian knight, beautifully forged from folded steel, and honed to a bright, hard edge. They looked like specimen weapons, never used nor worn, never nicked nor dented. They all knew better. When the Count was waist-deep in the ground, he rested his weapons in the bottom of the ditch, and, planting his hands firmly on either side of the hole, he lifted his body and legs through the aperture.

Laban was young and idealistic, and could not countenance seconding the beast, so he held Gilead's blades, and Fithvael stood at the Count's side. No words passed between any of them.

Dressed in nothing but their shirts and breeches, Gilead and the Count took their weapons and saluted one another across several yards of ground. Fithvael and Laban retired to either side of the allotted area.

The combatants circled, first clockwise and then anti-clockwise, neither lifting a weapon to the other. Gilead measured the size of the Count's stride, the softness in his knees, the weight of his shoulders. He counted his blink. He watched to see which side the Count favoured, which hand was strongest, which leg he trusted his weight to. He detected a flinching of a hamstring in the Count's right leg, suggesting that he preferred to lunge forwards and step backwards on the left, so he would tend to fight across his body. Conversely the Count tended to turn his head to the left, suggesting that sight or hearing were more efficient, more acute on the right.

The Vampire Count used his time to stride out the ground, checking the size of the arena in which he must fight, the position of the moons in the sky. He listened for any life that might be close by, any beasts or hidden audience. He eyed up the long, lean forms of the attendants, watching them breathe, discovering who was anxious or likely to intervene in the combat. He knew Gilead already. He knew that the missing digit did not seem to affect the elf's blade skills, and that he preferred to be the aggressor, attacking, always moving forwards. He knew that his concentration was impeccable, that no bird taking wing nor clap of thunder would surprise or trouble him, nor the movement of the earth beneath his feet, nor a blade driven hard towards him would throw him off balance.

Gilead was a consummate warrior elf, and he was everything that a knight should be and more.

After several minutes of striding back and forth, and of watching each other, Laban began to relax, wondering if anything would happen, after all. Then the Vampire Count spoke.

'If I am to die, this night,' he said, 'I die with honour at your hand.'

Laban stood up straighter and opened his eyes wider.

'If I should die before dawn comes,' said Gilead, 'I die at the sword-edge of a worthy opponent.'

The Count's statement was not a matter of form, however, not one of the many rituals he adhered to so fervently to make him feel human again.

'The skaven,' said the Count.

'What of the skaven?' asked Fithvael. 'What of the ratmen, bloodless one?'

It was too late, Fithvael's words were lost in the first crash of steel on steel, the first slide of blade against blade, the first exhalation of breath, the first dance of feet through the dust of the arena.

Gilead turned the Count's attacking blade, lowering it and causing his opponent to pull it back closer to his body to prepare for another attack. The second time that swords crossed they did so high. This time, the Count thrust his weight into Gilead, breaking the contact, but the elf was too deft for the knight and his second blade crossed the first, its tip hooking into the basket hilt of his opponent's secondary weapon. The Count had to adjust his balance and hold hard to his dagger to prevent its loss.

He escaped and turned, arcing his dagger through the air. Gilead did not try to make weapon contact, he simply moved his head three inches, and the blade whistled past his face, cutting through a thick lock of his white hair. He was inside the Count's reach, and his opponent had clearly forgotten that he was without his armour. The Count's left flank was exposed from the armpit to the hip. Gilead drove home the advantage, slicing through the fine linen shirt and into the creature's tough flesh. There was no blood. Gilead had expected none, but he knew that his blade had hit its target. The Count appeared to feel no pain, but he closed his guard and brought both of his blades up in a defensive posture.

Less than a second later, Gilead and the Count were nose to nose, looking through the V-shaped gaps their long blades made in front of their faces.

'Came you in search of me, my lord?' Gilead asked, exhaling, and then clenching his teeth as the Count continued to bring pressure to bear on the impasse.

'I came in search of death,' said the Count, breaking and bouncing away, out of reach of Gilead's blades.

The combatants circled one another again, kicking through the mass of footprints left in the dust, marking their combat as if it were a dance.

'I followed the curse,' said the Count, lunging forwards on his right leg, against the elf's expectations, catching the deep fold of linen under the arm of Gilead's shirt, rending a long slit in it, but not touching his skin.

Gilead's response was a less well-judged slice of his short blade that tangled with the Count's sword, the tip of which, embedded in the fabric, did rather more damage to the shirt than was strictly necessary.

Gilead stepped to the side, defending his left arm and clearing the Count's reach.

'The curse?' asked Gilead. 'Who is the curse?'

'Think not whom,' said the Count, adjusting his grip on his long sword, and resting his left hand on his hip before swinging at the shoulder.

Gilead registered that the left shoulder had some weakness he had exploited by accident, and decided that his next move must be to rid the Count of the second of his blades.

Meantime, the Count came forwards on his left leg, extending his knee joint and pushing his right shoulder forwards into a punishing thrust with the sword. Only Gilead's slender frame saved him from a potentially fatal injury. The blade pierced skin for the first time, but only skin and an inch thickness of flesh.

'Think what,' said the Count. 'Think of the cursed plague that rids the lands of their riches. Think of the barrenness of the beasts of the field and of the womenfolk.'

Gilead brought his attack heavily to the Count's left side, wielding both weapons: his sword in a direct attack, his short blade across his body. The Count had no option but to recoil, and withdraw his bloody sword.

Gilead turned his narrow form with his right side, his bloody side, facing the Count, and came in with only his sword, thrusting, parrying and driving onwards, forcing the Count to back away across the arena, ensuring that he rely on his right leg, attacking the left shoulder, the weak point.

The Count defended well, parrying hard and rallying for a counter-attack, but a third forward thrust forced him back onto his right leg, and he felt the stiffness of his left shoulder. He must do something to force Gilead to fight on his other side. He tried to turn, but his right leg would not hold, so he shuffled clumsily, and dropped his sword below waist height. Gilead came in fast and strong, flicking the Count's shorter blade out of his left hand, and catching it by its basket hilt on his sword.

There was a sharp breath from the edge of the arena, over Gilead's shoulder to his right, as Laban gasped. The elf thought his young cousin might even applaud, and it made his lip curl slightly as if in a smile. He raised his sword and flicked the Count's secondary blade over his shoulder for Laban to hold for him.

'We call it the plague,' said Gilead, turning the tip of his sword in small circles at arm's length, pointing it high at the Count's head. 'What know you of it?'

The Count took hold of his sword in a double-handed grip and began to swing it in a great circle from the ground at his right boot-toe to high above his left shoulder. The momentum behind the swing was vast, and the blade arced towards Gilead's shoulder, making the air sing.

Gilead stepped lightly away from the swing, and then brought his own sword down on the Count's at the bottom of its arc, while driving in at neck level with his dagger. Gilead drove the point of his short blade down inside the Count's collarbone at an angle, but the small amount of flesh there was dense and leathery, and penetration was not deep enough to do fatal damage.

'It matters not,' said the Count, sliding off Gilead's knife and backing away, rolling the hilt of his sword between his hands, and preparing for a new onslaught. 'The amulet is buried for all time. It no longer carries its mortal threat.' With that the Count feinted, and then lunged on his strong left leg, attacking low, plunging his blade into Gilead's thigh. There was a short spurt of blood, and for a moment the Count looked painfully disappointed, if, indeed, any expression could be read on his undead face.

His disappointment was short-lived. Had Gilead been human and his femoral artery had been as exposed as a man's was, he might have met his death, but an elf's artery is protected deep in his thigh in a fine, but virtually impenetrable sheath of cartilage and bone. The damage was superficial.

The Count had made the mistake of taking a step back, thinking that he had bested his opponent, and Gilead quickly drove his advantage, attacking high to the left again, exposing the weakness in the Count's shoulder.

As Gilead forced the Count backwards, defending wildly, his sword beginning to weigh heavy even in his experienced hands, the elf spoke again.

'What if it is not buried?' he asked.

'Not buried?' asked the Count. 'The Rat King forsook the jewel? Broke faith with his master?'

The Count staggered backwards, blocking another vicious onslaught of paired blades. His hamstring gave way, and he found himself on one knee, leaning away from the blades that must surely finish him.

Laban took a step closer to the Count, watching him carefully, looking for any trick he might still deploy against his cousin. Gilead took a step back from his fallen adversary and thrust his shorter blade into his cousin's hand.

'But…' began Laban.

'We fight on equal terms,' said Gilead.

He offered the Vampire Count his hand, and helped him to his feet. His hand was cool and dry and smooth. The grip was strong and firm and the knuckles stood proud, but Gilead felt no revulsion touching it; it was less horrifying than touching the sweaty, flaccid palm of a terrified human.

Gilead swung the Count to his feet and stood back. They had been in close combat for some time, and neither had proven stronger than the other. They were at an impasse, except that the Count clearly had information that would be useful to Gilead, and the elf wanted to tease it out of the undead knight.

Keeping his eyes firmly on the Count, and his blade high, held firmly in his right hand, Gilead teased the fingers of his left hand into his boot and withdrew the stone. He flicked it into the air, and watched as the Vampire Count followed its trajectory with his staring red eyes.

He did not catch it, but let it fall in the dust before him.

'Is that it?' asked Gilead.

'I know not,' said the Count, adjusting his two-handed grip to one hand, as his eyes flicked back and forth between the amulet and Gilead's stare.

'The Rat King wore it around his neck on a hair-ribbon,' said Gilead. 'It wove a spell around him, and around his people. It altered the very rock that his great hall was hewn from.'

'Then it is everything his master claimed it must be,' said the Count. He rocked his weight from one foot to the other, as if limbering up to defend himself from the coming attack, but Gilead stayed where he was, his sword up, but his feet firmly planted.

'You talk of a master? Another great skaven king? One

more powerful than the holder of the charm?' There was a sneer in Gilead's voice, as if he didn't believe the Vampire Count, as if this might be some kind of trick, some form of dissembling. 'I think not. Are you the master, then, come to claim your prize?'

'There is no prize,' said the Count, his gaze dropping and staying low. 'I followed power, and yet...'

'And yet?' asked Gilead, growing impatient, raising his blade in jerking movements, an inch at a time, menacing.

'I followed power that I might die, and yet...' said the Count. His voice was fading, as if he were remembering. 'I wished to honour my liege lord, and my liege lady. I wished only to perform one noble act before I died at the hand of the greatest warrior to ever meet with me in mortal combat.'

'What noble act?' asked Gilead.

'The noble act that you performed in my stead,' answered the Count. 'You were taken, and it mattered not, for I knew that you would best the skaven thugs, that you would out-wit and outfight them. I knew that you would recognise the amulet for the evil that it might do, for the plague that it has spread through the skaven horde, and I knew that you would destroy it, or return it. I could not restore the world, as you could. I have neither the honour nor the nobility I once had.'

'Return it?' asked Gilead.

The two warriors were circling each other again. They paced out the arena, watching one another. Laban and Fithvael stood on either side of the space, watching, unable to intervene, but silently praying for Gilead's life. The battle had been hard fought in flashes of brilliant swordsmanship, punctuated by long periods of walking and watching, circling and preparing.

Then the combatants were both at the centre of the arena;

once more, blades screamed against each other in a flurry of attacks and counter-attacks, of lunges, thrusts, ripostes and parries. One leg of the Count's breeches was cut away, almost entirely, as Gilead turned and drew his sword violently upwards and outwards, missing his target by the depth of the cloth and leather it was clad in. The Count was faster without his armour than Gilead had anticipated, and nimble too.

Gilead's reach was longer, so he was at the advantage on the attack, but the Count's defence was nigh-impenetrable. When Gilead did break through, the Count's hide was tough; he did not bleed, and he appeared to feel no pain.

Gilead had a graze on his chin, as if he had shaved badly, his hair was partly shorn away and his shirt was irreparable. The blood in his thigh had clotted quickly, and a clean scab had formed almost instantaneously, or so it seemed to the Count. Other creatures bled long and profusely – even the smaller mammals had served as a decent meal for him – but this elf did not bleed. He could not find his veins and exploit their weaknesses.

Laban had thought to help, to do something, and made to throw his cousin his second blade, but Fithvael, ever watchful, caught the youth's eye and slowly shook his head. Laban's eyes flicked back to the fight; the astonishment on his face made Fithvael turn in the direction that he was looking.

Suddenly, Gilead was no longer visible in one place. He was high and low, wide and fast, close, and then away again. Laban could see the Vampire Count swinging his weapon, always too slowly, never in the right direction. Gilead's sword had a new momentum. He took a piece of flesh out of an upper arm, carved a hole in a shoulder, hacked away a cheek, and thrust right through the gut.

Gilead was shadowfast. The world and everything in it seemed to stand still. He could not only see every move the Count would make before he made it, he could counter it and exploit it. The Count was good, his instincts sound, so this would be no easy kill, but Gilead knew, at last, that he would kill the unnatural being.

Laban sat down heavily. He had not seen a shadowfast elf before. He had known it was part of his family legend, had heard the tales, the old myths, but he had never seen it, and had never thought to see it as long as he lived. He pinched himself, wondering if he were dreaming, and at the same time trying to catch sight of the whirlwind that was his cousin.

The only light was from twin moons suspended high in the sky above. There were few clouds, and nothing more than a breeze in the air, but in the darkness Laban could hardly see Fithvael on the other side of the arena, and could see only the glints and flashes of Gilead's blade. He wondered if the Count could see anything.

Then, it stopped.

The Count and Gilead stood as close as two beings could stand one to the other. Laban noted that he could see no blood on the Count's clothes, and then remembered that the Count did not bleed. The young elf got to his feet and took a careful step closer to his cousin. He almost tripped over the Count's sword, sticking out of the earth at a low angle, close to his feet.

Laban took the sword by its hilt and freed it from the earth. He held it high in the air that Fithvael might see it, but the old elf was already drawing close.

Gilead had the blade of his sword hard against the Vampire Count's throat, ready to sever the creature's head from its body.

'Do it,' said the Count, its cold, red eyes, staring into Gilead's, willing him to end his miserable existence. 'Raise a pyre for me, that I may not return. Dismember and decapitate my corpse, leave no chance that I might escape this fate.'

'I will do all of those things,' said Gilead. 'It will be my honour to serve you in death, but first, tell me what I need to know.'

'What need you of my knowledge?' asked the Vampire Count. 'My tale is apocryphal at best. Trust me not, for I fear to trust me will do you nothing but harm.'

'I have nothing else,' said Gilead. 'Tell me simply, tell me truly, only that which you know. Embellish nothing. Give me only your truth.'

'It was always the skaven,' said the Vampire Count. 'They spread the plague, but it only resides in them, uses them, and disables them. It originates elsewhere, in the hearts and minds of the southern places, in the lost souls of the sands, in the broken people of the stone sarcophagi, and in their golden leaders.'

Gilead's hold on the Vampire Count strengthened as the creature began to lose all sense of himself in the bliss that was its demise.

'Kill me,' he said. 'Kill me now. I have nothing more for you, nothing more to say.'

Gilead gestured to Laban, beckoning him to bring the sword.

When he was close, Gilead let go his grasp on the Count, and, in that same movement, took the warrior's sword from his cousin and pressed it into his adversary's hands.

Then Gilead swung, bringing the hilt of his sword from his left shoulder, whirling the blade in a gleaming arc. By the time the hilt of the sword, still held in both hands, was resting against his right shoulder, the Vampire Count's body was falling.

Gilead had felt the flex in the blade as it cut through leather and petrified sinew and on through empty veins and calcified trachea. Then he felt the jarring sensation in his arms as the blade hit something that it could not strike through. The vertebrae still holding the Vampire Count upright were harder than the steel of his sword, and would not be divided by it in one swing.

The Count's head did not separate from his body, but lolled like some grotesque doll's head, bloodlessly. The legs buckled beneath the Count, the right first, tilting his torso awkwardly to one side as his head bounced for a moment at the extremity of his spine.

Gilead turned and walked away. He handed his sword to Fithvael and approached the hedgerow, which he began to rip away with his hands, quickly gathering dry, twisting twigs and lengths of half-dead wood.

'We must build a pyre,' said Gilead. 'We must honour our dead, and when we have held vigil and seen the bones scattered, we turn south.'

Chapter 22

Every tale must take its twists and turns where they may fall. I have no say in the unfolding of this story, and can only retell the events told to me. Gilead's saga is a long and complex one. He has lived too many lifespans, fought too many foes and saved too many lives, for these tales to take a simple course. The Rat King was dead, and the noble Vampire Count dispatched, and yet the threat was not expunged from the land, and Gilead and his faithful companions made their way to Nuln in pursuit of they knew not what.

Gather round, listen closely, and take heed. A tale has only the value of its telling and of its message, and you might all learn something from Gilead te tuin Tor Anrok. I know that I have.

In a matter of days, Gilead was on the road again with Fithvael and Laban at his side. He had not thought to travel with an entourage, but then he had been confident that he would find his quarry in the great north lands and was not a little surprised to find he was travelling south again, back through the Empire to the great city of Nuln.

The journey was not a difficult or arduous one. Gilead retrieved his palfrey, and a few hours of tracking brought the elves to the Vampire Count's war steed, which was broad of back and comfortably seated both Fithvael and the youth. They removed its armour, sigils and other adornments, and threw a blanket over its back in place of the heavy saddle that it was accustomed to. The horse was big and bulky, but looked as much like a carthorse as anything else by the time it was stripped of its finery, and it drew few glances on the roads they travelled, mostly in darkness.

'Why think you to ride to Nuln?' Laban dared to ask when Gilead advised the elves of his plan.

'To save my legs,' said Gilead, clucking at his horse to move a little more quickly as the sun crawled idly over the horizon.

'I don't–' began Laban.

'In all things, we use our heads to save our legs,' said Fithvael. 'Thinking costs less than physical labour. Have you learnt nothing, lad?'

'Perhaps my education should begin here,' said Laban, finding his confidence. 'Perhaps it should begin with an explanation of what we are doing, and why.'

Gilead, who was a length or two ahead of the war steed, turned his horse and stopped so that it filled the path in front of Fithvael and Laban's shared mount.

'We are doing what we always do, what we were sworn to do, what we strive to do. When we need not serve ourselves we serve others. Now, we do both, and we do it with good grace, and with fewer questions, if we know what is good for us,' said Gilead, glaring at the youth.

'And by "we", you mean me?' asked Laban, making eye contact with Gilead over Fithvael's shoulder.

Gilead said no more, but turned his horse back in the direction they were heading. At the first opportunity, he made his way off the road and into a sparse stand of trees.

Once fed and sitting before a small, but comfortable, fire, Gilead explained his purpose in heading for Nuln after spending so much time in the north.

'The vampire sent me south. He did so for a reason.'

'I was there,' said Laban. 'I heard what the creature said, yet I could make neither head nor tail of it.'

'You speak like a human,' said Gilead, an edge of contempt creeping into his voice.

'Tell the lad,' said Fithvael, 'and tell me. I would follow you anywhere, te tuin, and you know it, but I, at least, deserve your confidence.'

'I have never had anything but confidence in you, old man,' said Gilead. 'You have ever been a valued teacher and a faithful friend, and I will not soon forget the great services you have performed for me, or for others besides.'

'Then tell us,' said Laban.

Gilead glanced at his young cousin, then turned back to direct his words at Fithvael.

'There is a scholar in Nuln,' said Gilead. 'You must remember him, I'm sure?'

'Is that wise?' asked Fithvael. 'He is a knowledge thief, a scoundrel and a liar… if he is the man I remember.'

'But he was refined,' said Gilead, 'and "genteel".'

'By human standards, perhaps,' said Fithvael. 'But I fear you are attempting a jest, my lord, and your demeanour confounds me.'

'Confounded,' said Gilead. 'I'm sure that's the very word, Fithvael. I am confounded, too. I must know where the threat comes from if I am to do battle with it. The land is dying. The creatures of the air, earth and water, the men, women and children of other, lesser, races are perishing, and now the plague has struck our own kind. Our own Benath has been taken from us. I would he had been longer in our lives and taken a slower route into our memories.'

'Aye,' said Laban, bowing his head.

'Aye,' said Fithvael.

'The scholar is an imperfect man, more so than many, but if he can help us, if he can direct us and fill the gaps in our knowledge, his debt to me, his debt to all our kind, will be paid.'

'My fear precisely,' said Fithvael. 'Can we gain the knowledge by no other means?'

'By many means,' said Gilead, 'by many means that will eat up time and miles, and lead us on a quest that could take a score of years or more to unweave the clues and mysteries that will no doubt be laid before us. I seek a shorter, surer route.'

'You seek a dangerous route.'

'So be it,' said Gilead. 'I will not trouble you to enter the city at my side.'

'It troubles me little,' said Fithvael, 'but the boy might be kept from the worst of the dangers.'

'I'm not a boy,' said Laban. 'I was sent to learn. I was given into your care to squire my cousin Gilead and to learn what he might teach me. Spare me nothing.'

'Fine words,' said Fithvael, feeding and banking up the small fire so that they might rest beside its warmth during the daylight hours before taking to the road once more.

'I've had no need of a squire these many years,' said Gilead.

'You had need of me,' said Fithvael.

'Of you, my friend, yes, but I would hardly call your services "squiring".'

'It matters little,' said Fithvael. 'Laban is right. Benath was a younger soul than I, and has left us already–'

'He left us prematurely,' said Gilead. 'I will not hear you speak of your death.'

'Time is short,' began Fithvael.

'Not for us,' said Gilead. 'Not once this malaise is thwarted.'

'Then let it be so,' said Fithvael, 'but do not deny the lad. He is right. He came to us from the High Council, and it is our duty... it is *your* duty to further his education, to make of him a strong, noble-minded cousin for our future.'

The roads into Nuln were much travelled. People came from far and wide to benefit from city-life. Artisans came to work, labourers and domestics to serve, and gentlemen to trade or teach in the universities. It was the university that Gilead planned to visit.

It was almost dusk when the three elves travelled the last mile of the Nuln Road to the north gate of the city. It saw more traffic on an hourly basis than any other single gate into the city, and the road was thronging with people exiting and entering Nuln as lights and lanterns began to be lit all over the city. The guard lit the brazier that stood at the gate, partly to keep the soldiers warm, and partly so that light was easily cast on the men and women scurrying back and forth from their places of work or learning, to their homes outside the city, or from their occupations on the surrounding land and beyond to their homes within its walls.

Gilead had chosen the route, because, as busy as it was,

there was a good chance that their passing would go unnoticed. On the other hand, if they were stopped, the volume of traffic through the gate would make it easy enough for Gilead to hand the guard a little coin by way of payment for ease of entrance into the city, without it being remarked upon by the hordes of people around them.

On this occasion, no move was made against the two steeds with their three riders, and the elves entered the city unmolested.

They travelled through the industrial district of the city, still busy and noisy despite the plague that had decimated the countryside. The malaise seemed not to have struck the towns so severely, although it soon became clear that locals were growing food on every available plot of land, and were utilising all outside space. Balconies which once held flowering plants now supplemented the household kitchens with small quantities of leafy vegetables and soft fruits. The plants were a little grey and threadbare, but the buildings around them seemed, somehow, to protect them.

The elves kept their hoods up and their sleeves down, covering as much as they could of their heads and hands, and they slumped down onto their mounts, bringing their knees up and curving their backs so as to seem of more human proportions. The postures they adopted were not comfortable, and Laban began to suffer quite quickly, but it was imperative that they not be seen or recognised.

In times of strife, prejudices are closer to the surface and more brutal, and anyone could fall under suspicion, any foreigner or non-human.

The elves were singular among the crowds, but went unnoticed.

The safest places in the cities were often also the most

dangerous. The slums, the hovels, the out-of-the-way, hole-in-the-wall places could effectively conceal the presence of a thief or murderer or even an elf, while, at the same time, in the same places, the most innocent woman or child might be brutalised physically or mentally for very little reward.

Gilead preferred these places where people chose not to look too closely at anything but coin. A relatively small amount of money could prevent prying eyes from noticing how tall the elves were, how slender, how upright, how pale... how *other*. Gilead preferred to go to the places in the city where everyone's eyes were cast down or away, where no one looked for the truth in the eyes of another. His elf eyes could speak true and still his otherness would cause anything from a faint or swoon to an unprovoked attack.

The elves found their route along Commercial Way and around the university into the Maze and the old slum districts of Neuestadt. The streets were narrow and crooked with overhanging roofs and odd junctions, and the three elves soon had to dismount and walk in single file. Gilead led them, and Fithvael brought up the rear. Laban walked between them, leading the old war steed.

'Why has he brought us here?' Laban asked over his shoulder. 'This place is full of filth and degradation, and thieves and assassins too, no doubt.'

'Speak up,' said Gilead. 'I'm sure your insults didn't reach the ears of our hosts.'

Laban turned to Fithvael, colouring slightly.

'There is much to learn,' he muttered.

'You'll learn it all, in due course. Give it time,' said Fithvael.

'"Give it time" will only waste *my* time and put us all in danger,' said Gilead. 'Better teach him to shut his mouth. Make that your first lesson, and learn it quickly.'

Laban scowled, but did not speak again.

Gilead suddenly disappeared through an arched gap in the wall to their left, over an earth step and into a narrow yard with a ramshackle lean-to roof against the wall of the adjacent building.

'What is this?' asked Laban.

A human head appeared through a hole in the wall above the makeshift roof. Backlit, it was impossible to determine the human's sex.

'Business?' it asked in a voice which offered no further indication as to the owner's gender.

'A room. One bed. Three meals,' said Gilead, raising neither his head nor his voice.

The little door that covered the hole in the wall closed abruptly.

'So we all eat, but only one of us sleeps?' asked Laban.

'You can sleep,' said Gilead, 'but if the horses are taken, you'll have to find more, and you won't find them here.'

'Where's the ostler?' asked Laban. 'The stable boy? The stable for that matter?'

'What do you suppose that to be?' asked Gilead, gesturing towards the lean-to roof on the opposite wall. Laban walked over to the wall, stepping under the roof that protruded from it like some semi-permanent awning. He toyed with a wrought-iron tether-ring driven into the wall at waist height and pulled at a sagging bag of old, damp straw. Having disturbed it, he stepped back from the unpleasant mouldy smell that emanated from it.

'You'll find something more wholesome for them to eat, too,' said Gilead, handing Laban the reins to his palfrey. 'You can use the straw for a mattress if you so desire but from that odour I suspect an infestation, so I wouldn't recommend it.'

'What of the bed?' asked Laban.

'For my cousin and faithful companion,' said Gilead. 'Have you no respect for your elders and betters?'

'I only wondered why we should not all benefit from rest,' said Laban.

'Rest does not benefit the restless,' said Gilead. 'There will be time to sleep when I must and an eternity of rest when I'm dead. For now, there is work to be done, and it is better done by night.'

'Food first,' said Fithvael, giving the broad war steed a reassuring slap on the rump to encourage it into the makeshift stable.

Laban strode over to the old elf's side, throwing his cloak over his shoulder.

'Not you,' said Gilead. 'I'll have yours sent out.' He turned back through the arch, followed by Fithvael, and ducked through a low door three or four yards further along the wall.

Laban was left in the small, grubby yard with no one for company but the horses and no light or heat to speak of. He decided that deprivation was something he must be bound to get used to if Gilead was to be his master, but he would not thank him for it.

Chapter 23

Gilead stepped into the darkened room. Some light bled in between the badly drawn drapes; not moonlight, but the light of a hundred lamps and candles lit in the various chambers of the university to enable the most serious of scholars, or the least able, to study long into the night. The university buildings were never truly dark, and light escaped from windows and doorways, around ill-fitting doors, or those left ajar, and between partially drawn curtains or from windows that were left naked. Gilead did not need the light to know how the furniture was arranged in the two small rooms, for nothing had moved, but he was grateful for the chance to see the piles of books and papers that had sprung up all around the little study and adjoining bedchamber in time to step over or around them. The room had been free of obstacles the last time he had been in it, but that was fifty years ago, and men are wont to accumulate things, as if ownership of objects made their lives somehow richer.

There was so much about humankind that Gilead did not understand, nor did he wish to.

The elf was familiar with the university buildings, and with these rooms in particular. He had been stealthy in his approach and had entered the quadrangle without being noticed. He had kept to the shadows and moved silently, close to the high stone walls, standing under one or other of the oriel windows on those occasions when someone appeared from a doorway to cross the quad or duck into a stairwell.

Gilead had taken the narrow spiral staircase in the north corner of the quad, and walked the length of the corridor on the third floor of the building. It was a more circuitous route than taking the imposing, carved-wooden staircase in the East Hall, erected long ago to commemorate the death of the last grand master of the scholars' guild. The East Hall was kept very well lit, because it was the main thoroughfare through the building. It was always full of people moving around the university or simply gathering to talk and exchange ideas. On Gilead's last visit, which had also been his first, Mondelblatt, the newly invested Professor of Ethnological and Corporeal Physick, had taken him to his rooms by the more private route, not wanting to be caught red-handed with one of the elder race and, as a consequence, be found out for the liar and cheat that the elf knew him to be.

Gilead had not forgotten the building, the layout of which was as clear in his mind as if he had visited yesterday, but he had forgotten how it, and the man he had undertaken to visit once more, had made him feel; the whole place made his flesh crawl.

He hadn't originally sought to frighten Mondelblatt, for he needed something from the man, but once at the university, Gilead felt no compunction, breaking silently into the professor's rooms by night so that he should be the first thing the so-called scholar saw when he awoke with a start.

Mondelblatt's eyes widened as he twitched awake, and Gilead thrust his hand over the man's mouth.

Mondelblatt blinked hard, and stared at Gilead. His mouth relaxed under the elf's hand, and Gilead was confident that the professor would not cry out.

Mondelblatt shook as he sat up, and then turned and placed his feet on the floor. Gilead looked down to see gnarled, purplish flesh, the second toe on the left hooked over its neighbour. He saw how thin the man's skin was, and how frail his hands as he reached for a walking stick that was propped against the nightstand.

The hair that stuck out in tufts from under a yellowing linen nightcap was sparse and white, and the professor's eyes were red-rimmed and rheumy.

'Is it you?' asked Mondelblatt. 'Have you come for me?'

'I've come to talk to you, old man,' said Gilead.

'It talks,' said Mondelblatt. 'Just as I knew it would.'

He turned to Gilead, standing in front of him barefoot, one hand on his cane and the other resting lightly on the elf's torso, close to his waist.

'I knew when my time came, it would be you,' said Mondelblatt. 'I am ready.'

Mondelblatt took his hand from Gilead's torso and looked at it.

'Your flesh is solid... and warm. What are you?'

'You know what I am, old man: *who* I am,' said Gilead.

'You are death,' said Mondelblatt, 'come to rescue me from

this hell-hole. I knew how you'd come to me. I knew I'd never
be forgiven for the elf. I have waited a long time: decades of
fear and loathing, and now it is as nothing to me.'

'What?' asked Gilead. 'Of what do you speak, old man?'

'I am not afraid. I am ready. It is right,' said Mondelblatt.

Gilead looked down at the shrivelled human, and then
around them. He took the old man by his slender, wrinkled
wrists and urged him, gently, to sit on the edge of the bed.
Then he took a taper and lit the lamp on the nightstand.
Next to a pile of books stood a pitcher of water, a tall beaker
and a pair of round, wire-rimmed eye-glasses.

Gilead picked up the glasses and put them gently in Mondelblatt's hands, folded, inert in his lap. Mondelblatt did not
move for a minute or two. He simply sat on the edge of the
bed, spectacles in his hands.

Gilead stood in front of the old man, next to the nightstand so that the lamp shed a good deal of its yellow light
on him.

'Put them on,' said Gilead. 'Take a proper look at me.'

'What need I of spectacles?' asked Mondelblatt. 'I know
what you look like, and if you were a being of my imagination or a spectre sent by Morr himself, you would still look
the same to me.'

'You speak of death as if it were nothing,' said Gilead. 'Only
the living do that.'

'Then who are you?' asked Mondelblatt, still calm, but
fussing with his spectacles to unweave the arms and bring
them up to his eyes.

'I am who you believe me to be,' said Gilead, 'but I do not
bring death.'

'Then what do you bring?' asked the old man, who had
risen again from his bed, his glasses on the end of his nose,

and was peering up into Gilead's face, which was distorted by the shadows cast by the lamplight below.

'Only questions, and no one else to go to with them,' said Gilead.

'I can answer questions,' said Mondelblatt. 'I used you, I lied my way into this job and, in the end, I learnt a very great deal from it.'

'How so?' asked Gilead. 'You feared I would return, and do you harm?'

'I feared I would be exposed as a cheat and a liar. I feared being found out, and the only cure for that kind of fear is to begin again, to learn everything and to prove I could earn my scholar's robes.'

'And have you, old man?' asked Gilead.

'More so than you would ever believe of an old liar,' said Mondelblatt.

Gilead had shared his stories with Fithvael, and his thoughts, too. The Rat King had been driven insane by his longevity, by the slowing of his manic life, and had died as a consequence, but not before what little brain he had turned to mush. The Vampire Count had tried to warn him too, and that had to be worth something.

Nuln seemed like the obvious place to come, despite Fithvael's misgivings, but he didn't have the answers that Gilead was looking for either.

Gilead did not yet trust Laban, and someone ought to stay with the horses lest they be stolen, so when Gilead went out into the night to find Mondelblatt, he and Fithvael left the tiny inn together. Fithvael took his own route in a wide circle around the university district. He skirted the schools, the quads and the buildings that made up the classrooms, the lecture theatres and the lodgings of the students. The oldest buildings stood low and squat towards the middle of the quarter, and Fithvael made careful mental notes of where they stood in relation to ōne another, which direction they faced, how they were adorned and ornamented, and how alive they were with the activities of the inhabitants.

Fithvael did not trust Mondelblatt, but he understood Gilead's need to see the old wretch. It was Fithvael's job to ensure that no harm or ill-will befell his friend. Fithvael walked around and around for an hour, and then two. Students and masters came and went, some with books and scrolls under their arms, one or two with flasks or bottles and several with hot, paper-wrapped foodstuffs bought at the pie shop on the south-east corner of the district, closest to the student lodgings.

Fithvael spent several minutes standing against the pie-shop wall, cast in shadow by the tall, apparently windowless building across the alley. Gilead was taking his time, and Fithvael, while not actually hungry, was looking for an excuse to do something, to interact with someone, to learn some tidbit of information while he was out and about.

He wondered why Gilead had hired a bed at all, since Fithvael had slept in it for less than three hours and saw no chance of getting back to it any time soon.

Two young men ducked out of the narrow doorway, bringing with them the smell of greasy pasties, the pastry clearly made with animal fats regardless of whether it contained meat or not. Fithvael saw the grease spots on the paper that wrapped at least two rancid-smelling savouries, and possibly more, and the ink on the long-fingered hand that held them. The first boy to emerge was almost as tall and almost as lean as an elf, and Fithvael surmised that the surfeit of pies must have been bought with the view to fattening the fellow up, for his friend, the young man carrying more than enough books for two to study, was quite fat enough already. Fithvael cast his gaze across the lit doorway and could clearly count three chins on the shorter, more rotund of the two humans.

'Have you heard what they're saying about old Mondel-blatt?' the tall, lean boy asked the other.

Fithvael's ears pricked, and he took a step closer to the end of the alley.

'Hear about it?' asked the rotund student. 'I was there!'

'Did it happen the way they're telling it?' asked the lean boy.

'I don't know,' said the other. 'What are they saying?'

'That he's insane,' said the lean boy. 'They say he was bab-bling about dust.'

'Sand,' said the fat boy. 'He lectured on sand for three hours, and even then he wouldn't have stopped if Doctor Kitzinger hadn't flounced in to claim the hall for his next lecture. Mondelblatt had run over by an hour, but he looked as if he'd barely begun on the subject.'

'Are you sure it was sand?' asked the lean boy. 'Not dust?'

'What do you mean?' asked the fat boy. 'Didn't I tell you I was there? Of course it was sand! Dust indeed. Who lectures about dust for three hours?'

'Who lectures on sand for three hours?' asked the lean boy.

'And his eyes were sparkly the whole time,' said the fat boy. 'You've never seen the like.'

The boys would soon be out of Fithvael's hearing, but he had heard enough. He turned in the alley and headed north, back through the precincts of the university, in search of Gilead.

Chapter 24

'Dry as a bone it is,' said Mondelblatt. He chafed at the neckline of his nightshirt, which didn't seem to Gilead to be restricting in any way. 'A man could choke, it's so dry.'

Gilead poured a tall beaker of water from the pitcher on the nightstand. He'd poured two already and watched Mondelblatt drink them, but nothing seemed to quench the old man's thirst.

'What of the skaven? What of the objects the Rat King collected?' he asked the old professor. 'Where did they come from? What do they signify?'

'I've told you,' said Mondelblatt. 'They have no meaning. That's not what you came for, and you don't trust me. Without trust, without everything, I can tell you nothing. I know there is more.'

Gilead stood and turned away as the old man downed the beaker of water that the elf had poured for him. Mondelblatt's nightcap fell from his head as he leaned back to drain the glass. Gilead noticed how thin and ragged his neck was, and how hard his throat worked to swallow the liquid. He also noticed that there was very little hair under the cap, not much more than he had seen around its perimeter, and that the old man's head shone white and was dappled with liver spots.

'How old you seem,' said Gilead.

'You don't,' said Mondelblatt. He reached out to place his beaker on the nightstand, but it was farther than an arm's length away, and he was too old and weary to get up, so he simply held it between his hands.

'You shouldn't be so old,' said Gilead.

'I'm not,' said Mondelblatt. 'I am… I forget how old. It was my birthday… No, I am not old, not terribly.'

'Then why?' asked Gilead.

'Can you not see that I am parched?' asked Mondelblatt, throwing the beaker at Gilead in exasperation.

Gilead took a step back, but said nothing.

'If you will not tell me the whole of it, I cannot… I *will* not help you,' said Mondelblatt. 'I thought once to owe you much, but I'll be damned if I'll be held to ransom. I knew nothing then, and what I knew I cheated and stole for, but those days are gone, and I am a scholar. I am a *scholar* I tell you, and as honourable as the next man… *more* honourable!'

Professor Mondelblatt was becoming agitated, and Gilead wondered if the man was quite sane. On the other hand, the elf *was* holding something back. He was holding something back because he couldn't quite bring himself to trust the human.

Perhaps it was time. Perhaps it was Mondelblatt's time. Fifty years had passed easily and quickly enough for the elf, but that was a life to a human, and Gilead began to wonder if he had misjudged the professor. The elf had sought *him* out, after all, not the other way around.

'Not here,' said Gilead.

'Then where?' asked Mondelblatt. 'And while you tell me, pour me some water. I'm more than parched!'

Gilead held Mondelblatt's beaker of water, which the old man gulped from periodically while he dressed, and finally, after the old man had trickled a thimbleful of urine into his empty chamber pot, the two left the professor's rooms and made their way back along the corridor and down the little spiral staircase.

Gilead looked left and right at the bottom of the stairs, and then placed a firm hand on Mondelblatt's wrist, indicating that he should stay where he was.

'Gilead,' said a voice behind him as the elf turned in the entrance to the stairwell.

'Fithvael?' asked Gilead. 'Why came you here?'

'A rumour,' said Fithvael. 'Nothing more, but we must return to our lodgings and discuss our progress. I fear things are not as you would wish.'

Both the elves heard a shuffling gait to their right and turned to look, stepping back beneath one of the large oriel windows that ran along the lengths of the east and west walls, facing into the quadrangle.

Mondelblatt stood for a moment in the light of the doorway, turning slowly in an odd, skipping dance.

Gilead made to step forwards, but Fithvael caught his arm. Gilead placed his hand over his friend's and said, calmly, 'It's Mondelblatt.'

'Has it been so very long?' asked Fithvael as the two elves stepped out, taking one of the old man's arms each and propelling him along the walkway and out at the south gate.

'Yes and no,' said Gilead.

'I heard he was quite mad,' said Fithvael.

'He is,' said Gilead, 'but not in the way that his own kind mean.'

Fithvael looked across the insignificant little man between them at his old friend.

'He's paid a price?' he asked.

'A high price,' said Gilead, 'but only to our advantage.'

'What now?' asked Fithvael.

'Now we take him back to our lodgings and tease out more of his truths.'

'Truths?' asked Fithvael. 'Does he know anything about the truth?'

'Sometimes it is only the dishonest who finally know the meaning of truth.'

'I hope you're right,' said Fithvael.

'What are you keeping from me?' asked Mondelblatt. 'I know you are keeping something from me... the most important something... the key to everything.'

'Not so loud, old man,' said Fithvael, holding Mondelblatt's wrist so that his agitated hand couldn't knock over the drinks on the table. The elf gestured with his other hand for the serving girl, the innkeeper's daughter, to replenish the old man's beaker yet again.

The girl had looked at Mondelblatt in disgust more than once and had kicked a chamber pot under the table, sure that the old man must need to use it soon, and knowing that she'd be the one to scrub the floors clean if he should lose control of his bladder. She wondered just how much liquid the old man could hold in his gaunt, fragile frame.

The ale she poured was pale and cloudy and tasted of fermentation. There was no distinctive flavour to suggest what it had been made from, but it was as honest as it could be in these troubled times, and they were lucky to have anything to brew with at all.

'The blonde child, the sky clematis, the orb and egg. I understand them all, but only as parts of a puzzle,' said Mondelblatt. 'Humankind, flora, the dwarf, insects, the elf – all are represented by the best, purest examples of their worth in the world, but there is more. There must be more.'

Gilead thought back to the Rat King's dank chamber deep below ground, of the niches in the wall of the strange anteroom, of the visions that had come so strongly to his mind, of the princess, of the destruction of the plant, of being inside the dwarf's head, of the shimmering carpet of the insects' carapaces. He thought of his reflection and of the depth of darkness of the obsidian ceiling in the great underground hall. He thought of the Rat King and of his amulet, the same amulet that nestled in the cuff of his breeches, inside his boot.

He had known all along that he would have to show the amulet to Mondelblatt, but he had also known what it had done to the Rat King, how sad and sorry his end had been... And he knew the scholar's weaknesses.

Gilead knew the prematurely aged man to be weak of will, greedy, selfish and filled with his own importance. He knew that those had been his key character traits fifty short years ago, and he believed that mankind was too brutal and too arrogant even to desire to change, let alone to accomplish any fundamental shift in personality. He doubted that Mondelblatt had changed enough not to be drawn in by the powers of the amulet and by the immortality it seemed to offer.

The elf was also unsure how the amulet was activated, since it seemed to have little or no effect on him or his companions. He had taken it out several times, tossed it to Fithvael, held it up to the light, breathed on it, polished it and subjected it to various tests of a more arcane nature dictated by the tenets of his kind.

The amulet had remained inert, dull.

He had also seen its effect on the skaven, on their king, and he had seen the magic that it could produce. He wondered how close to the skaven humankind really were. He wondered what triggered activity in the little stone.

Gilead sighed.

'I could wonder forever,' he said, 'but I fear we have precious little time.'

Gilead motioned to Fithvael, and the two put their heads together and lowered their voices.

'Are you quite sure of our old friend, te tuin?' Fithvael asked.

'No,' said Gilead, 'I am not. I am sure that this plague must end, and I am sure that time is of the essence. There has been enough destruction, and if we can put an end to it, sooner has to be better.'

'We have time,' said Fithvael as he saw the dull little stone, extracted from Gilead's boot, turning in the elf's fingers.

'No,' said Gilead. 'With Benath's death, time, even in our terms, is running short.'

They watched Mondelblatt rubbing his eyes and blinking.

'What is it, old man?' he asked.

'My eyes are dry,' said Mondelblatt. 'So very, very dry.'

Fithvael almost felt sorry for Mondelblatt, who seemed older and more frail than he should after fifty years, even for a human. He placed a reassuring hand over one of the old man's.

'You're tired,' he said, 'and it's late. I'll find a balm for you when we're done, and take you home to bed.'

Before Mondelblatt could answer, Gilead leaned in, his closed fist resting on the table's surface, close to the old man's trembling hands. The human looked from Fithvael to Gilead, and then down at the elf's fist.

'You have brought me something?' he asked.

'No,' said Gilead. 'I want to show you something. It is not mine to give, but if you can tell me something, anything about it…'

Mondelblatt turned his hand over for Gilead to drop whatever he was concealing in his fist into it. Instead, the elf simply held the amulet between his finger and thumb, one digit on the bottom of the oval stone and one on the top. When Mondelblatt reached out for it, Gilead moved it out of the old man's range.

Mondelblatt blinked once more, and when he opened his eyes, Fithvael noticed that large, salty droplets sat upon his lower lashes. Another blink and two bulging tears trickled down the old man's cheeks.

Mondelblatt blinked again and sighed.

The hand that had been wrapped around his beaker, constantly bringing it to his mouth for long gulps of the poor ale, uncurled and relaxed and both of his hands stopped trembling.

At the end of Mondelblatt's long exhalation, the small room fell quite quiet.

Then the serving girl with the large jug of ale shouted out.

'Hey!' she said. 'Someone's got to clean that up. Can't you make him go in the pot?'

Fithvael looked down to where the serving girl pointed at a growing puddle of pale liquid that was inching out across the worn flags of the floor.

Chapter 25

On the other side of the tavern wall, Laban te tuin Tor
Mahone started from a light sleep as the horses began to
snort and sniff and paw at the smooth-worn cobbles of the
yard. The young elf got up and looked around as the first
fat raindrop fell from the sky, landing on his shoulder and
trickling down the front of his cloak.

The larger horse rocked its neck and stamped its foreleg. As
a second drop fell from the sky, and then a third, Laban bent
to look at the horse's leg. He was surprised to see a rainbow-
sheened, carapaced insect, its shell as black as an oil slick
and iridescent with reflected colour. As he bent to scoop it
off, the carapace opened to reveal large bright wings, and the
insect made a clicking noise before flying away.

Laban patted the horse's shoulder and whispered in its ear,
trying to reassure the beast, while the palfrey huddled as close
to the wall under the ramshackle roof as she could manage.

The rain was unlike anything the elf had ever seen. The drops of water were unfeasibly large and apparently filled with light, shining whitely out, and then spraying across the darkening cobbles as they landed. As the frequency of the drops increased, the noise became almost deafening.

Laban wanted nothing more than to pull his cloak tightly around his shoulders and run to the entrance to the inn, in the hope that he wouldn't drown in the process, but he dared not disobey Gilead or Fithvael.

Seconds later, as the elf stood with his back pressed against the wall, he felt the water rising around his ankles, falling too fast for it to run off into the drains and soakaways at the lowest points in the yard.

He felt sure that the whole city would be flooded if the rain lasted for more than a few minutes, and he dreaded the death and destruction that would inevitably result from such a disaster.

He looked hard through the rain and into the sky beyond, and saw clear, bright moonlight, as if the rain were falling in a narrow band that he could see the edge of. He turned and looked in the opposite direction.

Laban stepped out into the rain, and dashed over the step and through the opening in the wall. By the time he had crossed the street, he was standing on pale, dry cobbles. He looked up, and could see only the blackness of the sky, punctuated by the light of twin moons and the stars that filled the firmament. The elf could see no rain clouds, and certainly none that could produce such a downpour; such clouds would surely have obscured the stars and moons.

Then Laban's mouth fell open as he watched the progress of the band of rain sweep away across the street and over the yard. Two minutes later, and certainly no longer, Laban was leaning into the yard through the arched opening. The cobbles were bone dry, and the horses, standing side by side under the awning, seemed as relaxed as ever. The palfrey looked up at him and blinked. Then she walked across the yard, and dropped her head down to drink from the shallow trough in the opposite corner. Laban noticed that it was about half full, just as it had been when the elves had arrived at the inn.

Laban pushed his cloak over his shoulder and, without a second thought, strode into the tavern. His head was uncovered, and his thick, pale hair, cut in a straight line at chin level, looked almost like spun silver in the lamplight.

There was an almighty clatter and splash as the serving girl dropped the half-full jug of poor ale that she was carrying, and it fell to the flagstone floor, sloshing its contents into the puddle of urine, making even more mess for her to clean up.

For such a little person, she let out a surprisingly loud scream.

The girl was indeed small, even by human standards, and feisty, too, but her lazy father worked her hard, so she was generally too tired to bother noticing the few odd people that found their way into his tavern. She was only glad to be able to earn an occasional tip from them, since her father always seemed to have some good reason not to pay her; today, it would no doubt be her own fault for spilling so much perfectly drinkable ale, even though her father never touched it and kept the decent stuff for himself.

As the scream and the clatter of the tumbling jug filled the small, low room with a cacophony of sound, Laban, who had to stand with his feet apart and his knees bent to avoid his head coming into contact with the room's ceiling beams, turned back and forth at the waist. He looked first to Gilead and Fithvael, who scowled at him, and then at the girl. When he looked at Gilead and Fithvael for the second time, he noticed the little old man who sat between them, wearing what appeared to be a nightcap and looking at the oval stone in Gilead's hand. Still, his companions offered him no assistance.

Before Laban knew what was happening, the girl's father had vaulted the table that stood across the corner of the room and served as a counter. The short, bulky man had what looked like an ancient musket in his hands, but he wielded it expertly, and its working parts were clean and well oiled.

'The rain!' exclaimed Laban. 'Did you see the rain?'

The serving girl's face was red, and her hips swayed as she began to wield a mop as if it were a deadly weapon, lunging it at Laban's legs as if she would take them out from under him with one keen sweep.

'Never mind the rain,' said the girl. 'Did you ever look in a mirror? What's the likes of you doin' in a place like this? What's the likes of you doin' *anywhere* in this city?'

Laban looked down at himself as if perhaps he hadn't looked carefully enough in the mirror and might be inappropriately dressed.

'I…' began the elf. 'I… It was the rain. You've never seen such precipitation!'

'I've never seen the likes of you, neither, and I don't plan on seein' you again,' said the girl, still jabbing at his legs with her filthy mop as her father watched from a slightly safer distance.

Gilead and Fithvael looked at one another, but said nothing. They had been together for long enough to know when their thoughts were in accord without the need to speak, and speaking now, cutting the tension in the air with more singsong elf tones, might not be a good idea. It was never their intention to disturb the people they came into contact with, and, in these poorest of places, people rarely looked at one another or listened too carefully to accents and speech patterns.

So far, Gilead and Fithvael had gone more or less unnoticed, and they did not want to cause any harm by allying themselves with Laban's foolishness.

Fithvael still had his hand over Mondelblatt's, unwilling to make a move lest he draw attention to himself. Mondelblatt blinked and looked around.

'Foolish girl,' he said, rather too loudly, cutting the air and causing the owner of the inn to swing his musket back in his direction.

'Who're you callin' foolish?' asked the innkeeper. 'And what's the likes of you doin' 'ere at this time of night, dressed like that? You're not one of us. You don't belong 'ere.'

Emboldened by his speech, the innkeeper stepped closer to the table.

Mondelblatt stood up in a single, rather jerky movement, but the action coincided badly with his general equilibrium and the pool of piss and poor ale, and his foot slid out from beneath him. His chin came down with an almighty *crack* on the table, and he collapsed into a heap, falling onto his stool before sliding inelegantly to the wet floor.

The crash triggered a series of events, beginning with the serving girl thrusting hard with the end of her mop at Laban's legs. The elf jumped instinctively over the obstacle, but seemed to have forgotten just how close his head was to the ceiling beams. The impact made a loud cracking sound, and Laban, his momentum suddenly halted, landed unceremoniously on the floor. Seeing his daughter strike out at the strange creature, the innkeeper shot at Laban. His aim was good, but his reflexes were somewhat slower than they had been when he was a member of the city watch, and the musket shot sprayed in a wide arc over the elf's head as he came down suddenly, landing on his backside instead of his feet.

Fithvael and Gilead glanced at one another, and, with a swivel of the eyes and a slight nod, they silently agreed on their course of action.

Gilead got up from the table, turned and took the warm barrel of the innkeeper's firearm in his hand. With a tug and a deft twist, the elf freed the weapon, and with one short swing he cuffed the innkeeper across the neck with the stock of the weapon, rendering the man unconscious, but essentially unharmed.

At the same time, Fithvael planted a foot heavily on the head of the mop that the serving girl was still wielding in anger. Her face was flushed, and she was clearly more ferocious than afraid, but she should be easy enough to subdue.

The girl raged when she couldn't free the head of the mop, and within moments she had thrust away the handle, and flown at Fithvael, fists flailing, screaming like a banshee. He had not expected the assault, despite other experiences that had shown him just how fiercely protective human women could be, how resourceful and how vicious.

Fithvael pulled his head and shoulders up so that the hail of blows fell harmlessly on his chest. Harmlessly to *him*, at least, but he also gave himself away.

The serving girl gasped, pulled her head back, and then spat in his face.

It was enough.

Fithvael stopped playing nice.

He grasped the girl by her shoulders and pinned her arms to her sides. She had landed in the elf's lap when she had lunged at him and sat there, pink-cheeked with fury, but also blue-lipped.

Fithvael quickly realised that his grip on the girl was constricting her breathing, and that if he hung on to her much longer, she might suffocate. He looked her in the eye and smiled, but when he loosened his grip she took a deep breath, and let out a scream that split the air in the room. The noise roused Mondelblatt, whose head suddenly appeared above the table-top.

Fithvael let go of the girl's left arm in order to place his hand over her mouth to quiet her, but as soon as his grip loosened, she brought her hand up to slap the elf or pull his hair, or gouge his eye. Fithvael didn't know what form the attack would take, but he had no trouble seeing it coming, and he caught the girl's wrist before she was able to do any damage.

She screamed again, but the cry subsided into sobs, and Fithvael couldn't help feeling sorry for the feisty girl, as well as rather impressed by her. He allowed his grasp on her to slacken a little, and, glancing down at his right hand, he noticed that the flesh around the girl's wrist was already darkening with the bruise that had resulted from his strong, lean hands.

Then Fithvael noticed the girl's hands. They were misshapen and badly swollen, and black bruising was appearing around her knuckles.

'You're hurt child,' he said. 'Calm yourself. Be still.'

'What are you? Who are you?' asked the serving girl between sobs. 'Take your hands off me! What have you done to my father?'

'Enough,' said Gilead, sloughing off the hood of his cloak, and sitting tall in his chair.

The girl stared at him. Between his exotic looks, the pains in her hands and the alien and authoritative tone of his voice, she fainted. She slumped in Fithvael's grip, and he arranged her gently against his narrow chest.

The room was suddenly quiet and still. The three elves listened for several seconds to discover whether the girl's screams had prompted any investigation from the neighbouring buildings on the narrow street, but they could hear nothing. In the backstreets and alleyways of the slums of most great cities, people pretended not to hear screams.

'Pick yourself up, boy, and take the old man out of the way,' Gilead said to Laban. 'I... I'm sorry...' said Laban, bowing his head to his better. 'It was... The rain was so...'

'You've done enough,' said Gilead, dismissing Laban. 'Clean up Mondelblatt so we can get him back to his rooms and get out of this place.'

'We must tend to the girl,' said Fithvael. 'She fought so hard, she has broken her hands on me.'

Gilead looked at the girl and then at Fithvael. He raised an eyebrow, almost as impressed as his friend was by the girl's will to fight against the odds.

'You'll have to do it fast and alone,' said Gilead. 'And you'll have to keep *him* out of it.' He gestured at the innkeeper, still unconscious on the floor.

Laban tried to pick Mondelblatt up, but the old man waved him off, and the elf was content not to have to deal with the professor's urine- and beer-soaked clothes.

Mondelblatt rubbed at his chin, which had a startling red spot on it, but was not blackening.

'I'm going nowhere,' said Mondelblatt, 'except where you go.'

'You'll tell us what we need to know, and you'll go back to the university where you belong,' said Gilead.

'Then who will help you?' asked Mondelblatt. 'Who will school you in the ways of your enemies? Who will lecture you in the mysteries of the sands?'

'You speak in riddles, old man,' said Gilead.

'Aye,' said Mondelblatt, 'and riddles will be your undoing if you do not heed me.'

Fithvael looked at Mondelblatt, remembering the conversation between the two students in the alleyway earlier that evening.

'Listen to him, te tuin,' said Fithvael quietly. 'The old man knows what it is. He knows what the stone can do. He knows who wields its power, and he knows why.'

'I wouldn't say that, exactly,' said Mondelblatt.

'Then what would you say, old man?' asked Gilead.

'I'd say that I know where to begin,' said Mondelblatt.

Chapter 26

They say the best storytellers fear nothing. I think they should fear everything. If we feel no fear then we must feel no compassion or empathy, either. Fear is our enemy unless we make bravery our friend.

I never learnt to conquer my fear, only the art of telling a tale, and of inspiring fear and compassion in others.

The skaven are a godless breed, but if we feel no sympathy for their plight, our hearts are more surely to be made of stone than of flesh.

The Vampire Count is a being of great strength and sadness, and if we feel no fear for him, our hearts are surely more foolish than sanguine. But men are fools, and storytellers too, so make of this next chapter what you will, for I know where terror treads, and with all my heart I wish that these tales were not my calling, for I know that I must lead you in her footsteps.

* * *

The sky over Nuln glowed with a strange yellow light that no one seemed to notice. The air was dry and cold and heady, and it seemed not to move at all. A door slammed closed in one quarter of the city and a window swung open in another. A whispered breath and a faint, atonal note hovered in the air, but seemed not to move or dissipate. One moment it hung over the university, and the next a stray student, alone in the quad, looked over his shoulder, sure that he'd heard a step behind him. The brilliant, green grass of the close-cut lawn, smooth as a billiard table, suddenly looked grey, and the student bent down to look at it, mesmerised for a moment by the apparent fissures in the baked earth that crumbled away to sand, and then rippled, the blades of grass perishing as if they had never existed. The student blinked, and suddenly the lawn was as verdant as ever, and someone was leaning out of an upper window shouting at him to leave the bloody grass alone.

The student stood and looked up at the window. The tutor had turned away, otherwise he might have seen how dry the boy's skin was, how old and tired he looked, how desiccated.

The old and the young and the sick died that night, and no one noticed. Cut flowers wilted and then dried to papery husks as vases and jugs were suddenly without water. Fruits and vegetables turned to dried husks in kitchen racks and on the little vines that many of the city-folk grew to supplement their meagre diets, and no one thought to question or complain. Such was the way of the plague. Nothing could be done.

The two moons of Mannslieb and Morrslieb hung in the firmament, flat, grey and featureless, shedding almost no light through the yellowish haze of the sky. It was as if they had turned their faces from the city, as if Nuln had somehow been abandoned.

* * *

They came by the South Gate into the city. The City Guard of Nuln gathered in the yellow haze that signalled the twilight of the rising sun, and began preparations for opening the gate. They trimmed the wicks and filled the reservoirs of their lamps, emptied the still-warm ash from the brazier, allowed to burn out at dusk the evening before, and primed and relit it. Their breath clouded the air in front of their faces, and they stamped their feet in the chill of the morning while they waited impatiently for the boy to bring their breakfasts.

The South Gate into the commercial quarter of the city had been quiet for months, and the guard expected no visitors so early in the day, except perhaps for a little foot traffic. It was not a market day and commerce was depressed.

The three guards, their weapons slung on their backs, gathered around the brazier as it began to give off a little heat. Within a few minutes the boy, unarmoured and unarmed, but for a long knife slotted into a leather loop at his belt, arrived with a greasy, brown-paper parcel that was leaking steam and an earthy smell.

Surn Strallan was particularly attached to his sheathless knife. It was guard issue and had been used by any number of men before him, but the boy was inordinately proud of it, so much so that he had honed the blade to remove every nick and dink that it had suffered over scores of years, and he had sharpened it so thoroughly that it cut cleanly through human hair. As a result, the blade was as narrow as a stiletto, and looked not unlike his uncle's, the butcher's, boning knife.

'Mutton... again?' asked the largest of the guardsmen, 'and old, too, if the smell's anything to go by.'

'Be grateful we're not eating discarded shoe-leather,' said

his younger, taller companion, the man in charge of the little band.

'I'm not sure we ain't,' said Surn, until the other men turned on him, scowling, and he handed the parcel to the old man, raising his hands, as if in surrender. 'I'm joking.'

'Not funny,' said the old man, freeing the corner of the largest and greasiest of the pies from its paper wrapping and carefully examining the pastry where some of the gravy had leaked out, sniffing it before taking a large, hot bite.

'Not remotely funny,' said another guard, a middle-aged man with scrawny arms and legs, which didn't nearly fill his breeches and sleeves, and a round belly, almost like that of a pregnant woman.

When the air moved a little around the men, making them even colder in its draught, they huddled together around the brazier, eating their pies and ruminating on the state of the city. They did not see the cart and its entourage cresting the rise that led to the last few hundred yards to the gate, and if they had seen it, they would have considered it unremarkable.

The figure that led the cart was stooped and cloaked. The man would have been taller than average, if he had stood up straight, but he leaned heavily on a staff and did not make the extra effort to draw himself up to his full height.

There was little noise in the air, just the wet chewing and snuffling of the guardsmen as they ate the too-hot pies that made their nostrils drip, and the crackle of the little fire in the brazier. They should have heard the cart in the stillness of the early morning, but it seemed to make almost no noise. The compacted earth of the road seemed to fall away, to desiccate, as the figure walked ahead of the cart, leaving a two- or three-inch-thick layer of fine, sandy dust for the cartwheels to roll through. The sound it made was not the usual clatter of steel rims on hard earth, but the light, gritty, shushing sound of sand being displaced.

The road behind the cart seemed to mend, firming to packed earth again, but with two deep grooves where the cartwheels had passed through it, filled with more of the sand. The cart had only two large wheels, and might have been pulled by a pair of horses, if the double yoke was any indication, but the little band was clearly impoverished, and the vehicle was being manhandled by two more slender, cloaked figures who pushed from behind the yokes rather than pulling as a horse would.

Their feet and hands were bound in dusty linen in the absence of cobbled shoes and stitched gloves, to protect them from the hazards along the road, and from the blisters and callouses that would result from driving the cart. Their bowed heads were shrouded in the hoods of their cloaks, and their faces were not visible.

Most of the cart's contents were roughly covered with a tarpaulin that looked almost as if it had been made from a great canvas banner or sail, but which was filthy and threadbare, held together by the gritty dust that penetrated its weave. Stacked further back on the rocking cart, roped in place, were several earthenware jars made of a clay that was too pale and yellow to have come from the Empire. The jars were of similar sizes, no bigger than eighteen inches tall. They were round of belly with narrowing shoulders and carved wooden lids sealed in place, and they were heavily inscribed in a language that appeared to consist of pictograms or hieroglyphs, which were so entirely alien that only two people living in Nuln at that time could decipher them, and one of them was now too old and too blind to attempt the task.

The shape under the tarpaulin was roughly human, although rather larger than a man; the arms appeared to be crossed, resting on the torso and the feet stuck up slightly, as if the figure were resting peacefully on its back.

The little group was only a matter of a few yards from the gate when Surn happened to look up from his hot breakfast.

The sight of the cart came as a shock to Surn as he had not heard it coming up the road, and he instinctively inhaled, when he should have swallowed, forcing a piece of gristle into his throat, so that he choked and gasped. The man standing next to him thumped Surn on the back with one bony fist, but his arms were so scrawny that there was little strength in them, and the lump of gristle remained lodged.

Surn's face reddened, and soon the fat man on the other side of him joined in the thumping, trying to revive the poor boy, whose mouth was still open, and who was trying to cough the scrap of food up with so little success that his lips were rapidly turning blue.

The sergeant continued to eat his breakfast, his back to the road.

Surn flapped and gestured, at the same time, distending his throat and neck, trying to dislodge the unfortunate blockage that was preventing him from warning his fellow guards of the arrival of the cart, not to mention cutting off his air supply.

The pantomime continued for a few more seconds, Surn becoming increasingly frantic for his life.

At last, the sergeant wiped his oily fingers on the greasy paper his pasty had arrived in, and balled it up before tossing it onto the little fire in the brazier where it spat and gave off the stink of burning rancid fat. Then he came behind Surn.

As he did so, the cart, pushed by its pair of human labour-ers, rolled past the guards as they shuffled back the few inches required to avoid having their feet crushed under its wheels. Not one of them noticed that a spray of sand, almost like the wake behind a fast-moving, small boat, came up over their boots, leaving a film of pale dust behind, unlike the dark, hard earth that the track on that side of the city was actually made of.

The guard boss raised a hand to the cart as it trundled past, noticing that the lead man lifted his staff a few extra inches off the ground, as if in acknowledgement as they passed beneath the arched portal that marked entry through the gate. Then he clasped Surn manfully around the torso from behind, and thrust his clenched fists into the boy's sternum, twice. The second thrust caused the piece of mutton gristle to burst dramatically from Surn's throat and hit the stone of the arch where it stuck, wetly, for a moment.

Surn placed a hand flat on his chest, bent double and heaved in a huge, gasping breath.

He blinked and looked down at his boots. He lifted one of them and the faint layer of sand that coated them shifted, col-lecting in the creases of the worn-out leather. Surn replaced his foot on the earth and looked after the cart, but he could neither see nor hear it.

'What was that?' he asked.

'A waste of good gristle,' said the hungry, fat guard.

'The cart,' said Surn, finally standing upright. He pointed through the archway and then down at his boots. 'What was the cart?'

'Just a cart,' said the skinny-legged man.

Surn looked his boss hard in the face.

'What?' asked his boss.

'I don't know,' said Surn. 'Only this.'

And with that, Surn pointed at his worn boot and then kicked the arched wall with the toe of it, sending a puffing cloud of gritty, yellow dust billowing up. He did the same with his other boot.

The boss took his chin in his hand and looked from Surn's face to his boots.

'So,' he said, 'your boots are dusty.'

'Yes,' said Surn, 'but so are yours, boss. And when are your boots ever dusty?'

The boss looked down at his boots. He took his white neckerchief from around his throat, and rested the toe of his left boot on the wall so that he could wipe it without bending double. Sandy yellow dust came away on the neckerchief, leaving a smudge of staining ochre on the clean linen.

The boss held the neckerchief up to his face and flinched slightly.

'It's hot,' he said, 'and it smells of… I don't know what.'

'It's just dust,' said the fat guard. 'Are you going to finish this pie, or shall I eat it before it goes cold?'

'Dust comes from somewhere,' said the boss. 'This dust didn't come from these parts. The earth here is brown, or grey since the plague, and sometimes it's black. There's the clay brought in from the west that comes in red, and a spot of chalk if you go far enough north, but this is yellow. Where's the nearest yellow earth?'

'So, they've come a long way,' said the fat guard.

'If they've come so far, why haven't they left the yellow earth far behind, why are they still scattering it?'

The boss looked at the cloth again, and sniffed it.

'What is it?' asked Surn. 'What does it smell of?'

'It smells of the hottest, driest day of the hottest, driest summer of your life, boy,' said the boss, 'and then some.'

The boss lifted his nose from his neckerchief and wheezed to catch his breath. As he coughed, his lips shrivelled and cracked, and he reached for his canteen, suddenly parched. Then, he blinked hard, his eyes suddenly tearless and gritty.

'Is the professor still talking about sand?' asked the girl, whose name was Gianna, and who had raided her father's supply of decent ale for her visitors.

'He is,' said Fithvael, 'but I feel sure he's getting to the point.'

'How long has it been?' asked Laban.

'Who asked you?' asked Gilead. 'What are you still doing here? It will soon be dawn, and the horses need tending.'

'Shall I never live it down?' asked Laban, slumping onto his elbows so that he was almost lying on his back on the hard flags of the tavern floor.

Gianna leaned over and touched Laban on the top of his head with her free hand, as if he were some child to be indulged.

'I've forgiven you already,' she said, smiling.

Gilead looked from Gianna to Laban.

'The horses,' he said.

Laban got elegantly and swiftly to his feet, making sure that he didn't lock out his knees, avoiding banging his head on the low ceiling-beams of the small room.

'Try not to be seen,' said Gilead, 'and close the door and the gate behind you.'

'It's the composition,' said Professor Mondelblatt. 'Every region has its very own combination of silica and quartz, and earth and stone compounds; every area has its own specific balance of biological matter and geological, so that with careful study it's possible to determine within a matter of miles where any sand sample originated from. Then there's the range of sizes and colours of the individual grains, the weight and density of a sample, how powdery it is, for example, how silty. There's a fine line to be drawn between silt and sand. I could talk about it for hours.'

'You *have*,' said Fithvael, 'and still I do not understand what it is you are trying to tell us, old man.'

'I can tell you nothing,' said Mondelblatt, surprised. 'By what means did you presume I could impart any knowledge to you about what is to come, what must befall?'

'Why are we here?' Fithvael asked Gilead.

'He knows,' said Gilead. 'You know, old man.'

'What I know,' said Mondelblatt, 'has taken a lifetime to learn. If only you trusted me, I might impart a small portion of it, but you will never trust me as you should.'

'You can keep us all locked up in here for as long as you like,' said Gianna, pouring more ale into Mondelblatt's glass. 'I can't say I mind, especially not with my old dad incapacitated for once, and serve him right. You brung the old professor here for a reason, though, and that big boy out there, he's worse than useless. So, if you get my drift, I'm thinking that you've run out of choices. Show the professor a bit of respect and find out what you need to know.'

Gilead did not look at Gianna nor answer her. She finished pouring, and harrumphed slightly before wandering away from the little table where the two elves and the old man continued to sit.

'She's right,' said Fithvael. 'What harm can it do?'

'To trust him?' asked Gilead.

'It's what you came for,' said Mondelblatt.

There was an almighty crash from somewhere above,

followed by a thud and the tinkle of falling glass. Fithvael was out of his chair in an instant, but Gianna, already on her feet, was quicker, and she flew up the wooden steps at the side of the room.

'He had to wake some time, and he'll be as mad as a bear,' she said, over her shoulder.

Mondelblatt's gaze followed the girl as she disappeared at the top of the steep staircase.

'See,' he said, pointing, 'look there. They're all over the city. All over my beautiful Nuln. It was only a matter of time.'

'We should go,' said Fithvael. 'It isn't fair to the girl to keep her father subdued.'

'I think she rather likes him like that,' said Gilead. 'Better to keep him unconscious and remain here than to render every man that sees us in the city unconscious. With Laban for company, we'll leave a trail of bodies.'

With that, Laban entered the tavern again.

'I heard a noise,' he said. 'A window broke. There was shouting.'

'See to it,' said Gilead, pointing up the stairs.

When Laban entered the room at the back of the tavern that looked out over the yard, he saw Gianna and her father in a stand-off, one on either side of the narrow bed. The tavern keeper was trying to grab at his daughter, growling at her like a bear with a sore head. Gianna was trying, not very hard, to placate him. The elves made her brave, and she had taken too much grief from her bullying parent for too long. She goaded him.

'I'll set them on you. I'll make you pay. You've paid already, you old goat. They've been drinking your ale all night long, and serve you right. I doubt they'll pay, either, since they can tie you up and do what they will with you.'

The tavern keeper growled again and lashed out, swinging his left arm across the bed, still trailing the length of rope that had restrained him, but which he had broken free of.

Laban reached out a hand, almost nonchalantly, and took a firm hold of the rope. With a twist and a tug, he turned the fat man onto his side and pulled him onto the bed, where he hogtied him.

'I'll see Sigmar's great wrath come down on you... you beast!' said the tavern keeper, but without any force in his words, since his face had paled and his heart was beating too fast. He did not like the elves. He did not understand them, and he was very much afraid of their presence in his establishment. He knew that if he should live long enough to see them leave, he would become the hero of his own modified tale about that night, but until then he was a coward and he knew it.

Laban sighed.

'Go on then,' said Gianna, gesturing towards her father with a look approximating glee on her small, pretty face.

Laban sighed again, and then cuffed the tavern keeper high on his shoulder, against his neck, so that he rendered the fat man unconscious once more while trying to inflict the least possible damage on him. As it was, he'd wake up with a fearful ache.

'I never could stand listening to the old goat whining,' said Gianna, 'and, Sigmar help me, I've been doing it for long enough. Now, what's next?'

Laban and Gianna emerged from the top of the staircase, the elf bending at the shoulder as he descended the stairs.

'He won't wake again anytime soon,' said Gianna, wiping her hands on her apron as she stepped off the bottom stair. 'Feels like breakfast time, if I'm not mistaken.'

'Then we stay,' said Gilead.

'What are all over Nuln?' he asked Mondelblatt. 'What are you talking about?'

'The signs,' said Mondelblatt. 'They are all over the city.'

'What signs?' asked Gilead.

'Signs of things to come,' said Mondelblatt. 'Signs carved into the fabric of my beautiful city. I see them everywhere. I see them in the gargoyles and waterspouts and drain covers of the temples and shrines. I see them in the gable-ends and muntins and keystones of the colleges of the university, and I see them in the fence posts and banisters, and handrails and beams of the taverns and houses.'

'And you see them here?' asked Gilead.

'Don't you?' asked Mondelblatt.

'I will when you show them to me,' said Gilead.

'Then we must begin,' said Mondelblatt.

'It's three blokes and a cart,' said the fat guard. 'How much trouble could they possibly be? Besides, they're in now, and what could we have stopped them for?'

'Don't we have a responsibility?' asked Surn. 'Aren't we here to keep the city safe?'

The fat guard and the one with the skinny limbs looked at Surn and then at each other, and then they laughed. The fat guard laughed so hard that he had to put his hands flat on his knees so as not to overbalance, and he stood like that for several long moments, laughing deep and soundlessly in his throat.

The sergeant, though not inclined to work harder than was absolutely necessary, did not join in with the merriment.

'What do you think we should do?' he asked Surn.

'We didn't stop them,' said Surn, 'so we didn't do our job. Did we?'

'Supposing we had stopped them?' asked his superior. 'What then?'

'We might have found a reason to turn them away,' said Surn.

'We might,' said the sergeant, 'and we might not. If we'd found a reason to turn them away, and they'd decided not to leave, what then?'

'Then we'd have driven them off,' said Surn. 'After all, it was just three blokes and a cart, and we're armed and trained.'

The fat guard bent low over his knees, his face crimson with mirth.

'They might have passed muster.'

'Then at least we would have done our duty,' said Surn.

'You think we neglected our duty?' asked the boss. 'That's a serious allegation.'

'I do,' said Surn, 'but can't we put it right?'

'How can we put it right and fully man the gate?' asked the boss. 'Traffic has been light, but the sun is rising steadily, and there are bound to be more pedestrians and more wagons and carts to check and clear. It could be a long day. Is it wise to begin at a disadvantage?'

'Three men can easily man the gate,' said Surn. 'There're only ever three guards on this gate, except when there's a trainee.'

'But you're the trainee,' said the skinny-limbed guard. 'You're the guard we can manage without.'

'Then I shall volunteer,' said Surn, standing tall, puffing out his chest, and resting his hand on the hilt of his stiletto blade.

'Volunteer for what?' asked the sergeant. 'No one asked for a volunteer for anything.'

'I volunteer to shadow the three blokes and their cart. I

volunteer to watch them, to see where they go and what they do. I volunteer to keep a close eye on them at all times and to report to the city guard if they transgress or circumvent any civil or criminal laws.'

The fat guard, his hands on his knees, and his head so low that all anyone could see of him was the puce bald spot on the crown of his head, rocked gently with his silent laughter.

'Since you put it like that,' said the sergeant, with a wry smile, 'you have my permission, for one shift only, to monitor said vehicle, and you may report back to me at the end of the allotted time.'

Beaming, Surn bowed slightly to his bemused superior, and ducked quickly through the city gate, hugging the wall, making himself as inconspicuous as he possibly could while drawing far too much attention to himself simply by moving as no one else was likely to in a month of Sundays. He could have sauntered or wandered through the gate and gone unnoticed, but he skulked; he bobbed and wove, and he sneaked and insinuated. If anyone had been within a hundred yards of him, he would surely have drawn their gazes, but nobody was within a hundred yards of him on the outside of the city wall, except for his fellow guardsmen, and anyone within a hundred yards of him on the inside of the city wall was not within sight of him as he wedged himself into the corners and crevices between buildings, and skulked in the alleys and byways that had no windows looking onto them.

'Well, that saves us finding errands for the boy to run today,' said the skinny-limbed guard.

'Don't think it saves you from doing your job, mind,' said the sergeant, 'just because the best of our conscience is absent.'

'He's not absent,' said the fat guard, looking up for the first time in several minutes, 'he's on a mission.'

Chapter 27

The horses were tended to, and everyone else was fed by Gianna, who was beginning to think of the elves and the old man as a sort of surrogate family. No group of men had ever kept her company for so long, nor been so polite as this one was, and, besides, they'd kept her father occupied and out of her hair for several hours in a row. It didn't seem to matter to her that she hadn't slept and she'd barely rested. She'd been treated with nothing but respect, and it was all she'd ever hoped for.

As they finished their breakfast, Fithvael pointed up the staircase.

'Who carved the newel posts for the stairs?' he asked Gianna, as if it were an idle enough question.

'What's a newel post?' asked Gianna.

'It's a hundred years old,' said Mondelblatt, 'this little room, or two hundred, perhaps. You forget how short our human lives are, elf.'

'So you don't know who carved the wood for the tavern?' asked Fithvael.

'Know them?' asked Gianna. 'Only that they were ancestors. Six generations... No... Seven. How does it work? Six greats. My six greats-grandad was the first tavern keeper here. Well, not here. His first tavern was a hole in the wall, a shack, but it was right on this spot. It was on the outskirts of the city, then, a backwater. He had this place built when my five greats-grandad joined the family business. They needed a cellar for brewing by then. That's when they did the upstairs.'

'Not much more than a hundred years, then,' said Mondelblatt.

'Seven generations,' said Fithvael, 'in a hundred years. Isn't that a lot, even for humans?'

'Something over a hundred years, or so,' said Mondelblatt. 'How old are you, girl?' he asked, catching Gianna lightly by the hand.

'Old enough,' said Gianna.

'It's not a trick,' said Mondelblatt, 'just an innocent question.'

'Fourteen,' said Gianna, flushing slightly.

'How old's your father?' asked Mondelblatt.

'Don't know,' said Gianna. 'Don't care. Old.'

'Your mother?' asked Mondelblatt.

'Died when she was twenty,' said Gianna.

'Poor child,' said Fithvael, 'not to remember your mother.'

'I remember her very well,' said Gianna. 'Why wouldn't I? I was nearly seven when she died, and my brothers and sisters with her.'

'You don't have children?' asked Mondelblatt.

Gianna shook her head.

'Academically speaking,' said Mondelblatt, 'we measure

a city generation in the Empire in fifteen-year increments. Seven generations makes one hundred and thirty-five years; closer to a hundred years than two.'

'Where were you one hundred and thirty-five years ago, te tuin?' asked Fithvael.

The elves' eyes met, neither one needing a reminder of where they had been together, and what they had endured during their decades of questing and adventuring. Time was nothing to them. They felt things as deeply now as they had five decades ago, or eight or twelve. Time changed nothing.

Gianna laughed a nervous laugh, but stopped when she saw the expressions on the elves' faces.

'Strange, ain't they?' she said, changing the subject and breaking the spell. 'I can't say I ever noticed them before.' She stepped over to the newel post at the bottom of the stairs and ran her hand over the carvings in the wood with their hundred or so years of wear and patina.

'That's local,' said Mondelblatt, 'religious, Sigmarite. It's a ward of sorts, not common now, but brought in from the countryside, from the superstitions of the innocent folk coming to the city and changing their fortunes for better or worse, but forever. That's the one, though, higher up,' he said, craning his neck and pointing towards the top of the staircase.

Gianna skipped up the steps to examine what was carved there. She ran her hand over it and peered at it. Then she traced the edges of it with a finger.

'I don't know what it is,' she said. 'I can't believe it's been here my whole life and I've never looked at it before.'

'Humans aren't subtle creatures,' said Gilead, 'but not to know your surroundings is crass even by the standards of your own species.'

'Don't berate the child,' said Fithvael, rising from his seat at the table and following Gianna up the stairs.

'Let me see, child, what is it?' he asked.

'I've never seen its like,' said Gianna, tracing its edges with her fingertips.

'I know what it is,' said Mondelblatt, 'and I can show you where there's another like it, and then another, and a hundred more in Nuln, and then I can show you other things just as odd, and just as portentous.'

'It's a portent?' asked Gianna, her eyes widening in her startled face and her hand snatching away from the carving as if it could somehow do her harm.

'Everything is a portent,' said Fithvael, trying to placate the scared girl. 'A portent is a useful thing. Without them we wouldn't know what to fear or guard against.'

The elf looked at the carving, and turned to Gilead.

'It is what you described,' he said. 'It is what you saw below the ground, in the Rat King's lair. It was in your vision.'

'The beetle,' said Mondelblatt. 'One of the myriad. You saw an oil slick of throbbing wing cases, and you heard the clacking of carapaces and the clicking of exoskeletons. The air thrummed with them, if I am not mistaken.'

'It's a bug?' asked Gianna. 'I've never seen anything like it in these parts, not in Nuln, not ever.'

'They're not from around here,' said Mondelblatt. 'You'd have to travel south for many a day to find such a creature, or any of his cousins, into the very heart of the dead lands of the deserts.'

'What's deserts?'

'Empty places where nothing green grows, where there is no rain, only the heat of the day and the cold of the night, only the sun or the moons. Empty skies where there are no clouds, and where, if the air moves, it takes the sand with it. Empty places where there is nothing but dry dust and death, and heat and sand.'

'And bugs,' said Gianna.

'And bugs,' said Mondelblatt, snapping out of his odd reverie.

'Why is it here, then?' asked Gianna. 'If it doesn't belong?'

'They were here before,' said Mondelblatt. 'I knew that they would return. I knew when the plagues came, and I expanded my studies; I knew when I transcribed the language of their symbols; I knew when you told me of the artefacts you had seen; I knew that they would come back. I knew that they would seek to change the Empire forever. All this, I knew.'

'What do you know, old man?' asked Gilead. 'Why do you hesitate?'

'Only now,' said Mondelblatt, 'am I sure why you were sent to me.'

'I was not sent,' said Gilead. 'I came to you for answers. I came because you are the only man I know who might be able to explain what I experienced, what it means, and how it relates to the plague. I do not trust you. I do not truly believe that you have the answers, but I had to try. My people, too, are dying.'

'I do not have the answers,' said Mondelblatt. 'And yet, I do have the answers.'

'Riddle us no riddles, old man,' said Fithvael. 'You're frightening the girl.'

'It is simple,' said Mondelblatt. 'The answer stands before you. Or rather, he sits. Gilead te tuin Tor Anrok is the answer.'

'Then you had better tell us what the question is,' said Fithvael.

* * *

The cart rolled soundlessly over the cobbles in the backstreets of Nuln, save for the low shushing of sand displacing
beneath its wheels. The figures propelling the vehicle along
its course bowed their heads and shuffled their linen-covered
feet, driven by their master. His hood shrouded his face, but
he adjusted it once or twice with bandaged hands, so that
he could tip his head back or tilt it to one side and peer up
at an eave or mullion, or down at a foundation stone or a
kerb. He saw what he was looking for everywhere, and he
followed where the carved symbols and hieroglyphs led.

For the first half a mile, as they wove a way into the southern quarters of the walled city, the trio encountered no one.
They skirted the slums of the Faulestadt region, and the
small-scale industrial areas that were little occupied in these
times of strife. The tanneries were all but abandoned, since
few cattle had survived the plague, and those that remained
were too valuable for their milk to be killed for their meat
and leather. The same applied to the hardy goats, which had
fared a little better than their bovine cousins. One or two
leather workers managed to eke out their trade by repurpos-
ing old leather goods, turning worn wineskins into satchels
and old saddle-leather into sheaths and scabbards, but much
of the district was deserted.

On the corner of Aver Street, as the cart turned towards the
docklands and the Great Bridge, a child, sitting on a kerbstone, chewing at a stub of meat that his grandmother had
dried three winters since (being a wise woman of old, country habits), heard an odd shushing sound, and turned his
head. The wheels of the wagon passed inches from his feet,
spraying a wake of fine sand over them, the grit reaching his
face and the tough, sinewy morsel in his hand.

The child breathed in as the cart drew away, only to find that he could not breathe out. His hand spasmed as he panicked, and he dropped the precious scrap of meat, which landed in a pool of sand at his feet. He reached for his throat and tried to cough. Then he tried to retch. His fingers felt hard and bony against the flesh of his throat, and then the skin of his neck felt dry and papery under his petrified hands. His eyes widened, and were too dry for him to be able to blink them closed again. His gums receded in an instant, his teeth looking like pegs in the face of a dried-up old corpse. He did not slump or sag. He simply fell, sideways. There was no softness left in his body, all the suppleness had been sucked out of him, dried up, desiccated. His clothes hung off his dead body, a body that looked as if it had perished a thousand years before and had been locked in a dry, airless vault for all eternity.

No one knew the child. No one claimed the corpse. It was an abomination. Its mother didn't recognise it, though she hunted for days for her lost son.

A rumour soon spread about the tiny, papery corpse. The local people whispered speculation about the course the plague must be taking, but they did so in hushed tones, not wanting to believe that such a terrible fate might befall them. Better to live with the everyday inconveniences heaped one upon another over the years since the plague had begun to spread across the Empire, and better to ignore the atrocities that no one understood or could adequately explain.

The religious prayed, and the superstitious touched their talismans of good fortune, and all turned their backs on others' misfortunes, grateful that the worst had befallen someone else.

That was how the cart passed unnoticed through the poorer districts of Nuln. It passed unnoticed because it was safer not to heed its existence. The city-folk of Nuln kept themselves to themselves, turning away, even from their neighbours and cousins, when there was nothing left to believe in and no one left to trust.

No one but Surn Strallan took any notice of the cart with its figures of burden pushing it through the narrow streets, or its guide looking for a path to follow. The vehicle was distinctive and easy to spot at a junction of streets from more than a hundred yards away. Strallan did not want to get close. The sand bothered him. Where was the sand coming from? There was no sand in Nuln. There was dirt and filth and cobbles and hard-packed earth, and, when the river was low, there was the clay and silt of the exposed mudflats, but there was no sand.

Strallan ducked and wove, running ahead to a cross street, so that he could sit on a kerbstone and watch the cart coming towards him. He sat facing the cart, looking between its wheels at the street beneath. There was no sight of any sand trickling from one of the vessels on the back of the wagon. There was no sign of a sack of sand that might have been punctured. There was no sign of a barrel, or even a wineskin that might have been filled with the stuff. And yet, as the wheels turned they ground into sand, cutting through it and spreading a wake of it behind them. Sand collected in the gutters of the streets of Nuln, and against the kerbstones.

Surn Strallan wondered, if he were to brush it all up and collect it in a sack, just how much sand he would have, and reckoned, after following the cart for an hour, that it would be too much for one man to carry on his back.

As the cart approached him, Strallan hopped back to his feet and ducked down another alley, winding a path north, parallel to Aver Street. He was sure that the vehicle was heading towards the bridge, and planned to reach it first. Sometimes, it was better to follow from in front.

He turned his head to the right as he heard an intake of breath, and he almost fell over an old man, tapping his way along the narrow, uneven pavement, with a stick that was so tall he had to hold it a third of the way down its length.

'I've never seen such a terrible thing,' said the old man, to no one in particular, 'and I hope I never shall again. Such a strange creature, such a peculiar sight.'

'What was it, old man?' asked Surn. 'What did you see?'

He looked out past the old man's shoulder and saw the cart rumbling towards him, towards the bridge.

'The body of I don't know what, an ancient child corpse, or a shrunken thing, wrinkled and weathered, and older than time, lying on its side in the gutter. How did such a thing come to be there? What will the plague bring to our doors next?'

Strallan shuddered, but did not answer the old man, who wasn't looking at him, and hadn't really been talking to him in any case; he'd simply needed to say what was on his mind, and the boy happened to offer a convenient ear.

'What will the plague bring, indeed?' asked Strallan, ducking out of the old man's path and onto the southern docks as the cart approached within ten or a dozen yards of his position.

'When will it come?' asked Fithvael. 'What form will it take? How will we know the evil when it arrives in Nuln?'

'I do not know,' said Mondelblatt. 'I do not know, and I do not know. Gilead is here, and that is enough. If the elf is here, the other will come, and when it comes, Gilead will find it and destroy it.'

'You know where to look,' said Gilead. 'I am not the answer. The answers are to be found in your texts and scholarly works. If you have become the professor that you claim to be, if you stopped lying and began to earn the career and the reputation that you stole and cheated for, then you must know where to find the answers. You must know what references will lead you to the key to this plague, and to unravelling the mysteries that surround it.'

Gilead rose from his chair and gestured to Fithvael.

'We leave for the university,' he said.

'All of us?' asked Gianna.

'Stay here,' said Fithvael, kindly. 'Keep this place locked and safe for us to return to. Feed your father and rest awhile, and we will return.'

'Promise nothing,' Gilead told his old companion, sternly.

'We will return,' said Fithvael, looking directly at Gianna.

She tugged free the cloth that hung from her apron string and wrapped it tightly around the remains of the black bread and cheese rind on the table, and she stoppered a half-full jug of ale.

'There's nothing to eat at the university. The students are all so thin. Take this,' she said, 'and you'll have to come back to return the cloth and the jug.'

Fithvael took them from her, and smiled. Mondelblatt stood awkwardly, and then sat down again, heavily. He had been sitting for several hours, and, while he did not need a very great deal of sleep, staying in one position for any length of time rather seized up his joints.

Fithvael stepped in and took the old man's arm as Mondelblatt planted his stick more firmly between the flags and made a second, more successful attempt to rise.

'Perhaps we should take the palfrey, after all,' said Fithvael.

'No,' said Mondelblatt, 'if anyone should see me riding into the university the staff will begin to whisper. Besides, someone must cover a great deal of ground in the city, mapping the signs.'

'The bugs,' said Gianna.

'We cannot send Laban,' said Gilead. 'The boy is far too conspicuous.'

'I think he has learnt his lesson,' said Fithvael. 'He seeks only to do his master's bidding, and his master is nothing if not demanding.'

Gilead said nothing.

'Or, I could do it, if you prefer,' said Fithvael.

'I do,' said Gilead.

'What am I to look for, old man?' asked Fithvael.

Mondelblatt sniggered slightly, and Fithvael frowned at him.

'You called me old,' said the professor, 'and yet you must be three times my age.'

'Older than that,' said Fithvael, 'but only by comparison to your race.'

'Older than that, and wiser too,' said Mondelblatt. He was rummaging around in the deep pockets of the academic gown that he wore, and soon pulled out the stub of a pencil and a notebook made of ancient, woven paper, stitched together at the spine.

'Sit for a moment,' said Mondelblatt. 'My skills as a draughtsman are rudimentary at best, but I shall do my best to convey the shapes of the sigils you are looking for. Mark them as accurately as you can on a map that you must buy from the man, I don't recall his name, halfway down Eyk's End: the green, windowless doorway. No one makes a better map, and precision will make all the difference. A plague of the old beasts will descend. The beasts of the southlands, the beasts of the sigils.'

Gilead nodded at Fithvael, who pulled his hood up over his head, lowered his knees and dropped his shoulders so that he was suddenly a foot shorter and more rounded of form than he naturally was. He would have little trouble passing for a man, especially in a city where everyone was afraid of what they might see if they chose to take notice of anything. He ducked out of the tavern, tucking Mondelblatt's notebook between the fastenings of his jerkin.

Within a very few minutes, he was steering the palfrey through the byways of the waking city, east towards Eyk's End and the North Gate, to begin his task.

Gianna brought Laban back into the tavern as Gilead lifted his hood. The elf was already standing low, almost stooping. He fit easily under the height of the beams now, and had clearly taken his mistakes to heart. Gilead looked at him, and Laban dropped his eyes to the floor.

'You will escort the professor,' said Gilead. 'Allow the old man to lead you back to the university. Do his bidding, but remain at his side.'

'Where will you be, cousin?' asked Laban.

'Everywhere,' said Gilead. 'Sometimes before you, and sometimes beside you, sometimes to your right and sometimes to your left. I will always have you in my sights. I will always be able to see and hear you, even if you cannot detect my presence. Go undetected, Laban te tuin.'

'You talk as if it is not safe,' said Laban.

'Do you know that it is?' asked Gilead.

'You know better than I do,' said Laban, bowing his head a little further, aware of his earlier transgressions.

'If I raise the alarm, shield Professor Mondelblatt and, if you are able and it is safe, return here,' said Gilead.

'If I am not able?' asked Laban.

'The professor will know what to do,' said Gilead as he and the old man exchanged a long look. 'At all and any cost, keep Mondelblatt safe. Our task is great, so great that we cannot fully understand it. Much as it pains me, I fear we need the professor and his knowledge if we are to prevent the demise of our race.'

'You'll do more than save your family, Gilead,' said Mondelblatt. 'You'll save the Empire.'

'Raise not your hopes, old man,' said Gilead. 'You must know that when it came time to save my family, I was found wanting. When it came time to save my brother, I failed. With everything to lose, I lost it all.

'Your only hope, old man, is that loss means nothing to me.'

Chapter 28

It is coming. If I live out these last few hours, I will live long enough to tell the end of this cursed tale. It should have been about the skaven, and it was in a way. It was about them, and it was not about them. If they were the beginning, then it is time to reveal what the end of the story is about, and that is the right way of things after all.

It is about riddles. It is about time and the tides. It is about men and mortality. It is about being caught in the middle of things. It is about how alike we are to other races, and how different we are from them.

I'm not alike to an elf, and neither are you, and yet… and yet…

In the end, we are more alike than you could possibly imagine. More alike to the skaven, too. We're all alpha, all mortal. We must all make ready to die.

The omega. There's no death to be had for the omega. No end in the end.

Enough of my riddles, I hear you cry, but they're the riddles that were told to me, and they're not nearly so taxing as the riddles that will unfold yet.

Come close and listen, and see if you can work out what old Professor Mondelblatt knew. I'm not sure Gilead ever did. Gather round, and don't try my patience with questions. It'll all come out, right or wrong. It'll all come out, eventually.

Professor Mondelblatt checked his timepiece. He held it to his ear, wound it, and checked it again. Then he turned an hourglass in his study, and then he turned another and another. There were a dozen or more of them sitting on a library table in an alcove beside the fireplace, pushed well back, and unlit, so that Gilead had not noticed them when he had been in the room before.

They were of different sizes, and the sands were of various colours and grades, some coarse, some fine, all moving at different speeds through apertures of different diameters. No two hourglasses were alike, and Gilead could not say with any certainty how much time each of them might measure, although a cursory examination of at least some of them would give him a reasonable idea of their durations.

'It is ironic, is it not,' said Mondelblatt, turning to the elf, 'that in the deepest depths of the Southlands where sand is the only constant, time is not measured in the stuff at all?'

'It isn't?' asked Gilead, humouring the old man.

'It isn't,' said Mondelblatt. 'In the Southlands, where water is scarce, where it is hard to find and very, very precious, it is, nonetheless, used to measure the passage of time. A double irony.'

Mondelblatt made an odd noise in the back of his throat, dry and rasping, and then began to cough extravagantly.

Gilead took a step towards the old man, a mixture of alarm and exasperation on his face. Mondelblatt held up a hand to stop the elf coming any closer, and wheezed.

'Don't you recognise a dying man's laugh?' he asked.

'A double irony?' asked Gilead, who didn't want to draw attention to his concerns for the old man.

'Sand does not represent time where the sands of time can never run dry,' said Mondelblatt.

'You talk in riddles, old man,' said Gilead.

'Our human riddles, our preoccupation with sex and death, are so alien to you, elf, but I suppose that should come as no surprise,' said Mondelblatt. 'We humans know that our lives are short. Look how I have aged since first we met, when I was little more than a youth, a callow, ambitious youth, but a youth, nonetheless, and look how little you are changed by the passage of the same quantity of sand through my hourglasses. Man is ruled by the sands of time. You are not... Or not so much, at least.'

'And the Southlanders?' asked Gilead.

'The South is all sand,' said Mondelblatt. 'The South is all sand and death, and time is measured in water, the bringer of life. Time and life mean nothing there.'

'More riddles,' said Gilead.

'You are ancient,' said Mondelblatt, 'and a very great deal of sand will flow before your end is nigh, a very great deal of sand indeed. I measure the span of my life in these glass bulbs of sand in their little wooden and brass and bone frames, but I could measure yours in the sand of a great desert, or in a mountain range of shifting dunes. The two are not so very different, one from the other. In the end, we are both mortal.

'There is not enough sand in the world to spend on the

existence of a Southland tomb-dweller, not enough sand for a single one of them. They do not live, of course, but they inhabit the world just the same. They inhabit it, and they seek to corrupt it, and when they are done we will all be dust and we will all be sand, and there will be only time and not a single mortal remaining to spend it.'

Gilead caught sight of something out of the corner of his eye, and he glanced at the table. Something had stilled. One of the dozen or so hourglasses had come to a stop. Time had trickled through from the upper reservoir, and the sand in the apparatus was no longer shifting, no longer passing. Time was standing still. The elf did not hesitate. He took a step towards the table, and with one swift movement he flipped the hourglass in its frame, and the sand began to trickle once more.

Mondelblatt looked into Gilead's eyes and breathed a sigh of a relief, as deep a sigh as he was capable of breathing.

Gilead looked down at the hand resting on the frame of the hourglass that he had just flipped as the almost black sand trickled through the aperture, two or three grains at a time. He cast his long, slender fingers up and down the dark wooden frame, tracing the lines and curves of the stylised shapes carved there.

The carvings were ancient and worn and indistinct, but Gilead recognised them, nonetheless: they were the same as the shaky drawings that Mondelblatt had made in his notebook before giving it to Fithvael; they were the same as the carvings on the newel posts in the hole-in-the-wall inn where they had stayed the night before. Gilead traced the images of scarabs and scorpions, of locusts and spiders, and snakes and serpents. He traced the outlines of desert-dwelling insects and arachnids, the outlines of the mythic creatures, the totems and sigils of the Southlanders.

'Is it about time?' asked Gilead. 'Or is it about sand?'

Mondelblatt made the odd sound in the back of his throat again, and again the elf thought that the old man might expire before he'd had a chance to learn all that he would need to know about what must surely befall Nuln... what must befall the Empire.

'It is about life and it is about death, and it is about life in death and death in life,' said Mondelblatt. 'There is no time.'

'Enough with the riddles, old man,' said Gilead. 'You surround yourself with timepieces and you fill your mind with knowledge about sand. There are reasons for that. I know that there are reasons for that.'

'I cheated you, elf. You know that I cheated and I stole from you,' said Mondelblatt.

'I should not trust you, old man,' said Gilead, 'but I would be a fool not to. You know things that I do not know. Your life is short and you have filled it with study for a reason, even if the only reasons are guilt and shame.'

'And pride,' said Mondelblatt. 'Pride is a great motivator.'

'Tell me,' said Gilead.

'That's another irony,' said the professor. 'What it has taken me a lifetime to learn... The knowledge it has taken fifty years for me to accrue cannot be translated to you in minutes or hours, or even in days or weeks or months. It is all for nothing. It is all useless.'

'Then tell me only what I need to know,' said Gilead.

'There is no shorthand,' said Mondelblatt. 'There is no shortcut, no direct route. A great artist becomes what he is, can draw a convincing portrait with a few quick flicks of his brush, only after a lifetime of practice. Those thirty seconds it takes to wield the brush mean nothing; it is the lifetime that enables him.'

'At least tell me what is coming, who is coming, and when and how,' said Gilead. 'You know that much.'

'I know everything, and I know nothing,' said Mondelblatt, 'and I am old and tired. I must rest for a while.'

Fithvael's visit to Eyk's End, as fascinating as it was, took rather longer than he hoped and expected, and he left wishing that he hadn't mentioned Professor Mondelblatt at all. The old man's name had the cartographer bustling back and forth, pulling open plan-chest drawers and offering a wide range of maps of the city of various scales and types. They showed all manner of features from topographical and geological studies to conventional street maps; some concentrated on industrial and commercial areas, others divided the city by ethnicity, prosperity, religion and any number of other permutations.

Fithvael decided on a simple, folded street map to a scale that was easy for him to handle as he travelled on foot across the city. It was critical that he worked quickly and without encumbrances, and continually referring to a map that needed to be spread out over several square feet was not practical. Then, after a moment's reflection, he asked for a second map, if such a thing existed, of the undercrofts, cellars and basements of the city. The cartographer tipped his head on one side for a moment and then disappeared behind the counter where he reached into the lowest of the plan-chest drawers. The map he retrieved was hand-drawn in black ink on grey paper and the calligraphy was quite different from the clean simple script on the street map; it also had fold lines in it so deep that the paper was separating in places. The cartographer began to lay the map out, and then thought better of it.

'No, I can't. I can't let you take it,' he said.

'It's very old,' said Fithvael.

'Just one. Just one of a kind,' said the cartographer. 'It should be in the museum, in the museum of the Puissant Fellowship of Skilled Cartographers, and it will be, too, just as soon as I'm dead.'

'May I look at it, at least?' asked Fithvael.

'Yes, do,' said the cartographer. 'Yes, do look, but don't touch. I can't let you take it.'

Fithvael peered at the map for several minutes, his fingers hovering over its surface. Every time they dipped to within an inch of the fragile, grey paper, the cartographer sucked his breath in sharply through his teeth, and Fithvael lifted his fingers away, not wanting to disconcert the little man who clearly wanted to assist him in any way he could.

Eventually, the elf looked up, to meet the gaze of the cartographer's rather too close-set eyes. He nodded at the little man, and gestured at the short, slender pencil that nestled in the tuft of hair above his left ear.

'May I borrow that?' asked the elf.

The cartographer removed the pencil, licked the lead in preparation for whatever Fithvael had in mind and handed the drawing implement to the elf.

'Oh yes,' he said. 'Oh yes. With pleasure.'

Quickly, and with deft strokes, Fithvael transferred the outlines of the undercrofts and cellars from the old map onto the street map, working out how the city beneath fitted with the city above, how the underground rooms followed the lines of the streets and buildings, clustered under the university, spread in a wide arc across half of the city, traversed districts that on the surface seemed separate, and formed discrete areas below ground where the city spread indiscriminately above ground.

The job done, Fithvael spent a few minutes thanking the cartographer, paying him and saying his farewells, all the time
wondering what, or who, he was reminded of. Then, he was
back in the centre of the city, starting with the university building and environs, and looking for anything that resembled the
little drawings that Mondelblatt had scribbled in his notebook.

It took him several minutes to find the first of them, a gar-
goyle high on the wall of the faculty residences of the university,
but soon he was seeing them everywhere: in the carvings on
the plinth of the Great Statue of Sebastian Veit and on the
architraves and mullions of the College of Engineering. Fithvael jotted notes on his street map, and continued on in wide
circles, spending much of the day working his way around the
city, marking the positions of various representations of the
creatures on his list. They were carved into wood and stone,
painted onto street and shop signs, and woven into letters and
numbers. They appeared at ground level in kerbstones and
foundation stones, in the wrought-iron grilles of storm drains,
and as spouts at the bottom of drainpipes. They were cast as
door knobs and knockers, and etched into locks and escutch-
eons, and the harder Fithvael looked the more evidence he
found of the exotic insects and reptiles.

It was as if the city of Nuln had been hiding some long-
lost secret, some mystery from those who dwelt and worked
within its walls. Fithvael looked around as he noted the
positions of a row of ornate, cast-iron street lamps close
to Magnus Gate. They were covered in a myriad renditions
of the creatures he had been seeking out for the past three
or four hours, teeming with a host of locusts crawling over
the backs of scorpions, who seemed to be wrestling with
scarabs extending their wing cases to escape the thronging
layers of insect life. Serpents writhed around the base of the

lamps, some smooth and fat with flat heads and great venomous fangs, others with broad, flaring throats and staring eyes. Fithvael had never seen an iron casting so complex, so impossibly intricate or so extraordinary, and yet no one seemed to pay the street furniture the slightest attention.

Fithvael walked from Altgate to Temple Gate and along the Commercial Way to the local coach house. Then the sigils took him in an arc through Neuestadt across the corner of Links Park, along Cake Street and back to Temple Gate. In only a few hours, his entire map was covered in dots, dashes, slashes to left and right, strokes and crescents. Sometimes a single mark was repeated over and over again in an area, sometimes two or more coincided, and, as with the street lamps, some areas of the elf's map were crosshatched with multiple marks.

The city and its people were quite different from the last time that Fithvael had been within its walls. It was too quiet. The hum of busy people going about their daily lives was subdued. Fithvael was not conspicuous, because no one looked at each other, and no one looked at him.

In any town or city, anywhere in the Empire, Fithvael, Gilead, Laban, *any* elf had to be circumspect. Elves had to dress appropriately, round their shoulders, stand low in their knees, cover their heads and hands as much as possible, speak as little as they could get away with and as low in their throats as possible. They had to keep to the scrappiest slums, the darkest corners, the most over-populated areas of town. They had to skulk and sneak and avoid being noticed at all and any costs.

Not here. Not now.

Except.

* * *

Surn Strallan was on the Great Bridge before the cart hit the stone slope that marked the approach. He hugged the left-hand wall of the bridge, not wanting to walk out in the open, but not at all sure why. Something wasn't right. For the first time in his life, Strallan could not feel the movement of air coming up the River Reik, driving a corridor of wind through the city, eternally responsible for its weather systems. The water and the air above it were never still... ever.

Strallan took a deep breath and looked over the side of the bridge. The water beneath was like a millpond. There was not the slightest ebb and flow. In fact, the water did not look liquid at all: it was dull and grey and lifeless. He had never seen it look like that before. Strallan stopped and placed his hand on one of the wall's capping stones.

He thought he felt a rumble under his feet, and he looked up as the cart with its strange beasts of burden shimmied onto the bridge, hissing slightly as it displaced yet more sand.

He thought it odd that he should feel the movement of the cart on a solid, stone bridge. He thought it odd that he should hear the strange *shushing* sound of sand being displaced from several yards away, over what should have been the everyday breath of the air, the lap of the water around the abutments, and the sounds of other traffic crossing the bridge. Then the stone under his hand began to shift and crumble.

Strallan was terrified. He was so afraid that he was rooted to the spot. He could not move his feet or remove his hand from where it lay on top of the bridge wall. He could not blink or peel his eyes away from the stone flags that made up the surface of the road beneath his feet, the road that the cart wheels were traversing, spewing and shifting their little drifts and wakes of sand along as they went.

His mouth was dry.

This much fear should have generated a drenching sweat, but there was nothing. His brow, his armpits, his palms, were all dry.

It was only after the cart had passed that Strallan was able to blink and turn his head. He watched the cart as it trundled away, his gaze homing in on the strange earthenware jars that stood in rows on the back of the vehicle with their wax seals in the shape of snakes and strange insects that he did not recognise.

When the cart dipped below the apex of the bridge and began its descent down the slope and into the north side of the city, the distant whisper of shifting sand disappeared in favour of a sound much closer to the boy. It was the sound of trickling sand.

The capping stone felt gritty under Strallan's palm, and he lifted his hand to find it covered in a layer of sandstone dust as if the bridge were corroding before his very eyes. Then he looked down to see that the mortar holding the stones together had ceased to adhere, and was drying and crumbling away. The trickling sound was of the dry, dusty mortar falling away from the joints and collecting around the boy's feet.

Surn Strallan was as afraid as he had ever been. He did not know what was happening, but he knew that they should have prevented the cart from entering the great city of Nuln, while they had the chance. He knew that he had not done his job, that his sergeant had not done his job. He could not go back there. It was too late.

Surn Strallan drew together what little courage he had left and was determined to take his fears to the city guards. He didn't know whether they would believe him. He didn't know how he would make them believe him, but he knew that he must try to make them understand.

The cart was strange, far too strange and threatening for one boy to comprehend on his own. It was from another world, a world that he did not understand. It filled him with fear and loathing, and with trepidation and dread.

He had tried to tell his boss that something was wrong, and nothing had come of it, except that now he was alone in the city with his fears. It was up to him to find someone who would listen to him, who would allay his fears, and who would fight for his city.

Everything was up to Surn Strallan, and the boy wasn't sure whether he was man enough for the task.

Strallan took a deep breath, rubbed his hands together to get rid of as much of the sandy stone grit as he could, waited for a minute or two to make sure that the cart had passed out of view, and then made a dash for the far side of the Great Bridge. He did not know which direction the cart would take, but he knew that he wouldn't have to encounter it again on his way across the city to one of the watch houses.

The Bridge watch house was one of the toughest in Nuln. The walled city was well protected and most of the inner-city watch houses did little more than deal with day-to-day policing matters. The Bridge Watch was different.

The Bridge Watch dealt with everything and everyone that came through the northern docks. The guards didn't just deal with petty crime and domestic disputes; they dealt with smuggling, racketeering and duty evasion; they dealt with merchant seamen and stevedores, and their drinking and brawling, not to mention their illicit trade in contraband and their whoring. They also dealt with insurrection and terrorism and other genuine threats to the security of the city and the safety of its inhabitants.

Surn Strallan couldn't decide whether this was a good thing, or a bad thing. He wasn't at all sure whether he would be taken seriously, and if he were taken seriously, and the Bridge Watch went after the strangers and their cart, he wasn't at all sure just how extreme their actions might turn out to be.

On the other hand, if Strallan was forced to turn right off the Great Bridge and find his way to the Handelbezirk Watch, there was a chance he could persuade them to do something. He had a cousin on the squad, even though he didn't like him very much, and wouldn't trust him further than he could throw him.

Handelbezirk was a mid-rent area of the city and when times were good it thrived peacefully enough. Since the famine had begun to take hold, it had become a sullen, grubbing place full of dissatisfaction and petulance. Strallan often thought that he preferred the truly poor and bereft, who seemed to have more spirit in their tired bones, who complained less and helped each other out when it was needed. This miserable lot only seemed to gripe behind each other's backs and snipe to each other's faces. There wasn't much crime, but what there was tended to be spiteful and destructive, mostly vandalism and domestic violence.

Even with a relation who might be willing to stand up for him, Strallan doubted whether the guards at the Handelbezirk watch house would take him seriously or be willing to spend any time or energy investigating one cart with its odd-shaped cargo and its rows of clay jars.

He was damned either way, but he had to do something.

As he stepped off the Great Bridge, Surn Strallan looked to the left, and then to the right, and shuddered. He didn't know whether he was shuddering because he'd spotted the cart driving out along the dock towards Kleinmoot, or because seeing it going in that direction meant that he had no choice but to turn left and make his way along Siden Strasse to the Bridge watch house.

Fithvael stepped deftly. He didn't quite cross the mouth of the alley, but hugged the shadows of the far wall, the west wall of a tall building two-thirds of the way down Hauptstrasse. It had been a beautifully kept emporium trading in antiques, but without regular custom it appeared to have been closed for some time, although the windows onto the street were obviously still cleaned regularly, so someone had some hope of business improving again, one day.

Surn Strallan stopped before he reached the entrance to the alley, and looked around.

It had been a long day. It had been a very long day, and he began to wonder when he had decided it was a good idea to follow the strange man. It was the looking. It was all the looking, and the mortar. That was what had drawn him. Besides, he couldn't bear to follow the strange cart after what had begun to happen on the Great Bridge, and he hadn't been able to make anybody at the watch house listen to him.

First, his superior on the South Gate had waved the cart through with barely a glance. He'd let Strallan follow it, but that was an indulgence, and a way of keeping the boy busy. He was more trouble than he was worth; he'd known from the start that being conscientious wouldn't get him very far, his cousin in the Handelbezirk watch house had warned him of that, but he didn't seem able to help himself. This strange, tall, slender, old man seemed conscientious. He looked at things, examined them, and he was methodical and meticulous. Strallan had noticed it immediately, and he liked those things about the stranger. Those things made him feel safe.

The guards at the Bridge watch house hadn't made him feel safe at all. They hadn't wanted to listen to him. They hadn't wanted to talk to him, and when he hadn't taken the hint, they'd laughed him out of the watch house. Anyone who could bully a merchant seaman willing to trade contraband on the north docks of Nuln wasn't going to take any nonsense from a raw recruit who belonged to a gate unit, and a second rate, poorly regarded gate unit at that. Strallan had left with his tail between his legs, a bruised jaw and the feeling that he ought to have known better.

Where had the strange fellow disappeared to?

Strallan took a step or two back the way he had come, and then stepped off the kerb and looked across the street, but the foot traffic was light, and there was no sign of the man in the hooded cloak. The boy reasoned that the man he was following must simply have quickened his pace, and so he hopped back onto the narrow pavement and continued on his way.

One arm came across Strallan's body and the other hand around his face so quickly that he didn't have time to draw breath, let alone scream, despite the fact that a stabbing pain shot through his jaw where he'd been thumped by the watch guard.

Strallan felt tears stinging his widening eyes, but when it came time for the drops to form in the corners of his eyes, nothing happened. In practice, he'd always managed to bite the hand that attacked him, but life wasn't like practice, and the hand holding his face felt like it had the tensile strength of a steel gauntlet without the unwieldiness.

Strallan tried to throw an elbow and defend himself that way, but the arm around his body pinned both of his elbows to his sides, and he couldn't move at all. Then he realised that the grip on his torso was so firm that he couldn't feel his hands properly, that his arms were very nearly numb, and that he really didn't have any room to inhale.

Strallan began to panic.

Just how strong was his assailant?

Then he remembered that he had legs.

He'd been pulled, bodily, into the alley, and he'd been virtually lifted off his feet in the fray, so all he'd been able to do was pinwheel his lower limbs, hitting empty air and scuffing the rough, uneven, cobbled surface of the alley with his boots. His attacker had placed him back on his feet, though, once he'd pulled him off the street, so, standing firm, Strallan had one last chance to fight back.

There was no point bringing a knee up, as his attacker still stood behind him, so Strallan tried throwing a heel backwards, hoping to drive it into a shin or groin. His foot went nowhere.

The man standing behind him was only as wide as he was, albeit he seemed to loom over him, so was clearly very much taller, but he seemed to be hewn not from human flesh but from something altogether firmer, stronger, less yielding, more… more…

Then it spoke.

'Calm down,' it said in the strangest accent. Its tone was light and calm and almost lyrical. It was a tuneful, musical, beautiful voice.

Surn would have felt his body relax, instinctively, had he been able to breathe.

Chapter 29

Fithvael felt the young man's body respond to his voice, and he relaxed the muscles in his left arm, which was wrapped all the way around the boy, his hand grasping Strallan's right forearm.

'Breathe.'

Surn took one short, shallow breath, breathed out a sigh of relief, and then filled his lungs.

Fithvael could feel the boy shaking slightly in his grasp, and made sure he held him upright so that he didn't fall in a faint, but not so firmly that he could not breathe. He must find out the boy's intentions, but he didn't want to do him any harm. This was one of very few people in the city who seemed really alive and engaged with the world. The elf was concerned that the majority of the people of Nuln seemed to take no heed of their surroundings; they seemed to walk around in a daze, as if there were nothing left worth fighting for, as if their lives were already over. They were like the dead walking.

'Don't move,' said Fithvael. 'Breathe.' He knew that the youngest members of the youngest races were always the most suggestible, and that a little magic can go a long way, so he used his knowledge to exert what mind control he could over the human youth to manage the situation. The last thing he wanted to do was hurt him.

Surn Strallan breathed in another deep breath. He wasn't quite sure what was happening to him, but he was aware that any panic he might have felt had entirely left his body. He still didn't know who had attacked him or what his assailant wanted from him, but he was no longer afraid of the tall, hard-bodied man who still held him in his muscular, martial embrace.

'Now tell me,' said Fithvael. 'Why are you following me?'

'It's the stuff you're looking at,' said Strallan. 'The bugs... They look like bugs, and snakes. What are those things? Why are you looking at them? Why are they on the jars on the back of that cart?'

'What cart?' asked Fithvael, his voice rising closer to its natural pitch as his guard dropped and his interest rose.

'The sand,' said Strallan. 'What's with all the sand?'

'I'm going to let go of you,' said Fithvael, 'and you're not going to run. Do you understand?'

'Why would I run?' asked Strallan. 'Something's happening, and you're the first one to take me seriously.'

'You understand?' asked Fithvael again.

'I understand,' said Surn Strallan, sighing deeply with a relief that he had no idea he would feel. 'I don't know what I understand, but as sure as Ulric's my god and the Knights of

the White Wolf are his martial lords of the Empire, I understand something.'

The streets of Nuln did not bustle. They did not throng. As
dawn turned to morning, people began to move around,
leaving their homes for their places of work, entering or
leaving the city as the routines of their lives dictated, going
about their business, but they did so with a lack of energy or
purpose born of too many seasons of want and deprivation.

The cart had travelled for days, weeks, months, grinding
out the miles, crossing the deserts of the Southlands, rolling ever northwards, skirting seas, scaling mountains, taking
no heed of the rising and setting of the sun, the waxing and
waning of the moons or the changing positions of the stars
in the night skies.

The travellers had one will, one purpose, one task to perform. They pushed the burden of the vehicle on the quietest
roads, through the loneliest regions of the most barren lands.
They had no reason to draw attention to their mission, no
desire to commingle. They were at the mercy of no mortal
functions, and heeded not the time that passed. It was as
nothing to them.

They neither ate nor slept, nor sweated nor defecated.
They did not drink so had no need to follow watercourses
or streams as other travellers must, and they did not breathe.
They did not communicate one with another. They were of
one purpose, and that purpose was all and everything to each
of them and to all of them, and it required no discussion
and no agreement. They needed nothing from one another,
practically, materially, spiritually or emotionally.

They were automata, but they were not machines. They
were beings, but they were not living.

Before they entered the South Gate of the city of Nuln, they had encountered nothing and no one that had stood in the way of their progress, by design, because of the routes that they travelled, and by the unbending nature of their intent.

It was nothing and everything to them to slice a carotid, pierce a femoral, gouge an iliac: always the arteries. When there had still been humans in the Southlands, that had been their pleasure. It had always been blood and sand, sand and blood: sand in all its perfect forms, and arterial blood, blazing hot and flaming red like the sun setting on the desert horizon. Only bloodless did a human body become something they recognised, only naked of its flesh could it be considered clean, and only clean could it be immortal. Dirt and death were the same. Heat and liquid, and food and faeces, were the same as dirt, were the same as death, were the essence of mortal life and the scourge of eternal life.

Once they entered the city of Nuln, whatever the temptations, however repellent the sounds and smells of meagre human life, however badly the three beings accompanying the cart wanted to shed the blood of the filthy mortal beings, however driven they were to disembowel and eviscerate the humans, cleansing and rebirthing them, purifying and sterilising, and desiccating and immortalising, they must cleave to their mission, and they must not falter.

They entered by the South Gate, apparently without incident. They did not even have to stop the cart. They did not have to look at the guards, despite being the only vehicle on the road, and potentially vulnerable. They kept their hoods up and their heads down, and they trundled on. They did not increase their speed, nor did they slow their pace. They were, if their minds comprehended such a concept, nonchalant, insouciant even. They were strangers, but they acted with the sort of composure that made them seem harmless, beyond reproach.

They did not see Surn Strallan's reaction to their entrance to the city, to the sand that gathered in the creases of his boots, and if they had noticed him following them, they would not have considered the boy a threat. They might have cut an artery because they could, but not because he forced their hands, not because they must.

There had been only one mistake on the road to the Great Bridge. They had not been prepared for the child.

The sand was their power, their magic. They needed the sand; they could not do without it. Where they travelled, it travelled in their wake. There was no halting its flow unless the cart halted, and when its wheels rolled once more, the sands trickled anew. They did not see the child sitting on the kerbstone. They did not see it because of its small size. They did not see it because of its utter lack of significance to them. They did not see its naked hands and feet. They did not know how susceptible it would be to the sands of time when they came into contact with its skin, when it breathed in their dusty particles.

The cart did not stop, and its beasts of burden and its lead man did not speak one to another. They did not need to speak to know that they were in accord. They could not counter a commotion. They could not reason away a death by desiccation. They could not justify the presence of the sand. They could only keep moving.

They must cross the Great Bridge, thankful that so few people were yet moving around the city, and then they would take the back roads and wider alleys. They would come into contact with fewer people. The few people they would come into contact with in the more private, hidden parts of the city, they would encounter more closely, fatally closely, perhaps, but there would be no more accidents. They would take control.

The cart turned right immediately after crossing the Great Bridge, instead of heading north along the main thoroughfare of Emmanuelplatz. When he caught sight of the Feierplatz opening up in front of him, and a small, but not insignificant number of people beginning to gather there, the leader of the trio signalled a left and drove them up the alley behind the Church of the Drunken where they encountered only the comatose forms of a pair of inebriated beggars in their squalor. The sand that rolled up to them, nestling in a drift against the backs of the legs of one of the pair, looked dense and grey in the dark shadow of the tall, black stone church, more like ash than sand. As the cart rolled on, and the man closest to the wall groaned and tried to turn over, the mortar between the stones above him began to trickle free of its joints, landing in gritty patches on his upturned face, making him spit and cough and choke.

The cart crossed Emmanuelplatz between the Dragon on one side of the thoroughfare and the Cooked Goose on the other. The smell of sex and secretions emanated from the first and cooked grease from the other, and the three strangers were reminded, once again, of the very earthbound nature of the beings that inhabited this great city that had once thrived under their great auspices. Not this city, but another like it, another on this site, straddling this great river, during an era when water had done more than measure the passage of time, during an era that lived beyond the memories even of these immortals. Not this city, although this Nuln still bore the marks of what had gone before, still wore the signs, still carried the totems and, by extension, a little of their magic, some memory of what had once been.

As tall and imposing as he was, the lead figure got a view across the corner of Reik Platz where the domestic barter market was in full swing, or what passed for full swing this season. Conversations were muted. No one wanted to haggle, and bartering had become popular again where need had supplanted greed. Trade was done for necessities. There was no frivolity. There were no luxuries, and trade took time. No one wanted to waste energy on too much talk or too heated an argument, but everyone wanted to secure what they needed, while only parting with what they could manage without. Everything was a trade-off and no trade-off seemed favourable to anyone.

The cart did not falter or linger, it merely trundled onwards at the same pace, at the same rate, never hesitating, its wheels turning and turning, and never ceasing. It turned corners without stopping or even seeming to slow down, and when it came time to cross a street there simply appeared to be a natural gap in whatever traffic there might be. The sand shushed and hissed, and shushed, and spread in its wake from the tall, hard wheels of the cart, and the beasts of burden continued their work, relentlessly, without tiring, without stopping, without talking.

They encountered no one as they traversed the north side of the Drog Strasse. The public spaces, once green and pleasant, had grown so depressingly beige that the few children who had been born or had managed to survive over the past few years were not taken there by their mothers to play, although their mothers had been taken there to play by their own dames only a score of years before.

The leader had chosen to cross north of the Drog Strasse because he could smell the testosterone of the guards of the Bridge Watch only a few hundred yards away on the other side of the park. It smelled stronger in their blood, sweat and waste than anything else, and smelled more pungently of mortality than any other physique composition known to the most famous anatomists of the Empire, currently resident at the city's university.

It was not difficult to avoid.

The cart turned right, where it must, at Rillingheim Platz adjacent to the Cartwright's Guild.

If they had been sentient, like men, the strangers might have understood the irony.

The cart that they had laboured to propel the thousands of miles and the hundreds of days from the depths of the Southlands through the Empire to the city of Nuln, with all the attendant privations – not that these undead automata registered want or need or desire in the fleshly, physical ways that mortals must – did not require repairs. The wheels had never, in all that time, after all those miles, required the services of a cartwright. The wheels ground the sands of time and the sands honed the wheels, and this perfect marriage kept the cart rolling interminably.

This was the end of their journey.

Against the south-west wall of the university, where human seed was spread and lost, and, at various intervals found a tenuous hold in one or other of the women that serviced the richer students and the academics, at the brothel of the Beloved Verena, the three strangers and their burden came to rest.

They drove the last few yards of their journey beneath the archway into the yard at the rear of the narrow building that not only hugged the high wall of the university, but penetrated it, the only unofficial entrance to the hallowed halls of one of the greatest educational establishments of the Empire.

The beasts of burden with their bound extremities almost did not know how to stop. The wheels of the cart almost did not stop. The yoke of the cart met the wall of the yard and the wheels kept spinning, and the sand kept hissing and shushing, and collecting in a wake until it was so deep that the wheels were buried to their hubs in sand and could no longer move.

The cart was immovable, solid, as if it had been there for a hundred years or a thousand, and the true work of the three strangers and the cargo that the cart had carried so far for so long was about to begin.

The seventeen women and two boys who worked in the bawdy house were dead within moments, none of them knowing what had hit them, all dying quickly, spraying arterial blood in all directions. Bodies desiccated fast under the influence of the magic brought by the strangers, and breathless silence reigned as they went to work.

The smallest of them removed his outer garments to reveal his bindings and his skeleton beneath, older than time, whiter than bone-white with a girdle of gold, decorated with turquoise scarabs, slung around his pelvis.

The second of them, obviously female, if it should matter at all, despite the structure of her bones being somewhat larger, also removed her outer coverings. Her hands and feet unencumbered by layers of rags, she moved swiftly and easily, adjusted the twin sigils of scorpion and locust on her ornamental breastplate, and joined her comrade.

Just as their pace on the road had been methodical and rhythmic, their movements unloading the jars from the back of the cart were meticulous and economical. Their strides were deliberate. There were no false steps, no half-swings. They did not falter, but were determined, as if every movement were inevitable, programmed eons ago, before the beginnings of time, as if the order of things were predestined.

The jars were taken one in each hand, hoisted one onto each shoulder, walked across the yard into the bawdy house, and taken directly down into the cellar where they were racked and shelved.

The tallest of the strangers, who had led the cart, had not yet disrobed, but he had swept the shelves clear of the supplies that had been racked there with one great sweep of his staff. Provisions lay in a heap on the floor, some of the jars broken and spilled, the last of the preserved and cured meats and pickled eggs already desiccating in the drying air. Soon there would be nothing but dust where they had been.

The greying cloth that wrapped the end of the staff caught on a nail in one of the shelves, and the bandage-wrapped finger bones grasped the haft harder, pulling to free it. The cloth uncurled and, once free, unwound in a long, lazy spiral that fell silently to the floor.

The staff was more than just a walking stick. It was also an impressive bladed weapon and some sort of religious artefact. The curved blade that made up the top third of the staff appeared to be made of solid gold, its honed edge glinting in what little light penetrated the darkness of the cool cellar. Hieroglyphics were carved into the inside of the curve, and a series of spikes crowned the anterior edge. The haft of the weapon appeared to be made from the long bone of some massive, but fine-boned animal, although it was impossible to tell what creature it might have come from. A long, horn-shaped hook was attached to the other end of the haft, making for a double-ended weapon that could prove spectacularly dangerous when wielded by an experienced combatant.

As the two Tomb Guards placed the last of the jars with their strange markings and their ancient wax seals on the shelves in the cool cellar, the Liche Priest divested himself of his robes and bindings, flexed his back and chest, rose to his full, impressive height, and wielded his staff, curving it in a two-handed arc into the brick wall at the rear of the cellar.

Every brick in the wall had been marked, each one cut into with a chisel, and carved with a sigil: a symbol of a winged scarab or a scuttling one, of a locust or a scorpion or an arachnid, or of a serpent or a hooded snake. The mortar between the bricks, solid only hours before, had been trickling away ever since the cart had wheeled into the yard and locked itself in place with the spinning of the irrevocable sands of time. When the heavy, blunt, rear edge of the blade connected with the centre of the wall, the bricks flew back into the room in all directions, rather than going with the direction of the force of the blow. The Liche Priest stood his ground, and none of the spiralling, revolving bricks hit him, but the Tomb Guards ducked, spreading their feet wide, so that they could lunge and dive away from the flying bricks without falling. Golden light poured from the cavity beyond the bricks, beams of it following the trajectories of the bricks as they began to bounce off the three remaining walls of the room beneath the recently vacated bawdy house.

The room beyond the bawdy-house cellar, the secret room buried beneath the University of Nuln, long forgotten, if it had ever been known of by the human inhabitants of that fair city, was as it should be, was as it had been left, was as they remembered it. A great golden plinth, which appeared to grow seamlessly out of the floor, and which was producing the golden illumination, stood at the centre of the room, oriented north to south. The walls were studded with turquoise

and gold, and bone-white and arterial blood-red, and the
same motifs occurred over and over again in various combi-
nations. Along the south wall a series of ornate gold sconces,
each with a carved sigil, held an ancient banner stained with
the dust of ages and of battles long ago fought and forgotten.
The room was part shrine and last resting place, but there
was one final rite to perform, a final rite that the Liche Priest
had returned to complete.

He took his position at the north end of the plinth, the
head, and waited.

He waited while the Tomb Guards returned to the cart. He
waited while they relieved the vehicle of its final burden, and
he waited while they returned to the shrine room with it.

The Liche Priest waited while the Tomb Guards placed the
sarcophagus gently but squarely on the plinth, its head at the
north end, its feet at the south. Then he waited while they
took up their positions, the male guard at the left shoulder
of the casket and the female guard at the right.

Still the Southlanders made no sound. The Tomb Guards
did not breathe heavily under the weight of their burden,
since the weight was as nothing to them, and there was no
reason for them to breathe. There was no gasp of wonder
or surprise, since they felt nothing so prosaic as wonder,
and, besides, there was no need for them to breathe. Their
understanding of their situation was complete. It was so old,
so well learned that there was no need for them to speak,
one to another, of any of it. Everything had gone to plan,
because the plan was too old, too honed, too irrefutable, too
unalterable.

The three companions had been together since long before
leaving the Southlands, and that had been long ago indeed,
and not a single word had passed between them since before

they had loaded the cart. There was no need for words. There should never be a need for any one of them to utter a word to any other of them.

There were rituals to perform, and many of those were wordless, too, but where words were required they would be articulated unerringly correctly through long knowledge of them, through millions of silent repetitions in the memory of the individual who would eventually bear the privilege of their utterance. Nothing more was required or desirable. Nothing more would add to the mission, and what did not add could only detract from the outcomes.

Mondelblatt had never had so many bodies in his room all at once. He never took more than two students for a tutorial in his study at any one time, and his colleagues had never cleaved to him very readily. He rather relished filling his rooms with so many people, so many people that he could think of as 'young', because they were strong and upright and quick of mind and straight of back, despite their bone ages, and so many of them Gilead's kind.

The study was a busy place, stacked with books and papers and with the timepieces, the hourglasses that the professor had begun to collect when he had first taken an interest in sand and time, not very long after he had gained tenure at the university.

They had quickly realised that there was no room to spread out, and had decided that the bed was the best place to examine Fithvael's findings. The old elf stood at the foot of the bed, smoothed the counterpane and spread out his street map with all its annotations. If Nuln were to be visited by a plague of insects, of arachnids and of serpents, the map showed where they would strike.

Surn Strallan stood nervously with his back flat against the door that led from the study out onto the staircase and, from there, to the communal and public areas of the university. He kept his hand firmly on the door knob at the small of his back so that he could be the first to escape, watching the others through the wide-open bedroom door.

Fithvael had managed to keep him fairly calm, using the trick with his voice, but now he was in the room adjacent to where the very strange, elderly professor was holding court. Academic types had always been a mystery to Strallan, and what's more, had been held up to him throughout his childhood, not only as the worst examples of the boogieman, but as the stuff of genuine nightmares, the sort that could come true at any moment. Under any other circumstances being in close proximity to an elderly, barely-continent academic would have been Surn Strallan's worst nightmare. Today, he had gone up against the Bridge Watch and had his face punched and his arse kicked, he had witnessed the infiltration of his beloved city by an undead host and he was talking tactics with a family of elves. Still, he wondered whether Professor Mondelblatt didn't pose the worst threat to his immediate safety.

Surn Strallan was pretty convinced that he was going to die. He wasn't sure whether he was simply going to fall down dead, because there was nothing else for it, or whether the events of the day marked the end of the world as he, or for that matter anyone else, knew it. It didn't matter; he remained convinced that he was going to die.

Then something happened.

Suddenly, everything seemed to go very quiet.

Gilead, for that was what the head elf was called, raised his head from where he was scrutinising Fithvael's map, to look around the room, his unblinking eyes penetrating every corner, every nook and cranny. Then he stepped back into the study. He looked at Strallan, and then walked over to the table full of hourglasses in the alcove.

Silence had fallen when the hourglasses had all run out of sand. All of the hourglasses had run out of sand at the very same moment.

Gilead raised the index finger of his right hand and pressed it against the empty glass bulb in the top half of one of the hourglasses. It swung slightly in its frame, but the elf did not put enough pressure on it to turn it over and begin the sands of time moving again.

Then the faint sound of moving sand could be heard. The shushing and hissing of trickling sand began to fill the room. Gilead looked at Strallan, and Strallan shrugged. All of the sand in all of the hourglasses had collected in the bottom bulbs. They were all dormant, all still. The passage of time had stopped. The sound of sand was not coming from the hourglasses.

Everyone was still for several long moments. Only the sound of their breathing, Mondelblatt's shallow wheeze and Strallan's rapid gasping racing away from the elves' slow, steady respiration, was audible over the faint trickling swish of falling sand.

'Look!' said Laban, pointing at the sill below the bedroom window.

'They are here,' said Mondelblatt. 'The boy was right. The cart is what we dreaded it might be.'

'They are in the city,' said Fithvael.

'Worse than that,' said Gilead. 'They have begun their work.'

Sand gathered slowly on the sill, and trickled gradually over its edge, falling onto the floor and forming a shallow ridge on the rug below, not so much a line in the sand as a line *of* sand.

'What… is… it?' asked Surn Strallan.

Mondelblatt looked at him and smiled.

'Didn't you know?' he asked. 'Glass is made of the sands of time, too. Dust to dust… ashes to ashes. Sand to glass… and back to sand.'

Chapter 30

This talk of sand makes me thirsty, and the sands of time continue to shift under me. I fear that my time is running out, that it *has* run out. All my hours and days are borrowed now, so let me borrow a little more of yours to get me to the end of this tale.

Lubricate my throat with a cup more of that good wine I know you keep below stairs, and I will round off this tale in the best way I know how, weaving the strands together one last time for this, my last audience, my final tale-telling.

I relish it, but my throat is parched, as parched as that boy's was in the professor's study high in the college rooms in the University of Nuln. He's dead, too, of course. I would have loved to have heard this story from his lips. He told it like no other, they say... But I am getting ahead of myself.

I'll give the ending away if I'm not careful, and all a story-teller has, in the end, is the care with which he tells his tale, and the climax he reaches in its telling. When it is his last tale, the one by which he will be forever remembered, then care in the telling must be paramount.

Good, my glass is full once more. Now draw a sip yourself; I should spill such a full cup before it reaches my lips with my unsteady hand.

Enough, enough, any more and you'll drain the cup. The rest is mine, just as the rest of this story is yours, yours to treasure or repeat, or to do with as you will. Only, do this last thing for me: remember it, and in remembering it, remember who told it to you. It's a wondrous tale, however badly an old bard recites it.

Laban raised his fingers and placed them on one of the small panes of glass high up in the bedroom window. It was as fragile as a sheet of spun sugar, so fine that it could not be measured with precision callipers, but finer than a baby's hair, certainly. It disintegrated almost before his fingers touched it, and he was left with a residue of the finest dust, like a pale yellow powder filling the whorls of his fingerprints.

'It moved,' said Surn Strallan.

The sound of his voice made everyone else in the room turn to him, and he wondered whether he could bear the gaze of so many extraordinary eyes upon him. He wanted, very badly, to blink, but found that he could not, dared not. If he blinked then he would die. If he breathed, he would die. He was going to die... He was going to die.

When he blinked, he noticed that his eyes felt very dry, and when he spoke, he noticed that his tongue felt like sandpaper against his lips and teeth and the roof of his mouth.

'I thought the carvings on the things moved,' he said,

gesturing, weakly, with one limp hand, at the table with the hourglasses on it. 'That isn't possible, is it?'

Mondelblatt looked at Strallan and made an odd, strangled noise in the back of his throat. The boy was suddenly less afraid that he was going to die and more afraid that he would find himself in a room with a dead professor, which was, in actual fact, a bigger nightmare than being in a room with a live professor. Mondelblatt noticed the boy's disquiet.

'Don't you recognise a dying man's laugh?' he asked, laughing again, and choking horribly.

Strallan said nothing. He did not like the old man, and of all things, preferred not to engage with him.

'You watch glass spontaneously turn to sand, and you wonder what remains to be proven impossible,' said Mondelblatt. 'Strange boy. A pragmatist of a sort, I suppose, but odd, nevertheless.'

Laban and Fithvael crossed to the alcove with its table of hourglasses, and picked one up, each. The one in Laban's hand disintegrated. The glass, by the same strange alchemy as the window glass, returned to its natural state, and the sand poured down his clothes and onto his boots. He shook it off in disgust, and tossed away the plain, brass frame that had housed the timepiece.

Fithvael had picked up a larger, heavier piece, and something very strange did seem to be happening to the ornate, carved frame. It was made of what looked like bone, and was carved with winged scarabs and serpents twined around the tops and bottoms of the columns, rendered in mirror images of each other, that stood at the four corners of the timepiece, connecting the bases. This hourglass was of a particularly ancient type that had to be turned over, entirely, rather than the bulbs being simply rotated in a static frame with a constant top and a constant bottom.

Fithvael thought about what Mondelblatt had said before, about ashes and dust and sand. The hourglass was large and heavy. The glass was very old and very thick, but, because it had spent hundreds or thousands of years in motion, the glass had never sunk, as old pane glass did, which was always thicker at the bottom than at the top, where gravity had been able to act on the dense liquid over protracted periods of time. This glass was of equal thickness, of equal density throughout.

It was rare glass and extremely beautiful.

Fithvael looked at it as he held it in his hands.

He thought to turn it over. He thought to start the sands of time moving once more. He thought to break whatever spell had been cast.

Could it really be as simple as that? Could he stop what had been begun?

Gilead looked to Fithvael, and then to Laban and Mondelblatt. They knew what he was going to do.

Surn Strallan took a little longer to realise what was about to happen.

Surn Strallan was more afraid than he had ever thought possible, and, very probably, more afraid than all the other people present in the professor's rooms put together.

Then he saw something.

He didn't know whether he saw it because he saw it, or whether he saw it because he had lost his mind, but he could not help himself. He had to speak.

'There!' he said. 'It moved.'

All over the city of Nuln things began to stir, small things, almost imperceptible things. It began with a winged insect hovering around the head of a child in the Reik Platz. He swatted at it happily, playing with it, not sure how to identify this kind of creature that he had never seen before in his short life.

The bright-green, iridescent wings buzzed in the air, humming as the bug, as big as the boy's hand, avoided the child's reach, circled, made figures of eight around his father's sloping shoulders, and then flew up into the sky and headed towards the university.

It was a locust, and had emerged from a street sign just north of the Commercial Way and west of the Town Hall.

The adults close to the child were so intent on their business and so subdued by their circumstances that they failed to notice the oddity. When he spoke of it later, the boy got a scolding from his mother and a clipped ear from his father for telling lies, serious lies in such terrible times, but he had seen it, and he knew that he had.

The long line of scarab beetles that walked the length of Hauptstrasse, end to end, in the ridge of the gutter, went entirely unnoticed and unmolested.

The serpents that uncoiled from the street lamps along the Wandstrasse, found their way underground via the storm drains and run-off grilles that punctuated the wider streets, and no one noticed that they were missing from the castings on the lamps, or from the wrought-iron grilles or from the carvings on foundation stones and boot scrapers, door furniture and street furniture, shop signs and architectural ornamentation.

Bugs and beasts and reptiles gathered and collected in swarms and slithers and clouds, unheeded, unnoticed.

They knew not that they had been dormant, trapped in stone and iron, in wood and words, in paint and pictures.

They knew not what or where they were. They knew only that they were newly awake, and that they had been awakened with a purpose, and they knew what that purpose was and why, and they knew who and what they served, and they questioned it not.

The wind did not blow through the city as it should, and the Reik did not flow as it always had.

The people had learned not to talk of the famine, of the plague, whatever it might be. It had been going on for too long, it had been too hard. They had lost their old and their young, and the children had stopped coming and the creatures were all dead. The gardens did not grow, food was bland and dry and unappetising, and all anyone could do was survive. There was nothing to talk about, nothing to celebrate. When there is nothing to live for, life is no longer cause for celebration on its own.

Everyone felt the stillness. Everyone felt that the air was too dry, and everyone saw that the water was too dull and too still, and no one talked about it. They believed, and they assumed what their neighbours believed, that this was just the next phase, that this was what they were used to, that this was attrition. Nothing need be said.

Mothers noticed that their fractious children produced no tears, no stringy snot, no drool. They noticed that their thirst was unquenchable and that they rubbed red and sore their dust-dry eyes. Their skin had lost its plumpness, and cheeks pinched in an attempt at good humour remained sunken for too long.

When they looked at their hands, the few women who had clung to any shred of vanity wondered why their skin looked so dry and old, and why their nails were so ridged and flaking. They wondered why their hair frizzed and flew away, despite there being no wind to catch it. They wondered why their gums seemed to have shrunk and their teeth to have spread. They looked at their reflections and touched their faces, and wondered why they looked so damned old.

The men wondered why they didn't sweat or piss, and why, when they blinked, their eyes were sore. They wondered where they'd get their next drink to soothe their parched mouths and throats.

They should have done more than wonder.

They should have gathered or rallied. They should have evacuated or battened down the hatches. They should have hidden or defended themselves. They did none of those things. They had not the will.

They did not look down at the black carapaced scarabs, or up at the iridescent wings of the locusts. They did not notice the absence of the symbols, sigils and totems that were suddenly missing from where they had long been carved, embossed and painted. They saw nothing, because they had not the energy to see.

The war of attrition was over, and they had already lost.

The Liche Priest, his staff held vertically in front of him, spoke. The words were unlike anything a human had ever heard and lived to tell of. The sounds held no real breath, nothing honestly inhaled and warmed by the flesh of a body and exhaled, nothing deoxygenated. The sounds, for they could hardly be described as words, seemed not to begin or end in any meaningful way. Where no vocal cords exist or where they are desiccated to the consistency of the cat-gut used by the poorest of luthiers on the cheapest of their instruments, it is hard to imagine anything more than a squawk or a rasp. When the instrument is a fleshless hollow of ancient bone, and the gut and sinew of the strings are as if they had been left in the desert for a thousand years to harden and tighten, it is difficult to imagine any cadence or rhythm in the vocal instrument, any passion or fervour, any intonation, anything that might resemble a speech pattern.

The only advantage the Liche Priest had, and it was small enough, was that his cranium and chest cavities were remarkably large, and the mechanism he used to move air across his hardened tissues generated a frequency that, while the sound was discordant and layered in the strangest way, was, at least, tuned low, rather than shrill.

Noises emanated from the Liche Priest's skeleton, not just from his wide-open mouth, but leaking out in thrums and whistles from anywhere that bones and sinews met in configurations that allowed sounds to be generated. As they came, the air in the cellar began to move, slowly whipping a dust cloud out of the mortar that had been lost from the wall dividing this room from the one below the bawdy house.

The dust scoured the walls of the room, generating more particles. It swept over and around the fallen bricks, corroding them in mere minutes, and those motes and specks joined the sandstorm that was powering around the room blasting all of the surfaces, including the bones of the three figures present.

The Liche Priest continued with his incantations as the storm raged around him. The displacement of air in the room adding to the volume and intensity of his words as they swept through his chest cavity and out through his mouth, between his ribs, squeezing between the vertebrae of his spine, squeaking and squealing like a badly played violcello string, squawking and spitting like the ill-judged breath of a beginner trying to master a reed instrument.

The words ended. The Liche Priest closed his mouth, but the squeals and squawks continued on, supplemented by similar sounds made by the configurations of bones and connective tissues of the two Tomb Guards, the differences in their bodies evident in the tonal qualities of the sounds they produced.

The Liche Priest raised both of his arms high in the air, his staff wielded firmly in his right hand. The wind that had formed the sand and dust into an impenetrable cloud gathered around his figure in a tornado, and, as the air at its epicentre stilled, and as the air around it ceased to move, as all the movement was contained in that spinning vortex of gritty particulates, the sounds abated, all but the hissing and shushing of dust and sand particles moving through the air and grinding against one another.

The Liche Priest leaned out high over the sarcophagus with his staff, and the tornado travelled its length before spreading out in a low flat-bottomed cloud above the tomb, the stilled sand suspended in the air by some unearthly magic.

Utter silence prevailed once more, until the wooden outer casing of the ancient casket began to creak, its fibres so old and so dry it was held together only by the magic that suffused it. It creaked and spat like new wood being split as the lid of the vessel separated from the base and the top half levitated slowly towards the sand cloud.

The air did not move, so that no scent escaped from beneath the lid. There was no taint of the musk oils used to anoint the Tomb King, no aroma of the unguents used to prepare the skin for mummification, no scent of the bandages used to wrap the precious body.

The Liche Priest lowered his arms and slumped slightly at the shoulders as if fatigued. Then he lifted his skull once more, and his arms came up, slowly and steadily, to shoulder height, and, with them came the second lid, the top half of a second vessel, snugly fitted inside the first.

This was richly painted and ornamented in turquoise and gold, arterial blood-red and black. It was covered in elaborate hieroglyphs, but also bore images of feet and hands and a face, and was recognisably masculine, handsome, warlike. The crossed hands carried weapons, one in each hand, and elaborate armour of segmented gold and turquoise adorned the majority of the figure, including its chest and limbs.

The inner casket had been made millennia before of reed pulp, and was lightweight, but strong. The material was versatile, and could be sculpted and moulded, so more closely resembled the form of a human man than did the wooden sarcophagus that protected it.

If the body inside the sarcophagus had ever been human it had been a long time ago, a very, very long time ago, when the elves and dwarfs still ruled their corners of the world, and before mankind had prospered. If the body inside the sarcophagus had ever been human it was before the Empire had been founded and settled, in times unremembered by any human lore.

Beneath the painted casket lay a mummified body wrapped in woven layers of ancient reeds, long since dried of any moisture they once contained.

The Liche Priest lowered his arms again, but this time his shoulders and head did not drop. This time he signalled to the Tomb Guards, who stepped away from the vessel and strode back to the shelves that held the canopic jars. As they did so, the Liche Priest walked the length of the sarcophagus from head to foot, slicing his blade through the centre of the reeds. Where they were cut, the edges sprang up and separated, and began to curl away from what was beneath, as if shrinking from having been pulled too tightly across the body for too long.

When all of the canopic jars were standing on the plinth around the sarcophagus, the Liche Priest cast his arms in the direction of the painted lid, which flew across the cellar to be caught by the Tomb Guards, who placed it on the shelves. Then the wooden sarcophagus lid flew towards them, and they caught and stored that, too.

As they took up their places again, at the shoulders of the Tomb King, the Liche Priest set the sands in motion once more, this time driving them around the perimeter of the room in a great swirling stream like a swarm or a comet. He stood in its path, at the head of the opened sarcophagus and opened his mouth once more, generating a storm of sound incorporating the chanting, fluting, bellowing and squawking made by his skeleton, and the shushing, hissing and scouring noises made by the action of the sand and dust on his bones and sinews. The music, for it was a kind of extraordinary, controlled tune, however discordant, filled the room, making the walls throb, making the canopic jars vibrate.

One by one, they began to open. Some lost the mud and earth that they were sealed with. It simply disintegrated back to sand and dust, drawn to the great swirling mass of the stuff that careened around the room, finding its extraordinary path through the Liche Priest as he turned and writhed to control its path and the music he made with it. In other instances, it was the clay of the pots that desiccated first, the jars themselves that were too fragile, too friable to withstand the frequency of a particular note, and crumbled or shattered.

Whatever caused the jars to break or to open, their contents were activated by the strange magic that the Liche Priest summoned with his sands of time, and soon the room was full of more of them, more beings, more ethereal figures, more impossible, incomplete, undead warriors. They stood and turned, and they looked around. They stared down at themselves for a moment, or across at each other, and then they dressed ranks around the sarcophagus and prepared for their master to appear.

They had been waiting for a long time, but as long, as impossibly long, as it had been, they had not forgotten. They had never forgotten what they had waited for, or why they had waited. They needed no words of reminder or of explanation. One look at themselves, one look at each other, one look at the Tomb Guards standing beside them, one look at the Liche Priest, one glance at the tomb or at the Tomb King that lay within, was all that any of them needed, and they were the least of them. They were the least of them and they required no order, no command. Their purpose was clear.

The Liche Priest, all his preparatory work complete, stepped out of the swirling sandstorm that continued to chase its way around the perimeter of the room, tearing at the banners that hung in their sconces on the wall, shredding them to nothing. The chant of his mouth and the wailing of the bones and sinews of his skeleton ceased as he took his place once more at the head of the mummified body of the Tomb King.

He turned to face the sandstorm as it raged past him, and he threw back his head and thrust his arms high into the air. The rush of sand was almost deafening. The particulates collided one with another, and with the walls of the room, scouring and sanding and buffeting for all they were worth, and then the tone changed from a shushing and hissing to an odd whispered squeak. The particles of sand changed colour from yellow to green, and some changed to darker browns and even to black. They grew too, and their movement in the air slowed.

The sounds changed again to the chittering clicking of swarming insects, as wing cases buzzed and crashed, and a million insects beat a path around and around the room in a shrill cacophony. The flightless bugs, carried as far as momentum would take them, began to fall through the flying bodies of their winged cousins, dropping to the ground onto six legs or eight, springing into action: scorpions thrust their stings high over their backs and brought their great foreclaws together in threatening postures, and spiders flexed their leg joints and bobbed their abdomens, spinning silk in preparation for long climbs back to the surface of the city.

Then the locusts began to do their work. They stopped flying around the room, and began to fly into the walls of the chamber, devouring the remains of the bricks and ragstones that separated this chamber beneath the university from others, giving the Tomb King and his minions access to all the underground rooms and byways of the city of Nuln.

Chapter 31

The lecture halls were empty, as were the seminar rooms, and the studies, and the libraries. The students stayed in their rooms or in each other's rooms. They skulked nervously, unsure of where they should be. Some of the youngest and the most nervous, and some of the richest, left the city entirely, by any means they could manage. Many simply slung a few belongings onto their backs and walked out of Nuln by the nearest gates, and some found that the nearest gates were not manned.

All of the windows of the university had begun to turn to sand. The change was not visible from outside the buildings. Everything looked remarkably normal. No one glanced at the buildings, but if they did, where once they would have seen black windows, now they might see black holes where the window glass had, until very recently, been, and they would not have noticed the difference. A very keen eye might

have realised that there were no glints or reflections off the
glass, but there were no keen eyes left in Nuln, or anywhere
else in the Empire. Fatigue had set in, fatigue and dread and
apathy.

The students standing and sitting in the rooms of the university had noticed. The students sitting at their narrow desks
around the perimeter of the library, under the high windows,
had noticed when sand had begun to trickle down onto the
pages of their open books. The students sitting in tutorials
had noticed the hissing and shushing of moving sand, and
had turned when they had felt draughts on the back of their
necks from the glassless windows.

Every room in the university that had a window also
contained a pile of sand, and some of the grandest lecture
theatres, meeting rooms, libraries and refectories with entire
walls of windows soon housed great drifts and dunes of
shifting sand, but were, in all other regards, deserted.

Once the glass was gone, the plaster began to crumble,
the moisture leaching away, as if by magic, leaving nothing
behind for the dust to cling to. When the plaster had drifted
and trickled away into its own pale dunes, the naked walls
remained, made of block and brick and ragstone, of flint and
cob and render; made, in short, of dust and sand, and water.

Fithvael still held the ancient hourglass in his hand, but
Surn Strallan was pointing past him at the collection of
instruments that stood, silent, on the table in the alcove.
The glass bulbs in one or two of the smallest had already
perished, returned to the sands from which they had been
made, and the materials had commingled with their contents, making strange marbled patterns of varying coloured
sands: streaks of light in dark, and dark in light, yellow in

grey, and black in orange, and pearly iridescent white in a rich sepia sand.

'There!' said Strallan, waving his pointing finger, or perhaps it waved because he was nervous; perhaps it merely shook.

He tried to lick his lips, to moisten them, but he could find no saliva in his mouth and could generate none in his throat.

He had never thought that the inability to sweat could be such a handicap. He had a great urge to wipe the sweat that should have appeared on his brow away with his sleeve, but none had risen there. He wished that it had. He was filled with fear and dread that it had not, and the fear was increased when still the sweat would not come.

A great, black, gleaming scorpion, its carapace grinding almost audibly against the dark, grey sand from which it emerged, crawled over the lip of the table, extending its sting towards them.

Then a spider, cast in the brass of one of the tall, slender ornate frames of a particularly grand hourglass, revivified, stretched high in its leg joints and began almost lazily to descend to the sand below.

Suddenly a locust, its wing cases clicking, flew from the same hourglass, and the flat, narrow head of a snake bobbed up from behind, glossy and golden, its eyes blinking, and a forked tongue darting from between lipless jaws.

A host of black scarabs swarmed over the remaining time-pieces as one of the largest of the old frames disintegrated into its component parts: hundreds of bugs, painstakingly carved from ancient bog oak that had been waxed and handled for hundreds of years, so that its patina was reflected in the impossibly glossy backs of the dung beetles as they dropped to the floor and began to scuttle around the room, looking for a route down, looking for their master.

Then Strallan's attention was drawn back to the ancient hourglass in Fithvael's hand as the glass finally disintegrated, and he was left holding the symmetrical frame. The sand of the glass was so fine as to be the finest of dust particles, floating in the sunbeams that penetrated the glassless windows of the room, and dancing in the air. Not falling, but apparently weightless, they drifted through the air like perfect, magical glitter motes.

Strallan expected the sand, captured in the glass globes for a millennium, or perhaps longer, to shower to the floor to be ground underfoot, but more magic happened as the boy gasped for another breath.

Every grain of sand, every particle, every speck, expanded in the air like a sponge in water. Every one of the thousands of tiny grains trapped inside the globes of glass unfurled and blossomed, passing from the ovum stage to nymph to adult locust in the blink of an eye, except that Surn Strallan no longer had the ability to blink.

Each grain became an entity a hundred times the size that it had appeared to be in the airtight, watertight glass globes that had housed them since before the dawn of modern memory. Each one exploded in size and colour and intensity. Each one squeaked and chittered, each one spread its wings and each one added to the yellow, green, speckled swarm that began to rise around the old elf warrior.

He felt the flesh crawl across his hands and a slight constriction around his wrists, and he looked down, but he could see nothing through the cloud of flitting insects that, with one mind, was forming frantic figures, exercising one consciousness, shaping one collective body with which to escape the room and find a way to the Tomb King.

Fithvael was no longer holding the hourglass, and yet he had not dropped it. It had come alive in his hands, filled the air with dust and insects, and, when the swarm cleared, he found that his hands and arms were covered in more of them, in a crust of creeping scarabs. He raised his hands and thrust them away from his body, and, in that action, a host of the hard, black bodies fell away. Some of them spread their wings mid-air and joined the other flying forms that were fleeing the room. Others fell to the floor and scuttled across rugs and over feet, clicking and scratching against the floorboards, finding the gaps between them and the fissures and knots that would allow them egress.

The snakes that wove and coiled around Fithvael's wrists and forearms, sprung newly formed from the ancient hourglass frame, flexed and constricted, but the warrior elf's flesh was strong and firm, and no harm was done to him, other than a slight tingling of his fingertips. He pulled his dagger from its scabbard at his waist, and inveigled the tip of the blade between the first serpent's scaly skin and the cloth of his shirt. The sharp blade cut cleanly through several coils of snake, rending the cloth against his skin, and slicing a long, neat, narrow line into his flesh, just deep enough to draw a bead of blood.

He repeated the process three times more, ridding himself of the snakes that fell in pieces through the air. As they were cut they appeared to be as complete as they could possibly be, with perfect, glossy scales, gleaming eyes and the appearance of healthy, muscular bodies, but as they fell it became clear that they produced no blood, nor any fluids of any kind. As they tumbled, the scales petrified, the muscles withered and the bones desiccated, and, finally, only dust drifted to the floor.

'It's happening,' said Mondelblatt.

Surn Strallan, Fithvael, Laban and Gilead turned to the professor, who wheezed his strange, disconcerting laugh, and then Gilead, his eyes widening slightly, slowly drew his sword. Fithvael circled away to his comrade's left and Laban looked from one to the other. Surn Strallan did not know what to do. He looked at Mondelblatt, at the table that seemed to heave under the weight of too much sand of too many colours and of the armoured bodies of far too many exotic insects. Then he looked, one by one, at the elves, who were circling the professor, all wielding weapons, but none actually attacking. Finally, he looked down at his body.

He squeaked and jumped, involuntarily, and started a strange hopping dance, patting at his arms and torso, slapping and flailing to relieve himself of the creatures that, finding nowhere else to go, had begun to climb up over his boots and breeches, and were making their way up his shirt-sleeves and jerkin. He had been so unnerved for so long, so immobile, so rooted, that to react, to respond honestly and urgently was a relief. He could not bear the notion that he might go the way of Mondelblatt.

Fithvael had freed himself of the creatures that had materialised out of the hourglass he had been holding, and none had invaded Gilead's or Laban's person. There was no apparent reason why, except that they were other, except that they were elf and not human.

The insects were infesting Surn Strallan, though.

They gathered and swarmed, and seemed to reach the collective consciousness. They sought to escape the confines of first the hourglasses and then the professor's rooms, as the magic that suffused the air of Nuln, the magic that leached out of the cellar beneath the university, the magic that had travelled through time and space, through millennia and thousands of miles, animated the Tomb King's familiars.

They wove their inexorable pathways downwards between floorboards, through crevices, behind wainscots and under doorjambs. They circled the room, and when they could not find a way down, they found a way out through the glassless windows, and followed exterior walls down to the ground level, and hence into storm drains and grilles and down through gratings and vents.

Gilead signalled to Laban to follow the creatures, and the young elf first looked out of the window and then thrust Surn Strallan aside so that he could open the door and quit the professor's apartments. As he did so, the swarm, with its single mind, took sudden notice, halted in mid-air, and changed direction, hurtling past a still alarmed Strallan and following the elf. To Strallan's surprise and delight, most of the bugs that still crawled about his person took the hint and followed their brethren out through the door.

Mondelblatt's strange, strangled laugh came again, weaker and breathier than ever. Fithvael looked to Gilead, and Gilead shrugged. Neither one of them had wielded his weapon. It was difficult to know just how to fight this particular enemy.

Mondelblatt stood in the doorway to his bedroom, his hands eight or ten inches from his body on each side, his feet slightly apart. His head was tilted a little to the left, and he looked almost beatific. There was the illusion of a halo around his head as light shone in from a small window above and behind him.

He might have looked like a god had he not looked so nearly like a monster. He was covered from head to foot in creeping, crawling insects. They climbed over one another and wove paths between their neighbours, covering every

inch of his body. As he blinked, they dropped from his eyelids onto his cheeks, which dislodged others moving there,
which fell to his chest, sending yet more cascading down
over his paunch onto his thighs and down to his shoes, from
where they simply began their ascent once more.

It was not malice, but expediency that had caused them
to land on the old man. He moved little, if at all. He was
an easy target. He was prey. The creature knew it. They took
advantage of him.

This was a plague like any other, a curse like any famine:
the old, the young, the weak and the tender die first and
most easily, and it was Professor Mondelblatt's turn.

There was no target for the elves to attack. If they thrust
their blades at his body, they were as likely to do the old man
damage as they were to kill the insects, and if the bugs died
there would simply be more of them, and yet more.

Gilead took a long, slow breath, and he stilled. Fithvael
took a step back, and away. He looked at Surn Strallan, and,
seeing that he continued to struggle, he quickly sheathed his
weapon and began to flick and toss the last of the insects
from the boy's clothes.

Gilead flicked the tip of his sword at Mondelblatt's legs
first, and then at his arms. He began in small, regular movements to weave a path over and around the professor's
limbs, inserting his blade beneath two or three overlapping
bugs and, with a turn of his wrist, tossing them free. The
bugs chittered and clicked. They opened their wing cases
and seemed to spring on their legs or shrug or sidestep, but
one by one, or in twos and threes, Gilead began to dislodge
the creatures.

Some of the insects suffered the loss of limbs or wings during the operation, one or two were dissected, some crumbled

to dust under the influence of Gilead's blade, but Mondelblatt suffered too.

He was still, because he was old, but no one is truly still, and the ancient least of all; even the shallow breaths of an old man will lead to the bobbing of his head or the shrugging of his shoulders, and old sinews, tired muscles and unresponsive nerves lead to spasms and jerks and palsies that cannot be helped.

Gilead read the warning signs of the professor's tics as well as he might, but not well enough, and, inevitably, the old man suffered a nick here and a slice there. A trickle of blood oozed from a wound in his wrist, and a sliced knuckle wept and dripped. Several long narrow traces were left in his right forearm and a piece of flesh the size of the last joint of a little finger came away from the hollow of his shoulder above his clavicle.

Mondelblatt did not complain.

He laughed once or twice, but the last time that strange sound emerged from his maw, a spider slipped between his broken teeth, and he did not like the sensation of it on his dry tongue. He could not spit it out, because without saliva, or sufficient breath, he was unable to propel the thing away, so he resorted, finally, to biting into the bitter-tasting, loathsome creature, which fell to ashen dust in his mouth.

Two minutes passed and Gilead, his sympathy much heightened for the plight of the old man, and his will to do him no further harm fully engaged, was, in the gathering of his next breath, shadowfast. There would be no more breathing as he suddenly saw every locust, every scarab, every spider, every scorpion and beetle in stark detail. He saw and could predict every move that every one of them would make, and could tease them off Mondelblatt's clothes and skin virtually effortlessly, skewering many of them as he flicked them into the air to land on the second blade that he had drawn ready. When he could collect no more, when the blade was full, he flicked them off with a swishing arc of the weapon. For his next round, he simply used the first blade to throw the bugs aside, and the second to dissect them as they hung before him in mid-air, as if he had all the time in the world to finish them off.

There were no more accidents, and no more of the professor's blood was drawn or spilt and no more flesh was excised, but when the battle was over the old man fell to the floor, pale and ill.

Fithvael dropped to his knees beside the old man, as Gilead breathed once more and sheathed his weapons. Strallan stared, and stared.

'You should blink,' said Gilead, 'for I know I am no longer shadowfast.'

'What?' asked Strallan, still staring.

'He's dying,' said Fithvael.

'He can't be,' said Strallan.

Fithvael and Gilead both turned to the boy, who dropped his head to his chest, embarrassed. He didn't want the old man to die, not because he pitied him, but because he feared him.

'They've killed him,' said Fithvael, pushing up the wide linen sleeve of the old man's shirt to show a series of pinprick holes in his pale, papery skin. 'The scorpions carry poison in their stings. Shadowfast isn't fast enough.'

'His riddles were our only answers,' said Gilead.

'We have the map,' said Strallan from the doorway where he'd taken up his position, as if ready and more than willing to leave.

Gilead and Fithvael looked at him.

'And?' asked Fithvael after several moments, during which, once again, Strallan failed to blink.

Strallan's cheeks paled, and then flushed. He swallowed a dry, saliva-less swallow that almost made him choke, and then he said, 'And the cart.'

'Good,' said Fithvael, looking at Gilead, and then down at Mondelblatt, before he turned his gaze back on Surn Strallan. 'And?'

Strallan stared back at Fithvael as if searching the old elf's face for the answer. He shuffled his feet in the sand that had spread across the floor of the apartments. Then he stopped and pointed downwards.

'There's the sand,' he said. 'The cart made sand, too.'

'And?' asked Fithvael, lifting Mondelblatt into his arms.

'Ulric's teeth!' said Strallan. 'Must we?'

'Must we what?' asked Fithvael, placing the professor gently on his bed, folding the street map and tucking it into his jacket. Gilead continued silently to follow the exchange between the human boy and his old mentor, while filling his pockets with the many colours and types of sand that had erupted from the hourglasses.

'Must we follow the wretched insects? Must we follow the creatures that killed the old man? Must we?'

'Indeed we must,' said Fithvael.

'We,' said Gilead. 'Not you.'

'Not me?' asked Surn Strallan, ready to sigh with an unwelcome mixture of relief and disappointment.

'You should remain here to look after the professor, make him as comfortable as you can in his final hours.'

Relief and disappointment turned to horror in Surn Strallan's eyes.

'No,' said Mondelblatt. 'I'm not done yet. I won't be put away. I won't be put to bed. I won't be left for dead. Not now, elf, not yet.'

'It's time for you to rest,' said Gilead more kindly.

'How can I rest,' asked Mondelblatt, 'when I'm the only fool that remembers the power of the amulet?'

Chapter 32

Laban's descent was almost vertical, out of Mondelblatt's apartments and down the stairs, past the exterior door through a low, adjacent arch and down narrow, curving, stone steps, illuminated by slender beams of golden light that cast an uneven grid pattern up the steps.

Laban moved slowly, cautiously, as he heard the odd sounds that emanated from below the building.

He found himself in a simple storage cellar, but the yellow light appeared to be seeping between the stones of the end wall against which a series of trunks and boxes were piled in a haphazard fashion. The insects that he had followed were disappearing, one or two at a time, into those narrow shafts of yellow light. Laban moved the boxes quickly and put his hand against the wall, which was vibrating. The mortar, turning to sand and disintegrating, trickled freely from the joins between the stones, letting more light and more sound escape, while allowing the insects to infiltrate in greater numbers. Soon they were all gone, and Laban was alone.

The elf could hardly hear the desiccated mortar falling over the sound of the clicking and squeaking and chittering of the insects. He recognised the swarming sounds that he had heard in Mondelblatt's rooms when Fithvael had unwittingly released the locusts from the hourglass, but this was on a bigger scale. This was on a very much bigger scale. The insects that he had followed down to this place represented only a tiny fraction of the host swarm.

Despite the scale of the swarm sounds, they, too, were overshadowed by other yet more disturbing noises, cries and bellows unlike anything the elf had ever heard. He thought the sounds must be organic; they were somehow bestial, sentient, almost musical, despite their discordance, for they had a strange, rhythmic quality not unlike speech or a melody. He knew, however, that they could not be human. They were tuned too low for the human voice, and the beginnings and ends of the sounds were too indistinct, and besides, they represented no language that he had ever heard. It was the accompaniment that truly baffled the elf though, it was the squeaks and bellows, and odd, reedy outbursts that disconcerted him.

Then the vibrations in the wall turned to rumbling and shaking, and Laban lifted his hand away and took three or four hasty strides backwards in alarm.

The entire building shook to its core, the golden light blazed, and the wall came tumbling down.

The room beneath the university was ablaze with golden light, the walls had all fallen away and the swarm of insects wove a mesmerising pattern through the air. The dressed ranks of warriors clutched their weapons, ready to act upon their master's every command, the Tomb Guards stood at his shoulders, expectant, and the Liche Priest prepared himself for his last, great rite.

As he reached out over the mummy of the Tomb King, a great cloud of golden locusts rose and dispersed back into the swarm, having devoured the woven blanket of reeds that served as his shroud.

Then the shadows fell; lean, noble shadows, the shadows of three elf warriors armed and ready to enter the fray.

Gilead arrived behind Laban as the young elf looked into the brightly lit room at the rite unfolding there. He was facing south, and had not been detected by the party of undead as the swarm surrounded them and they, too, faced south, the direction of their homelands. His shadow fell short of the dividing wall that lay in pieces all around him.

Fithvael carried Mondelblatt into the cellar, and Surn Strallan, pale and unsteady on his feet, followed them. The old elf placed the professor carefully on the floor against a remaining pillar, and indicated that Strallan should tend to him, but within seconds several locusts were already picking at the papery flesh of Mondelblatt's face and eating the linen of his shirt. Strallan tried to beat them away, but one or two simply switched allegiance, settling on the boy's wafting hands.

Gilead approached, his fist closed around something. He knelt low to the ground and began to move his hand as if he were writing. A trickle of multicoloured sand emerged from the space he made between his long slender index finger and thumb, and Strallan realised that the elf was indeed writing something.

The locusts on his hands hopped once, twice and then darted away, as if stung by some unseen swat.

Strallan looked down at the trails and loops and swirls of sand. He could not read the elf words, but they wove the most beautiful pattern he had ever seen, and they seemed to scintillate somehow and glimmer with power. It was something like the way that Fithvael had used his voice. It was some sort of spell, some warding magic. Surn Strallan didn't understand what it truly was, but he was very glad that it was there.

Gilead very quickly surrounded the two huddled figures with more of the writing until they were warded on all sides, and then he sprinkled the little sand that remained in his hand over them, as if he were anointing them, speaking lyrical words in his own tongue that sounded magical to Strallan's ears and made Mondelblatt sigh.

Then Fithvael, Laban and Gilead stood together, and walked towards the undead host, knowing where they must attack, and wondering who would turn first. They stood for a moment, casting their elegant shadows into the room, over the Tomb King in his sarcophagus and over the host that stood to protect him.

The swarm would not, could not, touch the elves. They gathered in a tornado around them, but could do no more, and from the eye of the storm, the elves were content to forge onwards, cutting and slicing through the heaving mass of insects, killing few by comparison to the very great numbers that engulfed them, but closing the distance between themselves and their true adversaries.

The swarm afforded the Liche Priest time.

With two sharp thrusts of his staff in the air, he turned the dressed ranks of the undead warriors to the left and right of the sarcophagus, confident that his troops would make short work of the foe.

Then the Liche Priest also turned to face the elves and with a third broad, arcing swing of his staff he dismissed the swarm, sending it forth into the city, sending it out to do his bidding, to take the streets, to rid Nuln of all that was organic and wasteful, of all that would putrefy and taint.

The dressed ranks of undead had turned, as one, with their narrow shields and spears and their curved swords, with their naked skeletal bodies, ragless and without armour, but with cuffs and headpieces, with anklets and simple badges of allegiance. The Tomb Guards turned to face each other across the widest part of the sarcophagus, ready to perish for their king, to end their millennia of immortality that he might begin another long reign, restored to this ancient city.

Gilead took point, his shield strapped across his back, wielding both of his blades. He cut wide and fast and repeatedly, separating jaws, wrists, kneecaps and ribs, and marking and bruising shields. Nothing died.

Nothing died because nothing lived.

Left and right of him, Fithvael and Laban, each a yard behind and to the side, ploughed into the undead host with equal vigour. Laban reasoned that he might sever heads, but managed, in most cases, only to dislodge them, or leave them rocking or wobbling on their spines. Still nothing died.

The skeleton warriors opened their mouths and allowed their surging actions to create their battle cries, the air moving through their torsos as they lunged at the elves with their spears and defended themselves with their shields. There was a cacophony of bone on bone, and bone on sinew, and bone on elf steel, and still nothing died.

Gilead severed a spine, a shoulder joint and an elbow of

one of the creatures as ribs dislocated and hung from a wilting sternum, and still the creature thrust its spear at the elf's throat, catching the lobe of his ear and a lock of his hair as it passed.

'Duck!' shouted Laban as a spear flew hard at Fithvael's left shoulder, and, as he lowered his body and the spear passed harmlessly over him, the host regrouped, the first rank turning as one, and the second stepping into the fray.

Laban was attacked by a broader, squatter creature with a taller headdress and shorter weapon, a bright, curved sword that it used to thrust and hack at the young elf. Laban could do little more than parry and swing, and try to return strike for strike.

There was no point thrusting.

Thrusting is for flesh. Thrusting is to pierce skin and muscle, and to damage organs and to spill blood. To thrust into a skeleton is to risk missing. To destroy these creatures the elves must dismember and decapitate, they must separate bone from sinew and scatter the component parts of the skeletal beasts.

Gilead and Fithvael swung and hacked by instinct when they saw the figures that confronted them. Laban, appalled, parried and reacted, defended too much and attacked too little.

The blow came to his thigh, and it came with the squealing of a sinew in his attacker's shoulder and a hard, high whistle between ribs swinging through the air. The fluting of air through teeth was nothing compared to the impact sound, the wet thud of metal slicing hard, bloody muscle.

Laban cried out, and Gilead turned.

The skeleton warrior had aimed for the femoral artery, but he was not dealing with a human foe, and he had missed.

The blood that came was from a minor vein, so although the wound was painful, and, being deep in the thigh muscle, somewhat inconvenient, it was by no means fatal.

Gilead's fury was boundless, but it was nothing compared to Laban's embarrassment. The young elf had wanted nothing more than to impress his illustrious cousin, and he felt that, so far, he had singularly failed to do so. He had fought decently against the skaven, but it had been a war of attrition rather than a great victory. Besides, he had made an utter fool of himself in front of the humans in the tavern the previous night. He would not, could not be defeated by these... these creatures.

Before Gilead could come to Laban's rescue the young elf had swung his sword twice more and discarded his shield in favour of drawing a second blade. He disarmed the skeleton with the curved sword, sliced through its spine in two places, above and below its ribcage, took out both of its knees and separated its jaw. Then he inserted the longer of his two blades between two of its ribs, forcibly removed the entire ribcage and, swinging his sword high, flung it over the heads of the host that was stamping and agitating to join the battle.

The remainder of the creature's bones were suddenly inanimate, tumbling to the floor to be kicked out of the way by the bony feet of the horde that filled the breach.

Laban did not falter.

Suddenly, his anger quenched, calm returned, and as fast as he had been dismembering the warrior that had wounded him, he was faster yet, swinging both of his blades in a perfect rhythm, crossing and recrossing their paths so that no weapon could penetrate, and every stroke hit a target: an arm here, a leg there, ribs smashed, shoulders dislocated, vertebrae dislodged, jaws separated, joints rent.

Within seconds, they began to fall. Broken skeletal bodies began to tumble, clogging up the fighting stage so that they were kicked out of the way or hauled unceremoniously and flung to one side or the other by their comrades.

Then it happened.

He didn't know how, or even why, and for what felt like minutes he didn't even realise that the state had engulfed him. He thought that some strange magic had occurred, that the rest of the world as he knew it had come to a strange, halting stop, that everything was happening in remarkably slow motion, as if the skeleton warriors were fighting their way through some otherworldly viscous substance and not through air, and yet he could move freely and easily. He realised, too, that he seemed not to need to inhale for minutes at a time, or to blink for that matter, and that he had complete control.

When he realised that he was shadowfast, Laban almost lost control of the situation, taking the heads of two of the foe in one oddly satisfying, but far too exaggerated arc of his long sword. He reined himself in, smiled and looked to Gilead.

When Gilead smiled back, moving at his own speed in this world that seemed so slow, Laban knew that his cousin, too, was shadowfast, that they were kindred in that place, in that time, in that battle, and he knew that he had come home.

As the two elves made their way through the ranks of skeleton warriors left and right of the sarcophagus, moving faster than he could register their movements, with Fithvael tidying up behind them, ensuring that every last warrior was truly dispatched, the Liche Priest turned back to the sarcophagus, raising his arms once more, and with them a second maelstrom.

A wind swept up around him, disturbing the remaining sands and lifting some of the lightest of the bones dislodged from the bodies of the skeleton warriors. The Liche Priest stepped into the fast-moving air, flexed the great cavity that was his chest and opened his mouth.

First he must protect his king and then he must complete his rite of summoning.

Chapter 33

As Gilead and Laban fought the skeleton warriors, as Fithvael faithfully followed in their footsteps ensuring that their work was complete, Surn Strallan shielded Professor Mondelblatt in the lea of the pillar as best he could. The old man seemed not to grow any weaker, although he continued to cough and wheeze periodically, and Strallan made sure that he didn't move, that he remained within the elf wards, that he didn't cross them or smudge them or in any way disturb the magic that he knew Gilead had created around them. Without those words, he feared that they would already be dead.

Then the Liche Priest summoned a new wind.

Strallan heard it first. He heard it in the vibrations of sinew against bone. He heard it in the thrum of chest cavities and the squeak of cartilage, and he heard it in every movement of every skeleton that swung a weapon or wielded a shield, and he feared that wind.

When he felt it, he feared it more, and when he heard the faint hissing and shushing of sand moving against stone, he feared it more than he could have believed.

The insects had gone, flown away. Some had seemed to take other routes through fissures between the stones of walls below ground, or up through the ceiling above, but most flew clean past Strallan and Mondelblatt's resting place and up the stairs that they had descended to this subterranean hell-hole, for that was how the boy characterised it, that was how he would talk about it, if his ordeal were ever over.

For long moments he dared not look down at the floor around them, but when he did dare, he was not surprised by what he saw. The lines of the script that Gilead had drawn there were indistinct. The characters that the elf had made with the stream of sand had blurred and smudged, and in some places there were only random smears of sand, tiny drifts and streaks caused by the action of the wind on the dusty substance. The sand was dull, too, having lost its gleam, its magic.

Strallan did not draw attention to their predicament, he did not need to. Mondelblatt leaned in to him and coughed his ancient man's laugh.

'Ephemeral,' he said. 'Sand. That's how I like it.'

The last of the skeleton warriors were smashed and broken with none to collect the bones for burial, for internment, for another battle in another age. It mattered not.

It mattered not, for the Liche Priest was prepared.

As the last of the skeleton warriors fell, the lids of the reed pulp inner sarcophagus and the wooden tomb flew back to hover over the mummified remains of the Tomb King. His shroud of reeds had been decimated by the locusts so his jewelled and polished armour and weapons, his ornate and ornamented garments, his headdress and jewels of office would all be marred by dust and time and decay if the rites of summoning were not completed as planned.

It was imperative that the Liche Priest complete the rites.

The Liche Priest raised his arms, and allowed one last, long intonation to emanate from his mouth, accompanied by the inevitable cacophony that radiated from his skeleton. It ended when the lids were back in place.

When it was done, the Liche Priest stepped a little away from the head of the great casket to the north of the room, closer to where Mondelblatt and Strallan hunched against the pillar, so that they could see him clearly for the first time.

Then the Tomb Guards rotated away from their master, turning their backs on his closed casket, ready to defend his honour that he might yet rise.

Laban was on the right of the tomb. His thigh ached and his vision blurred as he descended from the realms of the shadowfast back to a more normal state. He blinked, and willed himself to maintain the strength and speed that had seen him destroy so many with such ease.

The Tomb Guard appeared to be looking at him through sightless eyes, although his curved sword came up and his feet spread a little apart to enable him to swing effectively.

There was nothing but blood in the Tomb Guard's consciousness, nothing but vermillion, arterial blood, the blood whose letting would cleanse the filthy beast before him. He sliced at Laban's neck, but it was narrower than he expected, and the elf was taller, but slighter of frame, and the strike was sorely misjudged. The whistle that accompanied the strike was shrill, but broken, as if there were some fault in the machine that was not a machine, as if there were already some weakness, as if the Tomb Guard had already suffered some injury.

Laban ducked easily and adjusted for the second swing without attempting to make one of his own. When it came, it was to his groin, to the femoral artery, to where it might have been had the elf been human. He was not human, and his artery was not so close to the surface nor so anterior to the joint. Again, a surefooted sidestep and a parry, and Laban was safe, uninjured. Again, the Tomb Guard's body seemed to betray him, seemed not to be in tune with itself. There was a jarring squeak, but still Laban could not identify its exact source.

The young elf guessed, rightly, that the next attack would be to his abdomen, to the iliac, and he adjusted for the undead warrior's knowledge of human anatomy, and took the parry early, riposting effectively, and getting in a counter-attack and a second strike with his sinister blade. Now he had a fight on his hands. If he didn't redress the balance soon, the undead creature might make an attempt at the mesenteric artery, and, even if he missed badly, his attack would be central to the elf's body, and was bound to be messy, if not fatal, for Laban.

The Tomb Guard was fast and dedicated, but his approach was not subtle. He had no interest in disabling or disarming the elf, his aim was to spill his blood, his arterial blood, and nothing else would do. Laban could ensure that the beast had no hope of accomplishing that feat, while carrying out a long, slow war of attrition of his own.

He began at the Tomb Guard's extremities, taking finger bones, a kneecap, a number of teeth, with the edge of his sword slicing across them, drawing them sideways, making them slant and whistle when he moved the skull through the air.

Yet still there remained that strange, atonal, half-hearted squeak.

Laban took some delight in detaching the radius from one arm and the ulna from the other, playing with the Tomb Guard, who blundered on, aiming at the same three targets over and over again, and consistently missing them by several inches, when he could be inflicting any number of flesh wounds with considerable success.

Gilead's assailant was less ponderous and more versatile, and she was also bigger and more brutal, but Gilead was faster.

Gilead was shadowfast.

As the Tomb Guard hacked and swung and thrust at Gilead, as she parried and blocked and countered, he wove a dizzying array of sword strokes around and through her frame, with almost too much finesse. Only when he began to hack and slash, only when he swung and struck did he begin to disassemble the skeletal figure before him. When her left arm was gone, she wore her shield high at her shoulder. When several of her ribs were gone she adjusted the balance of her body. When she lost a kneecap she locked out her leg and did not bend it again, but as hard as she fought, and as long as she struggled, she could not defeat Gilead.

Finally, he switched his balance from his right foot to his left, drawing her to one side and away from the sarcophagus so that he could get in behind her. There he tucked his sword close to his body, his arm flat across his stomach, and, with all his strength, he drew his blade between her vertebrae, severing her spine between the pelvis and the ribcage. He thrust his knee up into her pelvis and kicked her broken knee, and the bottom half of her body disengaged and toppled. Her head turned and she looked startled as her upper body began to drop.

Gilead pulled his sword arm back across his body, and a second solid stroke separated two of the Tomb Guard's vertebrae just above her intact collarbones. She was still looking at him, surprise and horror on her face, when her skull fell to the stone floor, cracked and rolled away.

Laban attacked the other Tomb Guard's left shoulder joint, having dislodged the shield, which hung at a steep angle and was pulling his assailant off balance now that he had only half of his major bones still intact. The humerus dropped and hung limply by a length of taut sinew that should have perished centuries before. The arm was useless, and as the Tomb Guard tried to bring his weapon around for another attack, this time to Laban's femoral artery, his body squeaked once more.

Laban had learned not to thrust, and yet his instincts told him otherwise. He was tired and his thigh was sore, and he wanted the battle to be over. There was more to do, there was still a city to save. The battle was not over, and the elf wanted nothing more than to dispatch this creature and move on. His intuition told him to thrust, to lunge, and that was what he did. He avoided the golden girdle that hung from its pelvis, aiming higher, and he drove the tip of his sword squarely into the tenth thoracic vertebra. As he was about to strike it, Laban realised that the bone was a slightly different colour from the rest of the skeleton. It was browner and had a less solid appearance.

As the tip of his sword connected with the bone, it shattered to dust. The vertebra above it dropped, suddenly, causing the bones below to jump and twitch, and the pelvis to rock unsteadily. Then the remaining vertebrae above the break cascaded down, creating a domino effect.

The shock on the Tomb Guard's face was palpable, despite him having no flesh with which to form a living expression.

As the bones in his spine lost the memory of their placement, they had nothing left to cling to and they fell to the floor like so many dice or runes, like the bones carried in some shaman's pouch. Once the spine was gone, the ribcage fell and shattered on the floor, and then the skull, with its shocked expression, crashed to the stone flags, breaking into three pieces.

Fithvael stood before the Liche Priest at the head of the newly sealed sarcophagus. The undead monster was all but spent of his magical energies, his mystical resources. It was as much as he could do to continue to control the swarm that was flying out in two great arcs around Nuln, following above ground the course of the ancient city that had once belonged to the Tomb King, some of which remained in the undercrofts and cellars of the nether-city.

The elf and the undead sorcerer faced one another. Fithvael's eyes were locked on the shaman's skull, where its eyes should have been, and he thought that he could read something there, some warning, some threat, something terrible.

The warrior elf wanted to fell the undead creature, but he knew that he could not, should not, must not. His hand closed around the hilt of his sword, his warm, flat palm wrapping around the cool grip, the two becoming one with long years of familiarity in a moment. Then he let go his grasp, flexed his fingers and rested his hand at his side. He swung his shield across his back and stood before the creature, unarmed and with no means of defence.

The Liche Priest stood still. No sound emanated from him, not from his mouth and not from any of the joints in his bones and sinews that sang when he moved with the winds that he generated.

The Liche Priest was generating nothing below ground, nothing in this chamber. The bones of the skeleton warriors lay cold and grey on the floor of the cellar, which no longer glowed with the golden light that had so recently suffused the atmosphere. The Tomb Guards had mounted their final stand, but were falling fast at Gilead's and Laban's hands, and their undead bones would soon be mingled with those of the ranks who had fallen before them. The room would soon be dark and silent, and the tomb would be inert once more, so where was the energy being diverted to? Where was the danger?

What was happening above while the elves were below?

Chapter 34

The great city of Nuln was like a ghost town when the creatures began to pour up from below the ground, from the cellars beneath the university. They divided and spread east and west. To the west, they crossed the Reikplatz where the market had broken up, the stalls and barrows abandoned, and followed the Commercial Way towards the Altgate and the old city wall. To the west, the route above ground did not so neatly follow the route below ground, and the creatures crawled and slithered and flew a less direct path, crossing roads at odd angles, cutting corners and traversing alleys, almost as if they were tacking, like sailboats catching the prevailing winds. The arc was less smooth, but the intent was to reach Temple Gate, creating an almost perfect semicircle with the Wandstrasse at its diameter, engulfing the university and the College of Engineering and encompassing most of Neuestadt.

If the Liche Priest could resurrect the Tomb King, he would control a vast power base at the heart of the city, and from there, anything was possible.

Already the university was all but abandoned. The trickle of students leaving had turned into a steady flow and then a torrent, and by the middle of the afternoon, the professors were leaving on the grounds that if there were no students to teach, there was no reason to stay. They did not speak of the sand, of the piles and drifts of sand in all the rooms and the dunes that were beginning to ebb and flow in the quads. They talked of the old man, though, in whispered tones. They talked of Mondelblatt and his obsession, and they blamed him.

'Water,' said Mondelblatt.

'There is none,' said Strallan.

'Stupid boy,' said Mondelblatt. 'I can make water, if I can be trusted, of course.'

Laban and Gilead exchanged glances, and then looked at Fithvael once more. Gilead gestured, and Laban touched the old warrior gently on the arm.

'What?' asked Fithvael.

'You are needed, te tuin,' said Laban.

'I bear no title,' said Fithvael.

'You have earned it,' said Gilead. 'The boy is right. I have need of you.'

Laban sidestepped into Fithvael's position as the elf, reluctantly, stood down, tearing his eyes away from the Liche Priest's faceless skull only at the last moment.

Laban could not see what his mentor had been looking at. The skull looked inert to him, vacant, possessed of no thought or intent.

Fithvael pulled the map from inside his shirt as he and Gilead stepped towards the two humans huddled against the pillar.

'Water,' said Mondelblatt, again. 'You must trust me to make water.'

'Water?' asked Gilead.

'Hand me the amulet,' said Mondelblatt. 'It is time to make use of the stone.'

Then the wind came. It started with the cart. It started with the sand that had collected around the cartwheels, locking the vehicle in place. It started to whip up motes of dust, and then it began to shift drifts of sand. It spread throughout the city, and then it spread beyond the city.

A new wind came in from the south, from the road that the cart had driven in on. The wind collected up the sand, everything left in the wake of the cart, and it drove it into Nuln, sweeping it up the streets and boulevards, and whipping it up into clouds and mini-tornadoes. The sand hissed and shushed and tumbled. It collected and drifted and built up, and then it moved on again, driven by the warm winds, driven from the south.

As the insects in the Liche Priest's swarm found their sentry points, gathered in their ranks, and prepared to attack and decimate the city and any inhabitants they could find, the grains and motes and specks of sand and dust rose into the air, swelled, and grew.

Then they fell to the ground, slithered away as hatchlings, or pupated, grew wings and flew, or crawled away on six new legs or eight. There was no end to the numbers of new creatures that could be born of the desert sands, and there was no end to the sands that could be resurrected from the dying buildings in the great city.

* * *

The Liche Priest's cold, eyeless stare did not falter. Laban's face was no more than two feet away and he could detect nothing there, no movement, no emotion, no intellect. He could sense nothing.

Gilead looked once more at Mondelblatt, questioning the old man's honesty with his eyes, knowing that he could trust the professor or not, but that the last time he had trusted him he had been duped.

Gilead was an old being. He understood balance and he understood humans.

He reached his slender thumb and finger into the top of his boot and pulled something out. He held it up between his thumb and forefinger, and Strallan gasped and sighed.

Surn Strallan burst into silent tears. He made no noise, nor did his face crumble, but the tears flowed freely from his wide-open eyes and he drooled from loose lips. He felt his boots and shirt fill with the sweat that he should have been secreting for the last dozen hours, and the experience made him feel oddly calm. He did not even care that he found himself sitting in a very large pool of Mondelblatt's waste, and when he looked at the old man, he too was crying.

'Write in it,' said Mondelblatt, gesturing with one palsied hand at the pool of liquid gathering around the human pair. Then he held his hand out, palm upwards and waited.

Finally, Gilead dropped the amulet into the old man's palm and thrust his hand into one of his pockets. He turned to look at the Liche Priest and Laban, considered for a moment what he might inscribe, and then began.

He held his hand like a writing tool only an inch or so above the shallow pool, and began to allow the sand to trickle between his finger and thumb in a concentrated stream. The sand was grey, but turned to a blackish purple and glittered as it hit the liquid. It seemed to petrify, turning instantly to something permanent, to a glossy crystalline ridge standing slightly proud of the stone surface of the floor.

Fithvael did not need to turn when the sound came. He was already watching the Liche Priest. As soon as the first of the sand hit the old man's urine and the young man's sweat and tears, the old elf knew that some strange force was working its magic, that between them, the alchemy of the humans and of the elves and of this great city was somehow working in concert to fight the Liche Priest and his evil intentions.

The noise did not come as the other noises had come from winds generated by the Liche Priest, from air moving through the cavities of his body. The noise came from the cracking of bone on bone and of bone on sinew. The terrible noise came from failure and from the Liche Priest recognising his defeat. The sound of bones breaking echoed through the dark basement as the Liche Priest flagellated his body with his staff of office. He wielded it against his limbs and ribs and back, and, with his final impact, he broke his own skull.

All the while, he made no other sound. All the while, the air in the cellar was still, for there were no words to accompany this rite, no celebration, no incantation, no music.

'More sand,' said Mondelblatt after several long moments of silence. 'You must have more sand.'

All of the sand was gone. There would be no sand to be found anywhere in the city of Nuln, no matter who searched for it, for it had all been generated by the Southlanders, and it had all been turned by them into an army of familiars for the Tomb King.

All the sand was gone, except for the sand that resided in Gilead's pockets, the sand that even the Liche Priest had not the power to influence.

Mondelblatt shooed Surn Strallan out of the puddle that they had both made, and then gestured for a hand. Laban stepped forwards, but Fithvael lifted the old, damp man into his arms before the young elf was able.

'Draw the map,' said Mondelblatt. 'Draw the map of where Mr Fithvael found all the bugs. Draw it in our puddle... Do it. Your magic and mine, the sand and the amulet will quash the plague of insects, drown them in a mighty flood. Do it!'

Gilead filled his hand with the sand in his pocket, but Strallan grabbed hold of the elf's wrist. Gilead looked down at the boy's hand and then into his face.

Strallan swallowed. He was a little afraid, but it was, nevertheless, a great pleasure to swallow saliva after many hours with only dust in his mouth.

'North's that way,' said Strallan, pointing over Gilead's left shoulder.

'The boy has a point,' said Mondelblatt, breaking into his choking laugh, which came, on this occasion, with an odd gurgling sound.

Gilead shifted his position, studied the map and began to draw.

He drew a line to represent the Wandstrasse first. It formed a firm, solid ridge of square sepia crystals as soon as it hit the liquid. Then he drew two arcing arms, not quite meeting, which were somehow a deep blue. Then he filled in the areas inside the semicircle, which showed in a variety of hues and textures, the sizes and shapes of the crystals varying dramatically, but beginning to form a beautiful and accurate representation of that part of the city. Finally, Gilead drew a trapezium that joined the two arms to complete the semicircle. It stood firm and grey and somehow staunch and permanent where the university should be, and it completed the map.

A large drop of water fell from the stairwell behind the pillar where they were all sitting or standing, or squatting. Then another, and another. In a matter of seconds they could hear the rain drumming and pelting and sloshing down the steps.

Mondelblatt, still held firmly in Fithvael's arms, stabbed his finger into the air above his head, and, taking the hint, the old elf strode out of the cellar and began to climb the steps. They were soaked to the skin before they were halfway up.

The rain rolled over the old city wall of the Wandstrasse as if from nowhere. The sky turned black and the heavens opened, and the water poured in sheets, straight down, shredding everything in its vertical path and rinsing away the residue.

Gossamer wings dissolved on contact with single vast drops so heavy the sound of thousands of them landing together on the cobbled streets was enough to send shockwaves through the wing cases and carapaces of the insects that had not been hit by the rain yet, incapacitating them, stunning them, and killing them in their millions. Then the rains came and washed away the carcasses, battering them against stone streets and iron storm-drains, shredding them into millions of pieces, rendering them down to wet dust.

They had waited thousands of years, trapped in sand, stored in hourglasses, baked in deserts, had been brought back to life by magic and atmospheric pressure and humidity and luck, and a thousand other quirks, and by fate and by the machinations of the Liche Priest and by timing, and now the rains had come.

The Southlanders measured time in water. Mondelblatt measured time in sand.

Chapter 35

Mondelblatt insisted that Fithvael carry him through the city, in order that he could see, for himself, the damage that was done, and know that Nuln would survive, and that it would survive because of the fifty years that he had spent as a scholar. He died as Fithvael carried him across the Glory Bridge on the way to the Temple Shrine of Morr. The hand, still clutching the amulet, fell away, the fingers loosened, and the stone fell into the River Reik. The rain was falling so heavily that the sound of it falling was heard by no one, and the splash it made when it entered the turbulent water below went unnoticed. The old elf gathered Mondelblatt's arm back onto his chest, and thought that it was fitting that the professor should die at the very spot where the drowned, dragged out of the River Reik, were displayed for identification. Mondelblatt would have thought it fitting, too.

Surn Strallan wanted to stay with Gilead, except that he was afraid of the elf, more than he was afraid of Fithvael, but perhaps a little less than he feared the professor, certainly less than he feared a dying professor. When he was dismissed by Gilead, there was nothing for it but to leave, although he wasn't entirely sure where he should go. He wanted to go back to the Bridge watch house to gloat, except that was foolish, and he'd never be hailed a hero. Perhaps the South Gate? They'd mock him, but he belonged there. He'd never be able to prove his part in what had happened that day, but he stood a greater chance with those men than with any others.

He walked through the rain, wetter than wet, wetter than he had ever been, his skin stinging under the weight of the raindrops and the volume of them falling. When he reached the halfway mark on the Great Bridge he stopped and looked over the side. The wind blew and the River Reik was high and throbbing, foam peaking and running off the surging waves. He put his hand on the capping stone of the waist-high wall and it felt solid. He didn't know how he knew it, but he knew this marked the turning point of everything. The famine was over. The next harvest would be better. Prosperity would return to the Empire.

Gilead sent Laban back to Mondelblatt's rooms to lie on the old man's bed and rest his leg. When he got there, the rain was lashing in at the glassless windows and the floor was swimming in water. It was no longer a wooden floor made of planks, but had a hard shell-like sheen, a shiny gloss, the residue of the sand, now harmless, inert, even beautiful, like a great oil slick cast across the room.

Gilead stood on the steps of the cellar and watched the rain fall. The casket was still there, the sarcophagus that might yet yield some unknown, evil force.

It rained and it rained, and it rained. The cellar was ankle-deep in water in moments, and then it was knee-deep. Within minutes, Gilead had to climb higher up the steps lest he be standing in water. When he left, the cellar was under water, as were all the oldest parts of the city, all the parts that had been in existence before the current history of Nuln had begun, all the ancient cellars and undercrofts that had once belonged to other forces, other beings, undead, unnatural things that always lurked somewhere and might one day return. One day.

They had tried this day, Gilead's day, and he had turned them away. They would not try again in his lifetime.

There's a relief.

The cursed tale must only be told once by any bard, and the timing is all. Too soon and the curse might just come true, and not just for the teller; too late, and the tale might go untold. I am satisfied. I feel the end drawing swiftly on… I feel the end… Just a breath or two, now… my friends… I am content to go… My tale is told…

You will not remember… me… Try to remember the tale… Do remember Gilead… and Fithvael too… Such a noble man… Elf…

One last… I think… One last… One…

The hand that moments before had been holding a beaker with an inch of wine left in the bottom relaxed and the arm fell away. The beaker had been taken by another, seeing the old dame weaken, taken by someone who wanted the wine more than he cared that the old woman was dying. She'd been rambling for long enough, and he longed for the silence and the chance to sleep.

The wine was as cheap as everything else in the run-down doss-house in the back streets of the small town west of

Bolgasgrad. For this was Kislev, cold and bleak and unforgiving. There were no beds, only benches and floorspace, and it was better to be close to other warm bodies, except that her body wouldn't be warm for long, so her value was gone.

'I thought she'd never stop,' said the short, wide proprietor, wiping beakers with a filthy rag.

'Do you suppose it was as dull as it sounded?' asked his brother. 'It could have been a long list, a woman's list of need, of want, of demand, for all the passion in that creaky old voice.'

'What was the language, the accent?'

'Empire, to be sure,'

'They have no fire in their bellies, no adventure, no passion,' said the proprietor.

'It's true,' said his brother. 'Nothing ever happens in the Empire. If you want a real story, Kislev's the place.'

'I wonder what she was doing here, an old dame like that?'

'Did she pay in advance?' asked the brother.

'Yes,' said the proprietor. 'I suppose her business here was no other business of ours. If I'd known she'd drone on for days, with hardly a break, I'd have kept her out, and never mind her copper coin.'

With that, he dropped his dirty rag into the beaker he was wiping, strode over to where the old woman was slumped in her chair, lifted her frail corpse easily over one shoulder and took her out of his establishment. She had been tiresome these last few days, droning on in her foreign language that none could understand, never allowing for a moment's silence, but at least she had added to the warmth in the room.

The wolves would have her now, and good riddance.

Dan Abnett is a multiple *New York Times* bestselling author and an award-winning comic book writer. He has written over forty novels, including the acclaimed Gaunt's Ghosts series, and the Eisenhorn and Ravenor trilogies. His Horus Heresy novel *Prospero Burns* topped the SF charts in the UK and the US. In addition to writing for Black Library, Dan scripts audio dramas, movies, games, comics and bestselling novels for major publishers in Britain and America. He lives and works in Maidstone, Kent.

Nik Vincent has more than a dozen titles to her name, mostly children's fiction, but also educational and reference books, and comics, and she co-wrote *Gilead's Blood* and *The Hammers of Ulric* with her husband, Dan Abnett. She has finally succumbed to the lure of Warhammer 40,000, and hopes to have a long and rewarding career writing about the guys and girls, and villains and daemons that play games with her imagination.